THE GRAIL HUNTER

Searching for purpose &
love in her life, Rowena
Colleen becomes entwined
within a 900 year old quest
for the Grail

RORY DUFF

Copyright © 2019
ISBN 978-0-244-81370

The moral rights of the author has been asserted in accordance with the Copyrights, Designs and Patents Act 1988

The Author currently holds all the right to this publication and its contents

No part of this publication maybe reproduced, stored or transmitted in any form without the express written permission of the author

A Rowena Colleen book

For more information on Rory Duff's work

www.roryduff.com

Other books by Rory Duff

The Celtic Kingfisher
Grail Found
Grail Bound
The Key to the Secret of the Ancients
Goethe's Fairy Tale – A full interpretation

Contents

Chapter 1 – Escape	**5**
Off to France	7
Le Mans	11
Limoges	17
Tarascon-sur-Ariege	21
Rennes le Chateau	31
Montsegur	40
Tarascon-sur-Ariege	50
The Cave of Lombrives	55
Chapter 2 – Back to the UK	**69**
Chapter 3 – Back to France	**133**
Cahors	134
Montsaunes	138
St Martory	143
Tarascon-sur-Ariege	160
The Concert	170
The Train to Paris	181
Paris	194
Chartres	227
St Martory	251
Chapter 4 - Spain	**263**
Montserrat	264
Monzon	268
Zuera	275
Segovia	288
Gandia	301
Murcia	322
El Berro	329
Caravaca de la Cruz	349
St Eulalia Monastery	367
La Bas Tida	372
Epilogue	**383**

Chapter 1

Escape

I stood there and just watched him.

Laughing and flirting with that same damn blonde from last week. She was all over him again flashing her false eyelashes and sticking her chest out in that ridiculously low cut blouse.

I couldn't believe it. After having told him last week how embarrassing it was, he was at it again.

It was the end of the week, we were in the local pub and it was packed just like every Friday night. I half wanted to walk up to them both and confront them but I was sick of it. I was tired, I hated my job, I didn't really like the place and I didn't even feel like drinking any more. It was at that moment I realised I didn't really like him anymore either. I was bored and I just didn't care enough to keep, whatever we had, going any longer.

That was it. I'm out of here.

The cold air outside and the silence made a pleasant change but I was now seething inside. I'd wasted nearly two years of my life with him based on nothing more than worthless promises. We'd get married, get a house, have kids, all when the time was right. It was never right though. I got into my Mini and buckled up.

I reached to switch on the CD player but remembered what I'd been playing when I'd arrived. Not now Timberlake. Time for Queen.

This was better. I turned up the volume until I couldn't hear myself think and drove off. In my rear view mirror I noticed John bursting out of the pub waving his arms at me. Good. I felt better already.

A road sign jolted me back to my thoughts and, realising my speed, I slowed down. The phone was flashing. It was John. If I answered it now, I'd probably only say something I'd regret later. This wasn't just about him. My life was going nowhere and I couldn't see any possibility of things changing.

I'd spent three years doing a degree and had even tried starting a PhD. Unfortunately all of that had nothing to do with my current job which was meaningless and unfulfilling.

I missed my Dad. It was always good to talk to him. I soon found myself outside the block of flats where John and I lived. One small bedroom and a kitchen living room - all for a ridiculous amount of rent. I hated it and I hated myself for accepting it for so long. That's it. I'm out of here too. I rushed upstairs, grabbed my suitcase and started stuffing it full of clothes.

The phone rang again. I left it ringing and went into the bathroom to collect my creams and stuff. Ping. He'd left a message. I'd have to come back for the rest. This was as much as I could do tonight. I struggled down the stairs. It had all taken less than ten minutes. A new record for me - by far. I threw the case and bags onto the back seat and stopped for a moment. I'd forgotten something but was not quite sure what.

Passport. Wow. I ran back up wondering where that thought had suddenly come from. It must be some kind of sign.

I checked my petrol gauge. Three quarters full. Good. It was only 9.20pm, I could still make the midnight ferry from Portsmouth. I'd ring my Uncle in the morning. He'd understand. I'll listen to John's message later.

"Crikey. What am I doing?" I said out loud as I drove past the Ferry sign. "I'm way too young for a mid-life crisis."

There were places on the night ferry to Le Havre. I booked a cabin not wanting to try and sleep on a seat after a night like this. I'd not been to France since my Dad took me when I was thirteen. I wondered what he would be saying to me now. "If you fail to plan, you plan to fail." Well if he was right, this was all going to be a terrible mistake.

Off to France

I made my way to the top deck to look back at the lights of Portsmouth harbour. It was my father's habit. He said it gave you the necessary mindset that you needed as a traveller. As I breathed in the cold night air, I shivered and looked down at my watch. 12.25pm. Three hours ago I'd been in the pub watching all the flirting going on. It was not just John's fault of course, he just couldn't stop himself.

It wasn't for me anymore though. I'd asked him several times to stop. He'd agreed but I could see now that he'd never change. We just weren't right for each other. I should have seen it earlier but I'd mistakenly thought that I'd be able to make a difference.

I checked my messages. One from John, three from Katy. I opened hers first.

'What's up Ro?'

'U OK?'

'Call me tmrw if you want?'

I texted her back. 'All OK. On Ferry to France. Will call soon.'

'What!' She texted back almost immediately.

'Had enough. Will chat tmrw.' Katy understood more than my other friends. We did yoga together and she was going out with Steve who was also one of John's friends. I didn't want to say too much now as I wanted to deal with John first. I took a deep breath and played his message.

'What's up Ro? Why did you run off like that? Call me.'

'Typical' I thought. 'He doesn't even know what he did wrong. He's probably still out having fun. I wondered if the blonde was still with him. What was strange in thinking that was that I realised I wasn't angry any more. 'Wow. That's was quick'. It really was time for me to move on. 'She could have him'.

I loved ferries. The low hum of the engines….the slow rolling from side to side was all, somehow, soothing and comforting. It smelled of adventure too. Dad had taken me to Ireland and Norway on the Ferry after Mum had left. Always somewhere new he would say. Never go back. There was so much more to see and experience.

I hadn't been on holiday for years. Not since well before he died two years ago. Things had been tough for him. The divorce meant he'd had to re-mortgage the house to the maximum. She'd left to go abroad with an American and neither of us had seen her since. I got the occasional Christmas card at first but after a couple of years they'd stopped coming.

After funeral costs and paying off all the credit cards there was only a few thousand left in the Estate. Not much for a life working as a consultant in the mining industry. The little money I'd been left was sitting in a bank account. I'd been waiting to use it for a deposit on a house but I didn't know how on Earth that was going to be possible. I'd need an income of over £50,000 just to be able to get a mortgage on a tiny starter property. I was sick of it all. The whole thing was just stupid. Save all my life for little more than a hut. It would mean being saddled with a huge debt for 30 years as well as trying to pay off my student loan debt. I honestly didn't know what I was going to do. There must be an alternative way.

I sat alone in the cafeteria drinking a laté fiddling with my phone. I needed to send John a message and it couldn't wait any longer if I was going to get any sleep later. I'd deleted three already without finishing any of them. I tried again.

'John. I'm totally stressed out with everything – you included and you know what I am talking about with regards to tonight. I'm taking a few days off to think about what I want to do in my life. Sorry. You are not going to like this but we have given it two years and it's just not working for me. I'll pick up the rest of my things when I get back. Goodbye and I wish you all the very best. No point calling. I've made up my mind.'

Dad would have been proud of me with that. He always said I should wish the best for other people. How he'd managed it with Mum I just don't know but he never had a bad word said about her after she'd gone.

I switched to another social media page and scrolled down. A new post from an old university friend caught my eye. It was Pierre. He was now in a new relationship with Brian. They had moved in together down in some place called Tarascon in the South of France.

I hadn't seen Pierre for a couple of years but we had kept in touch every month or two. We had both done Geology degrees at London Uni. My Dad had tried to talk me out of it but I guess it was in the genes.

My mind continued to wander through past memories. I'd tried starting a PhD up in Edinburgh after leaving London. It was fun and interesting but financially impossible for me. Even if I'd used all of Dad's money, it wouldn't have got me to the end of another three year course. There was also no promise of any job at the end of it too.

I'd met John a couple of years ago at a party in London just before my Dad died. He'd helped me through a difficult time and I'll always be grateful to him for that. He'd understood my need to try and do the PhD and had even helped me with the move up to Scotland.

Unfortunately the bills were just too much for me I had to leave. John had suggested I come back South, move in with him and take a local job until I could find work that was more suited to my qualifications. With that thought I managed to snap myself out of going down memory lane. Instead I returned to thinking about Pierre. I knew he would love it if I dropped by to see him but Toulouse was quite a long way to the South. Another of Dad's sayings came to me. 'Best sleep on it and see how you feel in the morning'. It had always seemed to make sense though I never really understood why or even how it might work.

As I dropped off to sleep my thoughts were more positive. I was now imagining what the next few days would bring. Somehow I now felt I had much more chance of finding what I was really meant to be doing in life.

Having driven off the ferry, I sat in two lines of traffic waiting to drive through passport control in Le Havre. It was a sunny day and that made me smile. Something I felt I hadn't done in ages.

I drove tentatively on the right hand side of the road through the town. My first time. A giant blue Decathlon store on my right caught my eye. I would have been in there like a flash before. There would be loads of new and different sports equipment as well as gym and yoga outfits in there. However it just didn't seem important right now. I carried on and was soon heading South on the A28 to a city called Le Mans.

Le Mans

Large open, flat, yellow fields of wheat stretched out on both sides of me as the long dual carriageway slowly curved its way in a South Westerly direction.

I reached Le Mans by lunchtime so I pulled off the road and headed into the town just to have a break. I was starving but still smiling. I hadn't stopped since the passport office. I was now sitting in the central square in a café called 'Le Jet d'Eau'. It was opposite a colossal Cathedral. 'How on Earth did they manage to build that so long ago?' I wondered. 'We probably couldn't even build one like that today.' I thought a moment later.

My eyes were slowly drawn to the flying buttresses that supported its great height and weight. There were lots of extra spiky bits on top of them which gave the building a sort of prickly, bug-like look. Not exactly something that was very inviting but perhaps its design was like that for a reason – to keep evil away.

Black French coffee. Goodness what on Earth were we putting up with back in the UK. This was heaven. The tiredness from driving drained away with every sip. There were a few people sitting outside in the Sun like me. One or two seemed to be tourists. The season must have just started.

A young Frenchman smiled at me. Still happy I smiled back but quickly stopped and looked away just in case he got the wrong idea. Good, he was still in his seat and back reading his paper again.

Having finished the coffee, I got up to go to the till. There were bananas in a basket next to it. Hunger pangs in my stomach now grabbed my attention and I picked one up. It was then that I realised I had no cash on me. I had to pay for that and the coffee with a card. 'Failure to plan'. I put the banana in my bag and ambled slowly across the square to the Cathedral. I was here now. I might as well have a look inside.

I never liked churches. There was always something depressing about them which got worse whenever people tried to sing in them. Stepping inside an old tall Cathedral though, that was different. There is something about the height that I loved and the blue and red light that streamed in from the stained glass windows. This one certainly didn't disappoint in that respect. Modern cathedrals just didn't seem to give out an authentic feeling that the really old ones did. There was almost a lightheaded spacious sensation sometimes when you walk past the ancient stones.

I walked slowly down the aisle in the middle, conscious of the noise my favourite boots were making with every step I took. My neck arched back more and more as I looked up at the ceiling.

I stopped suddenly though, becoming aware of a man standing right in front of me. He too was looking upwards with his back to me. He hadn't noticed me behind him. I looked at his short black slightly curly hair and could smell some kind of sweet musky aftershave. Then, unexpectedly, he took a step back, treading on my foot.

He spun around in quite an athletic manner and immediately apologised. I think he was speaking Italian, I wasn't sure, but it was fast and rather nice. He had a tanned look and must have been in his early thirties. I took a step backwards and mumbled an apology too. He switched to English.

"I am so sorry Senora. My mistake." He spoke with a lovely unmistakeable accent.

He had blue eyes which distracted me again as I thought that that was strange for an Italian. Words for now escaped me and all I could do was nod back at him. I must have wobbled backwards as he reached out to touch me on the shoulder as if to steady me. Instinctively I took another step backwards. I was not used to strange men immediately touching me.

"Are you OK?" He asked.

I nodded again and tried to smile but turned to hide my face. That turn continued and the rest of my body moved round until I was now facing the exit. Without thinking I started to leave.

"Senora". He called after me. I walked slightly faster for the exit.

'What is wrong with me?' I thought when I was safely back in my car. Why had I reacted like that? He was just being friendly and helpful. He really was just being apologetic and I'd said nothing.

I looked around …..Strangers were everywhere. I thought about it for a moment.

If I was going to get anywhere in my life…………… I would have to start being more comfortable around strangers. But where on Earth had that fear come from. My father had always been good with strangers. He'd travelled a lot though. Maybe that was it.

I sat in silence ………..my mind pondering it all. He was probably with his family. What! Where did that thought suddenly come from? I couldn't believe I'd just thought that. I could have sworn that my next thought was 'I'll never know now'.

What's going on with me? Unhappy with myself, I drove off wanting new scenery so I could distract myself with new thoughts.

I was never going to be able to drive all the way to Toulouse in a day, even if I did eventually choose to go there. I decided to head for Limoges instead and find a place to stay there over night. The place sounded nice …Limoges…it had a nice soft, round vowel-sound to it. I wondered what I might find there. I could always go to Bordeaux after that or even across and down to the French Riviera and Marseilles.

It was Saturday afternoon and my Uncle would be out walking his dog somewhere. I could call him later when I had checked into a hotel. No messages from John. That was good. Somehow it also felt bad though. Did he really care that little for me? Not even enough to try and make it up?

As I drove I couldn't help running through the events of the last 24 hours again and again. Had I really done the right thing? How the hell was I going to find out what to do in my life while I was over here in France? I dismissed that thought again like I had many times already and looked again at the countryside.

There were more trees and woods now and it was much greener. It was a joy to drive in the Sun all the time. I could open my windows, turn the sound up and get back to smiling.

The smiles didn't come though. Something wasn't right. Was I missing something? Katy. I said I would give her a call today. Saturday afternoon would be a good time for her. I decided to stop at the next town and make the call.

It was a place called Tours which was on the river Loire. I was soon driving down an avenue of sycamore trees …iconic France. I loved it. I pulled in at a roadside café that overlooked the river.

'Hi Katy. U OK for a chat' I texted.

'Sure' came right back.

I rang. "What are you doing, where are you? You mad woman." she started half laughing.

"I'm not sure yet," I replied, "I'd just had enough….had to leave."

"I went to the toilet and when I'd got back you'd gone. What the hell happened?" She asked.

"John again. But it's not just him. He was just the final straw."

"Was it the blonde?"

"Why do you say that?" I asked surprised she'd picked up on that.

"Steve and I left the pub at around 10.30. John had had too much to drink but had wanted to stay. He'd been with that blonde. Every time I looked over she had her hands all over him. It was actually making me really annoyed. He didn't once try and stop her."

"Yes I know. I saw it too Katy. I'd asked him again last week to stop embarrassing me anymore when we went out together. With a few drinks inside him though, he just can help himself. It made me feel sick. It was also like he'd punched me in the gut. I just had to get away from there."

"By the time I was driving, I was sick of my work, sick of the way my life was and sick of the way the country's going."

"I was just so stressed I had to get away from it all."

"So where are you now?"

"France. In a place called Tours on the river Loire. I've got a nice glass of white wine in my hand and I am sitting at a table looking out across the water. It's lovely. I've got my shades on and I'm starting to tan."

"Very nice darling, but what are you going to do?"

"I haven't decided yet. I'm heading for Limoges tonight and could go in any one of three directions after that. Maybe down to the French Riviera, or perhaps down to Biarritz or possibly, down to the Pyrenees."

"Well that all sounds very exciting but it's not quite what I meant." She persisted.

I knew exactly what she meant but I wasn't ready to answer that question yet. I just wanted to keep this feeling of freedom and excitement for a while longer before I got serious again about the future. She was a friend though and deserved more of an answer. "Look Katy, I really don't know yet. I just couldn't stay there in that flat with him and that job. I was suffocating. I had to get away, relax and take a break. I really need some time to think about everything too. I also haven't had a holiday in years." I replied honestly.

"It's going to cost you loads. You'll eat into all your savings" She said sounding truly worried for me. She really was a good friend but I couldn't have told her before I left.

"Katy, if I'd spoken to you beforehand you'd have just talked me out of it. I don't know what it'll all cost but I can't imagine I'll be away that long."

"Well Steve's already spoken to John this morning." Here it comes I thought. "John's worried sick about you. Says he doesn't know why you took off like that."

So he didn't tell Steve about my text then. He must still believe I'll come running back to him. "It's over Katy. I texted him that last night. I'm not going back to him. It'll never work."

"That's Ok Ro. Look, you have a great time and come back fully recharged. It'll do you the world of good to have a break and get some sun." I could tell she didn't really believe me when I said it was over but there was no point in going there anymore.

"Well please don't worry about me Katy. By tomorrow I could be on a beach next to a bar with some music playing." My voice had become cheerier. "I'd better get on now though. I'll be in touch soon. Bye."

"Bye Ro ... don't do anything stupid."

"Bye."

"Send some pics." She added quickly.

Limoges

I hit the road again and three hours later I was in the heart of Limoges. I'd booked online whilst in Tours and found a lovely little hotel called the Jeanne d'Arc. Limoges was another typically lovely French town that sat astride a large river.

I checked in and got changed into my running outfit and headed off to a small park that was around the corner. It was only 6pm and the Sun was still shining. How nice was that.

The park was beautiful with fountains, trees and footpaths but a little small for me to run around so I headed down to the centre of the town and the river Vienne.

Running always made me feel good. I used to do all the heart rate analysis stuff, running within training zones, measuring times and distances but I'd scrapped all that only a few weeks ago. I'd even stopped listening to music when I ran and I loved my music. All the electronic stuff had stopped working for some reason and, since then, I'd found that I far preferred running free from all of it. It was my time now and it was as though I was suddenly free to think again. I now just ran as far as I wanted to. If I wasn't enjoying it I would just stop and walk and enjoy that instead.

Right or wrong it worked for me. The only problem was that occasionally I could lose myself in my head completely and that meant it was really easy to lose myself physically.

Having got back to the hotel I felt a whole lot better and I'd had time to think about what I could do and where I could go.

Something was drawing me South and I couldn't fight it. I would contact Pierre tonight and see if I could stay with him for a day or two. If he had no room I could stay in a nearby hotel. It would be good to have a chat with an old friend and to meet his new partner too. Before calling him though I wanted to speak to my Uncle.

"David. It's Rowena. How are you?" I said louder than normal as I knew his hearing was going a bit.

"Rowena, is that you?"

"Yes" I said slightly louder. "I'm in France Uncle David."

"What are you doing over there?"

"I had to get away for a few days. I've broken up with John."

"You didn't have to go that far away dear. You could have just popped round here."

"I know and thanks but it was a spur of the moment thing."

"That's not like you Ro. Are you all right?" he enquired.

"Yes I know and yes I am fine. I feel better already."

"Well you have a good time then and take care. Come round when you get back if you need a place to stay."

Uncle David was good like that, but I knew he could only take someone living with him for a few days. He had to have everything in order and all laid out where he knew where things were. Anyone else in the house for too long would start confusing him.

"Thanks David. I wanted to let you know anyway. I can still be reached on my phone if you need to call me."

"That's good Ro. All the best and I still have some of your Dad's stuff you need to go through." He always added that these last few months and it was something I was dreading. Going through old memories of Dad and deciding what to keep and what to chuck was something I'd been putting off. David had kindly helped with moving some of Dad's stuff out of the family home when it was sold. The furniture had all gone but there were mementos, pictures and papers that he'd kept back for me.

"I'll be round when I get back, thanks again."

"I'll be here, bye" he replied.

I liked my Uncle but I never found much he wanted to talk about so conversations with him tended to be quite short. He'd been an English teacher but had retired early on grounds of ill health brought on by stress. After his wife Julia had died, he'd found he just couldn't cope with the younger generation anymore. He spent most of his time reading. I think.

I decided to text Pierre first.

'Hi Pierre. Can you chat or are you busy?'

My phone rang. It was typically friendly of him to just call straightaway.

"Rowena, lovely to hear from you. What are you doing, where are you?"

"Pierre. Congratulations I see. How are things?" I replied.

"Well thank you Ro, Brian is so sweet, you will love him. We have been together for a month now. You must come and visit sometime."

"Pierre thanks and that's really why I contacted you. I'm in France."

"Where darling?" He said excitedly.

"North of you up in Limoges"

"Wow that's quite a way away – nearly four hours in the car. How come you're in Limoges?" he asked.

"Long story but if you are up for it, I would love to stop by."

"Great, would you like to stay a day or two, we have a spare bedroom".

"That would be lovely." I said.

"When will you be coming? No it doesn't matter. Just come anytime you can."

"I could be there by tomorrow evening I guess."

"Is everything OK Ro?"

"Yes and No. I broke up with John."

"Darling, he was never right for you, you know that. I told you that before too. I'm so glad for you. Look. Don't tell me anymore now. Get some sleep and head on down tomorrow and will catch up more over a meal."

"You're a star Pierre. Will you text me the address."

"No problem, ring me when you are nearby. Take care love."

I always felt better having spoken with Pierre. Nothing was ever really a problem for him. Not unless it was a really big one. Then we would all have to gather round and help him.

Sunday breakfast in the hotel was very different from normal - plenty of types of ham and cheese to choose from the buffet and there was a selection of honeyed croissant with cinnamon and raisins and chocolate in. All I really wanted was some porridge. The coffee made up for it though.

Pierre had texted me an address in a little place called Tarascon-sur-Ariége. It was further South of Toulouse than I expected and I worked out that it would take about 4 hours with stops along the way. I set out at 9.00am and planned to be there by lunch time.

Tarascon-sur- Ariége

I was now some way past Toulouse and making good time. I'd entered the low foothills of the Midi-Pyrenees and had eased off the speed to look around a bit more. The countryside here was adorable with long avenues of trees lining the roads for many kilometres. The low hills with their straight rows of crops soon gave way to high limestone mountains with small white patches appearing in amongst dense green bushes and trees. Steeply sloping woodland was everywhere. At the bottom of these valleys there were now narrow, deep and fast rivers that occasionally bubbled over small rocks and swept around large boulders.

15 mins away I pulled over and texted Pierre. I was to look for an Aldi on the left hand side of the main road into Tarascon. He would meet me there in the car park.

"Pierre." I shouted out, waving as he pulled in to the car park in his Citroen.

"Cherie. You look so good. You've grown your hair too." He waved and called back with his arm out of the window.

His wide smile beamed at me as he pulled in next to my Mini. He still knew how to make me feel good.

"Rowena meet mon ami Brian." Brian had nipped out and come around to the other side of the car to stand next to his partner whilst Pierre reached out to me with both arms. I went forward and embraced him back fully in the typical French way of moving shoulder and face from side to side and back again.

"Ami?" Brian smiled mockingly at Pierre.

"No, but of course, my 'partner'." He said still smiling at me and then back at Brian emphasising the word in English with a French accent. "It has been only a short while and you Ro, are the first English friend of mine who has met Brian."

"Nice to meet you Brian." I said moving in for a repeat performance of the warm French hello.

"Enchanté, Mademoiselle" Brian beamed back at me.

"How did you both meet?" I said

"We met at the University in Toulouse…" started Brian.

"…Brian was doing his 'masters' there in Water Engineering …." chipped in Pierre.

"We met during a lecture on Advanced Hydrology." added Brian.

They were already a good double act I thought with a twinge of envy that they had completed their higher studies.

"Come, we must celebrate. Let's go down to the Les Vallées." said Pierre.

Over a bottle of white wine, we sat talking for an hour sitting outside next to a bridge over the Ariége. The river here was wide but shallow with stony islands filled with bushes and trees growing on them. After having had a glass of wine, I'd relaxed and was now able to look all around me. The limestone mountains towered over the houses on the opposite bank. Both sides of the river bank had high, man-made walls that went right down to the water's edge. There were obviously times when a lot more water would pass through here.

Time flew by as we chatted about what had happened to us in the last two years. When we had covered just about everything the conversation fell silent for a moment and I began to think about what I was going to do now and why I was here. Pierre seemed to sense this.

"Come Ro. It is time for you to have some fun" said Pierre. "We are all going to go down to the Prehistory Park to throw some Stone Age spears and to draw some Cave art."

"What?" I was truly surprised.

The Parc Pyrénéen de l'Art Préhistorique was only a few minutes away and was really for families with kids but it was filled with the sort of information that curious minds like ours enjoyed dwelling upon. This whole region was full of people 14,000 years ago. The mountains around the area had loads of caves where they'd lived. These caves had names like the Grotte de Eglise and the Grotte de Niaux.

In addition to that there were numerous old burial chambers that could be found. These were generally constructed with three large upright stones and another large flat one that was laid down on top of them. Again, exotic sounding names had been given to them like the Dolmen de Quiernes and the Sem Dolmen. We weren't here to just learn that though. Pierre led us through and outside to a place where there was a target area.

In a field at the back of the park there were cardboard cut outs of prehistoric animals, spears and spear chuckers. A spear chucker, which is held in your hand and not released, propels the spear. There is a socket at its end which the back end of the spear sits in. This simple mechanism doubles the distance a spear can be thrown. Our ancestors were not simple or stupid in any way.

Soon we were in fits of laughter. It was not at all easy and our spears were going in all directions and nowhere near the targets. "Yes" I shouted gleefully, jumping up and down, as my 10th attempt had hit the cardboard cutout of an antelope.

"No way….that's only the edge of the target. You missed the animal."

We were useless and my admiration for the Stone Age hunters had shot up. "Time for some Art" said Brian rubbing his right shoulder. All three of us had the same ache. We went back inside into a room that looked like a large classroom. Some kids were already hard at work making a modern form of rock art by drawing pictures of animals on flat stones that they had been given.

Half an hour later, my hands were filthy and covered in the red ochre colour that had come from the stones we'd been given. My finished effort was no better than the ones the children had been creating. We were all laughing.

"So Ro. What are your plans now you are here?" started Pierre.

"I am not sure. I wanted to get away from everything at first but now I'd really like to try and find out what to do with my life." I replied.

"Get married and have kids." half joked Brian. The other half I think was just testing my reaction to what he'd said.

"Maybe someday. Not at the moment though. It just doesn't feel right. I want to get my teeth into something more individual and personal to myself before I settle down. I'm just not sure what that is yet. I also need to earn some money too." I replied.

"Why not look for work abroad. There must be jobs for Geologists somewhere." suggested Pierre.

"I've looked. I really have. It's terrible to say this but there just are not many and the ones that are out there are in the middle of nowhere…. either exploration mining or on the rigs.

"What about going back and finishing your PhD?" He tried helping.

"I'd like that, but I'd really need to find a good way of funding my way through it all, as you know."

"Find a sugar Daddy." smiled Brian. "I hear that's the popular thing in London these days." He chuckled mischievously

"Brian. Don't tease." rebuked Pierre.

"Thanks but no thanks" I said, recognising a well-disguised compliment but at the same time wanting to make a stand against his tease. I flicked some of the paint from my fingers at the overalls he was wearing that we'd all been given to protect our clothing. Damn, I thought, now noticing my nails. They're going to take some time to sort out. A few were chipped and broken, not surprising really but perhaps worth all the fun.

"Well you are welcome to stay a few days" said Pierre. "We are fairly busy this coming week with work all around the region but there are some cool places you could try visiting while you're here."

"Like what and where". I asked.

"Well you must visit the Cave de Lombrives." He began. "Then there is Foix – a beautiful market town with its own central castle on a rocky outcrop in the middle of it all."

"What about Rennes le Chateau and Montesegur" added Brian.

"Wow." I said not knowing anything about these places. "I didn't know there was so much to see around here."

"Darling you are in the heart of Cathar country. There is so much here you wouldn't believe it." said Pierre

"Cathar country?" I asked, having some vague memory of having heard the name before somewhere.

"Come. Let's get cleaned up and go back to our place. We'll tell you all about it over dinner."

Pierre and Brian had moved into a chalet type apartment tucked away behind the main square in Tarascon. It was small, cosy but modern and open plan. It suited them well. They began telling me more over a chicken provencale.

"Back in around 1170 AD this whole area was filled with people who had turned to the Cathar faith." started Pierre.

"I've not really heard about this faith, what was it, or is it?" I asked.

"Well the Cathars are thought to have originated from Greece or Armenia." continued Brian. "They spread further into Europe and they reached this region around 1160AD."

"They differed in their way of thinking from the Roman Catholic church in many ways." interrupted Pierre. "It was very Gnostic."

"Gnostic?" I asked.

"Yes, their followers believed that Jesus and his disciples Peter and John the Baptist were all really teaching a more spiritual version of Christianity than we see in the World today." said Brian. "They were essentially saying that the way to find God…"

"…or Enlightenment…." said Pierre.

"… was to look within yourself and to become a better person." finished Brian.

"Their leaders were called 'Perfects' or Bons Hommes – Good men in English." He added.

"That sounds a bit sexist" I said.

"Not at all Ro. In fact it was quite the opposite. They were way ahead of their time in establishing that men and women should be equal. Both could be leaders of their church or community." said Brian.

"It was one of the things that the Pope really hated about them." said Pierre.

"One of the more well-known women was Esclarmonde de Foix" continued Brian. "She was just one of a group of Cathars who helped rebuild the Castle at Montsegur."

"She herself set up many schools across the region as well as several hospitals. She was known to always be looking to help the poor too." He continued.

This Esclarmonde lady was beginning to interest me. She seemed to have been an amazing person and way back all that time ago too.

"The Cathars taught that God was some kind of Universal Spirit and that it was a kind of eternal love that was perfect and absolute." Brian added.

"The Cathars also said that the Roman Catholic church had become corrupt and wanted nothing to do with it." added Pierre.

"The Cathar leaders were not…….hmmm…...how do you say 'when people show off' in English?" continued Brian.

"Ostentatious?" I tried.

"But yes. Ostentatious. They were not ostentatious, they worked hard in the fields themselves and wore normal clothes like everyone else." said Brian.

"They seemed like a nice lot" I pointed out.

"They were, that's why so many people were joining them. They did view things a bit differently though. For example they viewed death differently. To them it just meant passing back into better existence." Pierre added further.

"They thought that if they had prepared well in this life they wouldn't have to come back here again" He continued.

"A bit like reincarnation." I added.

"Yes exactly." He replied.

"They used to hold a really important ceremony called the Consolamentum. It was carried out in the sacred caves around here and taken in order to prepare themselves for their next existence in their next life by wiping away all their sins." said Brian.

"Just to help them not come back again?" I asked.

"Presumably yes. Because of this way of thinking they didn't fear death as much. They were more afraid of coming back into this World again. The Pope, a chap called Innocent, if ever someone was wrongly named it was him, absolutely hated them." said Pierre.

"The number of people who were joining the Cathars kept on growing and this was another threat to the Pope as people were turning away from the Catholic church. The Cathars also absolutely refused to acknowledge the dominancy of the Catholic church." said Brian.

"In the end the Pope just hated everything about them because it was threatening his power base." added Pierre.

"So he started a crusade against them which was later called the Albigensian Crusade with the intention of not only wiping them all out but to also wipe out all knowledge of the Cathari way of thinking. He very nearly succeeded too." said Brian.

"Montsegur, which is only round the corner from here, is where they made their last stand. In 1243AD they were under siege for 10 months but in the following year the Pope's army finally broke through their defences." continued Brian.

"Two hundred and twenty Cathars were burnt alive in a field at the bottom of the mountain." Pierre said more solemnly. "It is said that four of them escaped the night before though." He added.

"There is a museum in Montsegur worth popping in and seeing and the walk to the top of the mountain is well worth doing too. It only takes about 30 mins to get to the top." suggested Brian.

"The place is only about 40min by car too so it's really not that far." said Pierre. "If you fancy going a bit further you could visit Rennes Le Chateau too."

"Is that where the Cathars were too?" I asked

"Yes but that's not the reason to go there. Have you ever heard the story about the priest Bérenger Saunière?" asked Pierre.

"No" I replied.

"Well I won't tell you much as you can find out much more when you get there. All I will say is that the place has been a magnet for treasure seekers for decades." said Pierre.

"Treasure?" again I sounded surprised.

"Yes. Treasure buried in one of the caves there. It was said to have been stolen from Rome by the Vizigoths. Much of it had been stolen by the Romans though in the first place as they had taken it from the Jews when they were in Jerusalem." said Pierre.

"The story goes that the Priest found it. The reason for that is because, mysteriously, he was suddenly able to spend huge amounts of money. You'll see what he spent some of it on when you get there." added Brian.

"It's also a magical place to look out over the countryside in all directions. You may even find some inspiration there as to what you want to do in life." Pierre added as an afterthought.

"Maybe she'll meet someone, the love of her life." Brian smiled cheekily.

"Brian stop it," Pierre quickly interrupted "Ro has only just split up from her partner, she's not going to want to get together with anyone again so soon. Isn't that right Ro?

"The last thing on my mind at the moment is another relationship." I stated quite firmly.

Having finished the meal they put on some music and we all went out to sit out on their small balcony. It was a classical piece with a composer I had never heard of but it seemed completely appropriate looking out into the dark of the night. If I strained my eyes I could just about see the dark background of the mountains against the night sky. Tarascon did indeed seem to be a magical place.

Rennes le Chateau

Monday morning. I called work and told them I was suffering from stress and needed a break. They weren't happy. They never were, so I told them to take it off my accrued holidays. That seemed to go down better with them. I didn't tell them I was unlikely to be coming back though. That call would have to come when I was feeling slightly stronger.

I decided to set off to Rennes le Chateau first, have lunch there and visit Montsegur in the afternoon. Whatever the day would bring, it would bring.

I got into my trusty little Mini and wondered about music. This morning it felt like time for Pink. An easy choice and she joined me as I drove North out of Tarascon looking for the turning to head East and the road to Lavelanet. I'd be in Rennes in under an hour. It was another fine day and it soon got me to thinking about how I too could have a bright future. The fun the day before with Pierre and Brian had taken the edge off my stress but there were still some burning questions. I decided to put my most optimistic hat on and wished hopefully that I might find some answers today.

The narrow winding road circled the base of the hill upon which Rennes Le Chateau sat. Either side were fields of grass filled with yellow buttercups. I slowed down a touch as I approached a right hand turn that led up to the top. The road curved round bends with walls of red sandstone and it was not long before I was higher up and driving past the dry white limestone walls of the houses on the outskirts of the village. The view to the right of me was becoming breath taking.

Now that I was entering the village I was passing the typical red tiled houses found in this area of France. The streets were also getting narrower and narrower. Seconds later I was squeezing past close walls and into the car park at the top which looked out over fields and wooded hills to the North.

I got out and started to explore. There was strange quiet about the place. I had expected more tourists but I suppose it was only early on a Monday morning.

I was drawn to start at the little church dedicated to Saint Mary. It wasn't at all what I expected. The entrance porch had a wooden shelter above it with yellow painted panels on the front of its own little roof.

Everyone who then walks inside the church immediately sees what looks like a 4 foot tall statue of the devil on their left. I found out later it was a statue of Asmodeus who was said to be a Demon King. How that differed from the Devil I had no idea but its wide staring eyes were enough to scare anyone away.

The church itself was tiny. No more than fifty people could have squeezed into it at a push. There was a half domed ceiling above the altar which was covered dark blue and that had hundreds of small stars dotted all over it. The paintwork seemed nowhere near the age of the church itself.

The pattern continued on the ceiling for the rest of the church but in light blue. My eyes were drawn to some water damage at the back. The damp had taken away the blue wash colour and underneath I could see large daisy-like petal shapes with 8 to 10 lobes. In the centre of these shapes little silver stars had been painted.

It was as though it had all been deliberately painted over. I found that most curious. My overall impression though was that a lot of money must have been spent on the interior to make it look very plush. It may well have been what the Priest had spent some of his money on. I did what everyone then does and pulled out my camera phone and went round taking snapshots at everything – including a selfie with the demon king. I could post that one to Katy later.

I walked around to the museum and booked a guided tour. In reality the tour was just the two of us. My guide was a retired local man. Unfortunately he spoke very little English. I listened, trying my best with my own attempts at translation, to the story about the Priest Bérenger Saunière.

Somehow he'd found the money to do up the church. He had also started to lead a far more lavish lifestyle. The original 9th Century church had fallen into disrepair and it was thought to have been restored by the Knights Templar in the 12th century. It was then left virtually untouched until Saunière arrived in 1885.

I thought that this might have been when the ceiling got a makeover and the patterns underneath were hidden. They may well have been original Templar patterns. It seemed that there were several theories on how the priest, who was known to have originally been poor, got the money. It could have been old treasure from Rome, brought and hidden by the Goths. It also could have been from the Knights Templar who had hidden a portion of their wealth behind in a nearby cave.

Others thought there was a third reason. This was that the priest had found some secret scrolls under a loose flagstone in the church. These were then said to have contained something that was potentially very damaging to the integrity of the church of Rome. The people that thought this, said that Sauniere had been blackmailing the church with this information and that he was being paid off for his silence.

33

Whatever it was, it didn't seem to interest me. I was not a treasure seeker. Years of life could be wasted and nothing found and I didn't want any part of that.

I left slightly dispirited by what I had seen and heard and headed out and down into the village to find something to eat. Around a corner I came across a restaurant called the Dragon of Rhedae. Its painted sign on the outside of the building did it for me. That looked much more fun.

I was the only one in there. The young man who took my order for a light salad spoke English quite well so, when he came over with it, I asked him about the name of the place. He gave me a look as though he had all the time in the World and moved around to the seat next to me in a friendly way.

"Ah. It is good you are interested – thank you. May I?" He said pulling out the chair from under the table.

"Yes, please do sit." I said. He was a slim built young man with very short hair – the type that was cut with a trimmer and not scissors. Not my type but he had a wide smile and lines around his cheeks that emphasised it even more. I could see that it gave him a sort of attractiveness that some women would like.

"Hello, my name is Arnaud."

"Rowena" I replied holding out my hand. He shook it gently.

"Enchanté. What do you think of this place Rowena?" he asked in a way that almost seemed as though he was checking me out. I decided to tell him.

"Actually not much so far. The church was small, a bit weird and the treasure stories all seem to be a bit inconclusive so they didn't really interest me. I liked the views though."

His face lit up a bit. "I agree," He started. "but what do you think about the location?" He spread his arms out to the sides looking around and twisting slightly.

"Well it's nice…." I began.

"….It's all about the location for me." He interrupted sounding more inspired. "I'm a caver and there's loads of caves to explore around here." He caught my strange look. "Don't get me wrong, I'm not a treasure hunter, I am a speleologist. I just like looking for new underground routes."

It was his passion that attracted me more than the news he was someone who like to crawl around dark holes. For some reason I felt like asking him some questions to find out some more.

"Go on, tell me what you have found so far" I asked.

"This is just a summer job for me. I'm from Toulouse, which is not far away, but to get enough time underground, I really have to be living in the area."

"Why caving though?" I asked.

"Freedom to explore, the joy of finding new things, the peacefulness, the exercise, the beauty of some caves, but for me it's really about finding new caves and new routes through from one place to another. But let me answer your first question." I looked slightly confused. "The one about the name of this place". He reminded me.

"Oh yes." I remembered.

"Well firstly this place is called Rhedae. Some people call it the hill of Rhedae. Long ago there were Stone Age people who lived in this area. I have found their bones in caves too." He said nodding. "Then the Romans came here, they built a large villa on the hill, the land around is good and fertile, see. Then in the 6th and 7th Century's the Vizigoths came here. They ruled the whole area and it is said they built a huge city of around 20,000 people to the South of here somewhere. No one quite knows where it was though. Some historians have called this city Rhedae, but I think it became a name for the whole area – this place included.

"So what about the Serpent or Dragon?" I asked, having started to eat my salad.

"Ah." He began in a way like all good story tellers, "Well that goes back to the local legends and who knows how far back they go. This has always been known as the place of snakes. Large snakes, serpents are also called Dragons you know. You see not all Dragons fly. Some are said to be so large they coil right around the Earth." I could see he was enjoying telling me this short little piece of information complete with all its hand and arm gestures.

"I went once to the Cathedral in Narbonne." He stated, "It is a town on the coast. I saw a Red Dragon on a window there. My friend said they were the enemy of the church and the Saints used to go around trying to kill them all. It all seemed a bit strange to me." He ended with a slightly confused look on his face.

"So that is how this place got its name The Dragon of Rhedae." I stated.

"Precisement. The legends say that these large snakes are found here right on top of this hill." he smiled. "These stories say that these snakes can be found in the caves. In all my time underground though, I have never seen any snakes. I found that strange." His expression now became one of complete bewilderment as though he was acting out his own non discovery having come out of another cave.

"So what have you found?" I got back to my early question.

"I have two first breakthrough routes already. In one cave and out of another. I had to crawl for two hours in one of them but I found a beautiful cave on the way there with stalagmites and stalactites. That was my best day out."

"That must have been amazing." I stated remembering my early geology lessons on the subject and which ones went up and which went down.

"For sure. I have pictures I can show you later if you like."

"So what else have you found?" I continued

"Well, have you heard of the Cathars?" he replied.

"Yes" Having just heard about them the day before from Pierre and Brian.

"Well they were here too. The authorities though came here many years ago and pretty much cleaned everything out of all the caves they knew. I did find one or two caves though that very few people know of. I keep them secret for reasons just mentioned and in case other cavers find them and discover routes in them before me.

Anyway, there is definite evidence that they used to use them for their sacred ceremonies."

"But how do you know this?" I asked noticing that I was strangely more interested than I would have been a week ago.

"They used to draw on the walls of their caves. A typical sign is a painting of a dove flying upwards. It is supposed to represent their souls going to heaven. They didn't use all the caves though or even the biggest or more appropriate ones. For some reason certain places were more sacred to them than others." He paused for a moment as though in deep thought before continuing. "It is said that their Perfects, their leaders, would hold ceremonies for the locals in these caves and then travel all the way to another sacred site. They would then hold another one for that community. They even have a name for these routes. They are called the Cathar paths – Les Chemins des Bonhommes."

"So what are you going to do Arnaud? What do you hope to do in life?" I asked him.

"Ah, a good question. For me I am going to stay here as long as I must stay here and do what I must do."

I felt really puzzled by his certainty and yet confused that this was his answer. There must be something more. I tried again "But what after that and how will you know when you have done what you are supposed to have done?"

"That is not a problem Rowena. Really." He added when he saw my expression. "Life will work things out. It always does."

I had to admire his positivity. "But what about plans for the future? Don't you make any?"

"For sure, I have dreams, who doesn't, but you never know when life turns on you and your dreams are gone. So many things go on in this World that are just out of my control, I cannot prepare for these. Short term goals, they are Ok. Where to go tomorrow? Which cave to try next? These are things more in my control. I just take life as it comes with a hope in my heart and not a picture in my mind. So far so good." He paused to look at me, then continued. "If I have hope, everything will work for me, n'est pas?" he added ending on a French note.

I was left feeling slightly perplexed at this approach to life - one so different from mine. Could I really learn to do this I thought? Would it even help me if I did?

"Arnaud. Thank you so much for sharing your thoughts with me. I really do appreciate it and I really admire your attitude to life. Do you have any contact details? It would be good to stay in touch."

"For sure Mademoiselle Rowena, we can do social media, here have this." He took out a small note pad and wrote out an email address and web address. My cave photos are on the site too. I must get back to work now anyway. All the best Rowena. It was lovely to meet with you." We both got up together to go. "Until we meet again." He added with an English version of 'Au revoir'.

"Bye Arnaud" I waved at the door.

I stepped out, turned to the right and walked back up to the car park wondering about my meeting with Arnaud. He seemed to just get by on positive expectation and by spending as much time as he could doing the things he enjoyed most - almost the exact opposite of my last two years since University. How could I possibly do that? It just seemed like escapism to me. I had nearly reached my car when a little old lady walked up to me with her hand outstretched. In it was a little posy of white and purple flowers.

"Monnaie …Mademoiselle s'il, vous plait." She was in little more than dark coloured rags and the car park was practically empty. She still had a basket full of them under her other arm too.

I gave in, as I sometimes do when it seemed right, and took out my purse. I had visited a cashpoint in Tours and had about four Euros left in change. I gave them all to her. She handed me what looked like a bunch of white heather with some purple lavender. It could be my new air freshener I thought.

"Merci Madame" I said taking the posy and handing her the coins.

"She smiled and nodded her head a few times and then stared at me. It was strangely startling to see the change come over her. She reached out and carefully took hold of the sleeve of my blouse. She then whispered to me something which I think translated into 'Look out for the Snakes' but I wasn't sure, my French was not that good and her accent made it harder.

I nodded back uncertain of what to think. She smiled and pointed at me and then at the mountains to the West. I nodded some more and she again pointed to me and then the mountains and said the word 'Serpentes' again. I definitely heard that word right.

I got in the car and drove off wondering more about how she had reacted rather than what she had said. It came across as a warning but the way she was behaving made it seem like she was trying to help me. Maybe I had misheard her and got the wrong translation. This was turning into quite a strange day. I looked at my CD's on the passenger seat. No. I'll stick with Pink for a bit longer. I was soon rocking away back down the hill. If I made good time I could be at Montsegur by 2.00pm and have plenty of time to go up the mountain.

Montsegur

There is something majestic about driving through steep limestone mountains with a deep blue sky behind them. Almost everywhere you looked had perfect photograph potential. The winding road up to Montsegur had several passing points and I stopped several times to take some snaps. To get to the museum, I had to drive past the mountain and then down some zig zag hair pin bends to get to the small village of Montsegur.

Once inside I soon learnt that the Castle sits on the Pog – the name of the high rock formation. It was a very old site with evidence showing that the Stone Age people lived there about 8,000 years ago. The Romans had even built a shrine at the top to their goddess Belissena and, apparently, the locals have always known it to be a sacred place. There'd been three castles built at the top over the years. The first and second ones had been destroyed and only the remains of the third one, the 17th Century one, now remained. The Cathars had built the second castle around the year 1200AD. It appears that they too thought that this mountain was a very sacred place.

The Geologist in me then wondered why people considered some places to be sacred whilst others were not. It was a novel concept for me and total unexplainable especially since I had started a project in Geobiology studying how some places could be bad for life. I parked the thought for the moment and continued on around the museum.

Esclarmonde de Foix had lived at Montsegur for a while. Her name meant 'Light of the World' in Occitan – the local language at the time. A grand name for a grand woman, I thought, thinking too that I would have liked to have met her. In another part of the museum it mentioned that the 'Perfects' used to walk directly across the hills from here to the Caves at Ussat where there was another one of their very sacred places.

It was curious to think that the Cathars always seemed to be following some kind of path. I had come across two already. One of these seemed to be following paths from one sacred place to another. The other path seemed to be the one they were trying to follow in life in order to help them avoid coming back into this World again.

It appeared that they believed that much of what they experienced in this life was preset for them. They thought that there were set challenges that a person had to overcome. If they could overcome these that would help make them a 'Perfect' person and that would increase their chances of not coming back here.

I could understand them wanting to follow the right path in life in order to become a better person. However, I really couldn't see how they could be really sure if they were on their right 'preset' path or not. It could not be as simple as going from one sacred site to another – could it? Even if they did do that, how would praying make a difference too?

I wasn't a religious person and I was not going to start now so there had to be something else here I was missing or I was really wasting my time trying to learn anything from them. I decided to leave the museum and go up to the top of the Pog. I needed the exercise anyway.

All that sat well with me at the moment was the Cathar idea of being a good person to everyone. I also liked their idea that Men and Women should be treated equally in all things. Talk of reincarnation, preset journeys with challenges in life was just too much. Still something intrigued me about them and I felt I was missing a vital piece of the puzzle. Maybe there was even something in all this that could be helpful to me in my life right now.

The path sloped gently upwards to begin with and I passed a large field to the right of me. This was still today called "Prat dels Cremats" which in the Occitan language meant 'Field of the burned'. Two hundred and twenty people burned alive in the name of religion...it could not have been nice. My mind turned to the events happening around the World today.

Hmm...not much has changed.

What followed was a slightly steeper path through the woods and then a final semi climb/walk to the top. I was certainly breathing more heavily when I got there. I'd even had to use my hands once or twice. Up some wooden steps and I was soon through the stone entrance into the 17th century castle. From the models in the museum it now bore little resemblance to where the Cathars had once lived. The views though were magnificent.

I thought I had the place all to myself, until an oldish man appeared through the opposite entrance. He had been admiring the view from the other side. He seemed to be heading my way and I was heading his. I wouldn't have spoken to strangers normally but in this situation it would have been awkward to avoid any communication.

"Good afternoon," he began first, beating me to it by speaking to me whilst still at least 10 paces away from me. He must have been about 65 but he could have been older. He had a well-groomed appearance, smart walking clothes and shiny new boots which all told me that he was a man who was not poor by any means. He also sounded American.

"Good afternoon to you too. Are you from America?" I tried not sounding sure.

"Canada." He replied. Damn. I thought I hope he was not too upset with me for misjudging like that.

"Not a problem" He added. He must have just noticed a tiny twinge of disappointed on my face. He was observant then.

"Sorry". I replied. "It's a lovely day isn't it?" I deliberately changed the subject.

"Indeed it is young lady". He stopped a few feet away in front of me.

"I have to say it is strange to meet someone as young as yourself up here on her own, on a week day afternoon,….." He paused as though considering his next words carefully. "…especially someone from England."

He said that in a way that I noticed was designed to be as respectful as possible in case he was wrong in his guess. He looked as though he was very sure of himself though. I wondered for a moment before replying. He looked harmless and well-intentioned but he was still a fair bit bigger than me and it was just the two of us up here. I decided to put aside any fears with the help of Pink who'd so recently been singing to me.

"Are you up here alone too?" I asked as politely as I could. There was a short pause as he looked at me.

"Nicely put, young lady. My name is Paul. Paul Cloutier from Quebec and yes I am alone."

43

"My name is Rowena, Rowena Colleen. What brings you up here?" I asked feeling slightly more at ease.

"The water is too warm for fishing at the moment and the Sun is still too high." Of all the answers he could have come up with, I didn't see that one coming. He could see my surprised look.

"I have come to do some trout fishing in the Ariége and to see the sites. My family originally came from the South of France and I like to come back from time to time." He said by way of explanation. "How about you?" he asked back. I could tell he had been straight we me so I decided to be straight back.

"I broke up with my partner on Friday night in the UK, I hate my job and my life was going nowhere so I took the ferry to France. Somehow I ended up right down here. A friend recommended I come up here and today it seemed like a good idea."

"I wouldn't have employed you." He said quickly.

"What?" I said more than a little taken aback by his words.

"You look too smart, you are obviously adventurous and there is something about you that good employers try and avoid."

"Excuse me....and just what would that be?" I said now slightly angry but at the same time confused as he'd included somewhat kinder observations in his remark. He had also managed to somehow intrigue me. In addition to all of that I was a bit in awe of how he'd managed to make me feel all those emotions at the same time and so quickly.

"Please don't get me wrong Rowena. You seem the type who will eventually run your own business. I used to own a company back in Canada that employed over a thousand people. I sold it a few years ago." He added. "I've hired and fired many people over the years." I listened wondering where he was going with all this. "There is a trick to it. You need to find people who will always want to work for someone else. If you hire someone who looks as though they will one day want to run their own business, they'll just learn everything they can from you and then start up on their own. The next thing is you have a competitor cutting into your profits." He said.

I paused for a moment to consider what he said.

"I hadn't thought of it like that." I could see his reasoning and it was certainly not something I had heard before. I'd never considered running my own business though. "Do I look like someone who would want to someday run their own business?" I asked.

"Most certainly you do and you are already acting like you do. You look like a searcher Rowena. My guess is that you are doing that right now. You have something special in you. I can tell. That is what I was good at – spotting special people to do business deals with." He was right with me searching for something, but 'special', I wasn't so sure.

"Have a look round up here….. We can walk down together if you want….We can talk more on the way if you wish. I want to be fishing by 5.00pm though so need to be down by 4.30." He spoke with a degree of finality. He went and leant against the wooden railings outside the main castle entrance and looked Southwards. I left to walk around the top for a while. The views to the North were nice but I was still wondering about what he meant.

In the end curiosity got the better of me and I strolled back across to him so we could walk down together. As if he knew what was on my mind he began. "You see Rowena, not everyone feels they have to make a difference in the World. Some people are quite happy to be gardeners, midwives, farmers. It's not all about money. Success comes in many ways for other people. There is nothing at all wrong with that. In fact it is a good thing as the World needs good dedicated gardeners, midwives and farmers." He paused for moment as though thinking carefully about his next words.

"We are conditioned by our parents, by our teachers, by our peers, by the media into thinking that other viewpoints are right and correct over ours. For years we listen to others and we generally don't listen enough to our own needs and desires." He stopped and turned to look at me for a moment as though he was reading my expression on what he'd said.

"What may be right for others, may not be right for ourselves." He continued on down again. "You for example are special and special people generally want to make a difference in the World."

"But everyone is special in their own way." I challenged.

"Yes, but there are different types of special. This type of 'special' is like being a leader, a pioneer. Contrary to what some people think, you cannot train someone to be a real leader. Oh you can certainly train someone into thinking they are a leader but real leaders, like you, are born to it."

He certainly knew how to say the right things I thought, feeling now better for it myself. "It's a bit like the Cathars that lived here. Not all of them were 'Perfects'. It was just too hard a journey for them. It was not their time, if you like. Not everyone has the same journey in life." He continued. "We all have to learn to grow and develop in ways that are right for ourselves. This is why we must strive to find out what that journey is."

"How do we do that?" I asked.

"Ah. That is a good question and one I still ask myself. It may seem as though I have the answers but in truth I have made huge mistakes in my life. True I am a leader, I built a huge financially successful business. However, my wife left me, my children won't speak to me and to be honest there are times when I feel quite lonely."

I looked at him. His head was down looking carefully at where he was putting his feet. The path was very uneven and rocky and it put pressure on the knees with the uneven height drops as you stepped down. I sensed he was being honest and not trying to spin me a story.

"What happened with your family?" I probed delicately wondering if I should ask at all.

"I was never around. I was always working and before I knew it, my wife had gone off with an old friend of hers. My children just became more and more angry with me for never being part of their lives. I wish I could change things, but they don't even want that." He paused for a few seconds.

"You see I was driven to be financially successful. I thought that was what was important. The ridiculous thing was that I thought I was doing it all for the family."

"So what should you have done? Looking back" I asked.

"I am honestly not too sure. If I had worked less, maybe I could have spent more time with them but then again, if I had taken my eyes off the business, I could have lost everything." He paused again to think.

"Several times, if I'd not been there, that would have happened........ I regret it all now though as I have all the money I need........ It will eventually all go to them anyway so maybe I'll finally be able to help that way......... Who knows?" he spoke with several short reflective pauses.

"There's still time is there not?" I added in a caring tone.

"Yes there is and I am optimistic my sons will see and understand one day. In the meantime I must keep learning myself. It seems that some people need to go a long way through life before they learn what they really should be doing. Others know straightaway."

We'd got down to the woods again and the going was easier. All that we had to be careful of now was to not trip over the tree roots crossing the path. "What I can tell you is this." He continued. "I did all the goal setting that was possible. I read all the books, did all the visualising, made plans and kept to them...... I failed loads of times. I learnt from those failures and eventually went from success to success. If you follow all the rules, it all works." He stopped and became silent for a while. I sensed there was still more to come. He breathed deeply and continued "I've a great life but now, deep down, I have regrets and I'm not sure now that I actually followed the right path."

"Maybe you had to do all that to get to a point where you are now." I replied trying to be optimistic for him, "Now all you have to do, perhaps, is to overcome this last challenge. Maybe you are actually on the right path and now you have this final challenge?" I asked.

"Maybe. But I think I got the balance wrong early on. Yes I have a challenge or two ahead but if I'd not been so controlling, so focused on being a millionaire, I could have perhaps helped my family more." We walked on in silence for a while until we'd come out of the woods and were now walking down a gently sloping field. We were nearly at the car park when he spoke again.

"You have a good questioning mind young lady. Keep asking the questions and you will find your way. I am sure of it. It's not all about the money. That will come when it's needed."

"Thanks for all your helpful words Paul. It's given me much to think about. Thanks for calling me special too. That was nice of you."

"Just remember Rowena, not everyone can be like you or even live up to your standards. If you want to catch a Salmon, don't go fishing in a Carp pond." With those slightly bizarre words he turned and smiled at me whilst standing next to his black four by four. Reaching down into his coat pocket he pulled out a card. "Here. Call me when you find out the answer." He chuckled as though laughing at his own joke.

I could tell he was serious though. It appeared that we are all searchers at one stage or another in our lives. Age has nothing to do with it. Maybe it was even something we all had to continually get used to doing? I watched him drive off and headed over to my Mini. What to make of all that I thought - all that money, yet lonely and with a deep sadness within him.

What seemed interesting however was that he knew that all the goal setting, visualisation etc. worked, but yet, at the end of it all, it hadn't given him what he'd really wanted all along. He'd either denied it, forgotten it or just suppressed it in order to get rich. Somehow his motivation from the start had been lost along the way.

I looked at my CD collection. It had been a heck of a different kind of day so I fancied something independent in a different way too. I had nothing on the seat next to me. I reached instead for my mp3 player and selected Rita Ora.

Chilling out nicely and now driving unhurriedly down the hill I saw a woman running on the side of the road. Her long blonde hair was tied at the back and it swung from side to side with every pace she took. Her figure was small but perfectly proportioned with strong shoulders. My first thought was actually that she must work out her upper body as well as being a natural runner.

As I passed her, I glanced quickly around and could see she had a calm and relaxed look. She didn't even notice me. Her eyes were gazing upwards and ahead of her. Her casual stride belied the speed she was actually moving at. I could tell she'd been a runner all her life. What moved me most was the sense of freedom on her face. She was happy and away with it all as though in deep meditation. I admired her immensely for that. I drove on thankful for the reminder of how life can be good.

That thought then led me to thinking again about my conversation with Paul. I think I knew now what I had to avoid but I was still unsure of just how to find the right path. I was not sure exactly where my next feeling came from. For some reason I thought about getting married and having a family. My gut had suddenly ached when I thought that. I'd never thought I wouldn't have a family, but this feeling made me think that it might not happen for quite a while – if at all.

Maybe if Paul had started a family later on in his life things would have worked better for him. But then, what motivated him to start was to provide for his family so maybe he may not have succeeded then either. I thought of all the social media videos I'd watched of the stars telling us the same old message of how visualisation and goal setting had worked for them and how rich they'd become. I'd also doubted many of these stories as you would often hear later on that many of them had also been doing drugs or alcohol and had actually been incredibly depressed. They always seem to have had several partners in their lives too.

No, they were not sending out the right message at all.

Still I had nothing to go on from here. No answers were coming through as to what I should really be doing. Maybe there was a connection to the Cathars that I was still missing - something that I could learn from them perhaps. I decided to see if I could find out more tomorrow. Tonight though, I wanted to cook a meal for the guys.

Tarascon-sur-Ariege

A quick check online and I found there was an Intermarché in Tarascon. It wasn't far away and soon I was there.

Oh…..My…. Goodness were my first thoughts on walking through the doors. This was nothing like the UK. The aisles were filled with loads of different types of food. There were many regional types of cheese and local breads. There were types of fish I couldn't recognise and a whole load of strange cuts of meat. I could have spent an hour in there easily just looking around at all the choices on offer. Not having the time though, I grabbed some vegetables, some pasta and some fresh sauces and herbs with a pasta bake in mind.

The guys loved having a meal cooked for them and for the first time in a long while I enjoyed preparing it. John had always been boring with his food and it had become a real chore for me. I again wondered why I'd stayed with him for so long.

It was another good night with plenty of laughter as we shared the experiences we'd all had that day.

It was sunny again in the morning. I could get used to this every day I thought. Then it occurred to me 'Well why not? What's stopping you?' Again. There is was. What should I be doing? There seemed to be no escape. I'd been on the run from my ex, my work and my life, but I couldn't escape my mind.

I picked up a casual yellow dress but it didn't seem to work in the bright light with my hair. Instead I put on shorts, a T-shirt and a light jacket. That would go better with the boots I might need to wear later on today. I'd decided to go to the Caves at Lombrives just down the road at Ussat-les-Bains. It was a spa village that had been popular at the turn of the century for people seeking cures for their ailments.

I'd checked online for details about the Cave and found that the only tour today started at 2.30pm. I had all morning to wait. Not wanting to stay in their apartment after Pierre and Brian had left for work, I decided to look around Tarascon. It was certainly pretty with its castle walls and towers and spectacular views but it still felt as though I was just searching for something as I walked around. In the end I sat down on a seat that overlooked the river and the town. It was not far from a tall round tower called Le Tour du Castella. The high landmark made it stand out from all its surroundings and I was using it to navigate my way around. I could have used the mobile maps but the geologist in me preferred to use my own bearings.

I checked for messages and sent a couple of photos to Katy. Again nothing from John. I smiled and then started to laugh a little thinking of where I was now, compared to where I was last week. I guess it must have sounded, and looked from behind, like I was crying, with my shoulders rising and falling between the short laughs, because a passing French woman came up next to me and asked in French if I was alright.

She sat down beside me and we exchanged meaningful looks. With the age difference she could have been my mother but she had a kind look to her that my mother never really had. I tried to explain that I was really just half laughing but I am not sure she believed me. Her English was as bad as my French but we continued to try and communicate.

"Ma petite fille," She started, "C'est d'accord …It's ok to cry"

"No, I am ok." I replied

"Yes, Yes it is ok" She continued. I resorted to smiling more and nodding. She nodded back with me.

"Good. Come with me…. have some coffee." I didn't feel I had much of a choice and it was a kind offer she'd made.

"Merci." I said in my best French accent.

"This way, I clean here….. once a week. It small place…..I can make coffee."

Only a few meters behind from where I was sitting there was a white terraced house with large, pine coloured, wooden double doors. Going inside, it didn't look as though anyone lived there at all. It was more like a garage or an old workshop. She moved through a side door and we went up some narrow stairs. She spoke as we walked up them.

"This is small private room…. Some friends of mine…. I clean it each week….. No one comes….. No one knows." I walked into the room behind her, gasped and held my breath.

"What is this place?" I managed to ask after a moment of looking around. It was only a small room, maybe 3 meters by 4 meters. The walls all had flat glass display tables around the sides and there were more of them in the middle of the room making up a sort of central table. On the walls were all sorts of pictures and written information.

"It is Gadal ….Cathar….Saint Graal….. Je pense." she replied.

There were all sorts of prehistoric bones of animals and humans, many small minerals of different sizes and colours and other bits and bods that seemed to have been found in the caves from all around Tarascon. In amongst it all were pictures of a man called Antonin Gadal – a man who had been born in Tarascon back in 1877. Gadal, it appeared, had been looking for the Holy Grail. He had searched hundreds of caves in the area and his findings were on display in this room.

In addition to that, it appeared that he was most interested in the Cathars. His interest in them apparently had been stimulated when he was young. He had lived next door to an old man called Adolphe Garrigou. Garrigou, it seems, was a historian who had specialised in compiling information about the Cathars and their Gnostic form of Christianity. Gadal had been carrying on his work looking, from what he had noted in his writings, for a 'pure form' of Christianity.

There was one hand written note under glass there that caught my eye. It was titled Le Graal dans les Pyrénées. I took a photo of it in order to translate it later. One line of words in French stood out for me.

It read 'Le chemin du Saint-Graal est le chemin de la perfection!' It translated to 'The way of the Grail is the way of perfection'.

This took me back a bit as I thought that the Grail was the Cup of Christ. To me it was the cup that collected his blood on the cross and the one that was passed around by his disciples at the last supper. This was now saying that the Grail was some kind of journey. Added to that I had never heard of a connection between the Grail and the Pyrénées and now, it seemed, there was some further connection to the Cathars.

I looked around some more and in another display case in the centre of the room there was another piece of paper filled with strange symbols. Outlined in the middle of the page a red rectangle had been drawn. Inside it were seven symbols all labelled with one word - Graal.

Could these all be symbols for the Holy Grail? I wondered

I stopped for a moment and thought 'why am I finding this interesting?' At that point the kind lady brought in two small cups of fresh expresso coffee for us both. There was nowhere to sit but she and I walked around the room with her pointing to certain photographs. Several were of Gadal. At times we tried exchanging a few words of French until she felt I understood what she was trying to tell me. We had nearly gone around the whole room when she pointed to a large rock sitting on a low stool on the floor.

"Météorite." She said and indeed there was a sign saying Météorite in front of it.

The trouble was that it was not a meteorite. I knew that well, not only because I was a geologist but because it was also very similar to the rock my father had kept at home. It was a piece of Haematite.

Indeed, in the room, there were lots of small fragments of haematite under the glass lids of the tray tables. The cavemen used to use them to draw on the walls. I knew that only too well myself recently. I also knew that haematite could form under certain conditions deep underground in limestone cave systems and it was exactly in this whole and complete form that was sitting on the stool. It was practically solid iron.

I bent down to try and pick it up. I was not weak but this small rock was probably around 40 kg in weight. It was hard to get a grip so I lifted it only a few inches and then put it down safely again.

"Wow". I said, Trés lourds. Heavy." I said looking at her.

"Oui. Certainment" she replied. I decided it would be too hard with my French to try and tell her that I didn't think it was a meteorite so I left that alone. I would discuss it with Pierre later though. We finished our coffees and I thanked her very much as she saw me out. I asked for her name though in case I had a chance to thank her again.

Wow, I thought when I was outside. That was all a bit strange to come across all that right then. It had to mean something. Just what though, eluded me. I walked back to where I'd parked my Mini near to the apartment and changed from my trainers into my walking boots. I'd need them for going through the cave.

The Cave of Lombrives

The drive was less than 7 mins away. In no time I was pulling into a small car park where there was a sort of road trolley bus waiting to take people up to the entrance of the cave. I could have walked but opted for this rather different approach and got in behind the waiting driver.

"Bonjour Madame" he said respectfully but indifferently getting back to look on his phone.

"Bonjour Monsiour" I replied. A few minutes later, the trolley bus, with just the two of us on it, pulled away and started up the steep, zig zag tarmac path on the way to the Cave of Lombrives. At the top there was a party of Chinese tourists who must have walked up earlier and together we all set off on a two hour tour. Our tour guide was a young Frenchman called Bernard. He spoke good English but no Chinese. The Chinese though had brought along their own Chinese to French interpreter who was busy giving a constant translation of everything Bernard was saying. We soon realised he could more easily translate from English to Chinese so Bernard was able to save time by just talking in English rather than saying everything in French and English.

Bernard first explained that this was the most extensive cave system in France that was open to the public. The first chamber we were in was called the 'Lair of Giants'. As we went further in we began to see the many symbols and names on the walls that people had drawn in the past. In no time we had reached the Cathedral Cave. We were told that it was 107 meters high and bigger than the Notre Dame cathedral in Paris.

Bernard also said that from time to time concerts would be held here. The sounds echoing off all the walls made for an amazing experience. One of the Chinese began to sing a note and it had a lovely reverberation to it. Soon we were all making strange noises.

"Our next concert is in two weeks time" Bernard said. "We have a local musician called Christian Koenig playing the Pan Pipes. He rarely performs any more but his performances are always eventually sold out. He plays wonderfully and the sound is truly amazing. If you ask at the front desk on the way out I think there may be one or two tickets left."

After leaving the Cathedral Cave we climbed some steps and passed limestone concretions that, because of their shapes, had been given various names over the years. There were names like 'The Mammoth, the Witch and the Virgin." On the way Bernard told us all about an even greater tragedy than the one at Montsegur and one that was almost unknown.

It seems that five hundred Cathars had hidden in the Lombrives Cave in order to escape being killed by Simon de Montfort – an Englishman who was the Earl of Leicester. He had been placed in charge of the Pope's army in the crusade against the poor Cathars. When he found out where they were hiding, he sealed them all inside the Cave and prevented any of them escaping. They all died from starvation and dehydration. Their bones were found many years later.

Again I had to wonder just how these peace loving people were such a threat to the Roman church back then. But then I remembered why. It hadn't been about religion it had been about power and money. Whilst we were walking as a group I had a chance to speak to Bernard and to ask him a question of my own. I started with one about the Cathars and asked whether this was one of their sacred Caves.

"Absolutely" He started. "This one, and one or two others nearby."

"What evidence do you have though for this?" I asked.

"Well evidence was found that this was where they held their Consolamentum ceremonies. There were signs and symbols on the walls that supported this too."

I then mentioned that I'd met a caver called Arnaud over at Rennes Le Chateau who had told me about the sign of the dove he had found in a Cathar Cave over there.

"Ah. You know Arnaud. He is a good friend and we have done several trips underground together. Yes the dove is one of the signs they used to put on the walls of the cave they used."

"I met him yesterday. He's a very friendly man." I said.

"Are you also into caving?" Bernard asked.

"Me, no. I have never done that." I replied.

"Pity." He went on. "As a friend of his I would have been happy to have showed you one later after this. It is very close to this one and a place that nearly no one knows about." I wondered about what he'd said for a moment. Was this an offer to go caving with him or had I missed the chance? If it was an offer would I even want to go? He seemed a nice guy so I decided to ask so more.

"Is it dangerous?"

"Mais non. It is just a little crawl to begin with. You might get your clothes a bit dirty, but it would be worth it. There are couple of nice caves to see in there." I was almost caught up with this.

"I think it was a special cave for the 'Perfects' too as there is a dove there." He continued. "That would be worth seeing." He smiled at me in a way that was full of typical Gallic charm.

"How long would it take? To get there and to go in and out?"

"About 30 minutes." He said in a take it or leave it manner.

"I would love to see it, if that is OK with you." I stated slightly surprised at my own confidence here. I was a geologist though and I was not sure that, if I'd turned the opportunity down, I could have lived with myself afterwards.

"Only because you know Arnaud." He hurriedly said. "You must never speak of this cave to anyone." He warned holding up his index finger.

"Of course." I replied.

After the tour was over, Bernard asked me to wait for around fifteen minutes while he finished his shift. What followed next was a bit of a scramble along the side of the limestone rock face. There was no path, so we moved between, and sometimes over, the shrubs and small bushes. The ground was angled quite steeply and covered with small stones and I slipped a little on several occasions.

After about 10 mins of this, Bernard stopped and looked around. We were well out of sight of the main cave entrance. He explained he was just checking to see if anyone was watching. Satisfied there was no one looking, he bent over and began to pull back some small branches that had been lent against the rock. Having done that, I could see a large round flattish boulder that was about a meter high. He slowly rolled it to the side and behind I could see a tiny opening.

"Here." He said handing me a couple of rags. "Tie these around your knees and elbows, it will help you to not get scratched by the sharp stones on the ground. Best to leave your jacket here too. It will be safe." I was lost for words, not expecting this, but did as he suggested. He then handed me a small torch.

"Good, now follow me. Don't worry about turning around and don't try to go backwards. You will be able to stand up and walk around in a couple of meters." With that he got down on his hands and knees and then stretched flat out onto the ground and proceeded to move into the tiny hole at the base of the small cliff face. Seconds later he'd disappeared from view by slithering his way forward.

"It is Ok, Rowena, you can come through now" I was about to just follow him without thinking but suddenly remembered I hardly knew him and I was about to enter a secret dark cave and, on top of that, nobody knew I was even here. He was a friend of Arnaud though. A mixture of positive and negative emotions ran through me. Should I give in to fear? No came a voice from inside my head which did not sound like my own voice at all.

"Coming." I replied and stooped down to the ground immediately thankful for the cotton wrapping protecting my knees. After several awkward shifts of my body later using my hips, toes and elbows to move along, I was fully inside what appeared to be a short tunnel. It felt very claustrophobic. I could hear my breathing get slightly faster. Was this the beginning of real panic? I was resting on my elbows and my head was already bent down so as to not touch the top of the tunnel. Where was my hard hat? I thought.

"Don't worry Rowena. Everything is OK. I can see you." He shone his torch down along the tunnel and I could see the light in my face.

It was not far to go. A few move shoves and I was through. I felt relieved as I started to get up and my breathing became more relaxed again. We were in a small cave with room for about ten people to stand up in with their arms out and hands touching. Our torches moved quick all around and shone out in all directions. Bernard's light fell upon a small painting of a dove about 6 feet up on the far wall.

"I think this was where they also held their private ceremonies" he said. I looked at the dove, thinking about the man or woman who had drawn it. It was simple and yet so meaningful. "But look here" he pointed to a thin crack in the wall. "We can squeeze through this gap and get into the next chamber. It is slightly larger than this one."

He turned sideways and started to squeeze through. It was a tight fit for him. He was slightly taller than me and was wider in the chest too. Something I noticed thankfully before it was my turn. For about 5 meters we edged our way into the next chamber. In this one there was a large stalactite which had a small stalagmite growing up beneath it. The cave was higher and about twice the size as the last one. On the walls were a few rough indecipherable drawings of various kinds of animal. There were also some marks that looked more like scratch patterns than symbols. The floor was littered with loose rubble along with some little pieces of broken haematite. Underneath that there was a flattened earth base.

"I think this was used in the Stone Age" said Bernard pointing his torch onto some of the drawings. I shone my light around the walls and walked slowly around the cave. There were little shallow alcoves or ledges that appeared to have been cut out of the limestone. On one of wider ledges there was a larger piece of broken haematite. It looked similar to the one my father had but really all the pieces here looked much the same. I reached out and picked it up and almost dropped it due to its weight. It needed both my hands to carry it. I showed it to Bernard.

"Yes there is lots of that in here." He said.

"Would anyone miss this if I took it as a memento?" I asked, not quite sure why or how I was going to carry it out.

"No, not at all. The museums have much too much of this to worry about one more. Here, let me carry it for you." He offered.

"Does this lead anywhere else?" I asked.

"Not that I can tell yet" he replied. "I have looked though as I thought it might link up with the Lombrives cave but I think that might need a bit of digging and I am not into that very much – too mucky for me. When I have some time I will come back and search some more though." We spent a few minutes there chatting about how I came to be in the Ariege while he explained what his plans were. After a while he apologised and said that he couldn't stay for much longer as he had promised to go back and help his sister with some chores.

We squeezed out of the caves with him letting me go first this time. Outside in the light I could see just how dirty I'd got. Wiping my hands on the pieces of cloth I had taken off my knees and elbows I was able to get my phone out of my jacket pocket. I pressed the mirror app and saw my face was covered in brown marks. Seeing this Barnard laughed and soon we were both laughing. Before we left Bernard hid the entrance with the round slab and the bushes and we set off. I'd slung my jacket over my shoulder and he very kindly took my lump of rock. We then stepped carefully back along the rock face wall again until we got to the Lombrives cave. It was then just a short walk from then back down to the car park and my Mini. His small blue Renault was even parked next to mine.

I liked him but I didn't feel anything back. I thought perhaps that he might have preferred Pierre or Brian to me, either that or he was one of the genuine ones and had a girlfriend. Either way, I asked if he'd any time later for a drink after he had helped his sister in return for his kindness at showing me the cave.

"I would like that Rowena but maybe another time." He said putting the rock in the car boot for me.

"I would like that" I replied.

We exchanged numbers, hugged in the French cheek to cheek way without our chests touching and promised each other we would call.

"If you would ever like tickets to a concert, let me know too. I can sometimes get them before others if you know what I mean." He called after me.

"Thanks. I would like that." I called after him. I sat down in my Mini and thought about my second full day down here in this beautiful countryside. It was almost too much to take in. From the private museum in the morning, the tour in the cave of Lombrives to squeezing myself into Bernard's private little cave. I'd done more in the last three days than I had in the last two years back in the UK. How was that possible I wondered and in such a short space of time? Was there some meaning to it all even? Was there even some message here for me with regards to my future life?

I'd ended up down here in order to escape but now I felt that I'd found something but not enough to know exactly what that was. Maybe Pierre and Brian could help me make some sense of it all.

They'd given me a key to their apartment and, with the state I was in, I really needed to get back and take a shower. By the time I'd just finished dressing I was in the early stages of thinking that it was time I moved on. I couldn't stay indefinitely, it would not be right. It had been lovely here and I'd met really interesting people. I'd even found out some things that should be helpful to me. I decided I would leave in the morning. I fancied heading to Carcassonne first to have a look around the old town there and the castle and then go on to Narbonne.

From there I could perhaps head further East to Marseilles. It was a city that I'd heard much about. It had a sort of cinematic draw to it with all the films that had been made about the place. As for where I actually decided to go, I would see how I felt in the morning. What I did decide to do though was to tell them over dinner tonight. It was also when I could ask them some questions about what I'd come across today.

When Pierre and Brian got back they'd already decided they wanted to take me out instead of eating in. They'd already booked a table at the Bellevue restaurant in the Terra Nostra hotel just over the bridge and opposite the café we had been to on the first day. Apparently it was also place with a good local fish menu.

By 7.00pm we were sitting down at a window table with the best view of the river below you could get. All of us ordered the trout. Over a glass of Sauvignon Blanc, I thanked them for being so kind in letting me stay with them. I then went on to say that I felt I ought to be moving on in the morning.

They did their best to try and get me to stay a bit longer but, in the end, they knew it was the right thing for me. They were now more concerned about where I was going to go than anything else and were full of suggestions for places I could try. When the meal came I asked them my first question. "Guys, what do you know about the Holy Grail and its connection with the Cathars?" They looked at each other and then back at me with very surprised expressions.

"Well," started Pierre, when he saw I was serious. "The Grail was just a dish in a story by Chretien de Troyes back in about 1280AD. It was nothing special. A Graal was just a French name for a dish at the time. There was a holy wafer that was held in the dish and some people say that this was what was special."

"Another story, one that came along after that, was a story that said that the Grail really was the Cup of Christ – the one at the last supper" said Brian.

"But the one I think you are talking about Ro is the one the Cathars were said to have found. Why do you ask though?" said Pierre.

"Well I had a strange experience this morning. I met this lady who was the cleaner for what looked like a private museum here in Tarascon – only a few hundred meters away in fact. She showed me into this room where we had a cup of coffee and she introduced me to the work done by a man called Antonin Gadal."

"Mon Dieu! Rowena" startled Brian. "Do you know how lucky you are? There are people who have lived here their whole life waiting to see inside that room. I myself would love to see it but have never had the chance."

"What was in there, what did you find?" asked Pierre.

I proceeded to explain all that I had seen to them with their eyes getting wider and wider. "I was wondering if you could help me by translating this." I pulled out my phone and showed them the picture I took of the French writing that Gadal had done with the title 'The Grail in the Pyrénées'. Pierre took my phone and together they looked at and slowly read out a translation.

"The Grail of the Pyrenees" began Pierre.

"The Grail, or Grasal or Grasala in the Occitan language, (The Holy Grail of the Temple Knights)" continued Brian.

"...has been explained and mysteriously spread in the Middle Ages thanks to three troubadours." chipped in Pierre.

"The 3 principle writers: Chretien de Troyes, Kyot – a Frenchman and Wolfram von Eschenbach – a German. (From 1150 to 1191)." read Brian.

"Perceval the Welshman, from Chretien de Troyes, opens the cycle of the Grail – the blood of Christ. The Perceval of Kyot takes the stone from the sky, a stone from the stars, and this is preserved by Wolfram's Perceval." read Pierre.

"Wagner, an amazing 'initié' – initiate, followed with his magnificent Perceval Trilogy preserving….." started Brian

"…. the stone from the stars in his work 'The Cup of the Grail'." finished Pierre.

"This much so far is what is generally known I think" said Brian.

"The five drops of the blood of Christ, or the stone that came from the stars, ……..representing Lucifer falling ….. from out of the Sky, are the same symbols of purity and of the perfection of Christ." said Pierre stopping a couple of times to try and get his translation right.

"This is old French too" he added. "Not so easy to translate some words."

"The way of the Holy Grail is the way to perfection." This is Gadal said Brian. "He is known for thinking this way. It is this he thinks the Cathars were trying to achieve in their lives."

"I will let you continue Brian." said Pierre. "You know much more about Gadal than me."

"The castle of the Grail is guarded by the service of the Temple Knights. A broken sword that could not be mended, meant that the Temple

Knights could not overcome evil as they were not perfect- This again is Gadal's way of thinking – his interpretation of the Grail story." Brian added.

"The place of Salvation, the mountain of Salvation, the fountain of Salvation after having encountered the Grail….

Then there are a few dashes" adds Brian…..

"….To see: The Grail on the Rose and the Rose on the Cross – the Cross of the Grail."

"This is a bit more cryptic for me." said Brian. "I am not sure what that last part means."

"Goodness Rowena, what you have brought into our lives in such a short time." started Pierre. "A true puzzle to solve. Did you see anything else there?"

"Just a few symbols of the Grail" I showed them the photo I took of the symbols.

"I don't really know much about symbols Ro. You should take them to someone who might know more" suggested Brian

"Or search online" said Pierre.

"Yes, online first would be good" added Brian. The trout had come and we eagerly started to eat. The translation had given us all an appetite.

"What do you think it means?" I asked.

"Well," Brian started, "I think Gadal was a Gnostic Christian himself – like the Cathars and he would have liked the quest for the Grail to be like the quest for becoming a better person in life. I think he was looking at interpreting the Grail stories in a way that would fit that way of thinking. What do you think Pierre?"

"I think you are right about Gadal putting a personal angle on the interpretation of the Grail – to fit his beliefs, but I think he was also on to something else. Those last two lines seem to me to show that he thought there was more to it than just a journey of perfection. If Gadal is right, it seems to be about a special place as well. It mentions a place of salvation and a mountain and a fountain of salvation. What is interesting is that it seems that these are places that come after the Grail is encountered."

"I was wondering about special places myself" I added. "The Cathars seemed to pick very specific sites as being sacred. I was also wondering just how they did that and why that might be."

"I do not know the answer to that Ro. Maybe that is for you to find out though?" Pierre smiled.

"What is this all about a stone from the stars?" I asked.

"There is talk of a special stone that came down from the heavens. Wolfram von Eschenbach writes about this as having come from the Middle East. I think they have stories over there about the same stones." said Brian.

"Probably meteorites" said Pierre. My mind immediately flashed back to the private room and the large piece of haematite labelled Meteorite. No. Gadal surely couldn't have thought it was a meteorite. I wondered. Maybe he even thought that this piece was the stone from the sky.

"What are you thinking Ro?" Pierre asked as I had stopped eating and had been still for a few seconds.

"There was a piece of haematite in the room and it was labelled meteorite." I said. "Do you think Gadal might have thought that was the stone from the skies?"

"No. Impossible" said Brian. "If it was, it wouldn't have been left there in a small museum. In addition to that, we don't actually have any proof that the Cathar stone even existed." He added.

"There are also a lot of rocks like that around here." added Pierre. "As I am sure you will have noticed Rowena. I'm not sure how anyone could tell which one was a special one either?"

"Gadal wasn't a Geologist anyway." I added. "A mistake like that could easily be made though. There are Iron Meteorites that could look similar." For some reason my mind went back to thinking about what I was going to do with my life. That was much more important right now. This Grail thing was fast becoming a distraction and one I couldn't really afford.

Back at the apartment, Pierre and Brian went to bed. They'd had a long day. I went on to the balcony to have one last night time look at Tarascon. I had to go back home right away. It was not a thought I had expected but it made sense and it began to resonate within me. I had to face the music and sort things out. Going on to Marseilles was not going to do that. That was just escaping again. The short break down here had been good for me though. I'd needed that.

I would stay with my Uncle for as few days as possible and get a small flat somewhere. I would use the time to find another job and that would give me some time to think about what I could do on a self-employed basis perhaps. Maybe Canadian Paul was right. I was unemployable and I needed to work for myself. I could do that. I went to bed happier. I felt I was beginning to sort out my life. I slept well.

In the morning I told the guys my change of plans and, bless them, they were again very supportive and said I could come back and stay any time I wanted. Come back here later on in the year, they'd said, we can look for the Grail together. We smiled and hugged cheek to cheek in a way the French call 'les bises' and I was off.

Chapter 2

Back to the UK

It would have been a 10 hour drive back to Le Havre so I stopped overnight in a B&B on the outskirts of Orleans. I'd gone right through my Coldplay and Ed Sheeran collections. Having caught the midday Ferry back to Portsmouth, I was now only minutes away from my Uncles house in Newbury. I'd phoned him earlier and he had very kindly said I could stay with him for a few days until I'd found my feet.

"Uncle David" I reached out to give him a hug when he opened his door. "It is so kind of you to put me up for a few days"

"Not at all dear. It's lovely to see you again." I brought my two bags in and took them up to his spare bedroom while he brewed up some Green tea. Sipping it always brought back fond memories of my Dad. I think David knew that too which is why he always liked to put on a pot for me.

I explained all that had gone on since I'd last seen him. He did his best to listen and he would occasionally ask a probing question, like the good teacher still within him, but his interest only really perked up when I began to talk about the Cathars and the Grail.

"Ro, that's absolutely wonderful you came across these things down there. Have you read any books on the Grail yet?"

"No Uncle." I replied not at all surprised he'd turned the conversation to books - his favourite subject.

"You know of course that the Grail was considered to be many different types of things." He continued whilst I nodded. "It was first a dish, then Robert de Boron wrote about it being a Cup. Then, as you know, Wolfram con Eschenbach finally got round to saying it was a stone that had fallen from the stars. But did you know that it was also said to be invisible?" He asked.

"What?" I was genuinely surprised.

"Yes by more than one writer as well." He got up off his chair whilst still talking on the subject and shuffled over to one of his bookcases. He had two of them in the sitting room and they took up nearly the whole wall from top to bottom and from end to end. "The book Perlesvaus was written just after Wolfram's Parzival. No one quite knows who wrote it but it is thought to have been a Cistertian monk or even one of the Knights Templar themselves. In both books they say that only the holiest of people can see the Grail. Those that can see it, also talk of seeing it change shape over time."

"Really? How can that be possible? That sounds ridiculous." I blurted out.

"Well I really don't know Rowena. These are just stories you know." He replied casually." Here, I thought I had a copy of them both. He pulled out two paperbacks from the second shelf down and handed them to me. "I would read Wolfram's book first. It will help set the scene for you with the Cathars and their Grail stone. The other version is a bit different, more spiritually orientated some say. I found it strangely different from all the other Grail stories myself."

"Thanks." I said taking the two books. "I am not sure when I will have time to read these but I will do what I can. I've really got to get my head around what I am going to be doing now." I paused for a moment wondering how I should put together my next few words. "Uncle. Do you think being self-employed would be something I could do well?"

"Hmm…." He sounded giving it some thought. "Hmmm." He sounded again. "You know what Ro, you just might be best suited to doing that. Much depends on what you choose to do though. It's much harder than being employed you know. I couldn't have done it….. Hmm."

I could tell he was tired and had drifted off into thoughts of his own. It was something he used to do more and more of since his wife had died.

I let him be with his cup of tea and went upstairs to unpack and settle in. It was then that I realized I'd left some important every day stuff back at my old apartment. It was 5.00pm. I'd been away for nearly a week. The apartment was all the way over in Reading which was about 40mins away. I felt up to the drive but was I up to seeing John again. No. I couldn't put it off any longer. If I did, I might change my mind and I didn't want that. I still had my key and reckoned he would be back from work by 6.00pm. If I left now, I could pack up and catch him as I was leaving.

I pulled up 45mins later and unlocked the door. The place was a mess. Typical. There was also a distinctly unpleasant odour that I hadn't remembered being there when I lived here. I went from room to room. The kitchen sink was full of uncleaned plates. I noticed something strange about it too. There were plates with the same food stains on. He must have shared a meal with someone here I thought. Didn't think to clear it up – damn him. I went through to the bedroom not really wanting to go in. My heart was also beating faster for some reason.

How could I have ever lived with him if he leaves the place like this? I thought. It looked as though he'd fought with the bed linen and just left it lying all over the place. I never left it like that – ever. I'd always made the bed in the morning. I realized then just how much I'd been used by him. The bathroom door was open and having moved more fully into the bedroom stepping over some of his dirty clothes on the floor, I saw something that made me stop in my tracks. I'd never had a pink toothbrush.

Anger began to build up inside me as I wondered if it belonged to the blonde woman from the pub, but strangely as soon as it came, the feeling started to go. The words of my friends 'He was never right for you' came into my head. I breathed out and felt more relaxed. It really was over and I knew now I really could get on with my own life.

Driving over here I was half thinking of having a blazing row with him at the door, but now I could see the power of where Dad had been coming from. I would sincerely wish him well instead. He needed all the help he could get – just not from me anymore.

I left the mess as it was and packed up the remains of my belongings. I'd borrowed a couple of boxes from my uncle and collected up some kitchen items of mine and the rest of my CD's. I used one of the boxes for my books. I left the sound system, he could have that along with the memories.

By 6.00pm, I was done. I'd packed it all up and had placed it into the back my car. I then waited. Sure enough at five past six John rolled up in his black VW. "Ro. It's good to see you." He began, holding both his arms out. "Glad you're back."

"No John." I ignored his offer of a hug, "I've just been inside to pick up my stuff. I left you the music system but took my kitchen knives."

"Oh." He almost sounded shocked.

"Listen John," I began, "Things have just not worked out for us. You know that. I have to move on with my life. It was going nowhere here. Look. I really wish you all the best for the future. I really mean that. I am sure you will do well in your work and you'll find someone else in no time." I said it all as sincerely as I could and without any feeling of animosity. "I won't be back as I have everything – even my toothbrush." I added for my own benefit.

He stood there in silence, not sure what to say. Good. Let it sink in, I thought He might one day then realize that I knew what he'd been doing. He had every right to of course, after all, I was the one that had split up with him. I hopped into my trusty little Mini and was off. It was the second time in a week I saw him looking surprised in my rear view mirror. I always wanted to be ahead of the game from now on. It felt really good.

If I hurried I could get to the 6.30 Yoga class and catch up with Katy. I pulled up to the leisure centre car park and about five minutes later I was standing in my yoga outfit in the changing rooms. I knew Katy would be doing this class and moments later she rushed through the door. "Ro." shouted Katy. "How the heck are you back here already? What's going on? How are you? Sorry just so many questions." She burst out all at once.

We hugged excitedly. "We can talk later, after the class if you have time?" I suggested.

"Of course. Great." She replied just as eager as I was to catch up. We all lined up for the Hatha yoga class. Our teacher, Sheila had been doing this for the last three years having spent the five previous ones in an Ashram in Northern India. She knew that the postures and sequences that she'd put together were challenging. It was why it was such a popular class too.

Although the holds and the transitions between them were done slowly, you knew you were getting a work out as well as becoming more relaxed. Sheila also taught several breathing methods which was a little more unusual in a teacher. I found it all very refreshing. There was always a nice balance between the sequences we were used to and the addition of new exercise. By the time it was over, you definitely needed a shower.

Katy and I went upstairs afterwards to the lounge bar and after about half an hour of talking, I had pretty much rushed through all that had happened up until the point I'd said goodbye to John. "Good one about the toothbrush. Can I tell Steve?" said Katy.

"I'd rather you didn't just yet." I said. "I was kind of hoping the information would filter back through Steve to you and you could then let me know he'd been found out."

"Yes. Better." she said. "But Ro, you seem to have done so much in such a short time. So much seems to have just happened. Time must have flown by."

"Yes it did really when I come to think about it. I cannot believe it's been nearly a week since I left." I replied.

"That's what happens when ……" Katy stopped mid-sentence realizing what she was going to say but then doubting whether she should.

"What happens when what? I asked. She looked at me.

"That's what happens when things are meant to be." She continued slowly. "There's a saying that 'Everything flows when you are on the right path'." She said concerned that what she had said might not have been very helpful or kind considering my situation. "I mean…"

"….I know what you mean Katy. It was meant to be. I was supposed to experience all that in preparation for what is to come back over here in the UK…..I think." I finished, not wanting her to feel bad in anyway. She was a friend who was just trying to help.

"Yes. Most probably" She agreed but I could see she was not sure about it. It was her mention about being on the right path that hit a nerve with me though and immediately connected me back to thinking about the Cathars and their paths.

We finished our drinks and made arrangements to meet again in a few days time at another yoga class the following week.

It had started raining when we got outside and I headed back with the windscreen wipers going full speed. Loads had happened again today and it had started all the way back at Orleans in the middle of France. It was getting hard to get my head around all the changes that were going on in my life.

I was back at my uncle's house by 9.00pm in time for him to say goodnight to me as he was going upstairs to bed. I grabbed a bite to eat from the fridge and went through into the sitting room. In the old days if I'd been on my own, I'd have just turned on the TV and watched something, but in the last year the desire to do that had just gone. There just seemed to be nothing I wanted to watch anymore. Nothing that was ever shown held any interest. The news normally just ended up with people talking up the importance and significance of events that really had nothing to do with most people in the country. It was like it had all become some kind of unending reality show. That name was ridiculous too - a complete oxymoron – those shows were nothing like reality.

I then saw the two books I'd left on the coffee table. Might as well, I thought and leant over and picked up Wolfram von Eschenbach's Parzival. Two hours flew by and then tiredness hit me. I couldn't believe how much I'd read in that time. I put the book down with jousting knights and maidens in distress in my mind and went to bed.

The cup of French coffee in the morning didn't remind me of coffee in France at all. The thought was brief. I had to get into action mode today. I called work and said I would be back in on Monday. They were not much impressed or pleased to hear from me. For me it was now just filling a gap. I turned to the job pages on the internet. An hour later and I'd been through dozens of sites. There was nothing in Geology that I could have applied for as they were all looking for existing experience. Things were not looking good.

I turned to look for more local jobs in the Reading and Newbury areas. I then expanded the area to include Basingstoke and Oxford. Time and time again I clicked through to find that they were not jobs but self-employed roles. You never get a filter button to screen those out either. It is such a time waster as they are not really self-employed as you are still tied to working for one company. There were a few jobs I could apply for but before I did, I checked the rental costs in the area.

Impossible. If I was to work 50 hours a week and do one and a half jobs, things still wouldn't add up. I looked at living further way and included the cost of commuting. It still didn't work financially. I would be losing money, losing my time and not gaining any good experience. Instead I'd be getting experience I didn't want and it wouldn't lead anywhere either. This country was going downhill fast.

By the end of the morning I was struggling to keep my spirits up. If I signed on, I would have to be doing this non-stop all day. That would be a killer. I was not sure what to do but I knew I needed a short break. My Uncle had gone out so I decided to nip into town to see if that might provide any inspiration or opportunities.

Ten minutes later I was walking through the town centre looking for message boards. I picked up a copy of the local paper Newbury Today and went through that over a cup of coffee. Having looked through that and checking their website on my mobile, I sent off my CV to a couple of possible employers. They were not career enhancing prospects but the hours were good and it meant I could possibly find extra work in the evening on top of that. That way I would at least perhaps be able to start saving.

Feeling better I turned to browsing through the paper and my eyes were drawn to an advert in the leisure section. Kundalini Yoga classes Monday, Tuesday, Wednesday & Thursday with Aliya at a new centre that had just opened. I had not tried that form of yoga before and had only been doing Hatha yoga with Katy. For some reason it stood out. I made a mental note of where the centre was and the times of the classes. Feeling slightly better I returned to my uncle's house.

"Hi Rowena." He said, "How are things going?" I mentioned my progress with job hunting. "Good, good, something will turn up" He said sounding as positive as he could manage, which was not that much after losing his wife.

"I started reading Parzival, Uncle." I changed the subject to one I thought would perk him up a bit. It did.

"Do you like it?" He asked almost reverting to the tone of his old schoolteacher role.

"Yes, the translation is a little 'Oldy English' and the names are very different so it's a bit hard to keep track of who's who and who's doing what, but the storyline is good." I remarked.

"Wolfram is certainly someone who likes building up the whole picture." I went on having just checked if he was still interested. He was.

"I quite like the sense of adventure it gives too. There's a 'freshness' to the story. It somehow maintains a good level of 'unpredictability' for what was probably quite a well-known story at the time. I've still not got to the point when the Grail appears though." I tried to answer as best as I could, like one of his top pupils, with as much of an explanation and reason as possible. Anything else would have only annoyed him to a greater or lesser extent depending on the answer.

"Yes, good. I am glad you spotted that. The freshness of course would have been important to Wolfram in order to grow his audiences. You will find too that he tries to do this in other ways as well. I won't spoil it for you though. Let me know when you finish it, if you would like to discuss it further."

"Yes of course." I replied. I was happy to have a casual chat at the end but unwilling to want to go through a 'grilling' session. It would be good to hear his views on the Grail though I conceded to myself.

I spent the rest of the day reading the book and then cooking us both some dinner. Whilst we sat eating, he told me that his son and his family were going to drop by on Saturday.

Saturday came and went with the awkward moments and questions I fully expected. 'How long was I going to stay? You know he will not be able to cope after a week with anyone else in the house don't you? When are you going to get a proper job? Even, when are you going to settle down and have a family? And more. What was wrong with John? And. Why did you not just make things work with him?

At the end I'd had enough but I refused to let them know that. When they left I was all smiles but underneath I was mix of anger and angst.

"Thank goodness for that" said my Uncle. "I do hate these manufactured visits now. I never hear from them for weeks and they then just descend on me. I would much rather a few more telephone calls every so often."

I was slightly surprised by that remark but did understand it. "I think they are just concerned for how you are doing Uncle." I tried.

"You can stay longer than a week too." He went on, "I heard that question. They had no right to ask that." I can still hear quite well you know.

"That's very kind of you Uncle, but I don't want to put you out for too long.

"I know, I know. Your father would have done the same though if the shoe had been on the other foot." He replied.

"How are you doing with the book?" He changed the subject.

"I should have finished by tonight if you have some time tomorrow, I'd love to talk about it with you."

"That's grand. I'll look forward to that." His long ago love of teaching seemingly returning.

I woke early on Sunday having finished reading the book last night in bed. My vivid dreams were all about mediaeval times as if I'd been actually reliving a past experience. Who knows maybe there was something in all this reincarnation I thought rubbing my eyes. I soon dismissed the thought though after I'd found I'd forgotten most of the dream already.

The book had certainly given me a few things to think about though. On the face of it, it was just another hero's tale. Parzival had become one of King Arthur's Knights and he and Sir Gawain were both searching for the Holy Grail. There was jousting, duels, maidens in distress, love, disguise, mistaken identity, a sorceress, morals, the upholding of honour and people dealing with failure and consequences of that failure.

Von Eschenbach had reported, quite late in the story, that the Grail was not a dish, like in Chretien's story, nor was it a Cup, as was told in de Boron's Grail story, but instead it was a stone. Not only that, but there was something invisible about it that could only be seen by a holy person, like a hermit or a 'Godly' Knight.

This stone seemed to also have properties of rejuvenation that kept people in its presence looking young. It also healed the sick and provided nourishment for the hungry. It was even said to provide the holder with immortality.

What I found curious was that it appeared that the Grail had a connection to the Middle East. A group of people, called the Pure Ones, had brought it to Europe from the Middle East where it was now kept at the Grail castle. It was said to have been guarded by Temple Knights who rode out every morning looking for adventure. What I also found interesting was that the sign for these Knights was a symbol of a Turtle dove on their horse's saddles. These Pure Ones sounded very much to me like the Cathar Perfects – especially with the symbol of the dove that was connected to their Grail. I needed to ask my Uncle what he thought but there was no way I was going into a conversation with him unprepared.

I made some notes of some of the key observations I'd had and tried to do some interpretation of it all. He would certainly ask me if I had found any deeper meaning to it. Not much later I was prepared as best I could be and I went down for some breakfast.

"Good morning" he started, with a cup of coffee in his hand. He had just finished a couple of boiled eggs and toast so I knew he was ready to talk. "Did you finish it?" I could tell he was interested in knowing what I thought. He rarely opened up a conversation this early in the morning.

"Morning Uncle David. Yes, I finished it. Let me get a coffee first." I begged.

"Of course." He replied, "I have to confess how much I am looking forward this. It reminds me of all those years ago when I started teaching and why I used to enjoy it so much. I had students then that were genuinely interested in what they were reading. In the last few years, none of the A-level students really cared. It was all about getting an A Grade to get into their chosen University and only then to study something completely different….. It wasn't about thinking anymore it was just about knowing the right or wrong answers and getting a good result."

"I know, Uncle." I sat down in front of him holding a mug of coffee in both hands. I knew he couldn't wait much longer so I began.

"Well, I liked the book. On the surface it is a fairly typical version of the hero's tale, perhaps I should say heroes though. The descriptions of the battles and the duels showed it was obviously written by a person who had some experience as a Knight, which Wolfram was thought to have been at one stage in his life." I added to show I had done a little external online homework on the story. "What was interesting was the trouble that Wolfram had gone to in order to try and make out that it was his story that was the original story of the Grail."

"Further to what I mentioned to you last time, which you asked me to look out for, he introduced an 'out of story' character called Kyot, a man from the Provencal region of France, and even another man called Flegetanis. He did this, I think, in order to give this originality some further credence."

"Good. Good." mumbled my Uncle in voice just loud enough to be heard.

"This, it seems, was all done to try and really explain to the audience that the Grail was not a dish or a cup but actually a stone and, perhaps more interestingly, a stone that had really originated from the Middle East. Wolfram spells the word Graal as Gral and I think that helped him to create this new way of thinking so his audience could more easily accept it. He probably pronounced it differently too."

"Why he went to the trouble of doing this seems to open up some big questions. One of them is that there are several possible hidden meanings to the overall interpretation of the story. I think that this is what Wolfram had always intended to do and why he needed to do this prepositioning." I mentioned as an aside. "What is confusing though is that he then says that the stone is invisible and that only holy people, like hermits, and spiritual Knights can see it." I added.

"I have a question for you about this later as I want to ask you more about what you think about this invisibility." I pointed out. My uncle looked up at me and slightly nodded his head a couple of times.

"However, to return to the story, the basic open message Wolfram appears to have wanted to convey was about the development of a Knight and the sort of things that they had to do in order to achieve that.

This, to me, now seems very similar to Chretien de Troyes goals with his story 'La Compte de Graal'. It was not just about being a better fighter, it was also about becoming a better and more spiritual person. I think there are also some more obvious similarities though. Wolfram includes Parzival's forgetfulness at asking the questions 'What ails you?' and 'Whom does the Grail serve?' the first time he meets the wounded King Anfortas."

"This, like Chretien's Perceval, indicates his lack of compassion to begin with. We learn too that he has not shown enough care for his mother when he left home. By not staying in touch with her, it breaks her heart and she dies. His lack of care continues and he becomes more influenced by the people around him. It is only later on in the story that he slowly realizes that he needs to become more spiritual and that he has to serve only the Holy Spirit itself."

"This theme of becoming a perfect spiritual person, and then being able to see an invisible stone, has an interesting connection with Kyot's remarks about the stone being brought to Europe from the Middle East by 'Pure ones'." I added.

"I think this is a reference to the Cathars and their 'Perfects'. When Wolfram wrote his story, the Cathars were at the height of their power in Southern France and I believe he was drawing an analogy of becoming a perfect spiritual Knight, with becoming one of the Cathar 'Perfects'."

"Wolfram's, almost open support of the Cathars here, along with saying the Grail was not the cup of Jesus, or a dish with a holy wafer on, seems to be openly challenging the church of Rome." I stated.

"If you were to now look at the critical question 'Whom does the Grail serve?'" I continued, "You might well ask if this is really asking the question does the Grail serve the Church of Rome or does it serve God?"

"This would have seemed heretical to the leaders of the Catholic church at the time and I think that Chretien, in his story, was also asking the same question but in a slightly different way." Having said this, my Uncle reached out his arm to make me pause while he kept looking ahead and down at the floor contemplating my words. I waited. A few moments later his outstretched hand ushered me to carry on.

"I know Chretien died before completing his story and I have to wonder, whether or not, the Church even had him killed because of the message he was trying to put out." I paused. My uncle made no response to that so I continued.

"The way a person answers this critical question of course seems to come down to whether you were a Gnostic Christian or a Roman Catholic Christian." I pointed out as clearly as I could with my hands out in front of me as though I was offering him a choice.

"I think the whole of Wolfram's story was a hidden metaphor for one of the big questions that was being asked at the time during the end of the 12th century and the beginning of the 13th. This eventually resulted in the Pope's crusade against the Gnostic way of thinking and the Cathars." I ended.

I could see him thinking deeply about what I said.

"There is probably more that can be read into the story," I added, "but as you know I've not had much time to fully analyse it. I do have some questions for you though." I added as an afterthought.

He sat quietly still thinking about it all. After a few moments he looked up at me and smiled.

"Well done Rowena. I really am very proud of you. I would have definitely given you an A for that, maybe even an A+." He began.

83

I have to say I felt a mixture of relief and pride.

"I think you have certainly grasped the main theme of the story of the development of a Knight and you have even added an interpretation that I'd not considered before – one that involved the conflict in religious thinking that was going on at the time. Well done."

"I like too how you made comparisons to Chretien's story and also how you saw through the pre-positioning Wolfram was trying to do with the introduction of Kyot's story and his version of the origins of the Grail."

"Tell me Rowena though, do you think Wolfram's Grail was the original Grail or not?" he asked.

"That's a double edged question Uncle," I replied, seeing how he was trying to catch me out. He smiled at my response. "The original Grail had to be Chretien's as he was the first person to use the Grail word. However if you are asking if the legend, and the Grail properties that Wolfram describes, were from an earlier time, then yes that is entirely possible." I continued. "In fact, Wolfram's idea of adding the properties of eternal nourishment, healing, rejuvenation and immortality to the story were almost certainly not original. They probably also came from an earlier legend which was more than likely to have also come from the Middle East."

"Nicely answered young lady and nicely avoided too if I might say...... Rowena I have to say how much it pleases me to find you have obtained such a grasp over this book in such a short period of time. It's a really pity in a way that you went into Geology. I think you would have made an excellent English Literature student." He said in typical schoolteacher style.

"Thanks Uncle, its very kind of you to say that. However, in this case, I was more interested in this book having just learnt about the Cathars over in France. That definitely made a difference." I pointed out. "I did want to ask you for your thoughts on a couple of things if that is ok." I asked him changing my tone a little.

"Certainly. If I can help, I will." He seemed to really like being consulted about it all.

"Firstly, I was thinking about the conversation between King Arthur and Parzival's step brother Fierfiz. They'd only just met and the King said that Parzival was off searching for the Grail. The thing is," I stated, "he said it in a way as though Fierfiz must have already known all about the Grail." I looked at my Uncle to see if he had any reaction to that. He looked up at me as I'd stopped.

"Do go on Rowena. You have my utmost attention."

"As you know Fierfiz was from the Middle East, so that would mean that King Arthur could have been naturally assuming that the Grail was well known over there as well as in Europe. That's really just the first part but would you agree so far?"

"Yes, I think that is perfectly reasonable. After all we can consider that the 'Pure one's' brought it from that area too." He replied looking as though he was still considering the question.

"Well that leads on to my second question. I think the Cathars had special places that they thought were sacred. Wolfram's story also talks about a mountain of salvation and a fountain of salvation in Europe." I was now getting to the important point I wanted to make and ask him about. "There seems to be some kind of connection with a geographical location and sacredness and also this idea of an invisible Grail. Do you think that this is at all possible?"

"Possibly." He said not fully agreeing with what I had said yet. "There is also one other thing you might like to also check," he continued by changing the subject slightly, "and that is if there is any reference to the Grail, or something like it, in any of the Middle East legends...... My memory fails me now but I think that I remember something called the Gral in an old Persian legend. It too was connected to a dove….. You might find a connection there to all the Grail properties that Wolfram mentions too." He added.

"Really." My curiosity piqued. "I'll certainly search for more on that online. Can you tell me anything else about it?" I asked.

"Not at the moment.... Sorry. I'll have to think about perhaps which book I may have read it in...... I will have a look for you later today. What other things do you have for me?" he asked seemingly becoming ever keener on it all.

"Well, it also follows on from that really. This invisible holy stone that has fallen from the skies sounds as though it could be a meteorite." I began.

"The trouble is that these stones are not invisible at all. From somewhere in my past though I think I heard something about certain meteorites in the Middle East being thought of as sacred. Can you recall anything like this?" I asked.

"Yes indeed." He replied quite quickly. "There are a couple that come to mind and they are associated with the Muslim religion."

"Firstly there is the 'Even ha'shettiya stone. That is a foundation stone at the Al-Aqsa mosque in Jerusalem. That was part of a meteorite apparently and it was also positioned in a very sacred place according to the Muslims. Then there is the Kaaba meteorite, which is found in Mecca. This was built into the walls of the central black square - the Kaaba there. That piece of meteorite I think was put there by the Sufi's who built the place." He paused for a moment to reflect. "There is also the Cintamani stone," he remembered, "which maybe just a story but I think that was said to have fallen from heaven." He concluded.

"How on Earth do you remember all that Uncle?" I asked very impressed with his knowledge.

"Rowena dear, I really have no idea. Some things I just remember clearly as though it was yesterday whilst other things have just completely left my mind." He replied with his face looking quite oblivious and blank to it all.

"Well that means that many people in the past thought meteorites were sacred. My question then is why would Wolfram try and then say they were invisible? In his writings too, he even seems to indicate that they can also only be seen at certain times of the year?" I asked him.

"You ask a good question there Rowena?" he replied. "There was one Grail searcher you should be aware of. His name was Otto Rahn. Have you come across him?"

"No." I replied, "Please tell me more." I asked.

"I don't think I have any of his books, you might like to search online for those……no, Otto Rahn was searching for the Grail around the South of France just before the second World War. I believe that he was very much in favour of the Cathar way of thinking too and had probably been influenced by Von Eschenbach as well…." He paused.

"….come to think about it, I think he may even have met and worked with that man you mentioned, Antonin Gadal." He mused.

I sat up, now very interested. "Rahn I think thought that it was not the stone that was significant but that it was some kind of divine presence that was trapped within the stone." He added.

"Really? What does that even mean?" I asked quickly.

"My dear I really have no idea. Perhaps that is for you to find out, as well as trying to find out why some locations are more sacred than others."

He stopped for a moment and then decided to change the subject. "I am going to get the Sunday papers now if that is OK. Have a read of the second book though. I think you will find that quite different." He paused. "That may even help you find what you are looking for." He added as if out of nowhere. With that he got up and left the breakfast table and walked off in search of his papers.

His last remark made me stop and think for a moment. He had somehow managed to pinpoint exactly why I was reading these books, even though I hadn't fully realized it myself. I wasn't just interested in reading them. It was as though there was an answer in them that was relevant for me in my life right now. It was perhaps this that I was looking for. I am fairly sure it wasn't about me becoming a Gnostic Christian. However developing as a person, and journeying to find out how to do this, did seem somehow relevant. It again all seemed to be about finding the right path.

I would have picked up the book straightaway, but I was desperate to go for a run. I'd not run around Newbury before though and I really didn't fancy driving 40 mins just to go to one of my usual routes. I'd also become a bit choosy about where I ran. To me it was just madness to run alongside a road with all the car fumes. I had a look on 'maps' on my mobile. There were two possible runs for me. The more promising one was along some bridle paths around Highclere and Burghclere but that was going to need some serious planning to avoid getting lost. I wasn't up for that now.

The Avon and Kennett canal footpath it was then. The stretch of path was about 5km which was fine. It was flat but with an 'out and back' run I could take my brain out, relax and enjoy it.

That feels much better, I thought as I got back into my Mini. My head had cleared and I'd developed the beginnings of a plan. I would go back to work tomorrow and stay as long as I could until I found some work in Geology. I would widen my search into areas that included Europe and other English speaking countries and if something came up, I would relocate to where the work was – wherever that may be.

I resolved to start the search later today and to send out some CV's. I was in no way ready to become self-employed but would keep it in mind to perhaps do in a few years time. The run had built up my positive feelings and I'd projected them into thinking about a new life and a new future.

After showering and having a quick lunch, I went online to search for jobs. Three hours later I was tired and drained from it all. I'd widened my scope to further afield and even broadened the range of work I would consider. I'd been onto loads of different jobsites, National and International. Yes there was work, but nothing fitted my abilities and qualifications. I'd sent out my CV to two jobs but I knew I was lacking the experience they were looking for.

It was the typical catch 22. I needed the job to get the experience but could get the job as I didn't have the experience. I had to stop and take a break as I was beginning to look at ridiculous options that didn't even lead to a potential career. I also needed time to think again. Maybe retraining would be what was needed. It may be costly but if I did it in conjunction with my current skills, openings may be more forthcoming. Going straight into searching down that avenue would have to wait though. I needed to be far more mentally refreshed for that.

In front of me was the second book my Uncle had found for me. 'The High book of the Grail' - a translation of the book Perlesvaus by Nigel Bryant. Its 'Christianised' cover reminded me of everything I disliked in religion. That put me off for a moment. The last thing I wanted was to have all that forced on me. However something inside me said no, that was not what it was about at all. I slowly lent across and picked it up off the coffee table. I would give it 5 mins and miss out the introduction and dive straight to the story. If that didn't work for me I'd put it down and do something else.

Well this was different. The story seemed the same but it also felt new. King Arthur's knights, Sir Gawain, Sir Lancelot and Perlesvaus were travelling though forests, sometimes together and sometimes on their own rescuing damsels in distress. There were also many different Castles with really strange names. I had to admit that this had a certain kind of appeal. I read on. I wasn't going to be able to finish it in one go though.

My uncle came in, saw I was reading it and smiled. I put the book down having read it for nearly 2 hours. "Well?" he asked.

"It's good," I replied. "Too early for questions though." I added.

"Of course." He answered. "How are things on the job front, I noticed you were looking again."

"Not so good. I will have to keep plugging away at it, until something comes up."

"Maybe." He replied rather enigmatically I thought as though he perhaps knew something I didn't. I left it unanswered though as I could tell when he wanted to talk more and when he wanted time to himself.

It was a much longer drive to work on Monday morning. I took the M4 and then the Bath road into the middle of the city. On a clear road it would have taken only 45 minutes but with the early morning commuters it took me an hour and a half. I'd underestimated it and was 10 mins late getting in. It had been noticed. I sat down at my desk and my supervisor immediately came over and asked me to come into their office.

What followed was not nice at all. She was an officious older lady who'd worked for the business for over nine years. It was almost her life and she viewed her role as being protective towards the company, almost like the baby she'd never had but probably never really wanted. I sat in silence whilst she went into 'telling mode' and then into 'threatening mode' with regards to being late and also just taking a week off like that without giving the proper notice and gaining the right permission.

My only living relative could have died and she would have been oblivious to that fact as reasons were just not important enough for her to even ask for any. I continued to nod my head at her, wondering if that was helping or actually making things worse.

She finished and directed me back to my desk by pointing. I got up having not heard the last couple of lines from her tirade. Something about HR. By the time I'd sat down, despite my best efforts, my energy levels were severely depleted. It was cloudy outside and it had started drizzling and my mood was beginning to match it.

The office had a no talking policy at work. Everything we did was scrutinized. Calls were recorded, internet time and sites were logged. Employees were virtually glued to their seat and most people worked through their lunch breaks at their desk eating snack meals.

I looked around me. In the time I'd been there, I could think of no friendships that had been made between people working on this floor. It was probably the way the managers wanted it. Sure we were all nice and polite to each other but that was about it. When 5.00pm came everyone just wanted to leave and get as far away as possible. It was then that I noticed that no one was smiling. I worked and watched waiting to spot the first smile. This was terrible and my mood sank lower. I began to realize that this environment was slowly killing me and draining any spirit left in me.

How on earth was I going to get through to lunch time, let alone the end of the day? How had I lasted this long here? How had I not noticed all this before? Ah yes I remembered. It was all about sacrifice. I sacrificed myself for the promise of a better future with John. I had no feeling of blame though. It'd been my choice. I'd allowed myself to believe a very slim possibility that something might lead on from all of this.

This was surely not how life was supposed to be. In the past this kind of work came with a full pension at the age of 60. If you were lucky you might reach the age of 70, maybe 75 on 2/3ds of your income. You could survive but couldn't do much. Today you wouldn't even get a third of that so why are we all doing it? The only answer that came to me was fear and it was a really big reason.

Getting up, leaving and walking out with no income coming in was what I was now contemplating and I could feel the fear growing in my stomach. Strangely I wondered where that feeling was when I'd stormed out of the pub just over a week ago. I sat rigid at my desk. It was nearly lunch time. I could see my supervisor looking at me. I put my head quickly back down to my desktop screen. 1.00pm came and I got up to go to the toilet. I picked up my bag and left.

I sat in the toilet for about ten minutes realizing I couldn't go back inside. All sorts of thoughts span around in my head. I was selling my soul to a devil I didn't even know. The image of Asmodeus appeared in my mind. He was grinning at my discomfort. My fear was keeping me sitting behind a locked door. This was just not right. I was frozen still. I grabbed all the energy, will and intent I could muster, stood up and stepped out of the cubicle. Another lady, one who usually sat the other side of the office from me, looked at me in the mirror.

She could see my face and I could see hers. I could both see and sense the fear that had suddenly come over her. I looked in the mirror and saw my own face. My eyes were filled with some kind of demonic determination as though I was about to kill someone with a kitchen knife. I looked back at her and saw her washing her hands more quickly. Her neck turned slightly towards me to see what I was doing next. She immediately looked away again as though she might catch something.

I looked back into the mirror. I couldn't walk out looking like this. I spent a moment to make myself look as terrific as I could. Hair, Lipstick,

Mascara, a light touch of shadow on my eyes and I was there. The worried lady had already hurriedly left. Right let's go. I never want to feel like that again. Not ever in my whole life.

I got to the door. I could go right and down the stairs and escape straightaway, or I could turn left and along to the Supervisor's office. I couldn't let it stand, I had to say something. I went left.

Without knocking, I opened her door and marched into her office. She was leaning back in her chair and eating out of sight behind her desktop screen. Her mouth was full. She looked up at me with an angry look at having being disturbed, or found out. I didn't care.

"Take a look around you," I began. She looked confused, her anger now gone. "When was the last time you saw someone smile in here?" she now looked even more confused wondering where I was going with all this and why I'd stormed into her office. "No one is happy here, there all just too scared to tell anyone. This whole business here is running people into the ground. This isn't life. Look at it. Everyone is totally stressed with it all and the way this office is run makes it even worse for them. No one cares, no matter what the directors say. This place is just another lifeless box and I've had enough of it. This may suit you, but it's not for me. I'm taking my life back." With that I turned and started to walk out.

At the door I turned around. She still had her mouth full and couldn't speak – Good. "And one last thing, there's no way I'm going to work out any notice and I don't need any damn reference either. Goodbye and good luck." My voice was slightly louder now so that people outside the room could hear. There'd be no lies about how or why I'd left.

I turned back and walked back past the desks in the office. The few ladies that were nearby and had heard me, quickly turned their heads back down to their screens as I passed. Goodness gracious, there's really no hope for some people, I thought. They're all paralysed by their own fear. I strode past the uniforms on reception and out into the damp air. It was still drizzling. I looked up and smiled. This was my freedom.

The light drops of water on my face began to make my mascara run. I didn't mind. It was a small price to pay for the new feelings arising within me. I could find a way. I would find my path.

I drove back along the old A4. It was beautifully free of cars this afternoon and the fields and woods either side made it even more relaxing. My mind wandered back in time to when the road was once a track in the old days. Horses and carriages would run along it taking wealthy ladies from London all the way to the spa town of Bath. It would take them several days and Newbury had been one of the stops along the way. I smiled again thinking the same would be true for me too one day. Newbury would be just one stop on the way to the rest of my life. I had no idea what that would be, but I knew I would do everything I could to make it work.

By the time I got back to my Uncle's house, I had decided to get any local job I could that would be fun. It may pay less but I needed stimulation, contact with other people and a chance to keep searching. I would start by going to the local Yoga class. Maybe I would meet someone there who knew of local work opportunities.

Uncle David was very supportive when I told him what I'd just done. He'd said that I reminded him of his brother. Not wishing to pursue the job hunting again so soon, I settled down to finish reading the book about Perlesvaus. As it was, I still hadn't completed it, when the time came to go to Yoga. I'd already formed some impressions of the story though.

Something that was immediately rather strange about it was that, although the book was about the Grail, there were really only a very few details written about the Grail. The story was mostly about knights and their adventures. It started by stating that the Grail was a Cup and that it was thought to be the Cup of Christ. But several times later on in the story it suggested that the Grail was also invisible and that it only appears on certain occasions and only to certain people.

It was generally thought that this story had been written after Wolfram von Eschenbach's Parzival, but this now meant that, in both books I'd read, there was this unexplained invisibility to the Grail. The story itself centred around a Knight called Perlesvaus and his travels and adventures but it also included the stories of the other Knights doing similar things. This mainly consisted of riding through large, deep and dark forests and finding and rescuing damsels and maidens in distress. What then followed were battles with evil knights and various other beasts and demons in order to rescue people and right the wrongs that had been done.

To do this they travelled, sometimes together and sometimes on their own, from one Castle to the next. At each Castle there was always a nearby chapel and at least one hermit and it was from the many exchanges of communication along the way between everyone that they learnt what had been done and what they must do to uphold their idea of honour. There were lots of these different Castles and what was immediately obvious was that they had many different and somewhat strange names.

The names of the Castles were not based on the names of the location, as you might expect, but they were named more by some link to what, or who, would be encountered at that Castle – whether it was either a physical or emotional challenge. Examples were the Castle of Enquiry, the Castle of Joy, the Castle of Lost Souls, the Castle of the Circle of Gold, the Castle of the Black Hermit, the Unassailable Castle. This Castle was rather bizarrely also called the 'Turning' Castle. There was also Castle Mortal and the Castle of the Copper Tower as well as the Castle of the Fisher King.

That the Castles were labeled this way almost made them like symbols. It was like it was inviting the reader to try and decipher what they really meant. This invitation could possibly even be extended to the whole story and I wondered if this too had some deeper overall underlying meaning. In addition to that, the heroes of the story seemed to always arrive just at the right time in order to win their challenges and the winners always seemed to be the Knights who were the best at striving to be a more spiritual Knight.

The book also seemed to be about a conflict that was going on in the land between what was called 'The Old Law' and 'The New Law'. The 'New Law' was the one which King Arthur and his Knights were trying to install. In the book the two laws were openly representing the Old law of Paganism and the New law of Christianity. However, bearing in mind Wolfram's story of Parzival, I had to wonder if the difference between the laws was really a hidden reference to the difference of opinion in the understanding of the teachings of Jesus. This hidden meaning would then really be depicting a difference between the new Gnostic way of thinking about Christianity and the Roman church's version of Christianity.

The Grail was still linked to the Castle of the Fisher king but now there was also a Chapel of the Grail where the Grail appeared to Perlesvaus. In addition to that, Sir Gawain had met a hermit who'd spent a long time at the Chapel of the Grail and he was said to have looked young in age but was really an old man. This seemed to be showing the power of the Grail to rejuvenate people.

When the Grail appeared before Sir Gawain, It was said that he stared at it and that he thought he saw a Chalice that appeared to float in mid-air. Sir Gawain was also said to have had visions of Jesus when looking at the Grail.

Just what the Grail looked like, according to the writer of Perlesvaus, seemed to become even more confused later on in the story as the writer later revealed that the Grail appeared 'in five forms. Later on in the book, it stated that these forms should not be revealed. King Arthur is said later to have seen all these forms and in the last form he saw the shape of a chalice.

I had to say, that although this was a story, it had thrown up several new ideas as to what the Grail looked like. On the other hand though, it had revealed that it had similar Grail properties. It was certainly an intriguing story but at the moment, I was still none the wiser as to what the overall message was about. I resolved to finish it later and then chat it all over with my Uncle. I knew he would really like that as well.

The Yoga class started at 6.00pm. Aliya had ten people in her class and I was the only new one. There were three men and seven women and it was immediately obvious that everyone was very friendly. I knew was going to like it.

Although I hadn't done this form of yoga before, I soon found that the all the poses were very similar if not exactly the same. It was not long though before I noticed the first difference. Things were faster. Instead of holding a particular posture, or asana, for very long, we were moving through sequences of them that were called Kriyas. Each time we did a Kriya, it was also seemingly related to a specific area of health in our bodies.

The slow breathing technique that I had been carefully practicing in Hatha yoga was now replaced with various faster breathing methods. What was very new to me though were the meditations and mantra's. It was not just the 'Ohm' sound we used in Hatha, these were longer phrases and I'd no idea what they meant.

Aliya explained that a very necessary part of the meditation was to imagine a snake coiled up at the base of my spine. Then we had to imagine it gradually rising and straightening as it slithered up the whole length of it to my neck and head. This apparently was opening up my energy pathway so energy could run freely up and down and through my body. It sounded weird.

I tried really hard to do this visualization but I was just full of questions. Serpents? Energy? In addition to that I had to practice clearing my mind. By the end of the class I was far more physically exercised than I had ever been doing Hatha yoga, but on the other hand I was nothing like as mentally relaxed. It was almost stressful. The time had flown by but my mind was all over the place trying to keep pace with what I should be thinking of as well as what positions to move into next. It was definitely frustrating.

The other students though knew it would be like this and they each in turn offered me praise for doing so well for my first time. The mental side would come and with that the relaxation and mental release. Aliya then came over to me.

"Well done Rowena. I can see you have done some yoga before. You have good posture." She said with genuine care in her voice.

"Thanks." I replied, "I was all over the place mentally though. I just cannot get this visualization thing with the snake. What's that all about?"

"Don't worry too much about that yet. It takes a while to master. It's best to just get used to the sequences and the breathing first. You'll be able to focus on the chanting next and then finally the visualisations." she explained.

It began to make sense of how I might be able to progress with it but still had no idea why a snake was a necessary part. For some reason I thought of the old lady selling lavender at Rennes Le Chateau. There couldn't be a connection surely, I thought.

"Thanks." I said to her, feeling more slightly more reassured now there was at least a process to follow.

"Look. I have a half hour break before my next class. Do you fancy a chat over a hot drink?" she asked sensing that some further conversation might be helpful. She was right.

"Yes, fine. That would be nice." I replied grateful to have a chance to know more about her too. The reception area to the multi-purpose studios had a few modern armchairs in it. We each sat back on a couple of them with a cup of herbal tea that she'd quickly made.

"Aliya is an interesting name. I'm not sure I have come across that before." I started. "Does that have a meaning and an origin from anywhere?" I asked.

"It is an old Arabic name meaning 'Exalted'." Aliya replied, "My father had too many high hopes for me I think. He's from Ethiopia, my mother though was from India. Quite a combination." She added, smiling at it herself.

"I don't think I have ever met anyone with that parentage before. It must be fairly rare." I remarked with a slight question in my voice.

"It is over here in the UK, but back in India it is a little bit more common. I think there was a lot more trade between the two countries back then. I learnt yoga from my mother. Her father, my Grandfather had been a great Yoga teacher." She sipped her tea.

"How did you end up here?" I asked as politely as I could but really interested in hearing more about how she'd found her way in life.

"Ah that is a longer story" She replied. "But what about you? What brought you here to tonight and how did you hear about us?"

I explained briefly where I'd seen the advert and gave her a rushed account of the last nine days up to the point I'd given up my job this lunchtime. For some reason I expected her to look surprised but instead she smiled more and more and at the end she was even chuckling. I smiled back at her and said "I suppose it does all sound a bit amusing."

"Sorry Rowena," She said still with a smile on her face, "I am smiling because I think I know what is happening. You are awakening and that always makes me happy."

"Awakening?" I said not quite understanding fully what she meant.

"Yes awakening. I went through this myself some years back. Well, still going through it really." She added. "It's called other names too but essentially it starts with the same sort of wake up call." She paused and I waited for her to continue. "Look, this is big. Certainly not something I can tell you in a few minutes. Essentially it is this. People all around the World are waking up to realizing that the work they are doing is not what they are supposed to be doing. They became trapped in a way of thinking that was not really theirs."

"Go on." I asked gently.

"I myself trained to be a GP. I studied hard and got into a practice up in Birmingham. After eleven years of it I was completely burned out......totally stressed with it all for so many reasons that I just cannot go into right now.......nothing was working for me and, it seemed, very little was working for my patients. I was prescribing all sorts of drugs and I kept seeing the same people and then more and more new people........ Eventually I just quit." She sat back and sipped her tea again.

"What did you do?" I asked, now even more interested in what she had to say.

"I went back to India for a while, stayed with relatives there and then came back to the UK looking for a new life. I did lots of unrelated jobs but learnt all the time. I studied modern gardening techniques and started teaching yoga. In fact, I did everything I felt drawn to do. Now I have a small market garden business of my own and I grow specialist Indian herbs and vegetables for restaurants in the region. I am also now training to be a herbal nutritionist."

"Wow, that's amazing..." I stated. "....and you have done all that on your own." I added in a way that was like a question too.

"Not on my own. No." She replied, noticing the meaning behind my remark. "Everyone helps me. I feel grateful to everyone on my journey. If it was not for each person I've met, I would not have found my way to where I am now."

"What do you mean?" I asked again now really not fully understanding.

"It could be the smallest of things people say, or do even, that made me stop and think. Everything is connected, we are all connected. It's like a Universal law." She stated. "We have to just rediscover this connection." She pointed out.

"For example, if I'd not gone back home to India, I'd not have discovered from a friend back there that a particular vegetable was being grown for export to the UK. I then remembered someone in the UK who was looking to try and grow this very same vegetable but was having trouble doing so. I did some investigation myself and found out what the problem was and how to solve it. I have to thank the people who posted the information I needed online too for that. Anyway, when I got back I started to put it all into practice to see for myself if it worked. With a few tweaks of my own, it did and now I have a nice small little business." She explained.

"That's amazing," I replied in awe at her achievement. "You could grow that into an even bigger business too." I added.

"I could. But then where would I be? How would my life change? How would the lives of others around me change? I can't begin to know the answers to these things. It may be the right thing to do, but when should I do this." She questioned looking at me. "You see Rowena, we can make decisions on our own but when we do, there are consequences that come from those decisions. It is how we make our decisions and when we make them that is really far more important, if we are to consider other people around us." She stopped and waited to see if anything had sunk in. I remembered Canadian Paul and how he built his successful business but then lost his family.

"Yes, I think I do see what you mean, but how do we know what to decide to do and when to do it?" I asked thinking this might be the six billion dollar question.

"You don't." she replied. She could see my puzzled look and so she continued. "Others around you will help you come to know when the time is right. As to what to do, all you need to do is to find your path in life and then try to stay on it." she pointed out. There it was again. Finding my path in life.

"That's all very well, but how do I find my path in life?" I said sounding puzzled again.

"I don't know how it will work for you Rowena. But for me I just feel gratitude for everything and everyone around me as many times as I can. With that feeling in my heart and trying to be as positive as I can, I just ask to be shown the way......every day......and I mean I ask every day. It is continuous."

"What happens next?" I asked.

"I just try to be aware as I can. Explore what comes my way and look to help others where possible too. Invariably something or someone comes along and this ends up providing me with another clue for me to follow up. It is all very synchronistic." She said positively. "Meeting you today for example," she continued. "I didn't know we were going to meet and I didn't know you quit your job this morning, but maybe, it was as though we should meet today." She suggested. "I don't know where this will lead us, but I could have easily not suggested we have a chat but then we'd have both missed having this conversation and any possibilities that may come from it for both of us." She paused to let it sink in.

I sat silent thinking more deeply about what she had said. "Look, my next class will start soon. Please do come back again when you can and we can chat some more. Just remember Rowena, go with the flow. Go with what's working for you, even though it may not make sense at the time. Trust your heart too." She got up to leave and I rose as well.

"Yes thanks, I will and thanks for your time too. Bye." I said. We smiled at each other and then left.

My mind was still awash with thoughts on it all to the extent that I fully forgot to put any music on whilst I drove back. I could see the path that Canadian Paul had taken and which he had assured me worked when it came to earning lots of money, but here, Aliya had taken quite a different path altogether. She was not obviously wealthy to the extent that she didn't have to work, in fact, it was almost as though she didn't want to not work.

She was happy keeping her business small and would only change that if the Universe told her to do it differently. This communication would then somehow come through what she picked up though her interactions with others. What was incredible was that she seemed happy to teach yoga…. and she was a fully qualified GP. On the face of it, it just didn't make sense, but looking at it another way, she was happy and not stressed. She seemed to have found this 'unfixed' path in life and was doing her best to follow it.

It was this idea of an 'unfixed' path that began to resonate within me. At the very least I wanted to find out what my 'unfixed' path was. I could then perhaps decide if I wanted to follow it or not. To do that though, it seemed as though I'd have to start being more grateful for everything and more thankful to everyone. Then look at what was working for me and just ask to go with the flow.

What had been working for me though? I thought. The only thing I could think of recently was my time in the Ariege meeting all the people down there and learning from them all. There was no way I could earn a living from that though.

I was now back at my Uncles house and it was nearly 8.00pm. We chatted briefly about the evening but he was tired and wanted to go to bed. I assured him I would have finished the book by the morning. Over some hastily cooked pasta, I carried on reading the book Perlesvaus. It was 11.00pm when I'd finished and again I slept with dreams of Knights battling to save maidens in distress and this time I was one of them.

I woke early and immediately felt something was wrong. I looked around. Everything seemed fine. Putting on my dressing gown I went downstairs. All fine there too. I stood a while in the kitchen wondering what it could be. Slowly it dawned on me that I was not going to work today.

There it was. The nagging feeling intensified a little in the pit of my stomach. I had no job and soon no money would be coming in. I had to stop this so I began to do some yoga stretches and then an asana that I had just learnt. That was better. 'Action dispels Fear', I seem to remember someone once telling me in the past. All I had to do was to remain active. I couldn't do yoga all the time though so I put my mind to thinking about what else I could do today. Five minutes of new yoga later, it seemed to work.

During breakfast I thought about the conversation I'd have with my Uncle about the book. I knew he was looking forward to it and now, having done some preparation, so was I. I'd picked up a thread in the book which had resonated with me in much the same way as Aliya's words had resonated.

"Good morning Rowena," said my Uncle entering the kitchen. "and how are you this fine morning?"

"Good thanks Uncle David." He poured himself a cup of coffee, sat down and looked up at me.

"Yes," I smiled at him. "I've finished it."

"Well." He went.

I started by relating to him the general gist of the story and how it was different from Wolfram's Parzival and then I came to some of the more interesting points.

"One of the main themes in this book is the concept of King Arthur and his Knights upholding a New law over an Old law. Within the story line we are led to the understanding that this is the New Christianity prevailing over the Old pagan way of thinking." I stated.

He nodded and had now closed his eyes to help himself concentrate more. I continued. "However I am now not sure that this was the actual message that the writer really intended to convey. I think there is a hidden message in here." I said, purposely trying to arouse my Uncle's curiosity. It worked. He'd opened his eyes and looked at me. "In fact the whole story appears to have been written as a kind of giant metaphor. The clues for that are in the strange names of the Castles. In nearly every 'Castle related adventure' there are relevant conversations with maidens and hermits at that location. These seem to indicate there is an underlying meaning to it all."

"Remind me Rowena, what sort of names for the Castles were there?" he asked.

"Well, for example there was the Castle of Joy, the Castle of Enquiry, the Castle of lost souls and the Unassailable Castle." I replied.

"Ah yes, I remember now." He replied. "Thank you, please continue."

"In addition to that, throughout the story, the Knights appear to be just riding from one Castle to the next one. It is as though they are not just upholding this new law but they are also upholding a new kind of honour too. They seemed to be continually looking to help people by righting the wrongs that have been done at each particular Castle in order to become better people themselves. The names of the Castle even seemed to indicate

105

the nature of the challenge they would face. In this way, I think, it is quite similar to Chretien's and Wolfram's idea of a Knight becoming a better Knight." I said.

"What I found interesting is that this hidden message is now similar to Wolfram von Eschenbach's hidden message." I pointed out.

"Wait stop a moment." My Uncle interrupted. "Are you suggesting somehow that these two writers were somehow working together to promote a similar message?"

"No. Not exactly working together but I think they were probably both supporters of an opposite point of view from the Roman Catholic church." I answered.

"Oh Right. Ok. Sorry, please do go on."

"So what I think is being hidden here is that the old law is really referring to the Roman Catholic form of Christianity, and not Paganism, and the new law is now referring to the Gnostic form of Christianity.

"Sorry this is important what you are saying Rowena, but can you give me an example of what you mean that supports this." Uncle David asked.

"Well," I began, "The first clue is that the Grail starts off as the Cup of Jesus but later on in the story it becomes invisible, like the invisible Grail that Wolfram refers to. We also learn later on that only a holy hermit or a holy Knight can see it. If this was a story with a strong Roman Catholic Christian message, like Robert de Boron's story, then the writer would still want the Grail to be associated with the Cup of Christ. They would not have made it invisible at all." I pointed out.

"OK. You have a fair point there Rowena and you may be right. Sorry please do go on." He relented.

"Well the final thing that struck me was how much this whole story was trying to tell us about our own journey through life. It is not just about a Knight becoming a better Knight and even becoming a more spiritual Knight through individual development, it is about how we can do this too." I stated.

"What do you mean?" He enquired.

"Well I spoke with my yoga teacher yesterday and it was a conversation with her that helped me see this connection. She'd said that everyone in her life that she'd met, and even those she had not met, had helped her get where she was today. She also wouldn't make a decision about what to do next unless she'd received some kind of Universal sign."

When I said that I could see that my Uncle had raised up an eyebrow. He would do that when he'd heard something that didn't seem to make sense. I continued on looking to try and explain further.

"To her everything is connected in this World, like some kind of law of the Universe. All she had to do was to follow some basic rules and she would be able to follow the right path for herself. She said she had to stay positive and 'go with the flow'. This seemed to mean looking to help and care for those people around her in any way she could."

His eyebrow had now dropped down. I saw him then close his eyes and starting to gently nod his head again.

"She would regularly thank people in her mind for everything they'd done to help her. After that she would ask the Universe for further guidance. Having done that, it was all about looking for any signs of any help that might be coming. She called this synchronicity."

"Ah. Synchronicity." mumbled my Uncle still keeping his eyes closed. I continued happy he was seemingly following what I was saying.

"To her 'going with the flow' was all about being on the right path. Strangely though this, to her, meant not actually knowing where she was actually going to, or heading towards."

"So she never has any long term goals" my Uncle asked. "How on Earth does she manage to achieve anything?" he asked now with both eyes open. "That doesn't seem very sensible to me. I can't see how that would work for her." He said.

"I know what you mean Uncle but she is successful in her own way. She was a GP for over eleven years but then retrained to do something she enjoyed and which was much less stressful. Look I am not saying this is the way everyone should live their life. All I am saying is that I think there is a comparison here with the way the Knights were leading their life in the book Perlesvaus."

"All right Rowena, please do continue and I promise not to interrupt you again."

"Anyway, when she'd looked at all she'd achieved in her life, she'd realised that it was nearly always down to what she'd learnt from other people and how much she'd been helped by other people. When I was reading the Perlesvaus story last night, it seemed to me that the Knights were not achieving it all by themselves either. They too had regular help." I said. "It almost seemed as though there was a stream of synchronicity running through the story that recognised that those Knights who were looking to help those in dire need, and who were following the right path, were receiving some sort of divine guidance and help." I started to explain.

"Ah, I see now where you are heading with this – good." He nodded.

"This synchronicity saved them many times from dying as other people would turn up to help them, just in the nick of time. In short this divine guidance would come to people who were looking to help others as much as they could along the way. This is actually even quite a Gnostic, even Cathari, way of thinking." I pointed out. "At times even the Knights were not sure where they were heading as adventures just appeared one after the other. They were just upholding their version of honour and following their new law as they travelled around the land."

"And this, you are saying, is similar to your friends attitude to life of not having any end goal but just focusing on the journey." stated my Uncle.

"Yes, that's right" I replied.

"I now see where you are coming from with all this but I am not quite sure I understand the reasoning behind it all yet."

"I am not sure of the reasoning too yet Uncle but what interests me is that some people find it works for them and now someone seems to be writing about this way of life in a book about the Grail."

"Interesting." He mused.

I carried on. "This new law, I think, is rather like the law of the Universe that my yoga teacher spoke about. It is also, in its way, similar to the Cathari way of thinking." I suggested. "The Knights in the story even seem to recognize this and that their destiny was in God's hands." I continued. "The phrase 'if it is of God will' was regularly said by the Knights as though they knew too that it was divine guidance that was helping them along their journey." I pointed out.

"This phrase is even similar to the Arabic phrase 'Inshallah' which means 'God willing'. This even gives us a link to Wolfram's story and his Grail connection to the Middle East." I explained further. "The key, as I see it now, is this synchronicity. This is the message that I think the writer was trying to convey at a much deeper hidden level." I stated. "The path, that the Knights were travelling along through the forests from Castle to Castle, is a metaphor for our own path through life."

I could see him nodding still. That was good.

"Just like the Knights, we too are also travelling along our path in life from one challenge, or opportunity, to the next one. This book I think contains a message for all of us on how to follow this special path." I paused to collect my thoughts for my next few words. My Uncle was silent and also expecting more. "This message is about some sort of Universal or Divine guidance that can help us through life to where we are supposed to be heading if we uphold a particular way of caring and thinking and then asking for help." I suggested, thinking now about Aliya's words too.

"At the end of the book," I started again. "Perlesvaus, after all his travelling, finally goes back again to the Grail castle where, we are told, he finally 'turns' to Jesus who he now calls 'The Saviour of the World'. This, I think, reveals to us the final hidden message." I stated, aiming to build to a finale for my Uncles benefit.

"Perlesvaus has gone back to the Grail near to the end of his life and at the end of his journey. It was as though it had been the Grail that he'd always been heading towards but not actually been looking for, during his life." I pointed out. "What became important to Perlesvaus was the journey through life and not just getting to the end of it." I added.

"So the quest for the Holy Grail was not actually a quest to find the Holy Grail." My uncle suddenly stated out loud as though a realization had hit him.

"Yes. Exactly" I replied, "It was really a lifelong quest to become a more perfect person, a more spiritual person. If you could do that, it seemed you would then be rewarded by finding and then seeing the invisible Grail at the end of your life. This now also ties in with what Gadal came to think about the Grail."

"Well well. You have quite possibly found a completely new interpretation to the story of the Grail Rowena. Fascinating." He seemed genuinely intrigued with it all.

I waited a moment then continued. "The Gnostics, like the Cathars, thought that Jesus represented the pinnacle of perfection. To them this ending to the book would have meant that Perlesvaus had finally reached perfection as a person but that he'd only managed to achieve this by following the right path throughout his life. He'd only succeeded because he had followed the new law, the Gnostic way of thinking, and because he'd followed the synchronicity that came his way." I finished, feeling quite pleased at the way I'd explained it all.

In doing so, I think it had actually helped me to understand more clearly myself as well. My Uncle was silent for a few moments considering what to say next.

"Well, well, my dear. You really have excelled yourself." He praised using a tone to his voice that made me feel really good. "Tell me though." He probed and I wondered immediately if I had missed something, "If that was the message, what was so dangerous about it that it had to remain hidden within this story and out of sight from the Roman church." He asked. He then continued on to clarify his question further. "I know, of course, that the Church were against the Cathars at that time, but this message about following synchronicity to find your own path in life is hardly heretical." He questioned.

"That's a good question Uncle." I replied, genuinely impressed at his ability to probe any possible weakness in a point of view. "All I can say is that it might be to do with how a person finds their synchronicity. There is a sort of freedom attached to the whole concept. Relying on synchronicity, or divine guidance, to get you through life, in order perhaps to learn the lessons you need to learn, takes away a person's fear." I replied, feeling more confident that I'd found the answer. "The Knights in the story were not afraid to die in battle at all. If it was 'Gods will' for them to die, they would die." I continued. "Freely helping others, being free to go where you were next directed, righting the wrongs done to others was fundamental to their way of life." I went on.

"This seems to be in direct contrast to the church's far more controlling approach to Christianity and to life itself. The Pope and his inner team of Cardinals were extraordinarily wealthy compared to nearly everyone else. They lived in luxury and did little of no work at all, whilst the poor labored long hours in the fields just to feed their families." I pointed out. "If these poor people had no fear, they couldn't be controlled. This might then threaten the way of life the Pope and his Cardinal's. After all they had worked long and hard to attain this power for themselves." I pointed out.

"As I see it, the Roman Church used to install fear in their congregation. Only by turning up to Church each Sunday and paying them money, could the congregation have their fears taken away. No fear, no congregation, no money, no power." I ended.

"You have a good point there Rowena and one that seems to match life today in a way." He pondered. "I can even see a comparison here with your own situation, but I sense you've probably seen it too." He remarked with a keen eye that hadn't gone unnoticed.

"Yes" I acknowledged, "You're right. I'm aware of that and all the help I've been getting from everyone recently." I accepted.

"Does all this information help you in your life now do you think?" He asked slightly tentatively but with genuine interest.

"I'll need some more time to think about that Uncle. There are still too many questions surrounding it all." I replied.

"Indeed there are, my dear. I have one or two for you too if we can get back to the story for a moment." He answered.

I nodded. I think he might have sensed some slight reluctance from me to pursue my own questions in life just yet. Just thinking of my own future again seemed to have sapped me of energy a little.

"Yes well, it might even help you." He began. "For example, why do you think that both Wolfram and the writer of Perlesvaus both made the Grail invisible and, if this was something that was real, what do you think that could possibly even be?" he paused for a second and I realized he'd skillfully returned back to me a question that I'd put to him some time ago myself. "My second question is with regards to the idea that this invisible object was said to change shape. How could that be the case too, if it was something that was supposedly real?" He asked again. He continued on. "I don't expect you to have answers to these questions at the moment of course but, my real question is this, do you at least think that they are an important part of the storyline and indeed do you think they might even represent another kind of message for us." He concluded.

"Wow. Uncle that's a bit deep for so early in the day." I replied. "Yes" I carried on, "I do think the fact that two writers have made the Grail invisible has some meaning and yes, if we could find out what that means, I am sure it would also be part of the overall Gnostic message for us. Just what all that is though, I have no idea." I replied as honestly as I could.

"Good, then you now have something you can try and find out." He stood up and stretched a bit than placed his hand on his stomach. I knew that was a sign he wanted to end the conversation. "I think I would like some boiled eggs on toast this morning." He said opening the fridge.

I sat wondering about his statement about me trying to find out about the Grail's invisibility. Somehow he seemed to have placed it back onto me in a way that he thought that it might be connected to my own future. Did he mean to do that, or had I just wrongly thought that? Maybe he was just getting tired with all the thinking so early in the morning.

I got up myself as well and moved into the sitting room with my cup of coffee. Questions were buzzing in my head though. Just what was synchronicity anyway? I decided to do some online searching.

In the short time I had done that, it had thrown up even more questions. Some of them were actually quite helpful though. Apparently, according to Wikipedia, synchronicity was a term that was originally invented by the Psychologist Carl Jung. To him it had originally meant a meaningful coincidence. Later in his life though, he'd further defined it by linking it to a series of meaningful coincidences. Towards the end of his life, he had begun to think it was related in some way to some kind energy and even the paranormal.

I checked other sites and also found that synchronicity was said to occur when you were on the right path in life. That definitely resonated with me but the article was unsubstantiated. I opened the search wider and now found a connection to following ones passion in life in order to find your own path in life. Again there was no proof or back up offered here but it did make me start to wonder. What was it that I was passionate about in life? Had I had any synchronicity in my life? I was also reminded by what Aliya had said about asking for help. Had I asked for help in the past in any way that may have led to me getting help?

The thought of Aliya's words and asking for synchronicity struck a chord within me. If the Universe could help, it would help, but only if I asked for it. This was very similar, in a way, to the Knights in Perlesvaus who prayed for help and guidance. It was at this point that I suddenly remembered about my Uncle asking me to help go through my Dads old stuff.

"Uncle David." I called through to the Kitchen.

"Yes"

"Where did you put my Dads old stuff that you wanted me to go through?"

"In the garage."

"Great. I'll make a start this morning on it."

"Wonderful." He replied.

Half an hour later I was rooting through boxes of old photos, old school reports and mementos. It was hard with all sorts of feelings re-emerging after many years. I'd begun to make two piles though - One to keep and one to chuck. The 'to keep' pile was somewhat smaller. I'd nearly finished the last box when I saw it – The dark brown piece of haematite that my Dad had found.

I lifted it out carefully. It was about the same size and shape as the one I had in the boot of my car. I placed it between the two piles not sure whether to chuck it or not. Minutes later I'd finished and placed the stuff to chuck in some bin liners to take to the tip. The other pile fitted into two medium sized boxes which I stacked carefully out of the way at the back of the garage. I was now left looking at the rock. I bent down to pick it up. It was very heavy for its size too. I walked over to the boot of my car and half dropped it next to the one I'd picked up in the small cave with Bernard. It rolled slightly and ended up right next to my piece.

I gasped. It almost looked as though they fitted together. I pushed them closer. The height was the same and the fracture pattern along the top surface was almost identical.

I then reached down into the boot and picked each one up - One in my right hand, one in my left. They were really very heavy but I managed to bring them slowly closer together scrutinizing the edges and their faces more closely to see if they really did match. My arms started to shake with the weight of them both.

The two of them fitted exactly except there was still a broken edge. It was like I now had only half of the whole original piece. I stood speechless and confused and pressed the two pieces together again.

How on Earth could this be? Dad got his from a cave near to the beach and mine was found over 100 kilometers away inland. I brought them both in to show my Uncle.

"Uncle, do you remember Dad saying where he found this rock?"

"Argeles sur Mer. Just south of Perpignan near to the Spanish border." He replied. "He kept going on about how he swam round the point and found this cave which he then swam into. He said he found it right at the back of the cave." He replied.

"Well look at this." I said holding out both rocks. "This is a piece I found last week in a Cave in Ussat in the Ariege over 100 kms away.

They are both from the same original piece. Can you explain that in any way?" I asked.

"Goodness no." he replied just as astounded as I still was.

"There is a piece missing still" I added.

"So it appears." He replied still with a puzzled look on his face.

"But it's more bizarre than that even Uncle. I was just thinking about synchronicity and our conversation earlier when I thought about clearing out Dad's stuff and then this huge lump of synchronicity occurs."

"Curiouser and Curiouser." He mused in a typical way that an English literature teacher might do when quoting Lewis Carroll. "What else were you thinking about?" he added. I thought back for a moment. "I was looking online at people's thoughts on synchronicity and finding ones path in life.... how to follow ones passion and what I found interesting." I answered.

"So what have you been finding of interest recently." He asked.

"Well the Grail stories in the books you gave me to read." I replied

"Before that…. Aside from trying to work out what to do in your life, what was interesting you when you were in France?" He probed further.

"The Cathars" I began and then thought for a moment, "Their sacred places!" I almost shouted it out as though I had the right answer in class.

"What about these places?" He asked.

"I was wondering why certain places should be sacred while others were not. I couldn't understand that from a geological point of view. I was wondering if there was something from a scientific viewpoint that linked up all these sacred places."

"Aha." He noted out loud. "That then may be an avenue for you to explore." At that he began to wander off, feeling pleased with himself. It was just like him not to dwell on anything for too long these days. He was right though. As he'd said it all, I felt a welling of interest inside me again. There must be some connection between these sacred places and it might well be geological in some way.

I then remembered the project I'd started with my PhD course in Paleaontology and Geobiology at Edinburgh University. It was all about the effects of natural radiation on the biology in a particular area of the Southern uplands in Scotland. There was a Pitchblende deposit there that outcropped on the coast. It could easily be seen in a large quartz vein on the rocks right next to the beach. It had massive levels of Uranium radiation streaming out of it. My Geiger counter had had readings of over 30,000 clicks per minute. It was well over normal safety limits.

No one talked about it of course even though it had been known about for over 40 years. Going public on that, would have caused far too much of a problem. What I'd been planning to do was to collect biological samples around the outcrop, on the shore and inland, to see if I could find out how much it had affected life.

What I'd now come across though was almost the exact opposite. This new interest in sacred places, were places which were probably good for life. I'd been about to research places that were probably bad for life. It now looked as though that it might be my path in life to study why a place should be considered sacred or good for life. It now also seemed possible that all this could be related to the rather new subject of Geobiology – the study of how life affects the Earth and how the Earth affects life. Just how I was going to find out more about all this eluded me for now.

The only 'synchronistic' clue I'd been given were these two pieces of haematite that fitted together in half a lump – not exactly science.

At that point my Uncle reappeared. "Rowena, I have remembered something that may be important. I was trying to find that book I mentioned before…..about the old Persian legend and a dove when I remembered something else. It was something that Otto Rahn had mentioned in one of his books." He spoke quickly. It was almost as though he was out of breath trying to tell me. "I read it so very long ago though. You probably need to check up on this too. The Cathars had a sacred stone, that we know, but I think there was a story about when they were under siege at Montsegur. They didn't want their holy stone to be captured by the Pope's armies."

"Really." I interrupted.

"Yes. The story goes that four of them, in the middle of the night, descended down the cliffs on the far side of the mountain from the army so they were out of sight. Apparently they then took the stone and hid it in a cave somewhere miles away." He said in a way that was almost like he was telling me a secret.

"Ok but that was one stone Uncle." I replied.

"Yes but some people have speculated that it was deliberately broken in case they were captured. Each of the four then escaped in different directions with their piece of the stone." He went on.

"They would have most likely then travelled along the secret paths that only they knew about – the Cathar paths." I added enthusiastically.

"But wait a minute Uncle. You're not suggesting that these two pieces are two of the four pieces of their sacred stone are you?" I questioned.

"No. Not for sure. No." He replied holding up his index finger. "But it has to be a possibility and it may even explain why they were both found so far apart…. and both found in caves. May be the sea cave was also a sacred place of theirs?" he suggested.

"Wow. Uncle. I really don't know what to say."

"Well, have a think about it, I would. See what comes up." He replied as helpfully as he could. "It's the best I can do." He said almost apologetically.

"Thanks Uncle. I am sure it is significant. It is perhaps just a bit too difficult to get my head around just yet." I replied.

The events of the morning had shaken me quite a lot. All the memories of my dad, finding stones fitted together and now the suggestions from my uncle that they might be part of some holy Cathar stone that was once kept at the Castle of Montsegur. It was all a bit too surreal. I needed some grounding.

I started with job hunting again online. In no time at all I felt thoroughly deflated. I stopped after only a few minutes of this. What on Earth was I doing? A few moments ago I had been feeling much more excited. Confused yes, but at least I felt good. Now I had successfully brought my whole energy down to almost zero. I was essentially just trying to jump onto any path I could find in life. What was I thinking? I had to stop and reconsider things. I needed to go out for a walk. It would help clear my mind and to think better.

I walked, more slowly than usual, along a footpath beside the road that led to my Uncle's house. My mind kept coming back to this past idea that certain places in the World were held to be sacred. Was it because they were in caves, I wondered. Could it be down to the Geology in some way? Perhaps the Earth itself somehow made some places special and some places dangerous like areas where there was natural radiation? I began to wonder if it might perhaps be my path was to investigate this further. I might even be able to go back to Edinburgh University to continue studying it. At the moment though, I'd no evidence at all to support any scientific study. It was with that thought that I'd arrived at the gates of a local park.

Walking through them I was confronted by a large map of the park and all its paths. What immediately drew my attention were two diagonally straight paths that crossed over each other right in the middle of the park. It suddenly occurred to me that Cathar paths might also cross in the same way. If Montsegur was at the central crossing point then Rennes Le Chateau and its caves would be at the end of the path to the North East and Ussat and the Cave of Lombrives would be at the end of the path to the South West. This would mean that my father's sea cave, down by Perpignan would be at the end of the path to the South East.

This now meant that the path to the North West could also end up with a cave. Could it be that the four Cathars had secreted down the steep far side of the Pog, each with their piece of haematite stone? Had they then each made their way through enemy lines and along these four Cathar paths to these separate caves? With the two pieces I had, it would then mean that the other two would be in a cave at Rennes le Chateau and some other cave to the North West. I could perhaps check with Arnaud to see if he'd come across a piece that might fit in the Rennes area.

I stopped myself. What was I thinking? I can't go on some wild goose chase looking for two more pieces of haematite. My Dad and I had come across two pieces by chance. There would be loads of caves to have to find and then search and there would be many pieces of Haematite lying around. I hadn't got the money or time to waste on something like that either. On the other hand, this did seem like another clue. Was I supposed to keep looking? Maybe this would then lead me to finding out why some places were more sacred than others. I decided to check the map on my phone for areas that might have caves to the North West of Montsegur.

The nearest town in that direction was Foix. That had a mediaeval Cathar Castle but I couldn't find any cave systems around there. I kept looking. Further to the North West was the Maz d'Azil cave. It was a possible site but there was a road running through it. It sounded far too big and too obvious a place to hide anything or even to hold any secret ceremonies in. The place seemed to have more of a link to the Stone Age people rather than the Cathars.

After coming up with nothing else, I then tried searching online on my phone for old Cathar caves. I could find nothing obvious here though. In a final desperate attempt I added Knights Templar sites to the search because the church at Rennes le Chateau had been one of their places. This proved more promising. There was an old Templar chapel at a place called Montsaunes and not far from that were some caves at a place called Saint Martory. I decided to look into these places in more detail when I got back.

It was after midday when I got in and my Uncle had gone out. I took out my laptop and started to investigate. There was very little to be found about Montsaunes. The chapel there had been completed in 1180AD and the Templars had been there since 1146AD. Inside the chapel very some very strange drawings on the walls and ceiling – one of the guides described them as esoteric. It also went on to say that no one had yet figured out what they all meant.

For some reason that intrigued me so I switched to look for images of these drawings. They were indeed strange but one set of patterns caught my eye. They were the same as the ones I'd seen on the ceiling under the paintwork at the Church at Rennes Le Chateau. This may well indicate some kind of connection between the two places. I couldn't really tell though. It may be somewhere I should look at more closely I thought. I pushed on to look at the St. Martory caves. The only thing I could find was that local cavers had explored them but nothing else. It was not much to go on. The question on my mind now though was what to do next with it all. I'd reached about as far as I could go with it over here in the UK.

If I went back over there though, what would I be doing? What would I be looking for? If I was to follow Aliya's advice, it would be to just 'go with the flow'. Her idea was that I should just follow where the Universe was taking me, I would then meet the people I was supposed to meet and they would guide me to find what I was supposed to find. If she was right then 'the flow' was taking me in the direction of the Cathars, their stone, their sacred places and perhaps my growing interest in understanding why these places were where they were. If I was ever going to answer that question, I needed to go with the flow and trust that I would meet the right people along the way. That meant returning to the South of France.

I checked my finances. Not great, but if I took a tent and some camping gear I could cut my costs a bit. The travelling and food would be the main expense. I could probably spend a month down there and have at least a couple of thousand pounds leftover from what my father had left me. It was a big gamble. I decided to talk it all through with my Uncle and see what he thought.

He arrived back after about half an hour having been doing some shopping. I helped him put it away and made a cup of tea for us both. I explained all my thinking to him and asked what he thought.

"Well you are right." He began. "You can't go down there on the pretence of looking for the rest of a piece of stone. That's ridiculous.

However I am curious that you see a connection between this and Geobiology. For example why can't a place be sacred just because people have regularly prayed somewhere?"

"True, but why would the place itself make any difference?" I replied. "Surely the Cathars could just go into any old cave and have their ceremony. Instead, they kept choosing the same ones. And also..." I added. "...would a place remain sacred after they had finished their ceremony? If it did, how could that be so?"

"There seems to be evidence that different cultures used the same places for their prayers for over a thousand years. The Pog for example at Montsegur also had a Roman shrine on it and before that there were a Celtic shrine and who knows, there could even have been a sacred Stone Age site there too." I stated. "That again points to the significance of the location rather than just the congregation." I finished.

"You've a fair point," He relented. "You do seem to be on to something. Perhaps the answer is tied up with this invisible Grail. After all it also only seems to appear in certain places too. Maybe the Grail is connected to specific locations."

"My goodness Uncle you could be right. I'd forgotten about the invisibility angle." My Uncle thought for a while whilst walking around the table to sit down with his cup of tea. He then continued.

"So I guess why you need to go back over there, is to try and establish what all these sacred places have got in common. Not only that though. You'll need to find out, if what you find, also applies to sacred places all around the World." He pointed out.

"Hmm." I went. It was a tall order I know and I wondered if anyone else had tried in the past. It then dawned on me. Of course they had. The quest for the Grail must have been along the same lines. They were searching by going from one castle to another castle in order to see if the Grail appeared there. It may have been their way of checking if they had reached a level of spiritual perfection that allowed them to now see the Grail. These castles could now perhaps each represent different sacred locations.

I remembered Perlesvaus had been going from one castle to the next in his travels looking for the one where the Grail would appear. It did now seem as though every castle had the ability to host a Grail but seeing one was another matter. That was now down to the person in some way. I was sure I was onto something but still not quite sure what yet.

"Uncle." I started slowly, "Do you not think that the search for the reason why a place is sacred is now similar to the search for the Grail itself?"

He was about to bring his cup to his lips but it had now stopped in midair about 6 inches from his face. He paused like that for about 3 seconds and then moved it the rest of the way to take a drink. It was not until he put his cup down did he speak next.

"Rowena, my dear. I am not often surprised these days but you have certainly made me think - Probably in a way, that I have not thought for many, many years." He paused again.

"Actually, I think you might be right. I have been wondering myself recently, with you having read the books and our discussions on them, that there might well be more than one Grail. I'm not talking about Chretien's shallow bowl here...... With the possibility that the legends started in the Middle East and with these sacred stones being found at many sacred sites, it could well be that a Grail could be found at all these sites. It was perhaps just a matter of being in the right frame of mind, or state of spirituality, that would then allow you to see it or not."

"That still leaves us with the question of what the Grail is though." I pointed out.

"Well one clue, I think we can get, came from one of Otto Rahn's books. If my memory serves me, I think Rahn thought that what was invisible was something he called 'a divine presence'. He thought that these stones could hold this divine presence in some way. I think that he too also thought that this divine presence could only be found at certain sacred sites."

"Maybe this divine presence is actually some kind of invisible gas," I suggested, "Or even some kind of radiation? Gravity even? Something perhaps that might make people feel special in some way." I further suggested.

"Well that may be something for you to find out." He said. "What do you think you should do next?"

"I was thinking of going back over to France Uncle but first I need to do some preparation. I have to work out what I might need to take and what I need to establish over there. I was thinking of getting back in touch with my PhD tutor. I may be able to adapt the Geobiology project I'd started and continue my studies with all this in mind."

"Hmm." He pondered.

"In order to do that though," I carried on, "I would need to be able to come up with some kind evidence to present to my tutor that's worth following up with more detailed scientific research."

"Well, that's one possible route," he said. "There may be others of course." He added in a rather cryptic manner. With that he finished his tea and left me to go and watch the news. His last words now sounded like something Aliya might have said to me. Ah yes, I thought. I could do her class tonight and maybe, if she had time, she could answer a couple of questions I had.

We were all waiting at five to six in the studio. It was good to see several people from the previous class. I think they were also happy to see that I'd come back again and that I'd not been put off. Aliya burst through the double doors about a minute before 6.00pm. She was looking serenely confident and all smiles. With her light brown complexion she looked well under 30 but I'd done the Maths and she had to be closer to 40. With the music on, we went straight into a session that was similar to the one we'd done the day before. There were a couple of new sequences of movements though, one of which I found quite hard to keep up with. By the end I was dripping in sweat and loving it.

"Hi Aliya. Thanks for a great session tonight" I said.

"Thanks. I was really up for a good one myself tonight," she replied. "One of those days when everything changes. I feel fine now. How about you?"

"I found it easier than before but that last asana was really tough. I still haven't got the hang of this serpent energy thing though. What is that all about?"

"Kundalini," she replied. She could see I was none the wiser. "Chi or Ki energy. The energy of the universe" She went on.

"What energy is that then?" I asked.

"I'm not sure I can describe it more than that" she replied. "It is a sort of two-way feeling that goes up and down your spine. The Yin and the Yang if you like."

"Ah." I said not sounding as though I really understood. "I have heard of those. I always thought that was just something you imagined." I half asked.

"Well, in a way it is. But it is very real too and very powerful when you tap into it."

"Powerful? In what way?" I asked

"It can heal the body, it can provide great strength. It can make you look younger and it has been said that it will even help you live longer."

"Really!" I said sounding surprised. The things she had just mentioned where almost exactly the same as the Grail properties I had been reading about. "But what exactly is this energy Aliya?"

"Ah Rowena. You have your Western scientific hat on tonight that's for sure. People have searched the answer to that for centuries. It's a long subject that's probably best researched online rather than hearing about it from me."

"Do you have time for a drink before your next class?" I asked.

"Actually, my next class has been cancelled so yes. Why don't we go round the corner for a glass of wine though?" she suggested.

"That would be great." I replied.

We were soon sitting down with two glasses of chilled French Sauvignon Blanc in an old style pub. It was almost empty with just a couple of old timers cuddling their half's of bitter in a corner.

"So much has happened since yesterday," I started. "I haven't stopped thinking about what you said too. You were talking about finding my path. Well, I think I may have found it."

"Arre wah" she exclaimed. "So quickly too. Do tell me more." She said sitting forward keenly. I told her about my past research in bad Earth locations due to radiation and how my interest had now been kindled in sacred locations and a geobiological connection between them all.

"I think there is something that connects all these sacred sites." I said. "I am just not sure yet what it is, but my feeling is, that it connects to the Earth in some way." I stated more exactly at the end.

"Now that does interest me," she replied. "I think a lot of people would really like to know about a connection like that if one existed. But what makes you sure there might be?" she asked.

I then explained more about the caves and the two pieces of haematite. I'd not mentioned the piece of haematite that I'd picked up in the cave the last time I was with her as it hadn't seemed important back then.

I now told her about the second piece of my father's and how the two pieces had fitted together perfectly. I also mentioned the possibility that there were two more pieces and that they may have once been the holy stone of the Cathars.

When I'd finished, her mouth was wide open.

"Oh my." She began. "Well if that is not a sign, I don't know what is." she said.

"A sign.......in what way?" I asked.

"A sign to go back and explore more." she replied.

"Yes, I was sort of coming round to that conclusion myself. I can't of course go back just to look for the other half of the stone but I am not sure quite what I'll be looking for and where I'll start."

"Rowena." She sat forward and reached out and touched my hand. "These are the moments in life we wait for. These are the times when we either rise to the occasion, or we sit back down. There are no easy decisions. These moments are also quite rare in life but they tell us we have found the path we are individually supposed to be following. Every one of us will have these moments, sometimes not till quite later on in life. Many of us will not recognize them. Some of us will see them, but sit back down."

I sat dead still listening to her speak. It was as though I was seeping everything she said into each pore of my body.

"We cannot judge these people for their decisions though because, for the very few of us who stand up and follow the path, it is hard. You will be challenged." She paused, "constantly. You will feel like giving up" she paused again, "on many occasions. But you will also be helped along the way. No task, no problem will ever be too great for you. You will always be pushed just the right amount and no more." She shuffled closer to me.

"Listen," I think she'd sensed I was frightened. I was. "All you have to do is to lose your ego. It's not about you. Don't be full of it, don't do the 'selfie' stuff, that will just send you the wrong way and off the path."

I shook my head. I wasn't really into that anyway.

"I'm going to tell you what I see as the truth now and it has taken me years to understand this myself and I'm still not good at it……." she paused and looked me in the eye. "…..your challenge is not to find the connection between these sacred sites. You many think it is, but it's not. You may never find the answer to that. That is just a question you set out with. That's what gets you going. There will be other things you find out along the way that may be, and will be, far more important to find out."

"But how will I know these things?" I asked.

"You will know." She said assuredly, "Your challenge is actually to lose your fear and to stay positive. If you can do that, everything will flow and everything you are supposed to come across will appear in front of you. Be grateful for what you have and for everyone who had helped you. Do not be afraid of asking for help. Just be as precise as you can be when you ask. If you need money for example – ask for money to come into your life. If you

129

can do all this, synchronicities will keep coming along. It will be like life is conspiring to help you in your journey – which of course it will be."

"Thanks," I said quietly.

"Listen, stay in touch with me on this if you want." She suggested. "If I can help, I would like to." She said handing me her card with some contact details on. "I'd really love to hear how you are getting on anyway." I listened but remained quiet trying to take in everything she'd just said. "One of the things I've always wanted Rowena was to have a yoga centre of my very own. What kept me back was that I wanted it to be in a very special place – a sacred place even. The trouble was that I was never sure where this place might be. I've been waiting for the right time and the right signs. Now, with you and your journey, I can see how that might be possible. There are sacred sites all around the World. Why are they where they are? It's a huge question Rowena. I really wish you all the best with it."

"Thanks. I really have no idea where this is all going to take me." I answered.

"It's best not to think about it." Aliya suggested. "Just go where the flow takes you. If life wants you to know, you will know. When are you thinking of going?"

"I was thinking tomorrow." I replied. "I didn't feel as though there was any reason to delay it really."

"That's good. It's always good to act quickly when the time is right." she added. We chatted some more, finished our wine and then hugged and said goodbye.

I drove back thinking of what I should take with me when I remembered Katy and our yoga session the next day. I sat in the car outside my Uncles house and called her.

"Ro." How are you doing?" she asked.

"Fine Katy. How about yourself?"

"All Ok, not a lot is happening at the moment in work or in my life but I'm happy, which is good."

"Yes happy is indeed good." I replied

"What about you?" she asked again

"Well, are you sitting down?" I asked. She said she was and I ran through everything that had been going on since I last saw her. Every now and again she broke her silence with a few gasps and OMG's. After about 5mins I dropped the news.

"Having said all the Katy, I've had to make some changes to my plans. I am not going to be able to make yoga tomorrow night, which is why I am also calling. I've decided to go back to the South of France."

"That's ok Ro. I kind of guessed from what you just said that might be why you were calling. We can catch up when you get back. You just do as best you can when you are over there."

"Thanks Katy." I replied. "I'll do my best. Bye"

I went inside and told my Uncle the same news. I'd be off tomorrow. He was very supportive and he'd said that I was very welcome to come back whenever I was ready. He did though make me promise to keep him up to date with anything related to the Grail and the Cathar stone. I said I would.

Chapter 3

Back to France

Midnight. I was on the upper deck of the Ferry again looking back at the lights of Portsmouth. This time though I had very different feelings to accompany me. Instead of escaping without knowing what I was doing, I was now adventuring forward with a purpose. It felt good and now the even more familiar territory of the boat was comforting. It was difficult not to smile. I'd spent the day getting my car serviced, buying some necessary items and packing. My little Mini was almost completely full. I'd planned to head for Montsaunes first and the nearby caves. I wasn't sure what I was going to find there but it was going with the flow so I was going to trust in synchronicity.

I awoke refreshed after a good sleep in my cabin and was raring to get started. My aim was to get as far South as I could today and to then look for a late hotel booking in that area. Camping was an option but probably not the best one after a long drive.

The journey South flew by. Now I knew where I was heading I was making good progress. I drove right by the turning for Le Mans, with a brief memory of the good looking Italian man flashing through my mind. I passed Tours just before midday where I'd stopped to call Katy on the banks of the Loire river. The turning for Limoges came up at around 4.00pm but I still felt like pressing on.

I was now on the A20 and had passed Brives la Gaillarde. It was nearly 5.30pm when I saw a sign saying Cahors (Centre). That was enough for me today. I turned off and headed that way. Coming up to the first roundabout outside the town I noticed the Hotel Campanile Cahors. Easy parking, free Wifi, breakfast included and late checkout. It was just what I needed so I pulled in.

Cahors

Friday morning. Having done some homework the night before after a long hot bath, I'd found out that access to the chapel at Montsaunes was only from 3.00pm to 5.00pm on a Friday and it was closed on the weekends. It was only a 2 hour drive so I didn't need to leave Cahors until 1.00pm. That gave me the time to explore the town in the morning.

The brochures in the hotel lobby gave me some more information. Cahors had been quite a large centre right back to Celtic times when it used to be called Divona by the Cadurci tribe. Divona was the name of the fountain of Chartreaux which was next to the river here. The river Lot flowed in a large horseshoe bend and the city of Cahors sat on the inside of that. When the Romans came they had defeated the Celts and then taken over the whole area. It was them that had turned the place into a large city.

Of the sites now left to see, the main one was probably the Valentre Bridge which had six Gothic arches and three square towers. The locals apparently called it the Devil bridge because of the difficulties and length of time it took to be built. In the 14th century it had taken them 70 years to finish it. The locals had said that the devil was unhappy with it and kept causing the builders problems which was why it had taken so long to complete. What struck me as interesting was that it was also part of a pilgrimage walking trail.

It was enough to give me something to aim for when walking around the town. The local pink line number 3 bus ran directly to the city centre. It also stopped right next to the hotel so I nipped onto it. It took me right to the Marie, the central city hall. I was back to experiencing the delights of French cities and towns. Tree lined streets, French cafes and the Sun, it was lovely. I walked South down the Boulevard Leon Gambetta to the Place Fenelon to see its fountains. After taking some photos there, I ambled over towards the Cathedral St Etienne where the cobblestoned streets got narrower and narrower.

After about an hour of drifting in and out of indoor markets and delicatessens I headed down to the Pont Valentre. On the way I'd managed to buy a selection of food 'delicacies' for the rest of my journey. The bridge was now just a footbridge and in order to cross it, you had to go under the arches of the three square towers. It was mid-morning and it was busy with tourists and street vendors. I was happy to take my time, stopping in several good positions to take pictures.

"Mademoiselle …ici…" One male vendor tried to interest me.

"Non merci," I replied.

"Some nice souvenirs for you. key rings, necklace?" He tried again. How did he know I was from the UK? I'd used my best French accent too.

"Monnaie s'il vous plait." A voice from lower down reached my ears.

The voice had come from an old French lady squatting down against the wall next to the Key ring salesman.

"Non merci." I tried again.

"Je vous connais." The old lady continued on. "Je vous connais."

I stopped to do some mental translation. Is she saying she knows me I wondered?

I looked at her and then the key ring man. Is this a set up? The old lady then said something fast I didn't understand at all. "She said she saw you last night in her dreams." The key ring man said half-jokingly. The old lady started cackling with laughter. If this was a double act it was getting a bit scary.

"What does she mean?" I asked him

"Je sais pas." He replied quickly. The old lady then rattled off some more French I couldn't understand and that seemed to send her into fits and bursts of more cackling laughter. I looked again at the key ring man.

"She says she saw you in a cave of bones." His look showed me he was as confused as I was. I looked down at her again, somewhat surprised by that translation. Caves were what I was heading for. How could she possibly know that or even seen me in one in a dream. My face was obviously showing some concern.

"Don't worry Mademoiselle, she is a mad woman but I have to say I have never heard her laugh like that before. Hey Victor" He turned and called out to another vendor a few feet away. "Have you ever heard her laugh like that before?"

"Jamais. She is just mad and miserable." Victor replied laughing too.

"What have you done to her young lady?" Key ring man said.

"Nothing. How could I? I've only just got here." My words seemed to set off the old lady talking again in very quick French, accompanied now with hand and arm gesticulation as though she was reaching up to point to something. I looked at Key ring man again.

"She says you must pay her for the rest of the dream." He said.

I knew it. This was a double act. But how had she come up with a cave? I stood watching her laughing. She didn't appear to be laughing at me,

136

which was a relief. She really seemed to be laughing at something though. I thought about it for a while and wondered what Katy would have done in this situation. She would have probably paid the woman some money just to hear what she would say next. Well what harm would it do, I thought and got my purse out. I gave her a five Euro note.

"Mademoiselle, please," said Key ring man, "For me too please, here I have a lovely one for you." He pulled out a key ring with the words Cahors on it and what looked like some city emblem. "Five Euro's" he grinned.

"Ok," I said "But only after you have translated what she says." I negotiated. Key ring man then spoke to the old lady and off she went again in a string of French syllables and laughter.

"She says you will find what you are looking for above the entrance." He stated.

"Entrance to what, the cave?" I asked.

"Here is your key ring, please five Euro's now." He held out the key ring in front of me and I gave him the note.

"She says nothing else Mademoiselle." I looked at her. She was clutching the note I had given her like it was all she had. I then noticed the cataracts in her eyes.

"Is she blind?" I asked.

"En peu." Key ring man replied. I squatted down in front of her. It looked as though she only had about half her sight left.

"Thank you for sharing your dream." I said in slow English. "I wish you the very best." My head nodding slightly as I spoke. She just smiled back at me and started laughing again. This time in a nicer way though. With that I got up, said goodbye and then continued over the bridge wondering what to make of it all. Perhaps I'd really just paid ten euro's for a key ring I didn't need but it would make a souvenir and perhaps the money will help them a bit.

I headed down the road the other side to the Fountain of Chartreux. Underneath an overhanging limestone cliff face there was a small cave that had a trickle of water coming out of it. It filled a pool of water that was at a higher level than the river. It was all quite serene and I wondered about all the past activity that would have gone here right back in Celtic times.

On the outer banks of the meandering river there was a ring of limestone cliffs. They shone white in the mid-morning Sun. It would have been lovely to run around the river. I walked back again wishing I could spend more time here. Crossing the bridge I nodded to the Key ring man. He was busy with other tourists but at least he smiled back at me which was nice of him.

The old lady was still sitting against the wall next to him. This time though she was not laughing but just holding out her hands begging. Perhaps back to her usual self I thought, but who knows. I pondered further on her remarks. She said she saw me in the cave of bones and that I would find what I'm looking for above the entrance. I had no idea if it was any kind of clue or not. What was it with these old French ladies and me? The one at Rennes Le Chateau had acted quite strangely too telling me to look out for snakes and pointing in the distance. The bus back to the hotel took only a few minutes and soon I was on my way driving South on the D820 listening to Taylor Swift.

Montsaunes

At five to three I'd pulled up outside the Marie, the small town hall in the village of Montsaunes. I'd swapped my passport for the keys to the chapel and was now driving round to it. I was certainly thankful for my online preparations beforehand. This place was only open four afternoons a week for a couple of hours only. It was no wonder so few people knew about what was inside.

I stood looking at the entrance. Above the door arch was a sign I'd seen before on line. It was a Chi Rho, a Christogram. It was made up of just two Greek letters. The consensus of opinion was that it stood for a shortened version of the word Christos.

This Chi Rho was slightly different though. There was also an Alpha and Omega sign either side of the cross, although much of the Omega sign had been damaged. Curiously too, around the vertical baseline of the P was what looked like a symbol for a coiled snake. I smiled with the thought of how many other things it could mean. Chi energy, Aliya had said, and my nickname Ro. 'Energy Rowena' it could almost be telling me.

Was this again some kind of sign to get my attention? Was the old lady on the bridge meaning for me to look above this entrance? Who knows? I decided to just take it as I sign that I was supposed to be where I was today, whatever that would mean or lead to. I'd had the feeling that I should visit this place as soon as I'd found out about it and now here I was.

All the online images completely fail to do the place justice. Initially I could see that it was essentially just one large room with a very tall ceiling and with a curved half circular wall at the far end.

My first thought was that it was very much like a small country chapel with its pews either side of a central aisle, a font just inside the entrance, a pulpit on one side and an altar at the far end. It also had some small stained glass windows high up near the ceiling at the back of the church and at the far end set in the circular wall section. What made it all spectacularly different though was the décor. The walls and ceiling were covered in strange drawings and graffiti like images. This was way out of my league. I had no idea what any of it meant.

It was then I noticed some of the patterns were exactly like those on the ceiling of St Mary's church in Rennes Le Chateau. These had been the ones that were appearing underneath due to the water damage. They almost looked like petals or even leaves.

With the Templars being present at both sites at the same time it could not have been a coincidence. It must have meant there was a similar way of thinking behind both of them.

These strange drawings meant that the Montsaunes chapel was a real mystery. I decided to photograph as much as I could so that I could look back on it in the future if something similar came up. I could also perhaps enlarge some of the pictures and that would help me see some of the ceiling art more clearly.

As I worked along the walls with my camera, I noticed Cup like shapes. Could these be Grail type signs? I wondered. No idea. As I looked up at the ceiling I saw a series of shapes which struck me as even stranger. Up until now there'd been some sort of order to the drawings. They were neat and all geometrically positioned. The ones on the ceiling though were all over the place and in no order at all apart from one long length of circular designs.

Of particular interest to me was that some of them looked as though they were cross sections of round castles. They looked like an arrangement of bricks laid end to end in a circle. Inside of these were a variety of different shapes.

I couldn't get the idea out of my head that they each represented a castle and that these were, in some strange way, linked to the castles in the book Perlesvaus. Those castles, with their curious names, seemed to be symbols for something and now these circular, round tower type, castle shapes also seemed to be symbols for something too. The story of Perlesvaus had been written around the time of 1200AD. This place had been completed around 1180AD. It was therefore possible that the writer knew about these things.

For the moment no answer came to me as to what all these symbols really meant so I just carried on photographing them. Having completed that task, I took the time to get a feeling for the place. I stood in the centre next to the altar and became as silent as I could.

Although it was a small chapel, it seemed to have the same feeling as being in the middle of a large cathedral. I wondered why and then slowly realized as I looked up. It had to be the high ceiling that was somehow giving me the feel good factor. Maybe the Templars had discovered this phenomenon which was why they built their Cathedrals so high. The builders here may well have known of the significance of having such a great height to width ratio's for their buildings.

I'd been in the chapel for nearly an hour and no one else had joined me. I was glad to have place all to myself but again it really surprised that most people had no idea about its existence. I guessed that if those Templar symbols were ever fully understood, it wouldn't take long before the place would be crowded out. They'd be selling tickets in no time.

After a few more minutes appreciating the silence, I walked back to the entrance and turned to get a better look at the three small stained glass windows high up at the far end. I turned up the zoom lens on my camera to the maximum and took photos of each of them. I had a quick look at the central one afterwards. It was Jesus holding what looked like a glass orb. The words underneath were 'Salvatore Mundi'. My translate button changed the Latin to English – Saviour of the World.

Both the stained glass image and the Latin words rang a bell. I searched the Latin words online on my phone. Up came a recent Leonardo da Vinci painting that was sold at auction for over 400 million dollars. It too was a picture of Jesus holding a crystal ball. At the bottom there were the same two Latin words. This caught me by surprise. A few searches later and I'd found nothing on line that was such a good match. After recent books and films nearly everyone knew that da Vinci used codes in his paintings. What did all this really mean? Did the da Vinci painting have anything to do with this much earlier stained glass window here at Montsaunes?

The other question now on my mind was whether or not the Montsaunes chapel qualified as a sacred place, in the same way the Cathars would have considered a place sacred.

At the moment I really couldn't tell. From a geological perspective I had looked around but I'd soon found out that there was nothing that I could actually examine. The area around the chapel was just flat. From all the work that had gone into building the chapel as well as its ceiling art, the people that built it certainly must have thought it was a special place. I couldn't tell why though.

I was still missing something. All I could do for now was to hand the key back, get my passport and move on to the B&B I'd booked up. I could then perhaps take some time to look through all the photographs. That might lead somewhere and I could always come back again.

I'd planned to do some investigations into the caves around St Martory. It was a small village a few miles away to the North West. There was one cave there that had been called the Cavern of Montsaunes and I was hoping to find it. I knew it was a long shot but if one of the four Cathars had escaped in this direction North West from Montsegur, they may have known of a sacred cave in this area. Previous Cathar caves had a symbol of a dove in them. My thinking was to see if I could find anyone who had knowledge of the caves in the area and then see if they knew any with a dove symbol in.

I knew it might take a few days but I wanted to see if there could be any truth to the Cathar stone story and also see if there were any potential sacred caves nearby that I could check out. There had to be a reason why the Cathars chose specific caves and places to hold their ceremonies. If I could find some idea of what might be happening here, I could maybe test that idea again in the caves around Rennes Le Chateau.

Something Aliya had said to me was also beginning to surface in my mind. It may be that this was all just an exercise I had to follow, in order to find out something else entirely. Although I had an idea to follow up, if I was following my own unique path, I had to be prepared for where that path might take me. The good thing though was that I still felt I was on my path.

St Martory

It was only a few minutes drive from Montsaunes to the place I'd arranged to stay. It was called the L'Escalère and had been described on the internet as a B&B. From the pictures online though, it looked more like a grand country hotel.

It was situated next to the beautiful Garonne river and was just half a kilometer from the village of St Martory. The beauty of the place finally made me book it up. It was more expensive than I'd wanted but it seemed to be the only place to stay around here and the alternative was to stay several miles away. What I was hoping for was a chance to meet and speak with some of the local people.

Coming out of the village I drove round a left hand bend with the river on the inside, I noticed a limestone cliff face on my right. A quick glance and I could see several small caves in it. A little further on and I saw some more. It dawned on me that this place had a lot more caves than I'd expected. This all could become far too time-consuming if I was not careful. I had to stay positive.

The turning to the B&B turned out to be a long driveway. It led up to the front of a large two story white building with a low angled red tiled roof. The stylish black railing balcony above the entrance doorway gave it character. It all had a very warm, welcoming and homely appeal to it.

Surrounding the house was a mown grass lawn that reached down to the edge of the banks of the Garonne. The place actually looked much more expensive than it really was.

I was greeted at reception by Madame LeBoeuf, the owner. She apologised that the hotel was fairly empty at the moment which I thought was strange but later, on reflection, I think she just didn't want anyone to feel lonely here. After checking in, showering and relaxing with a cup of tea I went down to have a walk around outside. I had about an hour before dinner which seemed to be at a set time tonight.

I had looked at the menu in the reception. There was a delicious wild mushroom soup and a fish risotto to look forward to. The price was quite high though. I thought for a moment that it would be much cheaper to eat down in the village. Somehow though eating down there didn't seem quite right. Walking into the dining room, I noticed that on the left hand side, near to the window, were a couple of tall bookshelves. I was drawn towards them. They were full of maps of different areas, local guide books, activity brochures and old French books. I looked along the shelves wondering if anything might stand out. At the end of the second shelf down in the far bookcase one book was sticking out further than the rest. For some reason it caught my eye.

I reached for it and pulled it out. On the cover was a man standing in a large cave with Stalactites hanging above him. It was called 'Ten years under the Earth' by Norbert Castaret. It was an English version too. Probably the only English book in here, I thought.

"Ah yes." A voice from behind me said. It was Madame LeBoeuf. "An Englishman left that behind for others. I think he was into his caving." She said in reasonable English. "Monsiour Casteret was from here." She added. "He was born here over 100 years ago. My father knew him."

"Would it be OK if I read it?" I asked.

144

"But of course." She replied. "Is this something that interests you?" she asked me.

"Yes and no." I said. "I am interested in visiting the Cavern of Montsaunes. I heard it was near here but I am not quite sure where."

"I have not heard of this cavern but my father may know." She replied looking out the window. "He is taking a nap right now before dinner. If you would like to join us later I am sure he would be happy to answer any questions. He used to go up to the local caves himself when he was much younger."

"Thank you." I said, not quite believing my luck and the fact that I'd nearly decided to eat in the village.

After our conversation I decided to stroll down the lawn to the river. There was a small hut amidst a few well-spaced trees. In front of it there was a wooden platform and next to that there were some sun loungers on the grass. I looked inside and saw that it was a sauna. It was one of the nicest settings for a sauna I'd ever seen. Next I stepped carefully down to the river's edge unsure what exactly was underneath the grass and whether it would take my weight. Once safely there I stood and looked around.

Slow languid waters passed from right to left in front of me. I looked down to see that it ran deep right next to the bank. Perhaps no quick dip in here after the sauna I thought. Getting out again could be a problem. A fisherman was wading downstream of me casting his line over the white water towards a deeper pool of water the other side. I wondered if it was Paul. If not, I am sure he would have loved this place. I sat down on one of the loungers and watched the angler. The slow cast of his rod was both mesmerizing and peaceful.

I took out my phone to take a photo. Having done so I started to scroll through the ones I had taken earlier in the chapel. Pierre and Bernard would really love to see these I thought. Tarascon-sur-Ariege was about an hour and a half away. I wanted to go back there some time to look at some more caves and had brought my tent so I could stay in a nearby campsite. I didn't want to impose on them again as I wasn't sure how long I'd be there for. I'd give them a call soon, I thought.

Flicking through the photos I stopped at the one with the petal like patterns on the walls and zoomed in. Following a train of thought I started to search online images that were similar. One phrase kept coming up to describe them – a flower of life. It was a geometric form that could be found in many different places around the world. They appeared to be circles intersecting with other circles which in turn seemed to represent more shapes. They were seemingly linked to some kind of early Alchemy and they could be found as far back as 6000 years ago. Even Leonardo da Vinci seemed to have spent time drawing variations of them.

Nowhere though could I find a common interpretation for what they meant apart from the fact that they represented something three dimensional. Perhaps all the symbols in the chapel were really representations of three dimensional things. The Castle like symbols may even represent real Castles. The idea that the Grail could change shape then came into my mind. Perhaps these symbols were representations of the invisible changing shape of the Grail.

I was left wondering what on earth could be invisible and yet still be seen by holy people as something that could change shape. Did I feel I was still getting somewhere? I wasn't sure.

I turned to the book I'd recently taken off the book shelf. After having read a few pages I was totally absorbed by Mr Casteret's descriptions of his exploits underground. It seemed he was one of the early French pioneers in Caving and had made some major discoveries. Time raced by until my name was called by Madame LeBoeuf.

It was time for dinner. This was not like a restaurant at all. It felt like I'd joined a French family. We all sat around a long rectangular brown antique dining table. The bookcase was at one end and along the side was a typical French dresser complete with bowls and cups and plates. Madame LaBoeuf was at one end and her father was at the other end. There were two other guests, a French couple, and one empty seat. I sat next to her father who introduced himself to me.

"Enchanté, young lady. My name is Antoine. I hear from my daughter you are interested in the caves around here. Are you a caver?" He asked. His English was good. If it wasn't for his large bushy moustache, he could even pass for being an old English gentleman.

"Yes, in a way. Hi my name is Rowena" I replied holding my right hand out to shake his. He took it smiling and nodding his head at the very English way of introduction.

"Your English is very good" I pointed out. "Did you live in England at one time?"

"No not at all in fact. I worked for an Engineering company in Toulouse that was half owned by an English company. We worked together making products for the air industry there. Our meetings were nearly always in English."

"Amelie tells me you are reading Norbert's book." he continued.

"Yes, well, I've just started. It is very good though." I replied.

"I knew him you know. I was only a young man at the time and he was….. nearly 61." He stated in a way that showed he seemed to be keen to be factually correct about things. It was probably the engineer in him still, I thought. The wild mushroom soup was then brought in by a young man from the kitchen.

"Ah Fabien, that smells wonderful" said Amelie LeBoeuf at the other end of the table. Fabien smiled but said nothing as he brought the soup tureen in and placed it on a mat in the middle of the table before going back into the kitchen. We each in turn ladled some into our soup bowls. Freshly cooked small French buns were brought in next for us.

"Did you go caving with him?" I asked.

"Yes, he took me a few times to the caves he knew around here. He liked to do that with the youngsters in the village. I think he was looking to find someone else who might eventually share his passion. Me though.... I was too big really for it all really. Some of the spaces were too tight for me to crawl through."

"I was wondering if you knew the Cavern of Montsaunes?" I asked.

"Ah yes. That was one he did take me to. So many years ago now. It is not far from here. I can give you directions if you want to go there. I would take you myself but I'm really too old now. But please tell me, why do you want to go there?" He asked with genuine interest in his voice.

"I am doing a study on caves that might be sacred caves," I began. "I am hoping to see if I can find something common to them that makes them a sacred place." I then continued to tell him about the Cathar caves and the one Bernard had taken me to.

"It sounds interesting but I'm not sure you'll find what you're looking up at the Cavern now." He said nonchalantly.

"Have you ever come across a cave with drawings on the walls?" I asked.

"Yes. Several of the caves up there have drawings." He replied. "One is really quite hard to get to, but there are several there that are just one or two chamber caves. Are you looking for ones that might show signs that the Cathars were there?" He asked.

"Yes." I replied wanting to be honest with him. "Do you know of any?"

"Hmm........" He said thinking, "I'm not sure you'll find any of them........none that I know of anyway. Most of the cave art is really prehistoric. Drawings of animals you know." he said.

"I can show you where they are on a map after dinner if you like." I thanked him and that was all that was said about the subject as the conversation opened up on many different subjects between us all.

Just after we'd all finished the soup Antoine got up and went to the wine cellar. A few moments later he came back with a bottle of Pouilly Fumé. This white wine along with its slight smokiness went wonderfully with our next course – the fish risotto. The rice, the fresh vegetables, the herbes provencales and the small flakes of fresh trout had all been cooked perfectly with a moist texture. What crowned the dish though was a topping of coarse shreddings of dried smoked trout. The whole experience was like nothing I'd ever eaten before and totally mouthwatering. Fabien was an amazing chef.

After the meal Antoine kindly lent me a local map that outlined how I could find the Cavern and the other caves. It was not far from an old Limestone quarry and less than a couple of miles away.

I retired to my room to read the rest of Norbert's absorbing accounts of his caving exploits. At about 100 pages in, he started to talk about his childhood experiences in the local caves near to St Martory. I was in awe of the fact that, at the age of around six, he'd just been using candles and matches. The hair on the back of my neck began to stand on end as I read the next couple of lines.

He'd found an old pamphlet written by an Engineer and one of the pioneers of French Archaeology –a scholar called Edourde Harle. In it was the title 'The Hyena's lair in the Cavern of Montsaunes'. Apparently it was filled with old animal bones. Elephant, hippopotamus, wolf, beaver,

149

porcupine and even monkey bones had been found there. Norbert had been so intrigued by this that he had gone up there at night with his younger brother to investigate further. They pushed through and found a totally new cave system that night. The experience made a lasting impression on them that was to change both their lives.

Was this the cave of Bones, the old lady on the bridge had seen me in when she'd had her dream? The image of a laughing Hyena sprang to mind. No. This is ridiculous I thought as my right brain tried to reason with me that this was connected with her cackling laughter. It was just not possible to dream the future, my left brain kicked in. What this all meant, where it was leading to, I couldn't tell but there was one thing I was sure about. I was supposed to find the Cavern.

Saturday morning. I sat outside with a cup of French coffee warming my hands watching the river flow past. The Sun had come up but there was still dew on the grass and there was a light chill to the air. The French couple from last night came down and sat at a table a few yards away from me. They were obviously new lovers the way they were continually gazing at each other and whispering. I wondered how they'd met each other. I immediately stopped myself and blamed the romantic nature of the place for thinking such things. I had to focus.

I'd just finished reading Norbert Casteret's wonderful book. The descriptions he'd used had made me feel as though I was following behind him whilst he crawled and burrowed his way along the tight passages and down into cold dark running waters. It was no wonder that so many young people in France had been inspired by him to take up the hobby.

Madame LeBoeuf had been very friendly again this morning and had brought over some fresh croissants for us from the local bakery.

"I know you have only booked in for one night…" She said when she brought some more coffee, "… and you did say you may stay longer but my dad has asked if you would stop by and let him know how it went up at the caves before you leave." She asked.

I hadn't booked more than one night as I didn't know how long I was going to be here for. If I'd felt I needed longer I would have found somewhere to put up my tent. "Of course, I will come back, in any event, probably before tea time too." I replied.

"He has a nap at around 4.00pm so if you are back before that he would very much like that. He really would have loved to take you up there too you know." She added. I thanked her again and went back to contemplating the coming day.

Having looked at the map I found I could drive nearer to the cavern and it would only be a short five minute walk from there. The others caves were a short walk away from that one following the same line of rock strata.

As I approached where Antoine had marked the cavern on the map, all I could see was bushes. He'd said there might be a few but I think he'd underestimated the amount of growth that had gone on in the 40 years since he'd last been there. I'd come better prepared this time and was wearing stretch jeans and walking boots. I also had on a thick red shirt with long sleeves and a pair of suede gardening gloves. No scratches this time or broken nails.

The limestone face was almost hidden and it was not until I'd squeezed past the last of the branches that I saw the low opening to the cave. I'd brought my own flashlight with me and a small spare one as back up. An easy crawl through the entrance and I was soon able to stand up.

Shining the torch around the walls there now only showed up some French graffiti. No animal drawings. My light scanned the floor. No bones either. I'd expected that though as they would have been cleared out by the early explorers. What I'd hoped to find though was one or two small fragments.

There was nothing here now but a hardened mud. Looking around some more I could see that the ceiling was slanting slightly but there was nothing noteworthy on it. It was just part of a broad layer of slightly harder limestone that hadn't weathered away like the softer layer above and below it. At the back of the cavern I could see a small tunnel leading deeper into the system. It was where Norbert and his brother must have gone at the age of six. If they could do it, so could I.

I breathed deep and went for it. After a few short shoves from my feet, I'd got through. The passage was not as narrow as the one Bernard had taken me through but I still felt a sense of achievement the other side.

It was another chamber, this time slightly larger. I could hear the sound of water in the distance further on down the tunnel at the far side. Again I could find nothing of note in this chamber or its floor. If this had been a Cathar cave, I doubted they would have gone much deeper for their ceremonies, not if there were several of them involved. I tried staying silent in the hope I would feel something. Nothing. It was as though no one had been here for many, many years.

I headed back out slightly disappointed.

Having that sudden emotion shocked me a bit. If I was to get anywhere today I had to stay positive. I began to think how lucky I really was to be here instead of back in the horrible office I'd worked in for nearly two years. A positive feeling of hope began to return and with it I smiled. I felt free again. I clambered out between the branches again and took out the map. If I walked along the rock face for about ten minutes I'd find the other caves. I proceeded in that direction slowly checking the cliff wall occasionally in case I saw something.

After about five minutes I noticed a small animal path running through the bushes towards the rock face. I edged my way slowly along it to see where it went. At the end there was an old rotten stump. A tree had once been growing up and out of a vertical crack in the limestone wall. It had now fallen down and was almost totally covered by an undergrowth of bushes, their branches and some nettles.

The now visible vertical crack had probably started off millions of years ago as a small joint. It had then widened over many thousands of years into this vertical fissure. It must have once given protection to a small seed which had started to grow there. That seed had grown up into the tree I was now looking at. With it having fallen down, it had now left the narrow crack visible again. It went up about 7 feet where it then narrowed at the top. It had even gone right through the same hard limestone layer that had capped the ceiling of the Cavern I'd just been in.

However it was the other end of the fissure, down at ground level that had caught my attention. If the tree had still been upright and alive there was no way you could have seen the gap that was now visible. It was a gap that was now wide enough to crawl along at the bottom. The animal tracks also suggested that it led somewhere. I turned sideways and squeezed along it. Moments later I had squeezed through a hole and into a large chamber that was about the same size as the cave Bernard had taken me to.

I shone my torch around and almost immediately I saw drawings of all sorts of animals. There were antelope, rabbits, horses and even a bear. They were all drawn in red in a way that reminded me of the cave art I'd seen with Pierre and Brian at the Pre-History parc. They were also similar to the descriptions I'd just been reading about in Norbert's book on caving. What transfixed me though was the drawing of a dove that had been scratched onto a small part of the front wall just below the hard layer of limestone. It was almost exactly in the same style as the one I had seen in in the cave in Ussat. It had to have been drawn by a Cathar.

I started looking around me with growing excitement. The floor was flat dry earth with just a few small stones. There were no other exits. I could see no lumps of haematite though. That was a shame.

I calmed myself down by starting to breathe more deeply and slowly in order to relax more. I needed to still my mind. This way I could become more aware. The place felt special but not in any way I could describe. The ceiling was about 12 feet up. It extended upwards through the hard limestone band. For a small cave it really was quite high.

I looked around again, more carefully this time. A geologist is trained to spot anything out of the ordinary. It was always the small little differences in a mineral or a rock that would help tell its story. I'd learnt this having spent hours and hours looking at slides of thin sections of rocks and polished sections of metallic ores under the microscope.

That doesn't look right. I noticed a small shelf that the hard limestone layer had made just above the entrance. The softer layer of limestone above it had worn back a bit which had left room for placing things. I shone my torch closer. That was strange. The soft limestone there had a different tinge to it from the rock next to it. It actually looked unnatural. I took out my small geological hammer and started to tap it. It broke off but not in a way that limestone ought to break. It crumbled. I chipped away further and soon realized that this had been hand made.

After two minutes of careful knocking and scraping I'd revealed a small alcove that had been cut back into the rock. It had obviously been sealed up by some kind of mix of ground up limestone and water.

Inside the alcove were what looked like two rolled up pieces of parchment. They could even have been old scrolls. They looked fairly intact and solid. I touched one gently. It rolled slightly. I moved it again and found it was still flexible. As I really couldn't tell what they were, I reached up and put my fingers around the first one. It didn't disintegrate. I squeezed it a bit. It held. I then gently picked one of them up and laid it carefully down on the cave floor. I then did the same for the other one.

Each began to slowly unfold and with gentle prodding I soon had them fully open in front of me. Each scroll had some kind of writing on but it was nothing I could understand. I stopped for a moment wondering what to do next. There would be laws on what to do with finds like this. I tried my phone. No reception meant no internet search.

I was in no way prepared to transport them with any degree of care so I decided to photograph them and return them to their little ledge. I couldn't make up another limestone mix to seal them in so I decided I could hide them with some rocks from outside the cave for the time being. I'd come back another time better prepared.

It then dawned on me that this cave may not have been entered by anyone for centuries if the tree had been blocking the entrance. That was probably the only reason why these scrolls hadn't been found before now.

I took photos of them both under the light of my torch and also several of the wall art and the dove symbol. I then carefully placed the scrolls back where I'd found them and hid them with some stones. I was back outside in no time. It had been under an hour since I had left my car.

Wow, things can happen fast if you are in the flow, I thought. The old lady's dream was spot on. My right brain had suddenly just popped that thought into my head. I had found something above an entrance to a cave. My left brain had nothing to say.

I walked further along the cliff face to find and experience the other caves. They were just not the same at all. They were more like hollowed out shells which the odd animal would perhaps have used from time to time over the years.

The walk back to my car was filled with a variety of thoughts. The main ones were how to get these scrolls deciphered and what I should be doing about finding these things. There were probably specific authorities to report this to in France. I didn't mind of course, all I wanted to know was what was written on the scrolls as soon as possible. The more I thought about it, the more I felt I needed to chat about it with someone. I wondered about telling Antoine and Amelie. They would be upset if I didn't, especially after he had specifically asked me to let him know how it went.

I needed more than that though. I then realized that I wanted to talk it through with Pierre and Brian. They would understand more as I had shared much with them both already. It was still Saturday morning so I decided to call.

"Pierre," I began, "It's me Rowena."

"Rowena. It's so good to hear you again. Thanks for sending the photos too. How are you and what are you doing?" he asked sounding delighted I'd called. "Brian, it's Rowena on the phone….. He says hi." said Pierre.

"I'm having a great time thanks, but I need to show you something and have a chat about it." I said louder than I meant to.

"Of course, message me a picture of it on your phone, we can talk." Pierre replied.

"Can I come round?" I asked with my lips curling into a smile, knowing my words would surprise him.

"Zut alors where are you?" He exclaimed.

"I'm South of Toulouse in a place called St Martory."

"I thought you went back?" He said by way of a question.

"I did. But I had to come back over to finish what had been started. It's a long story." I stated.

"It always seems to be the case with you Rowena. You are the most interesting person I know I think. Of course come round." He replied with his voice now showing a more controlled excitement.

"I can be there around 3.00pm" I replied.

"Great…. No wait…. Brian and I are going out tonight to a concert."

"Can I come along?" I asked.

"Maybe but I am not sure there will be any tickets left. It's a concert up at the Cave of Lombrives. I will make a call and ring you back." He said.

"No wait. I have a friend who works there. Let me try to get a ticket I may have more luck." I replied thinking of Bernard.

"You just continue to amaze me Ro. Ok let me know and let me know when you are nearly here too. Bye." He ended.

"Bye." I rang Bernard.

"Hi Bernard, it's Rowena from the cave, a week ago."

"Aha. Hi Rowena, how are you?" He replied cheerily in a way that made me feel good.

"Well, really well. I have something I really want to show you, you will be amazed but I am after a favour. Can you get me a ticket for tonight's concert up at the Cave Lombrives?" I asked without trying to sound I was begging.

"Yes, I can do that. I actually know a friend who cannot make it now, they're not well." I will pick up their ticket and meet you there. I was going myself anyway." He replied.

"Good, you can meet my friends Pierre and Brian, you will love them."

"Fantastic Rowena, but tell me more. What is it you want to show me?"

"I found a new cave over here in St Martory. Have you heard of a man called Norbert Castaret?"

157

"Of course, he is one of Frances's greatest Cavers, but he is dead now." Bernard replied sounding slightly confused with me mentioning his name.

"Yes, I know, but I met a friend of his yesterday and he showed me where there were some caves around here. Look, I will tell you more tonight."

"I will look forward to it. I have so many questions in me for you too. I knew you were a special person Rowena. I very much look forward to seeing you again." He replied in a way that showed his curiosity had let slip his English.

"Me too you. Adieu." I replied.

"Jusqu'à plus tard." He rang off. I texted Pierre next to say that I'd arranged a ticket for the concert. One came quickly back.

'You are too much Rowena XXX'

I sat in the car and remembered the last time I was with Bernard. I twisted my rear view mirror around and saw my face was again smudged with dust all over it. For some reason I always managed to get my face dirty. Even as a kid.

Reaching for a packet of wipes, I started on it. Two minutes later with the help of my emergency make up bag in the passenger side door compartment, I was at least looking more presentable. My clothes were a bit muddy but I could change at the B&B.

Back at the B&B I gave Amelie the news that I wouldn't be staying but that I would be coming back sometime quite soon. I then asked if her father was around. He was having a mid-morning coffee by the river. I nipped into the toilet to change into a dress and then put my bags in the car. After settling the bill I went to join Antoine on the lawn. Amelie kindly came along few minutes later with a cup of black coffee for me. I was glad to see that she wanted to stay and listen too.

I related my morning experiences to them both and it was not until I showed them the pictures on my phone that I think they really believed me. On seeing them Antoine's tone became much more excited.

"Amelie look," he called out. "Look at these." Amelie moved round behind her Dad.

They were both now looking as he scrolled through them on my phone. He paused when he got to the ones of the scrolls. "Do you know what language they are written in by any chance?" I asked.

"I am not sure but I think it is a mixture of Latin and old French, maybe 'Le Langue d'Oc' what is also called Occitan." He suggested. I don't know anyone who could translate this though."

"Antoine, what are the laws in this country with regards to these things?" I asked.

"What the state wants, it takes." He stated. "If it does not want it, then anything worth anything is divided between the finder and the landowner." He paused thinking some more about it. "In this case I think the Archives Nationales in Paris would want to know about this. It is Saturday though, it will be closed today."

"Should I ring them?" I asked.

"You could try. I would email them though. That would give you proof you contacted them. Only send them a photo of one of the scrolls though. That will make them want to contact you more."

"Can you tell me more about how you found the cave?" He asked, in a way a child asks for a story to be told them at bedtime. I guessed that these days he liked stories of what was going on in the World – especially if they were personal ones. I explained what I had done in every detail I could remember about the morning and also about the tree covering the crack for probably over two hundred years which was also probably why no one had found the cave since the scrolls had been hidden there. He and Amelie just sat shaking their heads in disbelief.

"You may get extra bookings when this becomes well known." I mentioned.

"Peut être" said Antoine. "Maybe we shall just tell them we are fully booked." He smiled at me.

His daughter gave him a stern look. "He likes it when there are not many guests" she explained. "I think he prefers the peace."

I then explained to them both I had to visit friends now in Tarascon-sur-Ariege. I said my goodbyes to them both and thanked them again for all their help. I also said I would let them know what was going on with the scrolls.

Rhianna or Lady Gaga, I looked at both CD's for today's drive. Rhianna, and popped her into the player. I pulled out of the drive waving to them both and headed for the D117 and the road to Foix. From there I could take the N20 South to Tarascon again.

Tarascon sur Ariege

It was nearly 1.30pm when I reached Tarascon-sur-Ariege. It was market day and the streets were packed. I parked up and went directly towards it to pick up some food and wine for the guys as a gift. There were sheep and goats being herded past the stalls which were filled with jars and bottles containing all sorts of culinary delights. Fresh fruit, local cheeses and street cooking blended into a mixture of wonderfully new aromas for me.

I stood in line for a savoury crepe. One bite of it and I almost ordered another it tasted so good. Instead I found what could have been the ripest peaches ever. I bought three along with a variety of vegetables and moved on to the next stall. Here I picked up one hard and two soft cheeses with names I'd never heard of before. My last stop had bottles of local wines and oils. It was all so much more fun buying in the Sun rather than indoors.

I bought two bottles of a red burgundy I'd also never heard of - One for Bernard and one for Pierre and Brian. It didn't feel like a gamble at all out here. It was bound to taste good. I then went back to the car where I finished the crepe and one of the peaches whilst texting the guys and sending Katy a photo of the food stall with the goats in front of it.

I got a text back from Pierre saying they were at the Le Vallées bar where they'd taken me the first day I'd arrived. I texted them back. I'd be there in a few minutes. They had a glass of white wine ready for me. Life could not have been sweeter at that moment.

We sat and chatted about all that we'd been doing since I'd left. I deliberately missed out the part of the two pieces of haematite fitting together as I wanted to surprise them with that later. Eventually I got to the part about my cave trip that morning and I showed them the pictures.

"Crickey Ro" started Pierre, you went in there on your own? I wouldn't have done that."

"Yes you would have," Brian chipped in. "You're the brave one."

"Maybe, maybe." Pierre muttered whilst holding my phone and flicking through all the photos. "Is this one of the scrolls?" he turned the phone towards me so I could see it.

"Yes and the next few are too. I took several of them. Are either of you able to read any of the words?" I asked. Brian moved closer to look over Pierre's shoulder.

"Some," Brian said, "There are some strange symbols on there too though. I don't think they are any kind of words."

"No, I think not too," said Pierre.

"There are a few words I can tell are old French and some are Latin I think. But I can't be sure what they mean at all." said Brian having looked at them for several minutes.

"Brian, you have a friend nearby who may know how to translate this don't you?" suggested Pierre.

"Who, do you mean Albert?"

"Oui, Albert." Pierre replied. "Albert knows a bit of Latin and I am sure some Occitan."

"Who is Albert?" I asked.

"He is a local teacher. I think he used to teach Latin until that was stopped. From memory I think he liked researching old languages too. I will call him later. He is nearly 70 now I think."

"He still lives in Ussat?" asked Pierre.

"I think so." replied Brian.

"Maybe we can go round tonight before the concert. Ah yes the concert. Just how on Earth did you manage to get a ticket for tonight Ro?"

"Bernard." I replied. "He was the man who showed me the small cave near to the Lombrives caves. I remembered he said he could probably get me a last minute ticket if I wanted one."

"He must like you a lot Ro. Is he good looking?" asked Brian playfully. It made me blush a little. If it had not been for the wine, he wouldn't have noticed. "Aha. He is." He continued. "Maybe you like him a bit too." He teased.

I had to defend myself. "I think he would prefer Pierre if you know what I mean." I smiled back at him. Brian's smile dropped for a moment.

"Ah ha, you are joking Rowena, you nearly had me there." He went back to laughing and smiling.

We spent the next hour enjoying the time. The two of them were actually quite well known in the small town and several people stopped by to chat. Mostly men though.

"Guys, I am not sure how long I am going to be here and I don't want to intrude on you so I brought my tent along as I know there is a camp site nearby called Le Pre Lombard."

"Nonsense," said Pierre. "You must stay with us. I insist."

"That's very kind of you. Maybe for a night or two but I don't want to be in the way." I replied, grateful of their company as well as being able to save some money. "If I need to stay longer, I will go to the camp site, I insist." I stated. "Anyway, I have another surprise for you. I will show you at my car."

A few minutes later we were in the car park. I first gave them a bag of goodies that I'd picked up for them from the market. I then went round and opened the boot.

"Remember I told you that I'd picked up a lump of Haematite in the cave" I started.

"Yes" they both said.

"Well this is a piece that my father picked up in a sea cave down near Perpignan nearly 30 years ago. It's a bit weathered but have a look at this and tell me what you think." I picked up both pieces and brought them together so they fitted. Their eyes and mouths both opened wide at the same time.

"No way." said Pierre. "Let me see." He took them and tried it for himself looking really closely at the two sides that fitted perfectly.

"This is not possible. Brian what do you think?"

"I think she's found half of the sacred stone of the Cathars," Brian smiled when he said it.

"Seriously Brian," said Pierre again.

"Seriously, Pierre, I don't know what to think. It is just too much." He shrugged his shoulders.

I explained the thinking about the four Cathars following their sacred paths away from Montsegur which was why I wanted to see if there was a sacred cave over near Montsaunes. I'd found the cave with a dove symbol but unfortunately there'd been no piece of haematite there.

"You'll have to go to Rennes le Chateau Ro. The caving friend you met at the restaurant might be able to help you." started Pierre

"Arnaud" I added.

"Yes Arnaud. Did you not say that he knew of a cave with a dove symbol in over there?" asked Pierre.

"He did yes and I was going to go that way and see him. I will call him later and see what he thinks." I said.

Each of us was quiet in thought as we walked to their small apartment. Once we arrived I texted Arnaud to see if he had time for a quick chat. He texted me right back. 'OK now is good'. I called and asked him if he remembered what was in the cave with the dove symbol and if he had seen any large lumps of Haematite in it. He said that he knew it well but there was absolutely nothing in it now. He also reminded me that everything in nearly all the caves around Rennes had been cleaned out years ago by the authorities. The only ones left were the secret caves that only he and a couple of friends of his knew about and there were no lumps of haematite in those.

I mentioned that I'd met his friend Bernard. He told me that Bernard had called him several days ago to say he'd met me. I then told him about my cave at St Martory. You will become a caver too now he'd joked.

It was now nearly 4.00pm and Brian had called his friend Albert. It was agreed we could all meet up before the concert.

We pulled up at a small white house not far from the old thermal spring baths in the neighbouring village of Ussat. The extremely high limestone cliffs on both sides had narrowed together in a way that made the river valley we were in feel more like a gorge. The lack of light it got over the day gave the area a colder, slightly damper feel to it.

Albert was a grey haired man with a pale complexion who looked far older than his years. He lived alone in his mother's old house surrounded by his books. He greeted Brian affectionately as Brian's mother was an old friend of his. I took out my phone and showed him the photo's of the scrolls whilst Brian explained in French how I came to find them. Brian continued as the interpreter.

"He says they are a mixture of Latin and Occitan. He can translate some of it but there are six symbols he doesn't know about. He thinks they may be dates in some kind of code though. He is going to start to translate the first scroll now.

"*This is written by myself, brother Bertrand, in the year my master passed over into the next World. I write this* …something…something……*great work during his life. Brother R* ………..some name, I cannot say exactly what it is though from the writing,… *was one of the few who travelled to Jerusalem in the* …..something, something……..*in the tunnels he learnt of* ……something …something… *in a vision by our Lord. He came back with knowledge of*….I'm not sure what that says…. *drawings of the* ……something………..*and their sacred* ………something……….. *From Troyes he travelled South to Montsaunes in*……some date I think………. *where I had the good fortune to meet and join with him.*

With these words I promise to complete his work here according to his plans and designs so that we can all celebrate the …..something, something, something…. *here too long after we have all passed over.*

The last part starts with something, some date perhaps,……*We have now completed our sacred place of prayer here in Montsaunes as brother R*……….. *has instructed us. It has* ……….something something……….. *this is not the special place he had been looking for all his life. This path continues South to a place that is now in the hands of* ……something…………... *I will keep hoping and searching. God bless us all.*" Brian finished translating.

We sat silent for a moment. "Wait" said Brian. "The second scroll is written by someone else. He is going to try and translate that now."

"*This is written by myself, brother Thibault,* …..The next bit I am not sure about, it may be a date,………. *My master brother Bertrand passed over in* ……another date I think………….. *I hereby confirm that he completed the building of our place here at Montsaunes in the way brother R…….. indicated with all the signs drawn as he outlined as a way to pass on his work in secret to others who would come to understand later.*

I too have completed my work in writing about the Grail here ………something, something, something…………… Castle where our lord … sorry the next word I'm not sure of…….. I write this now at a time of great stress. Our good friends the Cathars have fallen at Montsegur burnt alive for their love of God. May God keep them now in peace. They have left in our care……..something something…… a holy stone that holds ……something, something ….. We must now move South and follow the path to the place of miracles in the hope that this is the sacred place we seek. I will take the …… something…………with me …..something….. … Cathar ……something, something…….. with two good Knights. God bless us all.

We looked at each other in silence for a moment. Albert began to speak again. I looked at Brian.

"Albert says that if these scrolls are established as having been written at the same time as the Cathars were burnt in 1244, this could be the most significant find in French Cathar history for many, many years." Brian translated.

"Albert also says he's not even heard of any sacred place or even about any Templar church at Montsaunes but these scrolls too have a huge significance for that place as well. You must inform the Archives Nationales as soon as possible." Brian said. I nodded back at Albert in recognition of his words.

"He says he has a friend who works for them in Paris who he thinks could give you a more complete translation but they would need to work from the originals. Do you have them?" he asked.

"Non." I replied, "I left them in the cave. I had nothing to put them in or to protect them in." Brian translated my English into French for Albert and I could see him nodding. It seemed I had done the right thing.

"Will you allow me to contact my friend in Paris about this?" Brian translated for me.

"Bien sur." I said. "As long as I can have a full translation I am happy to help."

"Do you have time for a cup of tea?" Brian translated again.

"Merci." I replied. We had an hour before the concert still. Albert went off to make a pot of tea and to call his friend. It allowed the three of us to talk about what we'd just heard.

"Rowena, this is so big," started Pierre. "Do you know what this means? Brian tell her"

"It means Rowena that your time will be taken up with endless paperwork and meetings you will get nothing for all your trouble."

"Brian, stop that again." interrupted Pierre.

"Seriously though," Brian began, "They will thank you but not immediately. Initially this is a headache for them. They will need to do all the checking to see if these are fake or not. This will mean carbon dating the scrolls which takes time. It may be six months before we know. But then, if they think this is all correct, they will celebrate your work Rowena. Probably there will be a special celebration at Montsegur and at Montsaunes. Big people from Paris will come down with their TV camera's… you know."

"Yes, thanks Brian," I began, "That's all very well, but what do you think the scrolls mean so far?"

"I think the first one, the one written by the monk called Bertrand, is talking about one of the original nine knights who went to Jerusalem. He seems to have learnt some great secrets and he ended up at Montsaunes wanting to build a sacred chapel there. He seems to have died before he finished though." said Pierre.

"And the second one seems to have been written later by a monk called Thibault whose master was the previous monk Bertrand. He is confirming that the chapel was built correctly but he also is saying that this wasn't the place the original Knight was looking for." said Brian.

"He also said something about writing a story about the Grail and Montsaunes being some kind of castle, I think." said Brian. "That scroll also must have been written in the year 1244AD when the Cathars were massacred." He continued. "He seems to have decided to leave Montsaunes, probably for his own safety. He then headed down South to somewhere referred to as a 'place of miracles'. I wonder where that place might be?" Brian pondered.

"I think he was also hoping that this 'place of miracles' was the holy place they were looking for." Pierre added.

"Maybe it was the place of the Holy Grail Castle that they were looking for." I added too.

"Yes possibly" Brian stated. Albert came in with the tea before we could imagine anything further. It was Earl Grey. He muttered something in French for the guys benefit. "One of the only things the English did right when they were building their empire." Brian translated for me and smiled as he did so.

I was grateful for the smoky bergamot flavour. Sitting, talking in this quite dark and dusty room had made my throat dry. Our host had started talking again and Brian translated for me as he spoke.

169

"Albert says he's called his friend who has said it is OK for you to send him the photos of the scrolls if you would like to. He will do his best to translate them but would like to do that with you directly. Here is his number. He speaks English fairly well so that should be no trouble." He then gave me a piece of paper with his name and number on. His name was Gaston LeMaitre. Whilst the others chatted in French I sent Gaston two messages with a picture of each scroll on in each of the messages. Moments later, I got one back. It said thanks and that he would be in touch tomorrow.

The discussion on what the scrolls might mean continued on for another half hour. It centred around the Grail and the names of the Knights who went to Jerusalem. As they spoke fast in French, I missed much of what was said so I tried searching online for possible names. Eventually I found them all. Two were apparently not Knights but monks. The name of one of them began with an R. He was called Rossal. It seemed possible that he could have well been the one who came back to Troyes with the other Knights, spent some years there, and then headed down to Montsaunes. I showed the others. Albert only agreed to an extent.

"Oui, Ca c'est possible, Je sais pas. Gaston will let us know." He smiled at me feeling proud of his attempt at English at the end.

The Concert

Having said our goodbyes, we set out for the Lombrives Cave. The car park was nearly full and the waiting trolley bus was about to leave. We'd come in Pierre's car and all I had with me was my small handbag. I searched inside and found the small mirror, some black mascara and my favourite lipstick. No eyeshadow though. I did what I could on what was a bumpy ride and wasn't entirely happy with the end result. It would have to do. Perfume? Perhaps not. It wasn't like it was a date.

Bernard was waiting at the top. His dark wavy hair shone in the last light of the setting Sun which was fast disappearing behind the Mountains to the West. From some angles he had the looks of a film star.

"Bernard." We 'bised' together with our heads dancing quickly from side to side.

"Rowena, How lovely to see you again." He said warmly.

"Bernard, this is Pierre and his partner Brian. They are good friends of mine who live in Tarascon." Brian looked at me briefly whilst Pierre gave Bernard the typical welcoming embrace. I could tell Brian had noticed Bernard's good looks and was now too not sure if I'd been joking before down at Le Vallées. Then it was his turn. When we were done, we headed in.

I guessed that there were over 200 people who had gathered in the Cathedral cave. It looked incredibly grand. All the uplighters at various different heights on the walls had now been turned on. It fully emphasized its height in a way I hadn't fully appreciated before. The overall effect managed to show off the complete majesty of the place. The audience had been placed on one side of the cave. The other side was a natural, slightly elevated section of the cave floor. There was enough room on it for a small orchestra. Somehow they had managed to make it look like a kind of rock stage.

The lights slowly dimmed and a hush came over us all. The silence in the darkness became more and more intense. Moments later a spot light appeared on a man with a loose dark grey shirt tucked into tight dark trousers. He could have looked just like a mediaeval troubadour but for the fact that he held to his lips a set of modern day South American panpipes.

"Flûte de Pan" Bernard whispered next to me. "That's Christian Koenig." A long and high haunting single note began the concert. It echoed around the cave from wall to wall in a way that produced a kind of natural 'surround sound'.

More notes followed breathing life into the air all around us. The haunting music moved smoothly and sinuously into a faster more playful beat. It lifted up ones spirit in a way that led to a feeling joy. Smiles began to appear on the faces around me.

As if we'd had too much of that a subtle shift of rhythm led us back down again. Lower and slower notes followed bringing a feeling of peace to the very soul of our hearts.

My more mellowed mind moved on and soon I was soaring with the wings of a swallow in the spring. The fresh air ran right through me refreshing me to the very core.

Now the tones switched to higher scales and, as they did, a tingling sensation ran up my spine as though I was now being personally tuned to the music by the pipes themselves.

What was happening? I tried to turn to the others but I was transfixed and spellbound like a child who'd been led gently into following behind the piper pied.

A tipsy light headedness filled my mind and the cave began to spin. It span and span for so long until the master, knowing it may be too much for many, moved his music on once more.

Down it went again with soothing basal notes that brought with it an emerging ache deep within me of a long lost love sweetly remembered.

I was being played and every cell in my body was resonating with everything around me. I was incapable of any more thoughts at all.

An unknown length of time later and my mind drifted back into slight awareness of what was going on around me. I slowly noticed that I was still upright but now being supported by Barnard who now held both my shoulders with a strong right arm across them both.

The music had ended and a dullness slowly swept across me. It felt as though I was being gradually let back down to the painful reality of living again in this physical World.

Bernard looked at me. Damn he had beautiful blue eyes and such a straight nose. "You nearly fell over Ro," he said softly looking directly into my eyes. It was too much for me. I looked away. He slowly released his arm until he was sure I could stand alone.

"Thank you. Bernard. I am not sure what came over me." I said feeling a little shaky on my feet.

"You were out of it for over half an hour Cherie." He said endearingly and lovingly. Does he really prefer men I wondered? Maybe my senses are wrong. Had I half hoped that? No. He didn't seem interested in still holding me anymore.

I breathed in deeply trying to work out what had happened. There was a pause in the music. The organisers had, perhaps wisely, arranged for an intermission. Maybe they already knew that too much of this music could be literally 'over the top' for some people.

Looking up I saw the ceiling over a hundred feet above me. The whole of the Cathedral cave seemed like one vast echo chamber. The sound must have bounced everywhere and back again. A thought blasted its way through from my right brain and into my left - A standing wave of sound. Standing sound waves that is what these high places can hold in place. With the right width and height and sound frequency all sorts of psychoacoustic phenomenon could be produced. Specific sounds must link with certain caves or cathedral dimensions.

If you got it right then the sort of resonant effects, like the one I'd just had, could probably be generated. Maybe I had even been on the way to some kind of experience that others in the past have called 'enlightenment' whatever that really meant. Had I even just had that experience? I didn't know. All I knew for now was that I was on to something.

Why not then just build these high Cathedrals anywhere? No. There had to be something more than that. The location they were built still had to be important. There were sacred sites outside with no walls or ceilings. That had to be factored in too somehow.

My heightened state of awareness was now making my mind race from one thought on to another. It got to the point that I wasn't sure what was going to suddenly think of next. There was no point trying to think about it all now in this state. My left brain was just not ready for it.

I tried refocusing my mind a bit by shuffling around on the spot switching attention to as many different unrelated things as I could as quickly as possible. I knew that would help break my association patterns and raise my high beta brainwave activity.

A few moments later and I felt able to communicate again without saying something stupid. The four of us chatted away for a while until the concert continued on again.

At 9.00pm it was over and we headed back down to our cars. Pierre had suggested we should all go back for something to eat and drink at La Mandoline an old style pizza restaurant in Tarascon. Bernard agreed and I went with him in his car. The Pizzeria was only a couple of minutes away but it gave me a chance to thank Bernard and pay him for the ticket. As I got in I gave him the bottle of burgundy I'd fetched from Pierre's car and some Euro's from my purse.

"Please no to the Euro's Rowena, but I will gladly take the wine, merci. Maybe you can tell me more about this new cave you found?" He asked as he pulled away from the car park. I insisted on paying him but he politely declined two more times. What could I do?

I proceeded to give him a short version of the story ending by saying that I was probably going to have to go back there sometime either to get the scrolls or to show someone where they were. I felt that I still owed him a lot so I asked if he would like to join me when I went back. In doing so, I tried to make him the offer in a way that didn't make him feel I was asking him for a date.

"I would like that very much Rowena. A cave for a cave. Now that is a good deal." He'd replied. Good, he hadn't thought I was asking him out.

The Italian restaurant had a covered outdoor seating area with lights attached to the wooded uprights. It was sheltered by the building itself on one side and several small trees on the other. It was typically Italian but it also had a nice Gallic feel to it. It was warm enough to sit outside and Brian chose a table at the back under a small tree.

Once we were seated I brought Bernard up to date with some of the details on the initial translation of the scrolls and the two pieces of haematite and we were all soon having fun speculating about the meaning of it all.

Towards the end of the evening, I started wondering what Bernard might say about the night. I think he knew I liked him but if he was playing it straight, he'd been pretty cool towards me in a way that could have meant that he just wanted to be friends. I was possibly just not his type. I didn't want to hear those words though. No girl does. I decided it best to play things cool too.

As we all walked back to the cars Bernard turned to us all and said thanks for the lovely time and that he hoped to see us all again soon. He apologised that had to get up early the next morning otherwise he would have loved for the evening to last longer. That was it. I was probably not his type, whether he was straight or not.

I needn't have worried though as Brian turned to me when Bernard had driven off. "Rowena, I didn't believe you for minute but yes you were right."

"Right? Right about what." I asked.

"Bernard, or course." he continued. "He's gay too."

"Really" I said, "How do you know for sure?"

"Ro. Brian is right. When you have been on the gay dating scene for a while you get to know fairly quickly you know." said Pierre.

"I wasn't sure," I replied, "sometimes I thought he definitely was and then perhaps not."

"That is one of the signs, is it not Pierre?" said Brian.

"Mais Oui." He replied. "There will be others Cherie." He smiled at me and I swung my bag casually at him in mock anger. He half dodged, the bag missed though and we all laughed together.

Sunday morning was another lovely sunny day and I decided to get up early and go for a run up to the nearby village of Niaux. It was all road but it was also likely to be fairly free of cars. I left the guys a message saying that I would be back in just over an hour and that I'd gone for a run.

Limestone mountains dotted with green shrubs, bushes and trees were visible both sides of me and I had a nice steady incline for about four and a half kilometers out up to Niaux. Ten 'K' was about my limit but this morning I felt terrific and it was going to be downhill all the way back. I pushed on and turned left by a small cemetery to go up to the Grotte de Niaux. It was closed but the view up there was great.

By the time I got back and showered I was starving. The guys were now up and cooking eggs. They added two more for me.

Around midday I got a called from an excited Gaston. He wouldn't tell me anything over the phone or send me anything. It felt very secretive of him. He had said he would be happy to pay my expenses to take the train to Paris. His department would also take care of hotel costs for me. I asked about the scrolls and whether I should bring them. Apparently not yet was the answer, he had to speak to another department who would arrange that with me. They would contact me sometime soon and meet me down there. Having covered all that, he finally said he would text me the details and see me on Tuesday at 10.00am in his office.

I came off the phone a little shocked at the speed of it all and how that had changed any plans I'd had for the next few days. I related it all to the guys. They just laughed at me for being so surprised.

"Rowena, you should never expect anything normal or usual with governments. They go slow, they go fast, they do nothing. Sometimes they do nothing right and sometimes they actually do the right thing. The trouble is you never know which of all those they will do." said Brian.

"For sure," said Pierre, "When you go, make sure they cover all your costs too when you are there. Don't wait for them to send money to you either."

"In fact," said Brian, "You should ask them for money. They probably have a fund for this sort of thing. After all they are taking up your time." They were right. They were taking up my time, but then again I was going to get the full translation. I didn't need the scrolls anyway. They were probably not worth anything anyway. Brian must have read my mind.

177

"Do you know Rowena," he started, "Those two scrolls are probably worth a lot of money to a collector. I would think hundreds of thousands of Euro's. What do you think Pierre?"

"No. Not that much, I think…." replied Pierre. "…probably only about fifty thousand. It is worth asking for some reward though. You never know as you are from the UK. That may make a difference. This after all was what you call an unexpected find, not an expected one. There is a difference in the law between them you know." he said. I mulled it all over and said I would certainly ask. French rail time tables were now on my mind.

Half an hour later I'd searched and booked tickets. I would leave on Monday just after 2.30pm from Tarascon station. I would have time on the train to collect my thoughts on everything and perhaps do some planning. For now though, I needed to unwind and relax.

With Pierre and Brian that meant going for a walk and that, for them, generally meant going up a mountain. Today they were going a small village called Vicdessos which was a little further on from Niaux where I'd run that morning. There was a place there they'd been meaning to visit. When I asked, they wouldn't tell me in order to try and get me to join them. It worked.

Half an hour later we were driving up a steep narrow single lane zigzag road to a small layby car park.

"It's not far from here, Ro. Only a short walk today." Pierre promised. "That's where we are heading." He continued pointing towards some rocks at the top of a cliff face in the distance.

Fortunately we were following a well-worn path which I took to be a good sign. I needn't have worried, it was only a slightly steeper path at the end and it had all taken less than ten minutes. As we neared the top we were treated with the magnificent sight of the Sem dolmen. A huge shining white, flat topped limestone boulder, probably weighing over 20 tons, was standing on two smaller lumps of limestone that were probably each over 2 tons themselves.

The big flat top stone was about 12 feet in length and between 3 ½ feet to 4 feet wide. It was only about 5 feet from ground level so it was possible to scramble up and stand on it.

My immediate thought was how could the builders have possibly moved these boulders up there. This was quickly followed by why. I asked the guys what they thought.

"You are always so full of questions Rowena. Just enjoy it up here. We can think later." said Brian. He was right of course so I leant back against it and just enjoyed being there. None of us talked. We just let the wonderful views all around us sink in. After a while I began to think of everyone I'd met recently who had helped me getting to this point in my life now where I was having such a lovely and memorable experience.

This place did feel very special. I began to see why some past chief or Stone Age priest had chosen this place to be buried. My mind drifted back to reasons again. Tops of mountains and hills were often sacred places, but not all of them were. My thoughts were interrupted by Pierre.

"Do you know Rowena…," he began, pointing to the North East, "…that you could draw a straight line from here through the Cave of Lombrives, through Montsegur and all the way to Rennes Le Chateau?" I was immediately drawn to his thinking.

"What? That cannot be right." I said, thinking he might be wrong but also very much interested as this was the line that followed one of the sacred Cathar paths.

"Yes. Look here on the map on my phone." He showed me and 'give or take' a few meters, it did looked fairly straight. "You were talking about these Cathar paths crossing at Montsegur. Well this is one of them and the other must run from Montsaunes down to around Perpignan."

He was right but I was not sure yet what it all meant. "I don't think it is significant." I replied. "Just a coincidence." In the back of my mind though I wasn't sure I was right.

"Brian. Why don't you tell Rowena your theory on how these were built?" Pierre said.

"OK. But I can tell you she will not like it."

"Oh do please tell me." I added. "I promise not to take the Micky." already sounding as though I was.

"Take the Micky?" Brian questioned emphasizing the word Micky. He looked over to Pierre for support.

"It's just a British expression Brian. It means she won't fool with you."

"Ah ha. I thought she'd already started. OK. My thinking is that these were placed here by using sound."

"What? How?" I asked.

"Well. Have you come across 'Acoustique Levitation'. It is when they can direct sound waves from different directions so that they can hold small objects, like a water droplet, suspended in midair."

"Yes I'd heard they'd done that. I've not seen it but surely that only works with very light objects like polystyrene." I argued.

"Mais Oui," continued Brian, "But what if they could get a much higher power of sound? What if they could then use some sound themselves with drums and horns. Maybe they could begin to make things lighter so they could be lifted?"

"Nice try." I said. "Theoretically it may be possible. But where would they get enough power?" I asked.

"Maybe the Earth itself?" he suggested. Extraordinarily it wasn't such a silly thing for him to say. We knew so little about the deep interior Earth.

"Ok I will give you a maybe." I relented and he immediately began to grin.

Was Brian on to something? Perhaps not, it was all far too technical to do and much too much precision would be needed. Way above the abilities of a Stone Age community.

After half an hour up there we walked slowly back to the car joking with each other about why our ancestors went to so much trouble to put the Dolmen up there.

The Train to Paris

Monday afternoon and the train pulled in on time at 2.50pm. Two mins later it left and I was on my way. I began to sift through all the things I'd recently come across, making notes on the way. I'd found in the past if I didn't do this, I would forget things. It was one of my faults. I would get too focused on what I was doing and it would distract me from other things I'd arranged to do.

The scenery though was a constant distraction. I kept looking out at the changing countryside. However after about ten minutes I eventually had my list and all of them were questions. The first half was about the information from the scrolls that Albert had given us, the second lot was more scientifically oriented.

Who was Rossal – the monk who went to Jerusalem?
Where was this 'Place of Miracles' to the South?
Why were these symbols at Montsaunes so important for the monks and what did they mean?
What did the monk mean when he said he had written about the Grail?
What was the reference to the Castle and the Lord all about?
Was the Holy Stone that was left a reference to the Cathar stone?
What were these Cathar paths and were they straight paths and, if they were, why were they straight?
How could a stone hold the 'divine' fast and what did that even mean?

The second half of the list contained the following:-

What made a place sacred?
What did a sacred place mean and were there any associated benefits to that place and do these relate to the Grail properties?
What connection was there to sound?
What would be needed for acoustic levitation to lift heavy objects?
What link is there, if any, to the natural sounds and vibrations that the Earth makes?
Are there places with good combinations of sound that are healthy for people to live in and are there places that have bad sounds that can lead to ill health and how much of an affect does that already have on our mental and physical health?

Lastly I had written:-

Are these two lists of questions and their answers linked in any way?

I was happy with the way things were going and now felt I had some structure to go on. I could also see a possible way forward from a financial perspective. I felt sure that people all around the World would want to know if a particular location was healthy or unhealthy.

After an hour and 20 mins the train pulled into the station in Toulouse. I had half an hour here to change trains and catch the TGV to Paris.

It was my first time on a double decker train so I naturally chose to sit upstairs. It was about half full which meant I could find a seat next to a window with a small table in front of me. After another five minutes the whistle blew. The carriage was nearly full now. The seat opposite me was still empty. I hardly noticed that we'd started to move. I'd heard these trains were smooth but this was amazing.

Moments later a large tall swarthy Australian man who looked as though he was in his middle twenties shuffled in with a large backpack. He turned to me and spoke slowly in English but with a heavy Aussie accent.

"Is … this…..seat….free?" He gave me a hopeful look.

I didn't know whether to nod or give the game away that I could speak English. I decided on the latter in case I was found out later on. After all, it would be a journey of nearly five hours.

"It's free." I replied smiling. If he shaved, had a haircut and dressed more smartly, there'd be many girls who'd think he was good looking. Now though, it looked as though he needed a good bath. He didn't seem to smell though for which I was thankful.

"Ah. A lady from good old England. Nice to meet you. My name is Ethan, Ethan Parker from Adelaide." He held out a strong hand. It was surprisingly clean so I shook hands and told him my name."

"Rowena, Rowena Colleen from….." I paused not exactly sure what to say next.

"…from the UK perhaps." He finished for me.

"Sorry yes, I have been moving around quite a bit lately and I don't really have a new base yet." He placed his backpack under the seat and sat down as I was speaking.

"Neither do I really. Last time I was in Adelaide was very probably nearly a year ago. So I guess I'm Ethan Parker from Oz." He laughed.

"Are you off back home?" he asked.

"No, I have a meeting in Paris tomorrow morning." I answered. "What about yourself?"

"I'm going to Paris to join a mate there for a couple of days and then on to London to see my sister and her husband for a day or two before I fly back." He explained, his accent becoming heavier the more he talked.

"Have you been away long?" I asked.

"A couple of months now I guess. I'm taking some time off as I've decided, after several years mind, to go back to Uni' to finish my psychology course. How about yourself?"

I paused before replying, wondering what exactly to say. "I am a research Geobiologist." I said slowly.

"Wow, you must be a smart one, I've never even heard of one of them. What does that mean you do?" He asked back actually sounding more than a bit baffled.

I paused again before I replied, thinking carefully after my recent experiences. "At the moment I am looking into how the Earth itself affects Humans in some areas of the World." I replied in as general a way as I could without drawing myself into any predetermined conclusion as to where my research was heading and also to perhaps put him off asking any further, perhaps more awkward questions. It didn't work.

"Like what effects?" he probed. I thought about it quickly and the experiences I had had recently in the Lombrives cave and before I knew it I came out with it.

"Sounds….. and how they can affect us in some places like caves….for example" I said not that happy at all with my answer.

"Ah…..Goodness….Yes…. I know a bit about that…. I guess." His answer took me completely by surprise.

"Pardon." The word just popped out. It was one I hardly ever used as well. He looked at me and realized from my face that more explanation was needed and being requested.

"Sorry," he began, "I've b'in some time in the bush ya' see….last summer…on a kind of work placement scheme…only it went on longer than I thought it would." He paused as though wondering how much to say next.

"Please do go on." I said remembering Aliya's comments to me that I should explore things more when unexpected meetings like this occurred. He seemed encouraged by my words.

"Well, I've been going for a few years now to the same place. It's near a place called Wilcannia in New South Wales. I worked up there with a group of Aborigine's. Well, only the ones with mental problems, which is quite a few of them really. Anyway, after a while some of them would tell me quite a bit about their background and their ways." He paused to think carefully about his next few words.

"Well they have special places in the land that are really sacred to them. Many of them are in caves too. I was taken to one once. It took a few days to get there mind." He added as if he was both remembering and reliving it.

"Anyway, when we get there, a place he calls 'dreamtime', he takes out this flat piece of wood on the end of some string. It's called a bullroarer. He then starts swinging it horizontally over his head, round and round, and it makes this low pulsing, whirling sound. He speeds up the swing a little and the sound gets a bit higher." At this point Ethan's own right arm had joined in with his description and he was now waving his arm around and around over his own head.

"Anyway he stops after a while and shortens the length of string a bit and does it again. This time he keeps his swinging arm constant and the pulsing sound becomes like a regular beat. After that he nods his head as though he's happy with something. Then he shortens the string again and this time he swings it round and round vertically up and down." Ethan's right arm was now simulating this action.

"Again he nods as though he is happy with that too." Ethan took a break to draw breath and continued on as though he was telling me a deep and personal secret.

"I have to tell you I'm pretty confused by now and wondering if he's been back on the spirits behind my back." Ethan said in a different tone as though he was sharing a secret.

By now he certainly had my full attention.

"So then he leads me deep into this cave until we reach this large chamber. At the bottom there is this tiny well of water – fresh water you know too. The ceiling above us is about 30 feet high so it's not a small place. I guess you could have had around 30 to 40 people in their quite easily at one time. He then tells me to tell no one I was here, well I didn't really know where 'here' was. We'd been driving all day in the desert, all over the place to try and find it, and I couldn't remember the way again if I tried, so now I know he's not thinking straight."

"Anyway he then starts to chant and at the same time he swings the bullroarer above his head." His right arm started up again too.

"The sound is going everywhere. I mean it's crazy too and its constant beat is now starting to mess with my head you know, when you've had a few too many, but this is different because your head still feels clear but in a strange way." He paused to see if I was still with him and if I was still listening.

I nodded. His experience was eerily similar to the one I had just had myself in the Cave of Lombrives, and he continued.

"Well he then starts spinning it faster and at all angles vertically and then back up horizontally again…." Again he matched what he was saying with his own arm moving in circles and demonstrating the action.

"…and then he swings it back down again and it seems like the whole cave is now spinning and he's the only one standing still. If I could have found my own way out, I would have taken it but it was like I was stuck to the ground."

"My head was now pounding…." Ethan continued. "… and all sorts of strange images started flying in front of my eyes and I'm beginning to wonder now if I've been secretly drinking the spirits without even knowing it." He pulled a confused look for a second as though to show me.

He then paused and leant back. I wondered how many times he'd told the story. After a moment he then slowly leant towards me again as though he's about to tell me another secret. In an even quieter voice than before Ethan started to talk again.

"Then he stops. I look over at him and he is now dead still looking into the deep black water down in the well." Ethan now moved his head forward and bent it over so he was now looking face down at the table as though he was looking down into the well too.

After holding his head still for a moment, Ethan looked up and directly into my eyes and spoke again.

"I shined my torch at him and it's as though he doesn't even know I'm there. He's in this deep, deep, deep trance now and I'm not sure what's going to happen or what to do even."

"It's b'in like this now for about ten minutes but it could be twenty. Then he seems to come out of this crazy state and he just hobbles over to me. Doesn't say a word. Just signs me to follow him out."

"Which of course I do. Can't wait to be honest." Ethan now said in a normal voice. "After several wrong turns by him, which worries me because he doesn't seem to be all there, and we've still got a desert to cross in the 'drover, he eventually finds the one that leads us out. Nice one I thought but no thanks, not again."

"Then once we're outside, he turns to me again and shows me the bullroarer and says this. 'A few white people think that this is a way we communicate to each other across the desert, well it is, but actually it is much more than that. You all call it a bullroarer, but it has many names. My tribe call it a Burliwarni. To us it's the voice of God. It goes back years. Some say more than 5000 years, 10,000 years maybe. I've heard told that the earliest peoples all around the World have these. To us, it helps us talk to God and to our Ancestors at these sacred places. I'm telling you this because I have been told to tell you but you must be careful who you tell or you'll have real bad luck.'"

"Well I can tell you I don't know if I was more spooked or shocked. He then just got into the 'drover and waited for me to start driving him back as though nothing had happened at all." With that Ethan also sat back, stopped talking and looked at me.

"Wow." It was all I could say.

"You know that's what I thought too." He sat forward again quickly and nodded vigourously as if in full agreement with me.

"You know I asked him some questions about it on the way back but he wouldn't say much. What he did eventually say though, I will always remember." He nearly had me leaning forward now but I sat still.

"He tells me he has to go back there every year in the middle of the summer. 'B'in doing it since he was eight. In the first few years he had to walk there, along the lines.'"

"Lines?" I asked.

"Yeah, they call them song lines. They're straight lines that cross the desert. Means they can never get lost. They say they go right round the World but I'm sure no one really knows 'cos none of them have ever walked right around the World. They're invisible too so they could be making anything up and we wouldn't know."

"Anyway they all have a story that goes with their part of the line that they guard. It's like a story of what was seen on the lines in the old days. They say that if all the guardians along the length of the line were out together one day, they'd have one long continuous story that would go on all the way across Australia. Strange thing is that these stories all have the same tune all along the line. It's like they hum them to help remember them."

"Hmmm....hmmmm." he started to make a sort of Aboriginal noise.

"Different lines in different directions have different tunes too apparently." He carried on. "Anyway he tells me that this place we've just been to was where some of these song lines cross over. They call it a 'dreamtime' place. It's somewhere they go to speak to their ancestors. Do you know what he said next?"

"No." I replied, now fully hooked in to his story.

"He said he'd been having a chat with his Grandfather back there. So I turned round and asked 'What did he say?'" Ethan leant forward again.

"You know what he said next….. He said… 'Why did you bring that idiot along?' …..His Grandfather was calling me an idiot." Ethan now leant quickly back upright into his seat.

"I have to say I wasn't chuffed with that, seeing as I had driven him all the way there, but anyway I asked him again. 'So what else did he tell you?' He turns and looks at me, and there's now a tear welling in his eye, and he says to me 'My grandfather says I can speak to my Dad next year?' and I says well that's nice and he says it's not because his Dad isn't dead yet…… I tell you that is one strange place."

"Did his Dad die?" I asked wondering if there had been any truth in any of it.

"I dunno. I've not seen him for 6 months. But I'll tell you, that chap certainly believed it."

"What was really weird was later on during the drive back. He told me that he'd had to show me all of this because he was told to do so in a dream."

"Here was I thinking he's b'in doing it just to mess with my head because he's always b'in saying that I've b'in messing with his."

"I tell you I'm done with all this psychoacoustic stuff. Time to get back to basic psychology I can tell you." This time he ended his story and again leant back against his seat. This time though he'd folded his arms as though to more fully emphasise the fact.

I guessed it was my turn to talk but I wasn't ready to share my own cave experience with anyone else just yet, more for the reason that it was just so recent. I hadn't thought about it enough and so didn't really know what to say just yet.

I decided to ask him some questions instead.

"So Ethan," I started, "What do you think it all means. I mean why do you think he was told show you all this in a dream and why then tell you to be careful who you told?" I asked.

"I wish I knew. To be honest I haven't told anyone for a long while. In fact I'd almost forgotten it, till you mentioned sounds in caves."

"I told me mates just after we got back and they just laughed at me and said that I'd been well and truly had. I'm not so sure though. Them things that happened to my mind in the cave felt real enough."

"What do you think? You're the expert who's researching this." He asked me.

I'd been put on the spot and I owed him some kind of answer.

"Ethan, I am only at the beginning of my research but I think that there are some places in the World where there are sounds coming from deep within the Earth that can be harmful for us or good for us. Somehow, when we make our own sounds, either with instruments, like the bullroarer or a horn, or if we chant sounds at the right frequency, we can manage to connect with these lower frequency Earth sounds." I paused to see if he was still interested.

He was so I continued.

"I think that when a connection is established it then probably depends on the particular frequency we've linked to. Some are good frequencies, some will be bad. It seems that our perceptual barriers in our brain are lowered when this connection occurs and we get experiences which, I think, may mirror those that can be achieved by taking psychedelic drugs."

"The trouble at the moment is that we are still trying to work out what psychedelic drugs do to our minds. I am just hoping to find out how the factor of the geology of the Earth comes in to play."

"So far I have found that some caves can lead to some people having these experiences but other caves do not lead to these effects. I think places like Cathedrals and mountain tops are also connected to these special locations too but, as I said, this is still all fairly new."

"Blimey," he replied. "Fair dinkum to ya for that. These old boys in the bush must have really been onto something then." He pointed out.

"Indeed. We've a lot to learn from all the indigenous peoples around the World." I added. "The fact that you've very kindly shared your story about these song lines and their sacred 'dreamtime' places where the lines crossover has to be significant. They may well be sound lines. It's one of the areas I want to investigate."

"Well I'm glad to have helped." He replied. "Do you fancy a cuppa?" he asked getting up off his seat. "With all this talk, I fancy a cuppa tea."

"Tea. Yes, thank you. That would be nice. Here let me get them." I reached for my purse. "No worries Rowena from the UK. These are on me." With that he strolled off in search of the buffet car.

I sat there thinking about everything I'd just heard. It really was quite strange that I'd been experiencing something in the Lombrives cave so recently and now I'd just heard of a similar sound experience in a cave in the middle of Australia. It was almost as though I was supposed to find out this information. As soon as I said that, I remembered Aliya's words 'If the Universe wants you to know, you will find out.' Everything had been flowing well for me since I'd returned to France. It must mean I was still on my path. It was encouraging to know that. My left brain, perhaps having enough of all the 'Universe' stuff then started to think about the possible science behind these sounds.

If sound was linked to location in some way, it had to be coming from the Earth itself in some way, a bit like the Earth's magnetic field. The position of the Magnetic North pole rotates as the Earth rotates because the magnetism comes from the centre of the Earth. From my degree I knew a bit about seismic waves, tectonic plate movements and Earthquakes. These produced low frequency sound waves that travelled both right through the Earth and along its surface. Sound waves were moving all over the place.

However when these waves were first measured they'd been linked to a very large Earthquake. It was expected that, after a while, these vibrations would die down and end after a certain period of time. The trouble was that they didn't. The scientists kept measuring a continuous background vibration. This meant that the Earth was continually vibrating. This in turn meant that the Earth was continually expanding and contracting by very small amounts and very slowly. Seismologists have been wondering what has been making this background vibration for many years. They'd even given it a phrase – The mysterious hum. Some of them had even thought that it might be the movements of the deep ocean currents going backwards and forwards over different depths of the ocean floor. Even after this background vibration was eliminated though, the hum was still there. The problem with it all was that it took weeks to measure some of these very low frequency vibrations.

An idea slowly grew in my mind. If I put sensors in areas that I knew had strong connections to sound, like the song lines and their intersections, I could perhaps compare the results to sensors where there were no sound intersections.

There was still a problem with that though. If I took the idea to my old professor, he would ask me 'What hypothesis was I testing?' I still had to find out a reasonable mechanism for what was generating this sound in the first place. Ethan returned with two cups of tea. The conversation turned to France and where he'd been around Europe. He'd been backpacking and was only taking the train now as he'd run out of time.

At ten past nine in the evening we pulled into Gare Montparnasse in Paris. We said goodbye having exchanged contact details. I'd promised to keep in touch and to keep him up to date with my research. He'd suggested

I start a blog but looking back on the last few days, I just didn't see the time for it at the moment.

I'd received a helpful text from Gaston with some directions. He'd recommended that I buy a carnet for the metro, the Paris underground train. A carnet was a bunch of ten tickets with one ticket meaning I could travel anywhere on it once. Ligne 13 would take me to the metro stop of the Basilique de St. Denis. Not far from that, he'd booked me into the Eurotel Paris Nord. From there it was only a short walk to Pierrefitte-sur-Seine where the Archives Nationales offices were located.

Paris

It was Tuesday morning in Paris and raining. It was not how I had imagined my first day in Paris to be like. The area was nice enough but there were no landmark Parisienne buildings nearby. Outside the hotel, I looked up at the grey sky. Nothing wrong with a little bit of rain I thought so I set off for a short 20min walk to the Archives offices.

It was a great chance to experience the Paris suburbs. The route on my mobile maps took me along the pavements of some of the major roads. The rush hour traffic stopped and started beside me. They were all heading in the opposite direction from me. It made me begin to feel that this new path I was on was somehow going against the grain. My journey now was so different from before that it made me smile.

As I neared the offices, I was amazed to see just how large they were. It was a modern structure with a mesh of crisscross white steelwork and long glass panels. There were several layers to it all with these rows of crosses covering different sections of the building. It looked like one long line of 'X's on top of another and another. It must have contained millions of French documents and secrets and it was not at all surprising to me that it was guarded by large metal gates and fences.

Gaston had arranged to meet me in the reception at 10.00am. Inside the large open plan interior the criss cross theme continued. It was now accompanied by a myriad of staircases going up and down in many directions to various different levels. Safety bannisters were everywhere. Overall there was a very clean and clinical look to it. The central atrium I was in had been carefully planned to lead off into all sorts of rooms - exhibition rooms, reading rooms, storage rooms, meeting rooms.

I was early so I sat and waited on a hard modern office type sofa trying to read the French brochure about the place that had been carefully placed on a nearby table. The pages were filled with pictures of the offices as they were being built. It seemed to have only just been opened in 2013.

I was interrupted by Gaston who came over and stopped about 3 meters away from me. "Good morning Rowena. I am so very glad you managed to come here. Thank you. Was the accommodation last night to your liking?" He asked holding out his hand to shake mine.

"Yes, thank you and thank you too for seeing me." I replied shaking his hand. His grip was gentle but not weak.

"Please do follow me," he headed for one of the sets of stairs, "I do apologise for all these steps Rowena. It keeps us old men fit though. My office is up here, we can then chat together more confidentially." I followed on up behind him on the stairs. He wore a dark brown corduroy jacket with some light brown chino trousers. What I thought strange was that he also had on some brown sandals without any socks. I looked around at other people and it seemed that this was not as uncommon as I'd first thought. He must have been about 60 years old and around the same age as Albert in Ussat. I wondered how they knew each other. As we reached the top of the steps I was able to more easily ask.

"Mr LeMaitre, can I ask how you and Albert came to know each other. He spoke very highly of you."

"Of course," he began, ushering me into his office. It was glass on all four sides but filled with bookshelves and filing cabinets. They were not in front of the outside window though. His desk faced the door.

"Albert and I were on the same course many years ago. The course was to help us learn the Occitan language. It was well before the days of digital learning of course." He added. "We kept in touch after that from year to year sharing pieces of old Occitan literature and poetry, you know how it is." He gestured me to sit down.

"Would you like a coffee?" I nodded and said thanks. "Good, let me just arrange that. He then went out of the door and he left me on my own for a moment. His desk was clear apart from a neatly arranged blank sheet of paper, a pen, an old style phone and a laptop. His neatness somehow impressed me. In a building filled with old documents I had imagined quite the opposite. Perhaps the open, see through design of the building had influenced him. He soon came back in again and sat down opposite me.

"Forgive me Rowena, I really would like to spend the whole day with you and to learn so much more about you and your work. Albert and I have spoken a bit on the phone of course and he has told me a little more about your discovery. This has all been such short notice as you know and I've only a short amount of time available this morning. I did however mention about you and your work to my daughter. She would also very much like to meet you too if that's all right with you. I have asked if she could take you for a bite to eat at lunchtime ….if that is OK with you of course?"

"That would be lovely, thank you but this is really all much more than I expected." I answered.

"Rowena," his tone changed to one that was slightly more serious, "I don't think you perhaps quite appreciate here what you may have found." He stops himself. "I say may, of course, because we still need to do some verification tests."

"No. I do understand, but again I have to say I'm quite taken aback by all this. It was just two scrolls after all and I don't yet know the complete translation of them. Therefore I'm not really sure of the implications in regards to it all."

"Ah. But of course, I forgot that. Yes. My apologies. I have indeed translated them and also conferred with a colleague of mine here to get their confirmation as well. We are all very excited you know. But we need to get these two scrolls carbon dated and do an examination of the cave you found." He paused, thinking about how best to say his next few words.

"If these are what we think they are, this could be one of the most important Templar finds in the last 100 years." He said interlocking his fingers and hands together as though in old fashioned prayer.

"Wow." Was all I could say. I really was lost for words.

At that moment a young man brought in two cups of coffee for us both. We both remained silent as we took them and drank. It was hot, but not too hot. I could feel its warmth and taste slowly energise me.

"Rowena, before I go on, I have to adhere to French law and ask you some questions."

"Ok, of course." I replied, expecting something like this but not sure what.

"What were you doing when you found the cave and can you prove that in any way?" He asked.

I wondered how much he wanted to know as I was mindful that there was a lot I could say and there was not really enough time.

"Well," I began, "I am currently out of work and looking for a purpose and direction in life. I had previously started to do research in Geobiology and I was now thinking that I might return to that research having found out a few things in the caves in the Ariege region."

"Well you have my full attention Rowena, please do explain more."

"I am wondering why some places in the World are considered sacred over the years and by different cultures. In my past I was aware that some locations can be bad for health and I was wondering if the reverse could be true." I'd started by purposely generalizing a little. Now though I needed to change tack. "To be more precise, I was wondering why the Cathars thought some caves were sacred places but not others. Some have a very special feeling and others don't. I am, at the moment, trying to find a hypothesis as to why this might the case." I added wanting to be as truthful as I could. "One of the clues that I'd found out about was that the Cathars used to draw a symbol of a dove in their special places." I paused to see if he was still taking me seriously. He was so I continued. "Anyway I'd heard of a place called the Cavern of Montsaunes and I wondered if there was a dove symbol in that cave or indeed one nearby. You see I'd already come across a symbol for a dove in a cave near to the Cave of Lombrives and I'd heard there was one in a cave at Rennes le Chateau."

"Yes" he interrupted me, "But what made you start looking in the Montsaunes region?" His words made me think of the Haematite stone but I didn't want to mention that just yet.

"It was because of what I found online that could be seen in the Montsaunes Chapel?" I replied.

"Ah yes. A place I must still go and see one day. Albert told me you had gone there. What was it by going there that led you to the connection to the Cathars though?"

"Well it was some of the designs on the walls that caught my attention. They are 'Flower of life' designs and they matched with designs I saw on the Rennes le Chateau church ceiling."

"But there are no 'Flower of life' designs on this ceiling. I have been there myself, several times in the past." He replied.

"Yes, I can understand you thinking that, but there was some water damage there recently and the light blue wash paint has worn away and you can see the designs underneath."

"Ah. I see. We must look into this. Please go on."

"Well, with the cave with the dove symbol being found near to Rennes Le Chateau, and it being an old Templar chapel it made me think that the Cathars and the Templars were much more closely associated with each other in that region than previously perhaps thought. I think they now probably shared similar beliefs and secrets." I continued.

"The Montsaunes chapel was another Templar chapel in the region so I thought it might be a good idea to look around that area for caves too. After a short internet search, I found there were a few near to the chapel which I thought were worth checking. That's when I came across the cave in St. Martory." I finished.

"I see now. A tenuous connection perhaps, but it has certainly yielded you results." He commented.

"So, from what you are telling me, you were not looking for things like scrolls, just symbols of doves and sacred caves. This is now very important Rowena. Was there anything else you were looking for?"

I remembered what Pierre and Brian had said to me and now realized why he was asking this. I could not be seen to have been specifically looking for treasure. The question on my mind though was the haematite stone and whether this was really treasure. To say I was looking for it would make me sound stupid, to not tell him would possibly leave me with problems later on. He also knew the full translation of the scroll and I didn't and I knew there was something about the Cathar stone in the scroll. I decided on the honest approach.

"Well there was one other thing," I began, "but if I tell you, you will think I am being stupid."

"Not at all." He seemed to relax a bit and leant back on his chair.

"Well, I found a piece of haematite in a cave in Ussat. For some reason I thought it might be part of the original Cathar stone."

"But why would you think that?" He asked quite reasonably.

I then explained all that I'd thought about the original stone being split into four pieces, then taken along four different paths and then hidden in four different caves. It was only when I added the part about my father's piece fitting perfectly with the one I had, did he react.

"Mon Dieu." He slipped back into French. I continued.

"I know you may think this will sound crazy, but I thought it might be that if I found the cave with the dove symbol, another piece of haematite might be there too. It wasn't though."

"Ah Rowena. This opens up so much more. I have heard of this theory of the four pieces of the Cathar stone. In fact my colleague here also strongly believes this to be the case. May I ask, where are these two stones you have now?"

I paused before answering his question. I realized I was at a point where I had a slight bargaining position. It might be the only time that came along as well.

"Monsieur LeMaitre, I appreciate everything you have done and I hope you see that I am being as honest as I can by answering your questions. You do though have me at a disadvantage." I breathed deep. "I am not someone who has the funds to continue looking for much longer. I am happy to tell you the exact location of the cave where I found the scrolls and will indeed guide you or any of your colleagues there. I don't actually need or want the two pieces of Haematite. They are sentimental and on their own are not worth anything to either you or me without the other two pieces. A good provenance to show that they were the original Cathar stone would also be necessary." I paused for breath and time to prepare my next words carefully.

"Monsieur I have a question for you. I know there is a French law on these things. At the moment I cannot see why the state would want these things as there is no value to them as they are. However, if all four pieces were found, there would be a value. My question to you is how much the state would want something that is currently of no value? For example are there any funds available that I could help me further my research for example, in return for what I have brought you already too?" I finished with a sense of hope in my voice.

"Yes of course you are right. Article 716 of the Civil Code says 'a treasure is anything hidden or buried for which no one can prove ownership, and which is discovered by pure chance'. It goes on to say that, if the state is not interested any discovery, it can be split with the Landowner. In this case you are also right too Rowena that we are in grey territory. We would be interested in the stones you have but perhaps not yet. We too would look fairly stupid to spend time and money going through all the paperwork just for two pieces of Haematite. However, we may have another piece already and the full translation does tell us some more about all this."

He must have heard my heart skip a beat when he mentioned a third piece.

"Listen. I do understand your financial position and maybe we can help here in a way but this is beyond me and what I can do for you. We are an organisation that answers to the 'Service Interministériel des Archives de France' – the French Archive Administration. They are part of the Ministry of Culture. The ministry will have funds available for these kinds of things. I will ask my Superior, when he gets back, to look into this for you. He will be most interested too, to hear you possibly have two of the pieces. He will of course want to see if our piece fits yours. For my part, from what you say, I am happy to tell the ministry that this find is an unexpected one. This will help you to get funds. I must insist though that the two pieces of Haematite are in our possession."

"I will agree on one condition, that I be present if and when the last piece is found and that I get recognition for finding the scrolls and at least half of the stone and if there is any reward financially from this find, that I get a fair share of this. Is that OK?" I asked him.

"That seems very reasonable to me. If it was up to me I would be happy to agree that. I will need confirmation of course and will get this for you soon. In the meantime we need to make some arrangements for you to meet with our representatives in the South to visit the cave and to pick up the scrolls. Are you Ok with this?" He asked. I didn't answer immediately but instead just looked at him. "Ok. I can cover your expenses of course and a little for your time from within my budget, but within reason." He offered. "If you give me your account details, I will arrange for a transfer of funds to help you in the meantime."

"Thanks. It will really help me considerably." I said and quickly wrote down my bank details for him.

"Good now let me show you the full translation. This, I have to tell you now, must not be revealed to anyone other than close friends. Those people you tell must not tell anyone either. Do you understand?" I nodded. "The reason is firstly, as you know, these scrolls have not been verified and secondly the information it contains is very sensitive. It has therefore taken on a 'political element' with regards to the timing of its release." He paused so he could be sure I was in agreement with this.

"I understand and thanks for at least allowing me to tell my friends." I replied.

"I can tell you that I had to work hard to be even allowed to give you this. It is only because Albert already translated most of it and gave it to you that I argued it would not make much difference. You also did the right thing by handing it all over to us. We have to be careful today in this World, Rowena. There are some people who, if they were in your shoes, would have looked to sell the scrolls on the black market. Indeed, speed is already important in case this knowledge has already fallen into the wrong hands. If it is possible I would like you to meet our recovery team in Montsaunes this Friday."

"That's fine with me I can assure you." I replied, thankful it wasn't going to take longer.

"Good I'll text you the arrangements as soon as I have them. I myself will not be able to attend unfortunately. Anyway, have a read of this. We have a little time afterwards for a chat but, as I said earlier, I have another meeting I cannot escape from. My daughter Gabrielle will be along shortly. I have asked her to come straight up to my office. With that he handed me a typed copy of a translation in English. He had labeled them the Bertrand scroll and the Thibault Scroll. He had written the following words on it:-

Bertrand Scroll

This is written by myself, brother Bertrand, in the year 1165 the year my master passed over into the next World. I write this as testament to his great work during his life. Brother Rossal was one of the few who travelled to Jerusalem in the year 1119 where in the tunnels he learnt of God's secrets that were told to him in a vision by our Lord. He came back with knowledge of the divine and drawings of the ancient paths and their sacred rose gardens. From Troyes he travelled South to Montsaunes in 1146 where I had the good fortune to meet and join with him. With these words I promise to complete his work here according to his plans and designs so that others can celebrate the divine here long after we have passed over.

1181 We have now completed our sacred place of prayer here in Montsaunes as brother Rossal had instructed us. It has great divine power but, as he finally suspected towards the end of his life, this is not the special place he had been looking for all this time. The path continues South to a place that is now in the hands of the Moors. I will keep hoping and searching. God bless us all.

Thibault scroll

This is written by myself, brother Thibault, in the year 1244. My master, brother Bertrand, passed over in the year 1210. I hereby confirm again that he completed the building of our chapel here at Montsaunes in the way brother Rossal indicated with all the signs drawn as he outlined as a way to pass on his work in secret to those who would know how to understand it later on. I too have now completed my work in writing about the Grail here in this Castle where our Lord appears. I write this now though at a time of great stress. Our good friends the Cathars have fallen at Montsegur burnt alive for their love of God. May the Holy Spirit hold them now in peace. They have left in our care a part of their holy stone that holds the divine fast but we must now move South and follow the path to the place of miracles in the hope that this is finally the sacred place we seek. I will take the stone with me with the Cathar who carried it here along with two good Knights. God bless us all.

Gaston had remained silent watching me as I read. It was obvious when I had finished by the look on my face and he began to talk as soon as I'd looked up.

"The dates gave me a problem for a while but eventually I tracked them down to being numbers from a Cistercian number cypher. I want to give you a personal thank you Rowena for that. It is moments like this translation that we live for in our business. It has given me great pleasure trying to decode these scrolls. Tell me, you don't think you missed anything when you took the photos do you?"

"No I am quite sure" I replied.

"That is good. What are your thoughts on them now you have read them?"

"My mind is just full of questions." I paused to think a bit more before I replied. Gaston kindly waited patiently. "I am not sure if you can help with some of these, but if you can, that would be really good." I asked.

"My first question is what else is known about Rossal? I did find him mentioned as one of the group of nine who went to Jerusalem under Hughes de Payens but could find out nothing else."

"My second question is what do we know about drawings and ancient paths and rose gardens when it comes to what was said to be found in tunnels under Jerusalem."

"Thirdly do you have any thoughts on where this 'place of miracles' South of Montsaunes might be because that may be where the 4th piece of the Cathar stone could be found?"

"All those questions are of course of interest to me but the last question I have is of most interest." I paused to gauge his reaction so far. He still sat patiently allowing me more time to talk if I needed it. I continued on.

"It seems to give the impression that the Montsaunes chapel was some kind of Grail castle and that there was more than one of these types of places. It also seems to be saying that this was not the one Rossal had been looking for and that seems to mean that he thought that there might be a bigger and more powerful Grail Castle – a place that is even more sacred than all the others – whatever that really means." I stopped and looked at him to see if he could answer any of my questions.

"Hmmm." He starts. "I can see why Albert liked you. You are quick to analyse and question. You isolate well what is important and what is not so important." He got up and started to walk slowly around his office. I swiveled my chair to watch him. "Hmm." He hummed again and then began his answer.

"It is true we do not know much about Rossal. He is named with one other person Gondamer as part of the original nine. We know nothing else about the two of them so I am sorry but I cannot help you there."

"As for the drawings, the ancient paths and the rose gardens, we don't know about any drawings either, this is the first I have heard of any such thing. The ancient paths have up to now just been a theory. There are Latin texts, of the Gallic wars I think, that tell of Julius Caesar mentioning about secret Celtic paths. Some people have even said that these straight tracks are from an earlier age than the Celts and that they ran across Europe over 2500 years ago. We have no real evidence of this though."

"The Rose Gardens I will leave to you to search on the internet. There is much I am sure you will find. What is true and what is not true is hard to say as they relate to places where the Grail is said to be found. The Grail researcher Otto Rahn has some words to say on the subject. You might like to read his books if you have not already." He suggested.

"Now. Your last question. I think this also ties in with your 'place of miracles' question. I can also understand why you find this the most interesting. It is also though, perhaps, the most dangerous question." He added in a cautionary tone. "This idea of one place being more special, or more sacred, than others, could do more harm than good, if different religions were involved. Finding this place is one thing, letting people know about it though could now be a very sensitive thing." He warned and went on. "These scrolls do seem to be proof that these two monks thought this was possible. All I can say on this again Rowena is that we must all be careful with this information for the time being. I can see you will probably want to find this 'place of miracles' but we have to consider it likely that this place is not in France. The scrolls talk about it once being in the hands of the Moors. This implies it is more likely to be in Spain. There I cannot help you and cannot be seen to be helping you."

"So as to where this place is, I don't know and, as of yet, I have not tried to search for this place. For me now, I must follow the right approach for this country and get the scrolls in safe hands and verified as soon as possible." At that moment there was a knock at the glass door.

"Entré mon chou." Gaston called out. In walked a good looking, well-dressed woman in high heels who looked as though she was in her early 30's. I immediately loved her red jacket. It had to be a designer special. It also exactly matched her bag, her lipstick and her shoes – all very stylish. What she was wearing was probably worth more than my car. I suddenly felt very under dressed.

"Ah Gabrielle, this is Rowena. Rowena meet my daughter Gabrielle. What good timing too. We were just finishing." They 'bised' cheek to cheek twice briefly and then she turned to me.

"Hi. Lovely to meet you," I said getting up off my seat.

"Enchanté. I am so pleased to meet you to." she replied. "Forgive me but my English is not as good as my father's."

"You seem to speak it very well," I praised her. "I have to say I just love your jacket." She smiled back in a way that I knew we were going to get along.

"Thank you, if we have time, I will show you the shop where I bought it. I don't think they sell this one any more though. Come let us go out and get something to eat. C'est d'accord mon pere?" she asked Gaston.

"But of course. I think we are finished here for the moment Rowena. If you do have any questions just call me. We will meet again soon, I am sure. Until then Au revoir."

"Au revoir et merci." I replied.

We walked down the steps and outside the building. Once outside Gabriella began to speak. "I have arranged to do no more work for the rest of the day so we can get to know each other." She strode along slightly in front of me towards a waiting taxi. It was almost hard to keep up with her. Even though she was only slightly taller, she had a pace about her that I guessed was just how she liked to live. "I have so much I want to ask you Rowena, if that's Ok of course." The taxi driver was now already out and opening the door for us. Once inside she turned to face me. "Are you hungry?" She asked in a way that was hoping I would say yes because she was hungry.

"A little" I replied.

"Good, I'm famished." She turned to face the driver. "Anton, s'il vous plait. Angelina's Rue de Rivoli…..Oh…via l'Arc de Triomphe… merci." She then turned back to me. "I think we are going to get along very well." She said. I smiled back. "You know, you are the only young woman my father has ever asked me to take to lunch. In the past it has been just older men."

"Does he ask you often?" I asked.

"Perhaps once or twice a year. It depends on how busy he is." She replied. "My mum refuses to do it anymore, but she is very busy too these days."

"What work does your mother do" I asked as politely as I could.

"She has an interior design business and I work with her in that. Anyway, what I thought we could do today is have some lunch at Angelina's. It is very popular with some of my clients. They call it a tea room but it so much more than that, you will see." I smiled and nodded. She continued. "Then I thought we could have a short walk past some shops, which I think you will like a lot." My smile broadened. "After that I was perhaps thinking of showing you a bit of Paris. I want to take you to see Notre Dame. I'll explain why when we get there. Then it is up to you, but if you feel like more, I have some idea's. What do you think?"

"That all sounds great Gabrielle. I am not sure how I can repay your kind hospitality though."

"Not at all, it is honestly my pleasure, but perhaps you can start by telling me more about your work." She asked.

I began at the beginning by explaining what I had done up until the point I'd found the scrolls and the two pieces of haematite. It seemed that her Dad had only shown her the translation of the scrolls. Because of that she asked me some questions on how the stone pieces were found. She seemed very interested in how things happened.

I was about to answer her last question when she stopped and started pointing out where we were as we came into the centre of Paris. She first pointed out the Arc to Triomphe as we headed towards it. I looked out to see a sea of cars going round what looked like an eight lane roundabout with a huge arch in the middle.

Our taxi pulled on to this circular racing track at quite a speed and then almost immediately turned off down the cobbled streets of the Champs Elysées passing shops like Cartier and Mont Blanc. She seemed to enjoy being my own personal tour guide. Next we passed by the Place de la Concorde, the Jeu de Paume and then on towards the Louvres.

Before we got there though the taxi pulled up and we got out. There was a stone arch colonnade with grand hotels and expensive shops underneath. One of them was Angelina's.

A gold coloured surround doorway opened up into what looked like the interior of a palace to me. Tall ceilings with panes of clear glass showed the clouds in the sky above us, white walls with arches were all surrounded with ornately shaped plasterwork. It all had an elegant charm that oozed wealth. I would have never contemplated eating here. I didn't even need to look at the menu to know the prices were way beyond what I could afford.

As if she could read my mind, she turned and said, "Don't worry Rowena, this will just be another business expense. Come let's get someone to find us a table. You have to have the African hot chocolate by the way, it's become World famous it's so good."

I ordered a Scandanavian club sandwich which was smoked salmon, boiled egg, goat's cheese and apple fries. Gabriella had the Caesar salad. Both of us ordered the African chocolate.

"Gabrielle," I started, whilst we were waiting, "I know your father is interested in what I've been doing, but can I ask you what you find interesting about it?"

"Of course you can Rowena. I have a deep interest in the Knights Templar and all things related to that. I will perhaps explain more later, but what really interests me is how people learn, grow and develop in their life. For instance, I can already see you have a passion for what you are doing. You seem to have also taken a keen interest in the Cathars as well. They too, are very interesting to me."

"My first question for you Rowena is to ask you what is it about the Cathars that you find so fascinating to the extent that you are now looking to find their sacred places. And secondly, how do you think you will find what you are looking for?"

They were fairly big questions and ones I really didn't expect her to start with. I began with my first thoughts.

"Well initially I liked it when I heard that the Cathars treated men and women equally and that both could be leaders of their communities...."

"…Yes, I liked that too…… Sorry, please go on" she interrupted.

"I also liked the simplicity of their life and their belief. To me, I saw that as just an expression of love for one another and for everything around them." I paused to think carefully before my next words.

"You see, I am not a religious person Gabrielle, I am just a scientist who is seeking the truth. I don't accept that God exists in the way that faiths around the World seem to talk about. However the idea that a Universal creative force might exist, this may be possible in some way, and something we can all benefit from. Now that is more interesting to me." I could see her keenly listening to what I had to say so I carried on.

"I know the Cathars were spiritual people who believed in God, but, to me, it was what they did and how they behaved that attracted me to them." I paused to see what reaction she had to what I'd said.

Gabrielle nodded as though she understood what I was saying.

"I think it may be possible that the Cathars had found a way to benefit from some kind of Universal force when they prayed in their special places."

"This may have even helped them to become better people and to do good for one another. I am not sure yet about their idea of us living after death, but I can't rule it out just yet either. Science can't really tell us one way or another at the moment."

"So you don't disbelieve God then," said Gabrielle. "What you are saying is that you just don't have any scientific theory yet to either prove or disprove God."

"If you like, yes." I replied.

"But, you may never find that science in your lifetime. That could mean a lifetime without God." she pointed out.

"Yes but I can still follow my own path to search for the truth. You see I'm not trying to disprove God exists or even trying to prove that he does." I replied. "There may well be some creative intelligent force in the Universe" I continued trying to justify my stance on it all.

"Aha. I knew you must be following some kind of path." Her voice seemed to light up again after hearing about my scientific stance on God. "When my dad mentioned you'd come across the two scrolls I thought it sounded too much like luck. There had to be something more to it than that." She added. "Sorry, please do tell me more. Do you believe there is a path just for you to follow or is it a path that everyone can follow?" she asked.

"Yes and No." I replied, thinking a little about my recent conversation with Aliya, "I have a choice. I can choose to try and follow my own path and then learn what I am supposed to learn in order to be a better person. If I do that, I can perhaps fulfill my own journey." I stated. "So my journey would not be the same as another person's." I continued. "We all seem to have our own path to tread."

"Yes, but how do you know you are on the path" she probed further.

The conversation was now getting much deeper than I'd expected. Nevertheless Gabrielle was definitely interested in what I thought and she seemed very genuine so I did my best to answer her.

"That's what I am still learning." I replied, "I can only be grateful, be positive and ask for signs to follow that will show me the way. If I do that, I will be led to find, and learn, what I am supposed to find and learn."

I paused before using the next word in my mind, wondering about the direction it might take our conversation. I decided to just go for it. "Synchronicity will then guide me." I stated. "I must just lose my fears and lose my ego. So far, it has worked well for me. Well, it has, at least, for the last few weeks." I ended.

"Ah. This is not so different then from the path I too try and follow." Gabrielle replied. "The difference seems to be though, that mine is with a belief in God. What puzzles me though is that you say you 'ask' to be shown the way but who do you ask?" she questioned.

"Well, at the moment," I replied again thinking carefully what I was going to say next, "it's like I ask the Universe. I'm not sure how it works but it's as though my subconscious mind has access to a sort of universal source of all knowledge."

"What do you mean Rowena?" she asked.

"Well. You know when you go to sleep at night and you need to wake up early, say 5.30am in the morning. Well if you ask your subconscious mind to wake you up then, you actually do get woken up at 5.30am. Have you found that?"

"Yes, it's actually something I do myself from time to time." She replied.

"Well you have to then consider that some mechanism exists where the subconscious mind can carry out an instruction to wake the conscious mind. This means there must be some two way communication going on between the two minds. If I ask my subconscious mind for help to stay on my path, then maybe it can carry out that instruction too."

"Yes but how would your subconscious mind know how to do that?" Gabrielle persisted. She had a fair point and I knew my answer was not a particularly strong one.

"Gabrielle, I can see why you ask that. I will do my best to tell you how I've come to see it over the years from a scientific perspective. I can't say it is right, just that it makes some sense to me."

"I see both order and chaos within life. Order naturally seems to arise from out of chaos. If order is a kind of natural plan for life then we have to ask what life is all about."

"That's not an easy question to answer," I continued, "but what is common to all life is growth. Everything living grows. So, to me, Life is all about growth, I can then ask for help to grow and develop. By asking my subconscious mind for help, to me, it's like becoming at one with the natural order in the Universe."

I paused to see if she was with me on what I had said so far. She was.

"If we all have the ability to become one with the natural order of things in the World, then it must mean that each of us has a natural, individual part to play in reaching that order. After all there are many different forms of life on the World and, we too, are all different and yet there is a form of harmony that exists between all life."

"So, if we each have a natural part to play, then there must be a natural path for me to take." I ended.

"But why would there be just one path you could or should take?" Gabrielle asked. "Why couldn't there be several paths you could take that would be good for you?"

"Again you make a good point and the answer is of course that we do have lots of paths we can take, but some are probably much better for us to take and which are also better for everyone else too that we take those better paths."

"This would also then mean there would be one path that would be the best path, albeit I openly admit that this would be a hard path for us to find and follow. We can perhaps just only try and do our best to find this path."

"The problem comes, of course, when we allow our own selfishness, our greed, perhaps to influence our conscious mind. We then try and get more of what we 'want' rather than what we actually 'need'. That path though will, almost certainly then, not help those around me either."

"Ok, go on, I can see that." Gabrielle agreed.

"If I allowed my ego to become selfish, then I would not now be playing the part I'm supposed to play in life. What then does my own greed do to the rest of the natural World and all life in it?" I pointed out.

"It would upset the natural balance of everything and there would be a lack or order and a step back into chaos." I said.

"Just look at how some humans are ruining the natural World around us due to their own selfishness and greed." I added.

"You have a fair point there, please do go on." She said.

"So when I ask for guidance or help, I consider that I am really just trying to connect my conscious mind with my subconscious mind to help me find this natural progression to a more ordered form of life and the particular part, or path that I have to play in it." I concluded.

"Do you see where I am coming from now when I say that I ask for help?" I asked her.

"Yes, I do Rowena and I quite like your answer. It does of course raise the question about the subconscious mind and what that is though. It could be that this is just part of a Universal mind and that could well be 'God-like' in its nature."

"Yes," I replied, "I could accept the concept of a kind of Universal Mind and perhaps Science will someday manage to explain how that could arise from out of the beginning of creation."

I could see we'd arrived at the point where it was impossible to take things further. Neither of us could really be sure what this ultimate truth was just yet.

I decided to change the subject and ask her about her path.

"If I may Gabrielle, you mentioned that you too follow a path. Can I ask you too follow your own path?"

"You will not know it by the name, I suspect, but we call it La Droit Humain."

She was about to explain more but the food and drinks came. "I will tell you more about it later. Let's eat first." She said.

Whilst we ate, I showed her the photo's I took. She showed an interest in all of them but it was the ones of the ceiling of Montsaunes chapel that she was most keen on. Once we'd both finished Gabrielle suggested we move on.

"Come we can talk more about this later." She'd said. "I think it's time for a walk." She kindly paid and we left to walk down the Rue de Rivoli towards the Louvre. We turned right under the arches and she showed me the glass pyramid in front of it.

"Rowena, I would love to show you round the Louvre one day, maybe when you are next in Paris. However right now, I think you might prefer some of our wonderful shops.

Three hours later, I'd seen more new types of clothes and shoes than ever before in my life. A massive indoor mall, the Forum des Halles, had so many shops and avenues in I thought I was going to get completely lost. There were just so many with names I'd never heard of as well. I could have spent a week there.

In the end I'd bought a black beret, a pair of low heeled red shoes, a white blouse and some red culottes that matched the shoes. Perhaps it had been Gabrielle's own jacket, bag and shoes that had been a colour influence on me.

With them all on, I could have easily passed as a fully-fledged Parisienne. They'd all also been in the sale so I'd spent less than 200 Euros. I'd justified it as an investment – a new look for a new career.

As for whether I needed it all, I fully recognised that in this World I had to make connections with other people and that, sometimes, meant dressing in a way that could help that happen. All women need a wardrobe with a wide ranging selection of clothes.

Gabrielle had picked up a small black hat, very chic and very expensive. She'd apparently been looking for one like that for weeks.

Before I knew it we were walking across a bridge over the river Seine and towards the towering Notre Dame. Looking at it now reminded me of Bernard when he'd told us it could fit into the Cave of Lombrives. He was just about right.

"Good, we are here and it's not too busy" started Gabrielle. "There are some things I really want to show you Rowena."

"This was one of several Gothic Cathedrals that the Templars had a large degree of influence over when they were being built. We know this because, within the overall design, we see some of their more peculiar ways of thinking. Let me show you what I mean." She led me around to the West facing entrance. Have a look at the carvings on the two sides of this door and tell me what you see."

"I looked closely and turned to her, "They look like signs of the zodiac" I said puzzled.

"They are. But don't try and look for answers just yet."

In the next half hour she'd showed me a statue of a 12th century alchemist complete with a Phrygian hat, 12 bas reliefs that showed a series of Alchemical processes. There was a statue of a man holding a shield and on it a snake was coiled around a long wand. It was very similar, if not the same, as the caduceus of Hermes from Greek mythology. With each new thing I saw, my curiosity grew and grew.

"If you look at other Gothic cathedrals in France that have had their designs influenced by the Templars, you'll also see signs of things like Alchemy. It is said they learnt it from the Sufi's." said Gabrielle.

"Reims, Amiens and Chartres all have more examples of their particular way of thinking. This was not at all the same as the thinking behind the Roman Catholic church. If you have time you should visit Chartres. It has a huge labyrinth there. There is nothing biblical about a labyrinth. It is also a very special place, if you know what I mean, with regards to what you've been talking about earlier today."

"Thanks Gabrielle, but what does this mean? Have you any thoughts on it all?" I said once we had come back outside again.

"Well, there is a school of thinking that the Templars discovered some secrets under the Temple of the Mount in Jerusalem." I gasped slightly at that and she turned around and saw my openmouthed expression.

"Yes, this ties in with your scroll." She explained.

As she answered Gabrielle and I had now walked fully across the river Seine and off the Ile de la Cité which was the island that the Cathedral had been built on.

We were now walking side by side along the South bank of the river heading towards to the botanical gardens.

"A few of the Templars seemed to have broken away from the Roman Catholic faith. We are not quite sure exactly what they did now believe, but we are fairly certain that they left clues behind for us to find and then interpret.

Unfortunately, the Templar order was eventually disbanded by the Pope in 1312AD at the Council of Vienne. Two years later their leader, Jacques de Molay, was burnt at the stake here in Paris."

"Some of the Templars escaped with their wealth and others went underground with their new beliefs. Some people believe, me included, that their way of thinking was preserved many years later by the Rosicrucians and after that by the Freemasons. Are you aware of what the Freemasons and the Rosicrucians do today?"

"No not at all." I replied truthfully.

"Well, we can perhaps come to that. What I find of interest though is the symbols that they left behind. We are all continually searching for new ones as they may contain new messages for us. This is why I was so interested in your photos at the Montsaunes chapel."

"But these are not new Gabrielle." I pointed out.

"I know but unfortunately, we've lived in a society for the last fifty years or so when there has not been much sharing of information. That we have a French Templar chapel that so few of us know about seems incredible, but it is true."

"Both my mum, my dad and I were unaware of the symbols on the ceiling of this church until you brought them to our attention. It is only since the internet that we are all becoming more aware of what is out there."

"Before, all we learnt was what was taught to us and what was taught has always been the same down through the ages. Little or no new knowledge came through."

"I can see the problem" I said. "This is why I quite like this new path I am following. I find what I am supposed to find. I am not waiting to be taught information that's not relevant to me." I pointed out to Gabrielle.

"What is relevant to me, I will find in the right time, if I can stay aware and on my path." I ended.

"I can see the advantages there, but you have one disadvantage, you are on your own. Within a group, we can help each other." She also pointed out.

"Yes I see that, but it's also what holds you back." I replied. "The confidences a group keeps between all its individuals mean secrets and that closes the mind. In time the group ceases to grow as well, and the knowledge that it has, becomes guarded. Less and less new information is brought in and shared that way." I pointed out back to her.

"I have my group of people all around me." I continued, "I just haven't met all of them yet. It's like we are all collectively working together, even though we are unaware of each other's work at the moment. It's as though we are all trying to play our natural part and walk our natural path." I stated.

"I do see your point of view and it does have a certain appeal……Maybe a bit of both is a good thing." Gabrielle conceded.

"We are not supposed to be on our own in life though." She continued again after a moment of thinking. "It's natural for humans to work together and to help each other. That is rewarding in itself and that too leads to self-improvement."

I had to agree with her on those points.

We continued talking over these things and also on what we thought the symbols at Montsaunes meant.

By the time we had walked around the gardens with their sandy, tree lined paths, Gabrielle turned to the subject she'd been about to talk to me about when our lunchtime food had come.

"'Le Droit humain' in English means 'The perfect person.' I feel you should know a little more about it as I have come to think it as similar in a way to the Cathari way of thinking. There may be something in it that you like or which resonates with you." She had certainly caught my attention.

"Indeed it might Gabrielle." I replied.

"I am a member of the lodge here in Paris. We are essentially truth seekers like you Rowena but for the differences which you have carefully pointed out to me earlier, without perhaps realizing it."

"I am telling you also because I am perhaps hoping we can have some ongoing connection in the future that will help us all."

"That's very kind of you to think these things." I replied.

"On a group level, we work to unite men and women who have a common way of spiritual thinking but who have different individual and cultural backgrounds. We too are all searching for the truth."

"We are, if you like, a combined male and female form of Freemasonry." She pointed out.

"Wow. That's different. I've never heard of that before." I said.

"Our members see men and women as equals, just like the Cathars did. Our lodge began back in 1901 so we are not a new organization. We have lodges all around the World and several million members."

221

"What we do is a bit like helping each other follow a spiritual path in life. It's a more structured one than yours though." She explained. "The structure is provided by 33 levels that members can progress along. These, if you like, represent stages of their understanding of their own path in life."

At this point we reached the front of a light sandstone block building with tall pillars extending vertically up from a first floor balcony. Above it was the writing Le Droit Humain.

"This is our lodge." Gabrielle announced proudly.

"It is certainly impressive" I replied.

"It's not open at the moment. I just wanted to show you as its round the corner from a lovely restaurant I wanted to take you to."

A few minutes later we were standing in front of a Morrocan restaurant called 'Au P'tit Cahoua'.

"It's one of my favourites. Come let me treat you." she offered.

I wasn't that hungry but I loved the kind gesture she was making, not only with food but also with her information. We went inside and were instantly hit by a variety of wonderful aromas.

"I have a date at 8.00pm tonight," she confided. "If you are Ok, I will see you on to the Metro beforehand that so you can get back to your hotel."

"Yes that is of course Ok" I replied. "Who is the date?"

"Ah, a new client. A young man from the North of Paris. He has his own 'tech' company. He's single but he wants me to look at his new apartment in town to freshen it up a bit before he moves in. I think he quite likes me because I've already seen the place and it needs next to nothing done to it at all. Anyway, we shall see."

"You must let me know how it goes." I smiled, "But why are you wanting to eat now? Surely he will take you out for a meal." I asked genuinely surprised.

"Of course he will, but not until later on in the evening. I don't want to appear hungry in front of him. What would he think if I finished my meal before him?" We both laughed but deep down I think she looked like she enjoyed her food.

We ordered the Chicken Tagine with mango, mint, figs and raisins and the Tajine Zaalouk which was monkfish with augbergine & lime.

While we were waiting Gabrielle went back to telling me about the 33 levels that their members took to journey along for their own path in life. I couldn't see that it would be for me though, but I thought it best to keep an open mind.

"Rowena, I'd like to tell you a bit more about Le Droit Humain because I think we might be able to reach some mutually beneficial arrangement between us in the future, if you are interested."

"That's fine with me but I am not sure how I can help you at the moment." I replied truthfully.

"Well, you have already. The scrolls you found with the information on them and bringing to our attention the Montsaunes chapel symbols are both going to be very helpful to us. I can tell you will find out more in the future too. That will also be of interest to us."

"Well I shall certainly let you know more if I find anything." I replied.

"We are also in a position to perhaps help financially in the future too." She added. "We can discuss that another time though. What I did want to do now though is to just explain one of two things that we do to find our paths that may help you in your own quest." She offered.

"Le Droit Humain, or the quest to become a perfect person, is indeed similar to the Cathar quest to do the same and also similar to the Knights Templars quest for the path to enlightenment. The difference between them was, I think, that the Templars also thought that they were fighting against the negative forces of darkness in the World who were opposing them."

I began to think of Perlesvaus and his journey through the forests from one castle to another looking for the Grail. Maybe what Gabrielle and her friends were doing was not too dissimilar.

"The first part of our journey is the quest for light." She began. "We have to awaken and become aware of our own personal spirituality. I think in your case you have certainly awoken to something." She pointed out.

I remembered Aliya laughing at me and saying it was because I had 'awakened'. Was this the same thing? I wondered.

"The second part we call the chapter of the Rosy cross. This is the quest to purify and strengthen the light within us so that it can help guide us through our life. I think there is a similarity here to your synchronicity and it guiding you." Gabrielle continued. "The Rosy cross is also linked very closely to the Rosicrucian way of thinking. You might like to look into this further some time."

Something was nagging me at the back of my mind when I thought about the words 'The Rosy cross'. My memory failed me at that moment so I carried on listening.

"The third part is the Holy quest. Here we try and find the path that allows us to make a positive difference to the World around us. You are already doing this in your own way whether you know it or not. That could be because you realize you only need to play the part you are supposed to play in order to make a positive difference around you. I quite like that about the way you are thinking there."

"Thank you." I replied.

"The last part is the quest for self-examination in order to find the truth."

"One of the things we are told at these higher levels is the importance of harmony. Harmony is perhaps the greatest secret of all. I have to say though that many of us are unsure exactly what this means."

"We have come to think about it meaning that we need the right balance in our life but I, for one, am not so sure. It could be that your work might even shed some light on this Rowena."

"Well, if I can, I'll let you know." I replied. "Thanks for sharing all that with me too. It has certainly given me a few things to be aware of going forward."

"Good." said Gabrielle. "I think there's much we can do together in the future Rowena. If I can help you in any way, please do let me know."

At that point the food arrived. It was scrumptious. Our conversation then continued and ranged on from the symbols at Montsaunes to the signs of the Rosy cross and to the shopping we'd done that day and strangeness at Notre dame. Time flew by.

At around 7.30pm she'd walked me to the Gare de L'Austerlitz Metro station. We said our good byes and I wished her good luck for the date. I also arranged to call her with an update on how things were going over the next few days.

It had been a lovely day with her but now I'd been looking forward to time on my own to think about the day and all the information I'd come across.

As I walked along the platform, I was thinking about the Templars and their Gothic cathedrals. At that moment, exactly when I thinking about the Chartres labyrinth, I saw a poster of Chartres Cathedral in front of me.

It was promoting the Sound and Light show around the city of Chartres at night. It looked fantastic. It was almost certainly another synchronous moment that I'd have to follow up.

With some quick calculations and a check on the rail times, I worked out that I could catch the train there tomorrow, stay one night and still be able to catch the train back to Paris and then back South to Tarascon. Brilliant.

The Metro train soon appeared from out of the dark tunnel. It was so different from the London Underground. The carriages ran on tyres which made it a smoother ride but also one that could go round sharper bends and up and down greater slopes. It was rather like a children's roller coaster ride.

I made a mental note to change trains at Invalides to get to Basilique St Denis.

I took out my mobile and started to make some notes.

Search Miracle sites in Spain with Templar connection
Look for 4th part of stone - possibly in Spain
More powerful place than Montsaunes - more powerful Grail site?

Ping. I had a message.

Money had been transferred into my account. I checked how much via my online banking app.

Wow. That's a nice end to the day. 1000 Euro's had been credited to my account. Then I remembered that Gaston had said it would be a part payment. Things really were looking up.

I changed trains at Invalides. There was time to read some of the posters on the wall that were promoting the place. It had been a hospital and retirement home for French war veterans but was now a museum. There really was so much to see in Paris.

Back on the Metro again, I went back to writing my notes.

Call Bernard re Friday visit to cave
Call Uncle David to update him on my progress.
Buy Otto Rahn books
Research Templar Alchemy and drawings and Montsaunes ceiling
Castle shape symbols - possible Grail message?
Research Rosicrucians and the rosy cross
Harmony secret?

Having written down my reminders I felt I could relax a bit. I pulled out my earphones and plugged in Adele.

Chartres

It was 10.00am and I was back at Gare Montparnasse. I was also now in my new French outfit. It felt great. There were posters all around the station advertising the Chartres light show. I couldn't wait. I'd manage to delete some of the action points off my list – the calls and the book orders which I'd arranged to have sent to Tarascon. They'd be there on Friday. The rest of the points were for the train ride. I'd also worked out that I would have just enough time to book into the hotel and get to the Cathedral by 12.00 noon.

I am not sure why I felt I had to be there at that time but I'd woken up with an urge inside me that this was important. I was still new to this approach of going with the flow so I wanted to go with this gut feeling and see where it led me.

227

No upper deck this time but nearly all the seats were empty. I chose one with the window to my right and facing the direction of travel. It just felt more positive.

My first search was on the Knights Templar & Alchemy. There'd been a clear connection between them at Notre Dame and I felt I had to learn more about it and to see if there was any connection to what I'd seen at Montsaunes.

After about fifteen minutes searching online, I'd almost given up. I was swamped with rubbish. There may have been gems in there but it would have been impossible for me to tell which ones they were. I had to find another approach. Going back to the flow seemed to echo through my mind. I opened up my digital photo album and looked at the images from inside the chapel again.

If I perhaps meditated on the symbols, I might get something. The round castle shapes with their circle within a circle seemed to be a theme. Inside them there were flower like symbols, spirals and the 'flower of life' type symbols. I looked at them in silence for a while. Nothing. Giving myself a short break, I looked out at the French countryside. It rushed by too fast so I focused on the buildings and trees in the distance.

The near smoothness of the train made my body rock slowly and gently from side to side. My mind soon began to drift into non thinking mode. After a while a thought broke through into my conscious mind. These symbols must be 2D representations of 3D shapes. There was nothing new in that of course, but it gave me a direction to think. The castle shapes on the ceiling could well link with the castles in the book Perlesvaus. Inside them all were the invisible changing Grail shapes. The long line of shapes could therefore have been drawn to represent this changing sequence. In each symbol there was a representation of each new shape as it changed. Someone, possibly Rossal himself, had somehow been able to see them.

I looked at them all carefully. It seemed to me that, to begin with, lots of circles were all moving towards each other. This led to the intersecting circles and the flower of life design. This then seem to lead on to a spiral shape design and then onto some kind of looping design.

I thought about these two for a while in a three dimensional way. It then dawned on me. These could be representing a Vortex and a Torus shape.

The castle walls had to also be invisible shapes. They could now be acting like containment fields for these changing shapes to form. In order for a large vortex to grow in water, it needs a circular current on the outside in order to contain it. This was not water though, but maybe, it could perhaps be some kind of sound.

Maybe some kind of sound containment field could possibly contain growing and changing sound shapes. Nature seems to have the same Universal rules after all. The changing shape of the Grail in the story could now be symbolic of a changing shape of sound energy. This is what could then be possibly found at these 'song line' or 'sound line' intersections.

Could being in these places of sound really have some kind of psychoacoustic effect on someone? Was this what the Templars discovered in the tunnels under Jerusalem? Was all this some long lost knowledge that had come from our earliest ancestors? Was this now even connected to some secret about harmony?

My mind was buzzing. Again I just had too many questions flying around. The only thing to do was to park it all for the time being. If I didn't I would lose myself in all sorts of crazy ideas. I knew I was onto something though. I could come back to it later and try and find a way to prove or disprove some of the more sensible ones.

I turned to my next action point – the rosy cross. This now seemed to connect with my previous thoughts. It was then that I remembered where I'd heard the phrase before. I'd come across it in the small museum in

Tarascon written by Gadal and his words on the Grail in the Pyrenees. "….To see: The Grail on the Rose and the Rose on the Cross – the Cross of the Grail."

Gadal must have thought that the symbol of the Rose and the Cross were connected to the Grail. If the cross now represented the crossing sound lines, then the rose in the middle could now represent the Grail in the middle of the Castle – the changing sound energy shape.

Gabrielle had told me that the cross symbol stemmed way back way in time before Jesus and his crucifixion, perhaps even further back past Egyptian times. It had represented eternal life or new life. The Rose in the middle was also said to represent light from the Sun. Did this now connect the Grail with the Sun in some way?

I thought about her words for a moment. There was no guarantee these interpretations were right of course. An eternal life meaning for the cross though did seem to match the Grail property of immortality though. The Rose could also be seen to be similar to the flower of life symbol. This could now mean that the flower of life was also a Grail symbol. Perhaps the petal shapes had a connection to renewed life. That would then make it tie in with the Grail properties of healing and rejuvenation.

The question now coming in from my left brain was what connection there might be between the light energy from the Sun and sound energy.

That needed more serious scientific investigation. There would perhaps be scientific papers on this I could search for. Again I felt I was getting somewhere but not yet anywhere specific. Maybe this was a feeling I had to get used to if I was following the right path.

Time had flown by and the train was now pulling into the station at Chartres. It was 11.25am. I'd booked a room at the nearby Timhotel Chartres Cathedral. It was clean and comfortable but more importantly for me, it was only a 10 minute walk from the Cathedral.

Having checked in I strolled towards its two tall towers in the distance. No map was necessary. It was exactly 12 noon when I walked towards the entrance. I wondered why the time had seemed so significant to me earlier.

Whatever it was, an air of expectation had given me a growing 'butterflies in my stomach' feeling as I walked. On entering the cathedral I immediately found myself drawn to looking upwards at the exceptionally tall ceiling. The blue stained glass windows either side drew my eyes right down the whole length of the building. Gradually returning my gaze down to the ground I saw that 'looking up' was commonplace. Nearly everyone was at it.

The one exception to this though was a small group of people standing in the middle of the central aisle.

As I moved further into the Cathedral I naturally came nearer and nearer towards them. After only a few more steps I noticed the dull yellow flagstones of the labyrinth outlined by a carefully carved, narrow dark grey paving. The two had been polished smooth together with years of feet.

Unfortunately, most of it was hidden due to the seats and backs of the chairs which had been placed in multiples of lines either side of the central aisle. A thought crossed my mind that this might even have been intentional. Someone, or some group of people, didn't want to encourage people to walk the labyrinth.

In front of me now was the small group of people I'd seen earlier. They were standing in what looked like central alcoves right in the centre of the labyrinth. Three men and two ladies stood deep in meditative silence. I stepped closer towards them.

Now only a few feet away, a tall elderly gentlemen on the far side of the group opened his eyes and looked right at me. He raised his right hand and beckoned me to join them on the one free remaining outline of an alcove. It was his warm and welcoming smile that made me move and take my place. We all stood with arms to our sides. Some had their eyes closed, others open. Everyone wore smiles. "Breathe in……." said the elderly gentlemen…. "and breathe out….."

I could hear the others doing this all together and watched as their chests rose and fell. It seemed appropriate to trust and join them. "Breathe love in…..and Breathe love out" The tall man continued. "Feel the love coming in to you……..now feel it going out into the World."

We stood in silence doing just that. There were no more instructions given. Slowly I began to feel it. The same tingling experience I'd felt in the Cave of Lombrives. It began in my hands and feet, then my arms and legs. It then slowly moved towards the core of my body. With each breath it became stronger. It soon felt as though every cell in my body had begun to resonate with each other. There was no dizziness in my head this time though. I was both calm and relaxed and yet also very much alive and highly sensitized to everything and everyone around me.

The feeling of love then began to grow and grow from within my heart. I just let it happen. It felt wonderful. A low hum began from the three men. The two ladies joined in with a slightly higher Ah sound. I went with it and did the same. The feeling I had already grew stronger. A hand either side of me touched mine. I looked down and they were all now holding hands. I added mine to theirs and the circle was complete. Any sense of time was now gone. I just wanted this to go on forever.

The humming faded away though and we released our hands and I opened my eyes. The smiles were still there. I now felt rooted to the spot. If I wanted to move, I don't think I could have just yet. The silence continued and we each looked around at each other knowing that we'd just shared something incredibly special.

Opposite me the elderly gentlemen was dressed in a tweed jacket and dark brown trousers. He looked English. To his right was an elderly lady in a medium length white dress covered with a variety of little red rose designs. She wore a pair of comfortable white low heeled shoes. She could have been

Spanish, I wasn't sure but she didn't look as though she was the gentleman's partner.

Next to her, and me, was a smartly dressed Japanese man who looked as though he was in his late 50's. He wore a light grey suit and a white shirt but no tie. How on Earth he ended up in the circle with us was the question most on my mind.

On the other side of me was a woman who was about 30 years old. She was standing in bare feet and had on a pair of denim shorts, a T-shirt and a long multi-coloured bead necklace. She could have been from any European country as she had a sort of multinational look to her.

The last person was a dark coloured man who could have been in his twenties, thirties or forties, it was hard to tell. He was wearing a combat jacket over a pair of tight black trousers that showed an underlying athletic body. He also wore what looked like a very expensive pair of trainers.

You couldn't have put us together as a typical group if you'd tried. We were all so seemingly different and yet here we all were. The elderly gentleman spoke first in a deep refined English voice. "Thank you." He paused. "Thank you for your journey here today from wherever you all came from. It is indeed a special time and day."

I wanted to ask a question but it didn't seem right here in the centre of the labyrinth for some reason.

"The energies here are still strong but we must move on and allow others to enjoy this place." He spoke again. I looked around and now, as he'd said that, I noticed one or two people watching us. "I will be outside for a few minutes if anyone would like to join me. Thank you so much. I hope our paths come together again sometime soon. I wish you all the very best." With that he backed away from the circle, gave us what looked like a slight bow, and slowly made his way to the same entrance we had all come through.

The Japanese man bowed to us all to and followed him out. Athlete guy followed him. The two other ladies stood still. I guessed they might still be rooted to the ground. Curious to know more I also followed them out. The four of us met outside the front entrance.

The Japanese man spoke first. "I must thank you all so kindly," his English was good but it came out bit by bit. "The Ki energy there was so very strong. With us all together - very powerful. I wish I could stay longer and chat to you. I will take this memory back with me to Japan in my heart. Thank you so very much, Thank you." He bowed low to us and took a step back and bowed again. He then turned and walked away as though he was already late for something or someone.

Athlete guy looked at me and smiled. I hadn't said a word up till now. "Qu'est ce que vous pense Mademoiselle?" he asked. I smiled, my new outfit had worked. He'd thought I was French.

"It was fantastique. The energy was amazing." I replied in English with just one French word. His expression was a joy to see and he switched to English.

"You surprised me Mademoiselle." He said with a laugh.

"Me too." said the English gentleman.

"That whole experience. What was that?" Athlete guy continued looking at us both. "I just came in to look around while my wife was in one of the shops. That was just incredible and I've never done that sort of stuff before either."

The elderly gentleman just smiled.

"It was pretty new for me too" I added. "Did anyone know each other before?" I asked.

"No." the elderly gentleman replied, "People turn up at the right time in the right place if it's to be." A distant memory came to me that I'd heard of this sort of thing happening before.

"It is a special day of the year today," he went on now addressing Athlete guy. "The energies are all in harmony today. That only happens four times a year."

'Harmony'. There was that word again, I thought.

"But why today?" Athlete guy said.

"It always happens the day before the Solstices and the Equinoxes" the elderly gentleman answered. "It's the Summer solstice tomorrow."

"But isn't that the more important day. Wouldn't the energies be more likely to be in harmony tomorrow?" Athlete guy stated.

"You might certainly think that. I used to think that once as well. But now, from what I've learnt, it is the day before." The elderly gentleman replied. At that moment Athlete guy's wife turned up. She waved to him with one arm. Over her other arm were several bags of shopping.

"Guys, Have to go." he started, "Thanks so much. I hope we meet up again some time." He bounded off to greet her. He looked and moved like a professional athlete – at least someone who could run very fast. He may well have even been paid to do some particular sport.

"Thanks again for joining us" The elderly gentleman said. He waved and we waved back. The elderly gentleman then turned to look at me.

"I hope you don't mind me asking but why is today special…." I asked, "….and what do you mean about the energies being in harmony."

"Might I suggest a nice cup of green tea at the Café Serpente over there" The elderly gentleman suggested, "It will give us time to become

235

calmer and more collected in our thoughts. I have about half an hour free anyway.

"Yes, thanks. That would be lovely." We walked across and sat down at an empty table outside the café.

"It has a lovely view of the Cathedral too. The prices are a bit steep but I've always liked the name of the place. It reminds me of 'Les Wouivres', as the French like to say, as they wind their way through the foundations of this so very sacred place." He said.

"Les Wouivres?" I asked.

"Yes. The old French legends about them talk of the dragons that cross the land to meet here. Some people call them Dragon lines or Serpent lines. The Chinese call them the Lung Mei, the Aborigine's call them Song lines. More recently some people have even referred to them as Energy lines." He turned to look at me and then continued. I was still thinking of his first words about serpents when he mentioned Song lines. Did he really say that I thought?

"Cultures all around the World have different legends about them. The Ouroborus is another name that has been used – these are serpents that are said to be so long that their bodies go right around the World so they can hold their own tail in their mouth." He ended.

"Yes but these are just legends." I replied testing him to find out more.

"Of course, but do you not find it strange that all around the World different cultures talk about something similar. I think it is far more likely that they are all local symbols for some common global truth."

For some reason I then remembered the old lady's words at Rennes Le Chateau. 'Look out for snakes!' I thought at the time I hadn't heard her very well and that my translation may have been wrong. I thought hard about what she'd actually said. It had been something like 'Regardez sssshhh serpents.' It was the shushing sound in the middle that had confused me. I thought perhaps that she was making a hissing sound like a snake. Thinking more about it now, it could have been the French word 'Cherche'. What she could have really being saying was 'Look, Look for the snakes.' It now dawned on me that what she may have been trying to tell me was to look for these 'Wouivres' and not real snakes at all. Why she would know to say that to me though. I had no idea. It was all very strange.

My mind then went back to thinking about Earth sounds again and his use of the words Energy lines. The elderly gentleman seemed happy to sit in silence with his face turned towards to the Sun. I held back my questions for a moment and enjoyed the Sun in silence as well.

A waiter soon appeared and took the elderly gentleman's order for two cups of fresh green tea.

I continued to let my mind think. If the Earth was producing these lines of sound, it too would be a global effect. After a while I returned to my original question again. "You mentioned earlier about energies being in harmony?" I asked. "What did you mean by that?"

"I will try and answer that question for you in a moment but first, have you had a chance to look around the Cathedral yet?" he asked back.

"No I've literally just got here." I replied.

"Well, you will find some interesting things here which are different from many other Cathedrals. You know the labyrinth of course, but, if you look you will notice that the direction of the place doesn't point East like many other Christian church's do." He paused to check if I was interested. "It was built along the line of the sunrise on the Summer Solstice. Here that is about 46.5 degrees to the North of East" The Cathedral was directly in front of us and he gestured the direction with his right arm.

"In fact" he continued, "when you begin to study the Templars you are forced to conclude that they were a very mixed bunch of people. I've come to think that one small group of them seem to have become very Pagan in their thinking. I am almost certain that this group was into some form of Sun worship." He turned to look directly at me. "Tomorrow is St John's day. It's a time of feasting, fun and enjoyment. This celebration has happened for centuries and that is probably why this day has been remembered for such a long time. What was forgotten though was what came before that."

"Which was?" I asked.

"Not many people know that the early Hebrew calendar was actually a solar calendar. It probably stemmed from a time even before them. The Hebrews considered that there were four days in the year that were exceptionally holy. Very few people were ever trusted with the knowledge of when these days occurred. It was never written down anywhere and was only handed down by word of mouth - probably only from high priest to high priest." He paused again as though deep in thought.

"I have been researching this for some time now and it appears to me that these early Hebrew holy days were always held on the last day of the Sun's cycle- something they called the Tekufah."

"The days of Solstices and the Equinoxes however are always held on the first day of the new cycle of the Sun. I think that the times of harmony are found right between these changing sun cycles."

"Today is the last day of the Sun cycle, tomorrow is the solstice and the day of celebration. It would only be natural that a day of celebration would follow after a day of prayer – don't you think?" He asked.

"So you think there is a connection between the Sun and these energies then?" I asked, now slightly concerned that he didn't think they were connected to the Earth and to Earth sounds but also now thinking about my thoughts on the train to Chartres about a connection between Light and Sound.

"My dear, these days everything seems connected when you look closer and closer at reality. Light and Sound for example are both energy and even they seem now to be connected in some way." He replied. It was as though he'd almost read my mind with his answer. I remained speechless with it all.

After a few moments of thought, he continued. "Sometimes we just have to be patient and the answers will come. But to answer your question……..Yes, I think there is a connection………. I am just not sure yet…….. quite what that is though."

This whole thing seemed to be opening up scientifically with these energies being possibly connected to both light and sound. I felt sure that all of this was going to be understood one day. I went back to some other questions I had.

"But why do you think they went to all that work in putting a labyrinth on the floor of the Cathedral?" I asked.

"Goodness me you are really full of questions." He replied and then carried on, pausing occasionally. "Well…………..., according to some people, this place is thought to have once been an earlier sacred site ……….and that's probably where the legends of all the Serpents come from." He added.

"The site also seems to have been important to the Templars. I think they were searching for ancient sacred sites like this one. As to why they built a labyrinth on it, that I think, is down to helping to attain the right feeling before praying…….. Have you ever walked a labyrinth?" he asked me.

"No." I said

"Then I suggest you do and you will know exactly what I mean." He left it at that and I realized he wasn't going to tell me for a reason. He wanted me to feel it.

"So what happens on these special harmony days with the energies?" I asked.

"Unfortunately I don't have a full understanding of that yet. My thinking though is that some of the Templars considered that these were times when all sorts of good things could happen to them."

"Like what?" I asked

"Things like manifestation, healing, rejuvenation, enlightenment." He replied. I sat still, in a form of numbed silence. They were all properties that had been applied to the Grail in the stories I'd been reading. Did this now make Chartres another Templar Grail site? Did they really think these things could actually happen?

A few moments later the tea came and we drank together looking up at the South Easterly side of the Cathedral now bathed in sunlight. "Have a look at the light inside when you go back in." He stated. "See if you find anything interesting in there."

"Should I look anywhere specific?" I asked.

"Only if you think that is a good strategy." He replied rather enigmatically. I left the thought hanging and changed the subject back to the Grail properties again.

"You mentioned manifestation. From a scientist's perspective have you any idea on how that might work?" I asked.

"My dear, I am afraid you are now asking questions that are way beyond my ability to help you with……….. I, myself, like to imagine the Universe, and everything in it, to be connected in some fundamental way………..."

"……….maybe to some base universal force…….. Who knows? If, when we are meditating, we can connect to this force in some way, then we may also be connecting with everything…….. maybe the sound of the Universe itself." He smiled as though he knew something but wasn't telling.

"If our thoughts are aligned in this way," he continued, "then our needs might be too……………… If we are following the right path, from the perspective of the Universe, then I like to think that it then conspires to help us……. a bit like some kind of natural order that arises from out of all the chaos………….. You might like to look into something called 'the law of attraction' ………….. I think there may well be a connection between that and manifestation." He paused and looked as though he was thinking even more carefully about what to say next.

I couldn't believe how similar this was to what I had just been saying to Gabrielle just the day before. What did that now mean?

"I am guessing you have come across Jung's concept of synchronicity." He began again.

"Yes." I answered now even more keenly listening to him.

"I like to think of it as coincidences that occur that are as a result of having asked for them in advance…………. Whether you know you are directly asking for help in your life ………or you are being indirectly helped by just being on the right path." He paused again as though to give me time to think about his words.

"You see, when you are on the right path everything just seems to flow. It is as though World is just conspiring to help you" He smiled again and briefly looked over at me.

I was without words. Nearly everything he seemed to be saying was information I'd either thought of myself or I'd come across recently from someone else. How could that be? I looked at him. He had a knowing smile about him as though he'd just been reminding me of something I'd known for years.

I drank my tea thinking about the things he'd just said. Life had certainly been conspiring to help me recently and I was very grateful for that. The elderly gentleman seemed like someone who liked to spend more time thinking than talking. Somehow, he'd managed to get me doing it too.

It was almost too many thoughts for me to cope with though so I sat back, relaxed and felt the Sun against my face. Maybe that was what he was also teaching me to do as I watched him doing the same thing. After a few minutes now of more peaceful silence I asked "How did all these people just turn up today?"

"My dear...... I have no idea..... It just seems to happen that way." He replied.

"You mean this sort of thing happens regularly to you?" I asked.

"Not exactly......these small gatherings on the four key days of the year have really only just begun....... I know of only around 15-16 of them happening around the World today...... There may be more....... I'd like to think so......... People just start gathering at sacred sites like this four times in a year. Today, I happened to be in this part of France so I came here. In the UK there are other places I go.

"Like where?" I asked.

"Modern and Ancient sacred sites"

"You seem to be a bit vague about it all?"

"Yes it does seem to be that way but too much organization and planning doesn't seem to work. These sorts of things seem to emerge organically. They then develop and grow with a life of their own and in their own time. You will find these places and others will find them too when they are ready and when they need to – just like indeed you and the others did today." He finished his cup and put it down on the table and started to rise. "It has been lovely to meet you today. Thank you so much again for coming along."

"No thank you." He was about to walk inside and pay the bill. "Can I ask who you are?" I asked him, "What is your name even?

"Who I am is really not important my dear. I am sure we will meet again if we are meant to." He replied. "Do enjoy yourself in the Cathedral. But if you do go back to the centre of the Labyrinth, don't spend too long there. It seems that too much of this is not good to begin with. I'll get these…. Have a lovely day." With that he left.

I sat there in the chair watching him pay and then walk off across to the small shrub garden square in front of the Cathedral entrance and then around the corner the other side.

He was obviously someone who'd been trying to follow his own particular path for some time. Meeting him had not only given me further things to think about, it had somehow given me hope too. The day was turning into a very special one indeed and I thought yesterday had already been a pretty good one. Yet again though, even though I'd found some answers, I'd ended up with even more questions.

I finished my tea and ventured back inside the Cathedral. There was no group in the middle waiting for me to join them this time. I took out my mobile and started doing the usual tourist thing by taking photos of nearly everything. I'd heard about the uniqueness of the stained glass windows and noticed with interest that some of them were called rose windows. The pattern they made was acutely similar to the flower of life designs I'd found previously. The rose shape must have been very special to the Templars.

I wandered around feeling tiny amidst the vastness of space inside it. Further along on the Southern facing side I found a whole stained glass window of zodiac signs. It was another indication that their thinking here

243

had really deviated a long way from that of the church of Rome. I reached the far end having sensed nothing out of the corner of my eye using a general sense of awareness. I turned around and walked back now instead focusing on what I could actually see in the designs of the windows.

I was already half way back down when I caught sight of an image of Jesus holding a glass sphere at the top of one of the windows. I'd missed it the first time as I was walking the other way and away from it. This time it was directly in my face.

What Jesus was portrayed doing was holding what looked like a crystal ball in his left hand. What shocked me though was how similar it was to the stained glass window titled Salvatore Mundi at Montsaunes. This of course then also made it very similar to the Da Vinci painting of that name. In addition to that, with the angle I was looking at it, the Sun was shining right through the circular section of glass that was representing the crystal ball. The result was that it was lit up so that the circular piece of glass looked as though the Sun itself was being held by Jesus.

It was obviously highly symbolic, but also very weird and very puzzling. I needed time to let it all sink in. Having spent a few moments there, I decided to go back to the hotel and freshen up before heading out for the evening light show. As I walked toward the exit I came nearer to the labyrinth again. It seemed to be drawing me toward the centre again. I stopped in the same alcove I'd been in earlier. Not being sure what to do this time, I just felt gratitude towards everyone and gratitude for being there.

When I had done that I asked to be guided to find my path and for whatever I needed to be able to do that. The power of the place was still there and even without meditating, my hands and feet were tingling. A voice in my head told me to move on. I did.

Once I was outside again my left brain stopped me. Was I going mad? I was now responding to hearing voices in my head! Ones too that didn't even sound as though they were mine either. I didn't know what to think.

My left brain had almost given up on me. It was a kind of day when it just had to be patient and wait for more information to work on.

It was nearly 2.30pm when I got back to my hotel room. On the way back I'd checked the map and found there was a river just south of the city centre with a footpath running along it. It was perfect for an out and back run.

I slipped into my running gear and ran along the main ring road and down the hill to the bridge. The path there soon took me through the beautiful parks and woods that were found along the river bank. On the way back I could see cathedral in the distance. It could now be clearly seen as being on the top of a small hill and, perhaps because of that, it seemed even more attractive when viewed from further away.

Instead of running back along the ring road, I ran up through the narrow 'pedestrian only' streets towards the Cathedral. On a couple of occasions I nearly stopped to nip into the shops. There was just so much more to Chartres than just the Cathedral. The city itself was a real nugget that no one seemed to be talking about. It was though the energy from the Cathedral had been streaming out for years making the whole city a peaceful, enjoyable place to both live in and visit. It made me want to get back, shower quickly and get out and explore it some more.

By 6.00pm I was exhausted and now hungry. I walked all around the centre, been into several shops and had completely fallen in love with the place. It was time to head back though. Not far from my hotel I'd noticed that there was a rather quaint Pizza place on the corner of Place Chatelet. It was called La Passacaille. I grabbed a menu and sat down at one of their outdoor tables at the side of the square. With one vegetable pizza and a glass of white wine ordered, I sat back and relaxed. I could perhaps now collect my thoughts on everything that had happened recently.

I decided to start with Le Droit Humain. Could I learn anything from Gabrielle's description of it all? What I liked about it was the support network it provided everyone. Likeminded people discussing their own spiritual journey had its up sides. I was not sure it was for me though. Having 33 levels seem a very rigid structure. It also felt very goal orientated where it seemed that one level had to be completed before you could go on to the next one. This could easily favour those at the top of some lodges where dispensing knowledge and wisdom could appear to be controlled or even controlling. Could this factor even hinder the learning progress I wondered?

On the other hand not everyone was free to move around, like I'd been doing. That alone might make it harder for some people to find their own unique path in life. Maybe that too was why Gabrielle wanted to stay in touch with me. We were all at different stages of a journey. Some might take only a short while to progress, whilst others may take a lifetime. Perhaps this extra structure was a better path for some people.

There was one thing that bothered me though. I liked the fact that women and men were working together and I liked it that accepted people from different faiths, the problem for me though, was whether faith was really necessary. Why did everyone have to believe in a single supreme being? The scientist in me just wasn't ready to accept that. Although I was looking for sacred sites, it was not really the right description for them. To me they were more like special sites than sacred sites.

With what the elderly gentleman had said this afternoon, I was beginning to think that maybe the Universe itself did have some way of influencing us. It somehow could make us think and feel things in ways that could be either helpful or unhelpful to us. I knew that order and chaos could be seen as two ends of a spectrum. Had this been turned into some kind of religious good and evil with a God and a Devil by a few 'power hungry', greedy, controlling individuals in our past? I didn't know.

For me, I would stick with just asking for help via my subconscious mind and then exploring any synchronicity that I came across. It had treated me well so far.

There was one other thing that had come up with Gabrielle though. It had also come up again today though. It was this harmony thing. Gabrielle had called it a great secret and that the current thinking was that it was all about maintaining the right balance in life. I could understand the need for balance in life but that wasn't exactly some kind of great secret.

What if this harmony secret had been really referring to something else? Something perhaps that I'd experienced today in the middle of the labyrinth?

My pizza had arrived. Its circular shape had been cut into six equal segments. Each was slightly different and yet together it made a whole pizza. There had been six of us at the centre of the labyrinth each standing in the six Templar laid alcoves. Had all our differences somehow made us a whole for the time we were there together?

The 'harmony' word was also a much more 'sound based' word. If these serpent or dragon energies and song lines were some kind of sound, maybe it was a combination of sounds that constantly changed? Maybe they were coming into some kind of sound harmony four times of the year at the end of the Sun's cycle just as the elderly gentleman had said? Did the Grail shapes then represent a changing form of harmonic sound? Could it be that this harmonic sound was actually vibrating and resonating with the cells in our bodies?

With the right frequencies, perhaps could this be an effect that was really very healthy for us? Maybe this was the secret. Again I just felt I had too many questions. Maybe it was all connected to the sounds of the Universe as the elderly gentlemen had almost knowingly suggested. I really needed to search to see if there were any scientific papers on these things.

I finished eating and went back to my room to rest. It wasn't until around ten that it would be dark enough for the light shows to start.

That afternoon, as I'd been walking though the city, I'd noticed tall rectangular metal structures about 12 feet high on the sides of some of the streets. At the time, I had no idea what they were there for. Now though, it had all become obvious. These were the light show tower sources. It wasn't just about the Cathedral. The walls of over 20 buildings around the city centre had been lit up with all sorts of repeating sound and light programs. There were even old black and white comedy movies displayed on one wall and all sorts of changing shapes and designs on others.

I was just one of thousands of people all moving around from one show to another watching in awe. I made my way towards to Cathedral and stood in silence with the numbers of people growing. We all stood and faced the main entrance waiting for the next show to start.

Classical music, opera singing, peaceful modern synthesizer music, organ ensembles each followed one after the other as the story of Chartres cathedral was projected with lighting that covered the whole of the front of the Cathedral and up each of its two towers. This wasn't just light though. This was computerized animation with images and moving graphic designs. It was absolutely mesmerizing. The Templars themselves would have surely loved seeing it. It was an uplifting, inspiring and almost an enlightening experience in itself. Every one of us was just looking up with our mouths open.

In the short periods of darkness between each of the different sets, strangers next to each would just start talking to one another about it all. It actually made you feel closer to everyone around you who was sharing it with you.

As it ended, I saw the young lady who'd been with me in the labyrinth earlier in the day. She was about four meters away with some friends. She looked up and straight at me and then smiled. I smiled back. It was as though we had developed some kind of special unspoken connection. I was about to move over to say hello, when she left her friends and came towards me.

"We should be friends." she said in an American accent as she came up to me and gave me a big hug.

"I think we already are" I replied hugging her back. We stood back and she took my hand and led me back to her friends. Her name was Tania and she was from Florida.

After some further introductions, we stood and chatted. She was with a group of travelling dancers that spent the summer doing shows all around Europe. She too had just joined in the group meditation a few minutes before me. The Athlete guy had then joined a few seconds after her.

I explained that I'd spoken to the English gentleman afterwards and that he'd told me that these sorts of gatherings were growing in numbers. It was all about being on a sacred site the day before the solstices and equinoxes. She'd liked the idea a lot and said she'd tell her friends to do the same.

It was getting late so we exchanged social media contacts and left. It wasn't about needing to meet up again, it was just a 'knowing' that we had become part of something both important and special. I think we both knew that we would be communicating more in the future.

I looked back at the Cathedral as the train pulled out of Chartres. Yet another place in France held my heart. I took out my phone and turned to my note pad page and added a few new things to mull over.

Crystal ball / Sun connection / Light & Sound connection
Sounds of the Universe – check scientific papers

Sun cycles
Ouroboros, Lung Mei, Dragon lines
Times of harmony
Six people six alcoves
Knights Templar connection to the Sun.

I'd caught the 9.35am train which would arrive in Gare Montparnasse by 10.50am. That would leave time for me to catch the 11.50 train to Toulouse. I could then change trains again and be back in Tarascon by 6.20pm. I texted the guys. They got back saying they were looking forward to hearing all about my time up here.

I was on the top deck of the TGV again drinking some tea when I got a text from Gaston. He asked if I could meet his team in the centre of St. Martory village at the bridge at midday on Friday. I texted back that I'd be there and thanked him for the money transfer.

I then texted Bernard to say we would need to leave around 9.00am in the morning. We would then be there early enough for just the two of us to go up to the cave first and then to go back down and meet Gaston's team at the bridge afterwards.

They guys met me at the station and I spent most of the evening going over everything that happened in Paris and Chartres. Brian had heard from Albert too. He'd also been given the full translation as well and they'd chatted about it. Albert had also come up with some possible places to look in Spain for the place of miracles. By 11.00pm it had become too late for us to talk anymore about it.

St Martory

On Friday morning Bernard met me at 9.00am at the Aldi car park. He insisted on driving me. I'd also brought the two pieces of haematite and placed them in the boot of his car, just in case the third piece was being brought along. I slipped three C.D.'s into my bag. He could have a choice, Katy Perry, Beyonce or Lady Gaga. I was surprised. I had him down for Katy Perry fan but he went for Lady Gaga.

It felt great to be driven around by a man again and it was fun with him from the start. So much so, that my mind went back to wondering if he really was gay or not. I slowly began to learn more about him. He was just a year older than me and lived with his mother and sister in Ussat.

He'd worked at the Lombrives cave for many years in the summer season. In the winter he was a part time ski guide. His sister was not well though and had some rare chronic problem which kept her indoors all the time. She also couldn't move without lots of pain.

This meant that either he or his mother always had to be in the house with her. His mother was a teacher in a local school so when she was working, he had to stay at home and vice versa. Today though, he'd managed to find a friend of his sisters to look after her. I'd asked about his aspirations for the future but he'd replied that, with the current situation, he couldn't think that far forward. He was studying languages at home though. He already spoke good Spanish, English and Italian. His passion was for Caving and Skiing. I then asked about past girlfriends. There was a pause and I began to wonder what he was going to say next.

"You know Rowena," He began, "I am sorry to say, I've had none. If I am to be honest with you, you are the first woman I have spent time with for many years. I find you interesting……passionate, fun…… I like you a lot….." he paused in a way that I knew he had more to say.

I thought that perhaps he was now about to tell me that he was gay. I was wrong though.

251

"…..The trouble is whether its girls, women or guys even, I just find that there's just some limit to what I can feel. I can like them….. I can even dislike them…… but never enough to either love or hate anyone." He paused, "I never seem to feel anything more than just a 'like'. I'm not even sure I know what love is."

My heart went out to him as I wondered why this might be the case. I turned the sound down on Lady Gaga. "I………" I started but then changed my mind, "Thank you for sharing that with me. It means a lot." Something was wrong, maybe something had happened to him in the past but it wasn't right for me to question him on it. It would have to come from him so I changed the subject.

"How is your Mother finding things with all she has to do with her work and with helping your sister?"

"It is hard for her. Especially since my father left us some time ago." He replied. I waited patiently whilst he thought about what he was going to say next. "He had a really hard time with it all. I don't think he could cope with all the family problems. It affected his work and after a while he lost his job." He paused again, this time for longer. "He left us three years ago…….. The police found him a few days later in his car at the bottom of a cliff…….. He was dead."

I couldn't say anything for a moment. I really felt his pain at that point. "I'm so sorry to hear that." I said touching his arm. After a few moments silence he spoke again.

"I don't think we were ever really close. He rarely even spoke to me. I never disliked him but I cannot say I ever really liked him. I know I didn't feel any love for him." I stayed silent hoping he might want to speak some more. "I think I find it hard now……you know….. to love…… or to feel love Rowena…….. Thank you though for wanting to share your time with me. It lifts me…. You lift me….." he started again. "….as for anything else,

I have nothing. I am not even sure I will either……. I'm sorry." He shuffled in his seat, sat up straight and continued to drive.

About 30 secs later he spoke again. "I can share with you my passion for caving though, if you would like that?" He'd changed his tone back to how it was before. It was as though he switched off something deep inside him.

"Do you know you are the first woman to show me a cave?" He looked over now smiling at me again. He then reached over and turned the sound back up on Lady Gaga. I knew then that the subject was closed for the time being.

We parked up at 10.30am exactly where I'd parked my Mini only a few days ago. I was wearing the same outfit as I'd had on then too. Walking past the Montsaunes Cavern entrance I pointed it out to Bernard. He said he would call Arnaud sometime and see if he wanted to come over one day and explore it with him. Minutes later we were pushing through the undergrowth and crawling past the old tree stump and into the cave.

"C'est merveilleux" he whispered. We shone our torches around the walls at all the animal drawings and the dove symbol. I then reached up to where I'd hidden the scrolls. They were still there. I breathed a sigh of relief. I brought one down and showed it to Bernard then replaced it. Turning back around we stood face to face with only a few inches between us.

I shone my torch up between us. The shadows on our faces made us look like two ghouls. It made him laugh. I felt like I wanted to put my arms around him and give him a hug so I did. His laugh stopped. I clicked off my torch. He did the same and we stood still there in darkness. I slowly felt his arms move around to my back and then felt the warmth of light hug back. I could smell the earthiness of the cave mixed with a light sensual odour coming from the side of his neck.

We stayed like that for about twenty seconds when he started to release his hands. I did the same. "Come, we must go." I said quickly and in a positive way. "You first this time." I needed to lighten the mood. It had been a nice hug but it had not ended in the way I'd hoped. I guessed he was just not yet ready for anything more.

Outside I could see that his enthusiasm had returned as he remembered all that was in there. "Rowena, I thought I'd shown you a small cave, but that was even smaller. What a find though. Your name will go down in the books for finding that one you know."

"What books?" I asked as we walked briskly back down to his car. He laughed and didn't answer. Once there, I quickly checked my face with my pocket mirror. Phew. No smudge marks this time.

At 12.00 midday we stood on the bridge over the Garonne river in the middle of St Martory at the other end from the arch that spanned over the road. A tall French man approached us from the far end of the bridge. He walked across favouring his right leg. It was hardly noticeable but it looked as though he was doing his best to disguise it. He was wearing a clean set of overalls that seemed to be covering a dark suit underneath. Behind him were two men in dark blue working overalls. They were wearing hard hats.

"Good morning. Rowena?" I nodded. He reached out his hand to shake mine, "My name is Dr. Hugo Benoite. I am a colleague of Gaston LeMaitre. I am so very pleased to meet you. I feel we have much in common, of which I will explain more about later." He then held out his hand and introduced himself to Bernard. Bernard replied in French and said he was just a friend of mine.

"Shall we follow you?" Hugo suggested. We agreed and in no time two cars and a van were parked up and we were all heading up the hill to the cave.

"Ah I can see the old tree stump here and how it hid the entrance. Amazing." said Hugo. "It could have been hidden for over 250 years."

"It may be best I take you in first" I said to him. "When we come out, the other two can come in. It is quite small."

"Fine. Do lead on." He replied. Inside he shone a very powerful two feet long torch around the cave. It almost completely lit the place up.

"Incroyable….Mon dieu…." He kept repeating to himself as his torch skirted around the floor of the cave, the walls and the ceiling.

"The two scrolls are up there" I pointed to the small ledge above the entrance.

"Incroyable." He whispered again. From out of his pocket he pulled out two white gloves. Having put them both on, he then reached up and took them both down one by one. He held them as though they were about to disintegrate. "I am going to take these outside now, will you come?" He asked.

"Yes of course." We left with me leading the way. He crawled out slowly behind me cradling both scrolls in his right hand whilst resting his weight on the back of his wrist. Once outside, he stood up and gave the other two some instructions. One of them had a camera, the other had some sampling tools and containers.

"They will be here for a few hours." He said to Bernard and I. "Come let's leave them to their work and go back down."

Once back at his car, Dr Beniote opened the boot and brought out a security case which he proceeded to open. He then carefully placed the two scrolls inside two silk bags and then settled them both down in the case with some bubble wrap so they wouldn't move. He then locked it and placed it back in the boot.

He then turned to us said. "I suggest we go somewhere we can talk and get something to eat."

"I know a lovely hotel near here." I suggested. "I stayed there before."

"Wonderful. Please do lead the way." He replied.

Amelie was overjoyed to see me again and even Antoine got up and came over to us all. Whilst some French onion soup was being prepared, Dr Benoite began to talk. "I have to tell you that I don't often get out into the field anymore but I just couldn't resist it this time. You see it's not just about the scrolls but also about the stone of the Cathars which was mentioned in them. As Gaston may have told you, I have had a theory for many years now that it was divided into four pieces and hidden. Imagine my delight when I heard you had the same idea and you thought you had two of the pieces."

"I was just as surprised when I heard that a third piece had been found. But please tell me, did you bring your piece along today?" I asked.

"Yes, did you bring yours?" he replied. I nodded.

"I suggest we get them and bring them back here." I said.

We each went back to the cars and came back with a bag each and placed them on the wooden table outside the hotel. We both opened our bags at the same time and I placed my two pieces together on the table so they fitted perfectly. Dr Benoite brought his piece closer turning it around as he saw how my two were joined. As he brought it closer we could all see how similar they looked. With only centimeters to go, we knew it would match. Antoine and Amelie were now looking on from behind and even they gasped as the three pieces came together.

We all fell silent until Dr. Benoite spoke. "Well Rowena, you really have made my day and indeed my year. Thank you" Bernard started clapping and soon everyone was but me. I didn't know where to look.

"A celebration, I think. Amelie. Go and fetch some champagne and some glasses." said Antoine.

Soon we were all toasting each other. Hugo and I were soon relating to the others the stories about how the three pieces of stone were found by us both and by my father.

The soup arrived and we settled down around the table. Dr Benoite had explained how he'd found his piece in a cave at Rennes Le Chateau. I'd asked him if there'd been a symbol of a dove in the cave. There had been. He then explained where I could find the cave. The conversation then turned to where the 4th piece might be. All thought of the scrolls and the cave we had just been in had gone for the moment.

After a while Dr Benoite held his hand up and we all fell quiet. "The unfortunate thing for me Rowena," Dr Benoite began, "is that I cannot be seen to investigate in Spain. The proper channels must be gone through. Permits obtained for each area I wanted to go. It could take years even if we knew where to look. If the stone was found, and it could be proved it was the 4th part, the paperwork would be possible and it would be quite quick." He paused and looked at me. "What we would need is for someone to perhaps initially look there for us. Perhaps even to just find the 'place of miracles'." He looked away and continued. "Of course, we could not be seen to be financing this sort of venture either and even if we were in some way, it could not be indefinite." He again looked back at me.

"That would be problem. I can see that." I answered, getting the picture. "Something like that could take several weeks, just to check out a few likely sites and to look around. Even then the 4th part may not be found." I ended.

257

"But if there was someone who could use their rather unusual skills and techniques at finding things," Dr Benoite added, "it may be worth investing something towards that venture, if we knew however that, if the 4th piece was found, the whole stone would automatically become French property."

"I suppose that would only be appropriate given it would be the holy stone of the Cathars, but the investment would need to be appropriate and, if paid in advance, it could be made to look like payment for other services previously given and deservedly rewarded." I replied.

"I think we could perhaps discuss the finer points after dinner, what do you think?" Dr Benoite suggested.

"That would be lovely." I replied.

The French onion soup had arrived in bowls for us all. A basket filled with small baguettes was then placed in the middle of the table.

Lunch had been most enjoyable and, with Hugo's help and permission, I'd brought Antoine and Amelie up to speed with the full translation of the scrolls. The location of the cave though had to be left unannounced for a while longer until all the research work had been done.

Dr Benoite and I then had a short walk together down to the river bank. He offered to pay me an advance of 5000 Euros which was technically payment for services rendered in finding the two scrolls. He also told me that he'd had permission to give me the same amount again if the 4th part of the stone was found. I pointed out though that with the 4th part, the stone was that much more valuable to everyone. I also mentioned that two weeks in Spain was no time at all and that I needed at least a month. That could cost me 5000 euros alone in time and expenses with hotels bills and other things. He had to agree with that and we finally agreed on an advance of 10,000 Euros with 10,000 extra on completion. What was now on my mind was that this left almost enough to help fund me through the rest of my PhD.

Dr Benoite had also agreed that I could take my two pieces with me so I could check any haematite samples I might find. What he required from me though was that, if I found it, I needed to make sure I could prove where I'd found it. This was necessary in order to help fully prove a 'provenance' to the whole stone. Everything also had to be done by the book, if the 4th part was found and if any Spanish authorities were involved.

One last point he'd agreed to was that I would be accredited with the find and my expenses would be covered to bring me over to any celebratory ceremonies that might occur when it went public. I just liked the idea of a few more days in Paris and perhaps some down here at their expense.

It was 3.00pm by the time Bernard and I headed back. I'd relented on the music after all it was his car, so the Eagles had now joined us. Not my usual choice in music but still OK. He must have got the taste for them from his Grandparents or someone that age.

As we headed South down the D117, an idea popped into my mind. I could get the keys to the Saint Christophe de Templier chapel again in Montsaunes. Bernard would enjoy that and it would give me a chance to test an idea I'd had. We drove round to the Marie to pick up the keys and then back round to the chapel. The chapel sat there on the side of the road looking innocent, as though it had nothing to hide. It was clearly guilty though.

With all the time I'd spent looking at my photos, the inside had become quite familiar to me. I showed Bernard around pointing out the various things that I'd found of interest. It was not really his cup of tea but I think he enjoyed it all the same.

It was now time for me to try some sound tests with some meditation. I wanted to see if this place gave me any similar effects to those that I'd felt at the Lombrives Cave and at Chartres on the labyrinth. I went and stood first in front of the altar. I breathed in and out slowly waiting to sense any feelings that might arise. After a few minutes I'd felt a slight tingling in my fingers.

I tried again but this time I hummed beginning with a low hum and then slowly rising up the frequencies. As I did this I tried to feel for anything different. At nearly the top of my vocal range, I switched to singing an 'Ahh' vowel sound. The sensation began. I kept singing the sound at that frequency and the tingling in my fingers began to spread up my arms. It seemed I had to find the right frequency in order for it to work.

I stopped and went outside the chapel and tried again by the car. Bernard followed, bemused by my activities. This time I had no feeling at all. I went back inside again and did the test once more again just inside the doorway – hardly anything.

I then went half way down the chapel main aisle. This time I felt the tingling rising again. I finally went back to the altar and now chanted at the same frequency but this time much louder. The echo around the interior was different. I looked up to find this part of the chapel had a curved ceiling like I was under a half dome. Maybe some spherical resonance was coming into play, I didn't know.

What I'd discovered though was that sound was making me feel different depending on where I stood. I had even discovered the most sensitive place in the chapel with regards to the sound. If the Templars had built a Labyrinth here, the middle of it would have been right in front of the altar. There was clearly not enough space for one though.

Bernard by this time had thought I'd gone slightly mad. I got him to try standing in front of the altar. He felt nothing. I hummed the same sound again. He remained silent as though wondering what to say. I hummed again and his lips curled into a smile.

"Does that feel good?" I asked.

"Something feels Ok" he replied.

"Where is that feeling? I asked.

"In my stomach. It tickles. But when you sing, it tickles more. Why is that?"

"I am not sure yet Bernard. All I know is that it is good you feel what you feel. Something is happening."

"Try it by the entrance." I suggested. We moved over there – he felt nothing. Having done that, we went back to the car and drove round to return the key. The tests on their own meant nothing scientifically but it did give me some ideas for further scientific testing with sound generators. It also gave me a quick way to determine whether I was on a sacred site or not and if I was on a sound line or not. That alone could be invaluable to me down in Spain.

Part 4

Down into Spain

Bernard and I had talked all the way back in the car but what had briefly happened between us in the cave was left unspoken. I was slightly sad about that but could do nothing about it for the moment. Given time, things may be different but he obviously had some issues to deal with still. I'd told him I'd like to see him again when I was coming back from Spain. He'd said that he'd look forward to it. I thought I'd noticed that his eyes had lit up a bit with my suggestion. Perhaps he was beginning to more than just like me.

Pierre and Brian had been great and we'd talked about all sorts of places I could try investigating in Spain. In the end I'd set three targets and a possible fourth. I'd spent the weekend with them doing some trip planning and also keeping in touch with everyone. My Otto Rahn books had arrived so now I also had something else to get my teeth into.

It was now early Monday morning, the Sun was shining and I was driving South on the N20 towards the Spanish border in the Pyrénées. My bank account had also never looked so good. In fact, everything was looking good and now I had Katy Perry for company. I'd decided to spend a maximum of two weeks looking at the target sights. If I'd nothing to go on, or to follow up on, after that, I'd head back and do what I could with the money I had left. Even if I didn't find the 4th piece of the stone, which I thought was fairly unlikely, I could still try and do some sound sensation tests at the target sites to see if I could learn anything more from that.

What I also really wanted to do was to enjoy it all more like a holiday. If I could do that and still be 'going with the flow' I'd be more than happy. If that then took me back to my PhD at University great, if not, that would be great too. One strategy I had for the target sites was to try and connect with the local people there. I also wanted to check any nearby caves for any dove symbols and to try and find out if the each site was known for any miracles back in the early 13th Century.

My ultimate aim though was to build a plan for my future research into areas that might have good healthy sound vibrations. The thought had also crossed my mind that the opposite might be important too. This meant that I should be looking out for regions that may display more negative signs that were down to unhealthy sound vibrations. If either of these could be established, my thinking was that it would generate huge interest in people and organisations wanting to know where these areas were. The example that sprang to mind was Aliya looking for a favourable place to site her own yoga studio.

Montserrat

I was now heading for Montserrat and the Santa Maria monastery. It was not far inland from Barcelona. It was not at the top of my list for the most likely place to find the 4th piece but it had some nearby caves. There was also a loose connection to Wolfram von Eschenback's Parzival story and more modern miracles were said to have occurred there.

The downside was that there was no clear evidence of the role the Knights Templars might have once played there. In Parzival, Wolfram had mentioned a place called Montsalvache where the Grail could be found. There were two main candidates for where this was. One was Montsegur; the other was Montserrat. Some people clearly thought Montserrat was where the Grail had once been and, because of that, I had to consider that it might have been down to a piece of the Cathar stone.

There was also a cave there called Santa Cova. In an old piece of writing, dated at 1239AD, it was said that back in the year 888AD some children had seen a great light fall from the sky. A little later on a beautiful song was heard coming from the mountain. This sound was said to have occurred there every week for four weeks. During these occasions a vision of the holy virgin Mary was also said to have been seen in the cave. This grotto could now be found in the chapel of the holy grotto which was now part of a 17th century Benedictine monastery complex.

In 1657 there was also talk of a miracle happening for a little girl at this monastery. Montserrat therefore had a history of miracles and that made it a possible candidate for being 'The place of miracles'. Aside from looking at the cave another thing I wanted to experience was the Vespers boys choir that sang in the monastery at 1.00pm every day. After the experience I'd had at the Lombrives Cave, I wanted to see if their singing affected me in any similar way.

At 12.10am after midday I arrived at the cable car station at the bottom of the limestone peaked mountain range. I got on and went up to the monastery where there was a small funicular railway that could take me a short distance back down the mountain to get a bit closer to the cave. The plan was to listen to the choir first and then go down the funicular to the cave.

The Basilica, where the boys choir sang, was really a large, wide arched, high ceilinged chapel. This one though had been expensively decorated throughout. It looked as though a lot of gold had been used. Not exactly an example of piety and humility from the church.

The boys singing had been beautiful and very touching but not in any 'cell-tingling' way at all. The notes just didn't resonate with my body at all. I left before the end to go down to the cave. The steep angle of the funicular made the train seem as though it was clinging on to the side of the mountain as it descended. It was safe, but it didn't look it. Once out, I had to follow a single path around the side of the mountain to get to the cave. On my left was a steep drop hundreds of feet down, on my right was pretty much a cliff face hundreds of feet high. It literally took my breath away and I was glad of the safety railings.

Passing through an enclosed cloistered area, I stepped into the small chapel of the Holy Grotto. I was alone apart from someone lighting a candle. It was one of many on a candle stand in the middle of the room. At the far end there was a bare rock face which was actually the back of the original cave. All that was there now was a petite reproduction statue of the Virgin Mary. There were no dove symbols and certainly no lumps of haematite. I thought for a moment and decided to meditate a little.

I almost immediately felt something. Not much but a tiny tingle in my fingers. I started to hum, the feeling began to build. "No hay sonido aquí." An angry voice hissed at me. The tone tore me abruptly back to my senses. Looking about I saw this black gowned man looking directly at me. I had no idea what he'd said but figured he made some kind of mistake and that I was someone else. I went back to what I was doing and started humming again.

"No hay sonido aquí." This time the man had walked towards me and had reached out to grab my arm. I batted it away before he touched me.

"Debes salir de aquí. No hay sonido aquí!" He now said even more menacingly. What was his problem?

"I am English. What are you doing? What are you saying" He tried to grab me again. This time I struck his arm out of the way with my right hand and started to back away from him. It seemed to anger him more. I had to get away from this. This was crazy. I backed towards the door. He stopped coming after me when he realized I was leaving. I turned and moved quickly through the door and the cloisters and out onto the narrow path outside. I continued on quickly for about another 10 meters before slowing down to a more casual walk. What on earth had just occurred?

All I'd been doing was humming. There surely can't have been a problem with that and, even if there was, what kind of reaction to it was that? I walked on with a feeling of growing anger and indignation building inside me. He'd no right to try and grab me like that either. That was totally wrong.

I would report him when I got back up to the main part of the monastery. 'Report what?' I thought a few moments later. It would be his word against mine and why would they be concerned about what I thought. The more I thought about it, the more annoyed I became. They obviously had some kind of rule there about having to be silent in the cave. But why? Had his reaction occurred just because I had hummed? Did they perhaps know about the effect of the place? Is that possibly why they made the rule in the first place? Perhaps they didn't want anyone to find out about the special effect that the place could have on a person?

It then dawned on me. OMG. What if some people high up in the church knew about the power of real sacred locations? The last thing they would want is for people to know about that. There were probably loads of churches all around the World that were not in sacred places. That would be disastrous for them. It would give all the power back to the people. It meant it wasn't about the church at all, it was about the location.

I had a problem. If my research proved successful, not everyone was going to like the fact. I could see now what Gaston had been thinking about when he told me in his office that my research might lead to sensitive information.

I reached the funicular. The beautiful views were not on my mind at all. It made me livid to think that religion would try and block the truth, but wasn't that how it had always been throughout the ages. I wasn't in the mood for this place anymore. I went up the funicular and then took the cable car back down to my car. Clearly there was something special going on back at the cave, I'd felt it. If the fourth part of the stone had been there though, it was probably long gone by now or alternatively locked up somewhere and forgotten about. If that was the case, I could kiss goodbye to any further payments from the French ministry of culture.

I'd planned to stay at a B&B near Montserrat. Instead I decided to save some time and go straight on to Monzon. It was only a couple of hours drive so I'd be there by 5.00pm. I calmed myself down a bit and then rang the hotel there and changed my booking to include tonight as well.

Monzon was my second most likely target place and the one I had a lot of hope for. It had a Bronze Age background and had been inhabited by the Romans and the Moors in the past. What was mainly drawing me there though was a large Knights Templar fort on top of a high hill that overlooked the whole area.

Nearby to it was the Ermita de la Alegría which was also called the Shrine of Joy. Apparently some modern day miracles had been witnessed there. The trouble was I'd not come across any reports online of any mediaeval miracles. This was one thing I wanted to check somehow. The other was the dates the Moors and Templars had been there.

Monzon

Driving to Monzon I dropped off Lady Gaga and picked up Beyonce for company along the way. She perked me up considerably as we crossed the relatively flat landscape of Northern Spain heading West.

About a kilometre out I could see the huge walls of the fort towering above the road I was on. It had been built on top of a large rock formation with cliffs on three sides. It was an impressive site and one that looked as though it could have never fallen to any enemies. I would be visiting it in the morning. For now though, I was heading for the Hotel MasMonzon, its gym and its spa.

It was a modern, minimalist looking building which had a white and grey theme going on, with the emphasis on the white. The overall clean look to it was just what I needed after a long day on the road and my trip up the mountain at Montserrat. I headed up to my room, changed and then headed down to the gym. It was small but I was lucky, it was empty. After a 30 min CV session with some light weight circuits, I headed for the sauna. There was a young Spanish couple in there. I said 'Hi' and introduced myself but they didn't speak any English at all.

Dinner in the restaurant was also uneventful and without conversation again. I was probably the only English speaking person in the Hotel and possibly the whole of the town. With no one to chat to I headed up to my room to start reading Otto Rahn's book 'Crusade against the Grail'. The only highlight so far was the Castillo de Monzon which I could see out of my window.

It had been all lit up by a series of spotlights that had been placed along the bottom of its walls. A yellow light now fell on the Castle stone and the rock it stood upon. With the black night sky above it and the dark rock face down below, it looked as though the whole castle had been suspended high in the air as it looked down over the town. It's almost magical night time setting made me think that tomorrow would surely be a better day.

After a light continental breakfast, I waited for a small minibus outside the front entrance of the hotel. There were five of us that had booked up for a guided tour of the Castle. The others were two Spanish couples in their sixties. They were very pleasant and smiled at me a lot. In their minds though I could tell they were wondering what on Earth I was doing there on my own in the middle of the week.

My earlier luck in France didn't seem to be holding down here in Spain unfortunately. The guide, the minibus driver, spoke almost no English. I nipped back inside the hotel and picked up an English brochure I'd seen earlier on in the reception area.

The minibus took us nearly the whole way up. Even at that height there were already great panoramic views over the town and countryside. The rest of the way was up a sloping walkway with a rounded cobblestone surface. Although it sloped upwards there was an occasional small step every few meters. To get to the inner courtyard at the top we had to go through the base of the James 1st tower. Coming out through that and onto the level ground I could see another tall square tower, a refectory and a chapel. The chapel was now on my right and, as it was that which interested me. I let the others go on ahead.

The first thing that was clearly visible was an old archway in the chapel wall which had been bricked up. It was the top of the arch that had now caught my eye. Around the top there was a collection of Templar symbols. Some were unmistakable but there were a couple that I couldn't recognise at all. The obvious ones were the six petal flower of life symbols. These were also surrounded by two circles which now made them very similar to the castle shapes at Montsaunes. In addition to them there were several circles within circles shapes as well as a four petal and a three petal flower of life.

Much of the masonry had been worn away. Some had even looked as though it had been purposely destroyed. Out of all of it, what most drew my attention was one particular four petal flower of life symbol. This was very similar to one of the changing shapes in the sequence of symbols on the Montsaunes ceiling. The reason why it had caught my eye was that here, it looked very much like the Knights Templar cross.

I fell silent contemplating the huge implications if I was right in what I was thinking. The Templar cross had never meant to represent the crucifix. If you reversed out the image, it wasn't the cross that could now be seen. It was the four white shapes to the sides of the cross. It was a four petal flower of life shape.

When the original group of Knights had formed the Knights Templar at Troyes in Northern France, they'd probably told the Roman Catholic Church that their new 'red cross' logo represented their version of the crucifix. In this way they had got away with hiding the truth in plain sight.

Gabrielle had mentioned to me that there had been an earlier Egyptian cross that represented eternal life. The Templars may have even been thinking of this too when they made the red cross their symbol. It was obviously now a really important sacred shape to them.

If, what I was thinking about the Templar cross was true, it seriously raised up the significance of this particular shape. It also now really confirmed a link between this shape here at Monzon with the four petal shape on the Montsaunes ceiling. If this sequence of shapes on that ceiling had anything to do with the invisible Grail then the Templar cross was actually now a symbol of one of the changing shapes of the Grail itself.

I snapped away with the camera on my mobile, zooming in on some of them so I could analyse them more closely in the future. After that I went inside the chapel to see if I could sense anything. This time I waited until I was alone before I started to hum. There was definitely a strong tingling sensation here but nothing like the feeling I'd felt at the altar in the Montsaunes chapel. I had no answers as to why, but, all in all, it confirmed to me that some kind of deeper connection also existed between the two places. The others in our small group were the far end of the Castle taking photographs. I read the brochure while I waited for them to return.

It seems that between the years 1130AD and 1136AD Monzon had been held by the Christians. They had then lost the town back to the Moors for the period 1136AD to 1141AD. The Templars had finally won it back in 1143AD. This unfortunately now presented a problem for me as the scroll message had clearly said that the place of miracles had been in the hands of the Moors in 1159AD. Monzon couldn't have been the place of miracles. However Thibault and his team may well have passed through here. They may even have stayed a while, but it had not been their final destination. My heart sank a little finding that out. There was no need to look for caves here or search for the stone. I had to move on.

My plan for the afternoon had been to investigate the sacred hermitage a few miles to the South of here. There'd been a history of miracles there that had seemed worth investigating before. I decided to still go though, if only to see if I could feel the same tingling sensation in my fingers.

Having been dropped off back down to the hotel by the minibus, I got in my car and drove straight out to the Ermita de la Alegría. It was a short journey and I found I could park right outside. It too was situated on top of a hill. That it was also on a hill, set my mind to thinking again about high pressure concentrations of sound. Perhaps hills and mountains, situated in relatively flat areas of the land, worked a bit like lightening conductors in reverse when it came to sound. If these sounds were coming out from the interior of the Earth, perhaps their favoured exit path from the Earth was via these areas of high ground. It might perhaps then also explain all the so called sacred mountains around the World.

I'd spent some time online looking for more ideas on how sounds like the mysterious hum might be generated but I'd found nothing. I really needed to find a hypothesis to test if I was going to be able to propose a change to my PhD program. So far I'd been trusting that something would come up but, as of yet, there'd been nothing.

With just a small amount of investigation I'd found out that the hermitage had been built originally in the 17th century. If miracles had occurred there, it had to have been after that. Inside there were images of the Virgin Mary and some stained glass windows. Although it was a lovely peaceful place, I found nothing when it came to meditating and sounding. There was just no tingling sensation in my fingers at all. I was actually quite surprised by that. Due to its proximity to the Castle, I had thought that any low frequency Earth sounds may have linked them. Whatever I was experiencing with regards to some locations, I was no closer at all in figuring it all out.

I spent another night in the hotel without finding anyone to have a conversation with. If it carried on like this, I was not only going to have a very boring time, I was also going to have a problem achieving anything.

With nothing else here in Monzon for me, I figured I had to move on to my next target.

It was a six hour journey to my next destination – a 13th century Catholic church near Segovia which had been built by the Knights Templar. I again had high hopes for this place. It had been my number one target for being the place of miracles. It was 8.00am and I was already back in the car and ready to go. It was going to be a long day so I started off with Amy Winehouse and slipped the CD into the player. Nothing. I pushed the knobs. Damn. The CD had jammed.

I carefully dug around with my nail file and got the disc out. I tried again. This time the tray wouldn't budge. I'd have to use the mp3 player on my mobile with the loudspeaker on. Nothing like as good, but still better than silence.

By 9.00am I'd by-passed the town of Huesca and had just started off down the E7 to Zaragoza when what looked like diversion signs took me off the main autovia and on to the road running alongside it. I guessed it had been the old road before the modern dual carriageway had been built.

The traffic had been pretty clear most of the way so it wasn't going to delay me much. I wasn't in a hurry either so I went back to thinking about the position I was in and what I should do. Things hadn't been going well since I'd arrived in Spain. All I'd found were a few Templar symbols at Monzon Castle and a potential connection with the Montsaunes chapel. Apart from that and the slight tingling sensation, I'd nothing else. This whole Spanish trip could well be becoming a total waste of time and money.

I'd crossed two places off my list and was no nearer in finding what I was looking for. I had to find a different way of tackling this otherwise the same thing might well happen with the last two places. As for the last piece of the Cathar stone, it was looking increasingly unlikely I was going to find it.

On that rather negative thought, out of the corner of my eye, I saw a large black animal flash into my vision. It was headed right in front of my car. I stamped on my brake and braced myself. Thump. No air bag – that was good. Oh God, I hope I haven't killed it or injured it too badly.

I'd only been going about 30 miles an hour when I saw it and had been going nothing like that fast when I hit it. My car had stopped at almost the same time as the bump. I sat there with both my hands gripped to the steering wheel. I looked in the mirror – nothing. Oh no. It must be under the car.

My heart was now beating fast and sweat seemed to have instantly appeared everywhere on me. I opened my door and got out. There was nothing in front of the car. I bent over and looked underneath - nothing there too. I went to look behind it – nothing. I stood upright again and looked right round me pivoting 360 degrees on the spot. The grass verges on the side of the road had some bushes. I walked slowly along the nearside of the road. About three yards away I saw a tuft of black fur and a drop of blood.

Whatever it was, it had to be alive. I strained my ears in case I could hear any signs of an animal in distress – nothing. I must have slowed down enough for it to have just been knocked slightly. It'd probably then just run off. I remembered the noise though. It had been one hell of a thump. I walked back to check the front of my car. There was a new dent in the front. It was clearly visible but it didn't seem to have caused any problems. I could get that sorted out when I got back to the UK. I wondered if my insurance would cover it. No idea. I'd have to read the small print.

Slightly shaken, I got back in my car. I drove slowly in silence for the next few minutes to get my confidence back. All seemed fine so I started to increase my speed. After a while the diversion ended and I was back on the main dual carriageway. I thought back to what had just happened. At the time all I'd been thinking about was myself and now some animal was probably in a great deal of pain and it still might die. I really hoped not. The idea of an animal having a long slow painful death didn't make me feel good at all. All my thoughts had been about me and now I felt awful. There was probably a connection. I couldn't keep focusing on myself and then expect the Universe to help me.

Twenty minutes later an alarm went off. One of the signs on my dashboard turned red. It looked like the radiator. I slowed down and pulled over on to the hard shoulder. As I did the steam started coming through the bonnet. I looked around and realised I was miles from anywhere. It looked safe to get out so I did. I checked my phone for reception. Good, at least one bar. I reached down to my door side pocket and pulled out the car documents and the travel insurance I had. Having glanced through it I found the international breakdown assistance number and rang them.

Someone would be out to me in about 45 mins. Although there were only a few cars on the road, I didn't fancy just sitting in the car with my back to the oncoming traffic. It only needed a half asleep lorry driver to drift off line a couple of feet and they'd hit me. I walked a few yards towards the traffic and half sat on the guard railing on the side of the dual carriageway.

I was in a flat, light brown, area of Spanish countryside with a few dry and pale looking bushes and trees. I reached down into my hand bag and pulled out some factor fifty cream and applied it to my face and arms. I left my legs. They needed all the sun they could get.

Zuera

The breakdown lorry pulled up about an hour later. I'd had more than enough Sun and waiting. A middle aged man in overalls jumped out and came over to me. He spoke little or no English but I was prepared for that this time. Whilst I'd been waiting I'd found and downloaded a 'Spanish to English' and an 'English to Spanish' voice translation app. We each spoke in turn into the microphone. I'd got the male and female voice selection wrong which made us both laugh. It was at least a good start.

He went round to look at the front of my car and then gestured for me to come over. He pointed to a small gash in the grill. After a few more voice translations I'd found out that wild boar are quite common around here and that it was more than likely something like a tusk had got though and punctured the radiator. It was lucky I'd not been going faster. Apparently, wild boar can quite easily survive collisions like this. Their large bulky bodies seem to provide them with enough protection. Cars on the other hand have sometimes had to be written off.

It would need a new radiator though. Just using a sealant would only be very temporary with a hole this size. He could get one ordered today from Zaragoza. It would come tomorrow morning. He could then have it fixed by tomorrow late morning before the siesta. He gave me a rough idea of the price and I asked him to also look at the CD tray to see if that could be fixed too. What he quoted seemed high but manageable financially for me. I nodded for him to go ahead.

He hitched my car up to tow it behind his breakdown recovery truck and I climbed into the passenger seat. The cab was extremely messy. Twenty minutes of Spanish radio music later and we'd pulled into his small garage on the outskirts of a small town called Zuera. It was about 25km North of the city of Zaragoza.

He then kindly gave me a lift into the centre and dropped me off at the entrance to a narrow street. He'd recommended a hotel called Hostal Pensión Aisa several times saying it was 'good value'. I didn't really have much of a choice. I walked pulling my suitcase along what appeared to be one of the main streets in the town. The brick buildings either side of it were about 4-5 stories high. All the windows had thin half-ledge balconies with railings. Occasionally there was a gap where a building had once stood. In these gaps there were either unfinished demolition jobs going on or unfinished buildings. From looking at them, I couldn't tell which.

As I walked, I slowly figured out why the streets were so narrow and the buildings were so high. I'd been walking in a much more welcoming cooler area due to the shade that was nearly always there between the buildings. Up ahead of me was a group of teenage boys who were playing with a football further along the street. As I got nearer to them I noticed that they were just a few yards past the hotel entrance.

"Oye, Senorita. Quieres jugar?" said the tallest boy. I had no idea what he said so I just smiled back and walked towards the entrance of the hotel.

"Por supuesto que ella quiere jugar pero no contigo." said the boy next to the tallest one. The others laughed and the eldest boy seemed to take a swipe at the boy who had just said that.

"Oye, Ven a jugar conmigo." said the smallest boy on the end of the five of them. I was just at the door but out of the corner of my eye I could see he was pretending to take his trousers down. They all started to laugh and I was glad the hotel had not been the other side of them. Whatever they'd been saying, it was fairly obvious to me now that they weren't being pleasant.

The room was basic but clean and it had air conditioning. After the morning I'd just had, it immediately felt like an oasis where I could rest up for a while. It was around midday and now very hot outside. I figured that that was how the young boys had got away with their actions. There was no one around then to stop them. Nothing was open until about 4.00pm because of the siesta. I unpacked, picked up Rahn's book and laid down on the bed to continue to read it.

At about 3.30pm I really needed to stretch my legs so I left the hotel and walked down to the river. Again there was hardly anyone around. As I walked I passed loads of wide open areas next to blocks of apartments. There weren't even many cars around. What I also couldn't see were any offices or industrial zones. The only answer I had was that this place must be some kind of satellite town for commuters going back and forth to Zaragoza every day.

As I walked back along the same path I could now see the river. There were large central islands of dry stones all over the place. There was very little running water. I stopped at a plaza around the corner from the hotel and sat down on a bench under the shade of a small lollipop shaped tree. I called it that because of the thin straight trunk and the perfectly spherical bush of branches at the top. There were several of them sticking up almost unnaturally amidst the stone benches and the grey white gravelly ground. What followed next happened fast and unexpectedly.

One minute I was looking at all the lollipop trees and the next I was surrounded by the same group of teenagers I'd seen earlier outside the hotel. This time though they weren't smiling. The tallest one made a lunge for my hand bag. I grabbed it towards me before he could get his hands on it. I immediately moved to stand up but hands behind me on my shoulders pulled me back down on to the hard stone seat.

I yelled at the tallest one and kicked out in his direction. I missed but he was taken aback a bit by that as though he hadn't expected me to fight back.

I felt a punch to the side of my head. It glanced off me and didn't hurt. It stirred me into more action though.

I spun round to my left where the punch had come from now grabbing my bag against my chest with both hands.

My turn had made the hands on my shoulders come off. I stood up and ran at the tallest boy shouting as I did. Another blow struck me from behind on my shoulder. I could feel that one.

The tall one threw a punch towards my face. I dropped my chin and his fist hit my forehead. I kicked out at his shin wishing I had my boots on and not my trainers. It would still hurt him though.

One of the others behind me must have then stuck his leg out. I fell towards the ground.

Still clutching my bag to my chest, I reached out with one of my hands to break my fall. It did but the force twisted me round and I was now on my back with all four of them around me looking down.

I kicked up and out at them with my two feet and one free arm. My skirt had now unfortunately slipped up around my thighs. I shouted louder furiously kicking my legs backwards and forwards so they couldn't get hold of them.

Someone must hear me. I shouted some more. One of my kicks then hit one of them between the legs and I could hear his groan.

Good. It seemed to stop the others a bit. He was doubled up in pain and the others looked at him not sure what to do next.

I scrambled quickly to my feet and began to run.

I headed towards the gap between the boy who was bent over and the smallest boy next to him. I knocked over the boy who was bent over with his hands shielding his crotch and started to run faster.

I then saw their football on the ground in front of me. I turned and kicked it to the side and on to the road. Maybe that would divert some of them. Hopefully they might chase off after the ball and not me.

I took a quick look behind me. The tallest one was catching up. There was no way I could outsprint him. I ran towards the shops that I knew were around the corner. What I didn't know was if any of them were open yet.

Turning the corner I was now about twenty meters from a café which looked as though it was the only thing that might be open. The tall one was right behind me now. A thought suddenly struck me. He was probably on his own.

If I stopped and confronted him I would be in stronger position, especially this close to the café. I stopped and span round. He almost ran into me trying to stop. I swung my bag at his head but he ducked in time. In doing that though, he'd swerved and ran into the road.

There were no cars but I felt I had an advantage now. I shouted again at him in English "Go Away! Leave me alone!" He looked at me uncertain what to do. His friends had now appeared further down the street and were now looking at the standoff between us.

I walked backwards slowly towards the café looking over my shoulder and keeping my eyes on him all the time.

The owner had now appeared at the door. I turned and ran towards him.

"Do you speak English?" I asked, now gasping for breath.

"A little" he replied.

"I have just been attacked by him," I pointed at the tall boy in the middle of the road who was still looking at me. "…and his buddies down the road there." I turned to point at the others at the corner of the road.

As soon as he saw me pointing at them, the tall boy turned and ran off back to his friends. "They were trying to steal my bag!" I exclaimed now panting.

It was then that I began to realise what had all just happened and my body started to shake. Before, I had just acted instinctively out of self-preservation but now the whole experience was fully dawning on me.

"Sit here, please Senorita." I sat down in the chair he'd pulled out for me. "I know those boys, they are trouble. I will call the police.

"They can sort it out." He bent down and looked at me carefully in the face. "Hmm…. They have hit you a few times it seems. How are you feeling?"

"A bit shaken." I replied. "Angry too." I added. "Why me?" I asked. "What have I done to them?"

"Nothing of course. Come let me get you a nice cup of coffee."

"Thank you. But why did they do this?" I asked again. He walked off to behind the bar.

"They are bored. There is little for them to do around here. They are always up to no good because of that. Every one of us has had problems with them stealing things, breaking things." He said whilst pouring me a cup from a half full cafeteria.

"Can't the police do something, or their parents?" I asked

"They try. But they get no support from the government. They are back on the streets in no time laughing at us. We have learnt to ignore them as best we can." He returned handing me the cup.

"But that is terrible." I said taking it and sipping.

My breathing was less rushed now and my heart beat was going back down again. I checked my bag. Everything seemed to be there, including my phone. Nothing had fallen out. If I'd lost my bag, it would have been a nightmare.

"But that is the World now Senorita." he sat down opposite me.

"I will ring the Policía. Just stay there and drink. They will be here soon."

About five minutes later a Police car pulled up. The owner of the café spoke to them for a few minutes. It all looked very casual as though these sorts of conversations regularly happened. A policeman had got out of his car and was now walking slowly over to me. He looked as though he was in his mid-forties and someone who used to be more athletic but who now had a slight stomach on him. His figure was probably down to a more sedentary family lifestyle. The ring on his thick marriage finger looked as though it wouldn't be able to come off easily either.

"Mateo has told me what happened and I can see you have been hit a few times. We know who they are and we will do what we can. Has anything been taken?" he said in a slightly apologetic manner.

"No." I replied, "They tried to take my bag but I wouldn't let them."

"You are very brave maybe and I hope this never happens to you again but if it does, be careful what you do……. To fight back can make the situation far worse…….. People have died from being stabbed because they fought back." He spoke slowly and carefully with English that showed he must have studied it carefully at some time in his past but hadn't used it in a long time.

"I will be more careful in the future." I replied, "I just reacted without thinking." I said shaking my head.

"I can take a statement and some photos if you wish and I will bring them in for questioning. They are too young though and my hands are tied. I suggest in the meantime you are careful where you go here. May I ask what brings you to this small town?"

I explained about the crash and the radiator. He nodded as I spoke. I also said I would be just staying the one night and be off by midday tomorrow. "If you would like me to take you to a surgery, I can do that, but

I don't think there is much they can really do. You just have a few small cuts and bruises. A good shower or bath would probably be the best thing." He suggested. "If you would like, I will come and pick you up tomorrow and take you to the garage. It will be no trouble." He offered.

"That would be very kind of you." I replied.

"Here just call this number in the morning when you need to go and I will come round. It is as much as I can do to help you for now." He then took out his camera and took a couple of photos of my injuries. I then gave him an account of what happened while he took some notes. After a few minutes we were done and he walked me back to the hotel. I thanked him again and went inside.

Upstairs in my room I undressed and headed for the shower. The sweat and the dirt from the ground had made me sticky, smelly and generally horrible all over. I wanted to wash off all memory of it. I caught a look at my face in the mirror as I entered the bathroom.

OMG. I looked terrible. I had a badly bruised left eye and there were cuts on left cheek and above my right eye. My hair was thick and matted. I hadn't noticed how I looked in the café as I was still running on adrenaline and reliving it all as it was being written down.

I got under the shower and started soaping myself all over. It was then that I discovered even more injuries. Bruises were now showing on my legs and hips where I had been kicked. My left wrist also began to ache which had come from breaking my fall to the ground. I looked and felt awful.

I stayed in the hot spray of water for about twenty minutes and washed my hair twice. By the end of it, I felt much cleaner but also weaker. Emotions had begun to sink in about what had happened and what could have happened. I was now unbelievably tired so I slipped under the bed covers and soon fell asleep.

At 10.00pm I woke up starving. After this afternoon's incident, I didn't fancy walking these narrow streets at night looking for a place to eat so the receptionist at the hotel kindly ordered a take away pizza for me. It arrived 20mins later. It was too late to call anyone so I sat thinking about things while I was eating.

Spain was not going well at all. Aliya had said I would be challenged. Was this what was happening right now? Was I being challenged? If I was, I hadn't expected this. But then again I hadn't been expecting any challenges either. The question on my mind now though was whether I was still on the right path or not. Had I somehow taken a wrong turn? Was I now on a wrong path or was I being challenged and still actually on the right path? I had to conclude it was the latter. I was here in Spain and not back working in that horrible office back in England.

I remembered now that Aliya had also said that I had to lose my ego. That must be it. If I hadn't been continually thinking about myself, I may have noticed the wild boar earlier and avoided hitting it. I wouldn't then have a damaged radiator and I wouldn't then have had to stop in this town to get it fixed. I wouldn't have then been beaten up by a bunch of bored teenagers. I could feel my bruises. I was still sore from it all. I was definitely being challenged to try and lose my ego.

If I kept on thinking about myself, I would keep on being challenged. One of the things that Aliya had also said was that reducing ones ego went hand in hand with reducing ones fears.

It was much easier said than done. I wasn't even sure how the two were connected up.

Was I even ready to look into all my fears? I'd never even asked the question before. How hard could it be? I decided to give it a try. I began to list them on my notes page, starting with the most recent fear.

1. Going outside for a walk in the streets at night and being attacked.

2. Having my bag stolen or losing it.
3. Running out of all my money.
4. Failing to find the 'Place of Miracles'.
5. Failing to find 4th piece of the stone.

Those had all been quite easy. I thought about it some more.

6. Failing to find my path in life & going back to work in the office.

That wouldn't be nice.

7. Failing to find love and a lifelong partner.

Wow. Where did that come from? Was I really afraid of that? I thought about it for a while. Yes I really did want to be with someone I loved. The problem was that I also knew how difficult it was to find someone who was compatible these days. If I thought about it, I was probably frightened about that to some degree. For some reason I then thought of Bernard. If he'd been with me, this wouldn't have happened. No it wasn't easy these days.

8. Being lonely.

Where did that feeling come from as well? Was I really fearful of being lonely? I'd always had friends and made friends easily. I felt sure I'd already conquered this fear but I supposed I could always still feel slightly lonely somewhere and at sometimes. It seemed that the total elimination of fear was nigh on impossible. A small amount of fear was always going to be with me. Perhaps that was how it was meant to be.

I tried to think about it another way. If I had somehow managed to totally get rid of a fear of snakes, I might perhaps think that I could go around picking up poisonous snakes. That would be madness though without the skill and knowledge to do it safely. A little bit of fear here would helpful. I could then proceed with caution. My fear might help also make me want to learn how to pick them up safely in the first place. It then dawned on me that I all I really had to do was to find a way of lowering any fears down to a more logical lower level – a helpful level even. It wasn't about eliminating them altogether. I felt sure I could do that.

I just had to find a way to reduce my more extreme levels of fear. If my challenges were going to become greater in the future; my fears would also become greater. It was a game I could never win unless I could find a way to cope with this. I needed to find a strategy to minimise my fear.

That was it. I could see it now. My fear. My focus was still on me. My ego was still concerned for myself. I could see now why I had my fears. It was because I'd still been focusing on my self. In order to have a minimal or a manageable amount of fear, I had to have a minimal, or manageable amount of ego. If I cared more about others rather than myself, any fears of my own would become minimal. They would then be down to a level that would be helpful to me. This strategy should work for all types of fear I thought.

If I focused on losing my ego, instead of focusing on fighting my fears, I could keep any fears low and under my control. I just had to think of others rather than myself more. It sounded ridiculous but for years I'd thought that the reverse was more likely to be true. In the past it had worked because my challenges had only been small ones. Looking at my old strategy now though, it seemed that this way was going to be virtually impossible if the challenges got bigger. That would only make my fears bigger.

It would have meant that my 'I', or my ego, would have to massively 'grow' in size in order to keep on conquering the bigger challenges. Controlling them would have got harder and harder. In the end they would become so hard that the challenges would be totally unachievable. I could see it now - the bigger the ego, the bigger the fear and the greater need for more control.

I could now also see now where things were going wrong in the World. Politicians and global multinational corporations were all seeking more control over their environment and everyone else. Their leaders tended to all have huge egos. It was no wonder they wanted to put so many controls in place with armies, policemen, surveillance devices, intelligence services. They were all paranoid and full of fear that it might all change and they would lose their power. It was a race that they and everyone else could never win.

The opposite focus was the only way forward. I had to focus and care about others and not myself. We all really had to start focusing and caring about others more. By caring for other people, my own ego would then diminish. I would then have less fear and not feel the need to control everything around me. It would actually help to set me free. Free to find my path in life.

My mind flashed back to the book I'd been recently reading. Was this what Parsival was finding out when he was on his travels? His lack of care for his mother was really down to his own fears and his own ego. This must then have been connected to him only thinking about himself at the beginning of his journey of development as a Knight. His adventures could now also be seen to be ones which were about conquering his own fears. Not being afraid to die in battle was the same as not being afraid of death. As he became more spiritual and he cared more for others, his ego began to go away and in return he became more fear less. Synchronicity was then able to guide him along his path. Was this the key to finding the Grail?

Was the Cathars knowledge of their own immortality and their lack of ego what helped them to not fear death? Was this what then kept them on their path? This was all very well but it was completely different in real life. It would also take time.

My fear now was still very real. I was in no way ready to go outside tonight and walk down the narrow streets – no matter how much I suddenly cared about others. My ego was in no way ready to give up that easily.

Maybe however, if I'd cared enough to stop and talk to the young boys in the street though, instead of allowing my fear to lead me quickly through and into the hotel, I could have made friends with them. If I'd done that, then maybe they wouldn't have wanted to attack me later. We might have even kicked the ball around together.

I was beginning to see how my fear and my ego could lead me into trouble in the first place if I wasn't 'care full'. I could now see that caring more in the present could help avoid future potential trouble and fear.

I made a note that fear was a state that I could never escape but that a small amount represented an opportunity for me to learn to keep my ego in check. With that I went to bed with lots on my mind.

Segovia

I got a call at 9.00am in the morning. It was the garage man telling me the total cost would be 495 Euros. He was checking it was still OK to go ahead. A fear of running out of money began to kick in. I dismissed it by thinking how the money would help the man in the garage and his family. I told him to please go ahead. He said it would all be done by 11.00am.

I still didn't feel up to walking there though. I rang the policeman and he very kindly called for me at the hotel, as he said he would. He then drove me round to the garage. On the way he had apologised again about the incident and hoped that this hadn't put me off Spain and his little town. He was obviously very proud of it and in its own way Zuera really was quite a nice place. I'd said it hadn't put me off, happy that he hadn't asked me that the day before.

I was on the road again by 11.30am and beginning to feel slightly better. Amy Winehouse was now singing to me via my repaired CD player and there was a wide open road ahead of me. In four and a half hours I would be in Segovia. I just hoped I'd have no more problems along the way. The idea of being stranded again worried me a bit but this time I was going to drive with much more focus and attention on others with the aim of trying not to think about myself at all.

I was heading for the Knights Templar church of Vera Cruz just to the North of Segovia. It had been built in 1208AD and the place had been used by the Moors and the Templars. It had got its name because it was said that a fragment of the wooden cross that Jesus had been crucified on had been brought to the site. The story went that a Knights Templar Grandmaster had been captured by the Sultan of Alexandria. The Sultan, who respected the Templars, then invited him to his banquet to celebrate his victory.

By way of offering friendship and in wanting to establish peace, the Sultan offered the Grandmaster any item he wanted from out of his treasury room. The room was filled with jewels, silver and gold and also the piece of the true cross. The Grandmaster chose the piece of the cross.

The Sultan then went over to pick it up. As he did so, he noticed that amongst his new treasure there was a silver Christian communion chalice. He picked that up as well. The Grandmaster then asked the Sultan to put the chalice back down as it was a holy vessel. The Sultan ignored the Grandmaster though and ordered that a refreshing drink be brought to him in it so he could drink from it.

The Grandmaster then suggested to the Sultan that he should touch the piece of the cross with the chalice when it had been filled. The Sultan did so and immediately the drink in the chalice turned to wine. The Sultan was now unable to drink the wine as it was against the Islamic religion. Nonetheless, he was impressed with the miracle.

Unfortunately this happened several times and the Sultan began to think that the Islam religion itself was being mocked by these repeating miracles. He therefore ordered that the Cup should be filled with molten gold and given to the Grandmaster to drink and obviously die.

At that point the story went that three of the Sultan's soldiers came into the room to take the chalice and the piece of the cross away to carry out the Sultan's orders. As soon as they did this though, the three of them, the two objects and the Grandmaster all disappeared.

They all then reappeared in the Church of our Lady in the town of Madruelo. The Knights Templar who had gathered in the church there to pray were astonished that the Grandmaster and the three soldiers had suddenly appeared from out of nowhere holding a piece of the true cross and the chalice.

When the church of the Vera Cruz (the church of the true cross) was built at Segovia, the holy relic of the piece of the cross was kept safe inside it.

For me this place now ticked all the boxes. It was known for its miracles, it was roughly to the South of Montsaunes and the time it was built fitted with the dates in the two scrolls. What I needed to find out was if any there was a good connection between this place and the chapel at Montsaunes. If there was, it might indicate that this was the place of miracles. I also wanted to see if any sound sensations could be felt there.

I'd driven down the E-90 road South from Zaragoza and had later turned right and on to the country roads so that I could come down the N-110 into Segovia. It had been a long journey.

It was 4.30pm by the time I was approaching the outskirts of the city. A road sign that I passed, proudly displayed that it was a World Heritage site. The city had a mediaeval wall surrounding it and a Gothic cathedral at its centre. This towered above all the other building around it. At the North West end there was an old fairy tale style royal palace – the Alcazar. This was surrounded on three sides by natural cliffs and it had clearly been built with defence in mind. The city itself though had been a special place since before the Celtic times. Even the Romans had lived here and there was an old aquaduct of theirs that was still standing today.

I'd booked in to the hotel don Felipe which was not far from the palace. Outside on the narrow streets you could hardly recognise it as a hotel. Inside though, it had been modernised with shiny white marble floors and glass doors. At the back there was a lawned wall garden with tables and chairs. It was just what I needed to relax in after hours of driving.

I checked in to the reception just after 5.00pm. I could visit the Church of the True Cross tomorrow. It was only about a 20min walk away. Having got to my room I started to look at the street map in more detail. The place had some lovely panoramic views and gardens and soon thoughts of relaxing were far from my mind. I wanted to explore. Yesterday was still fresh in my mind though and walking through unknown streets was a concern. I thought about it for a minute and decided that a short run would be better. No one would bother me then and I would be better prepared to just run away too.

With full leggings, running shorts, a top with sleeves and sunglasses, I'd covered all my cuts and bruises and now felt confident enough to venture out. I would stick to running in places where there were plenty of people around. That would be safer as well. I set out first to the gardens in front of the Alcazar. There would be load of people wandering around there. Its dark grey conical turrets strangely made it look very 'Disney-like' and not Spanish at all. The views to the North stretched for many miles and about a mile away and a few hundred feet below me, I could see the small round tower of the Templar church I was heading for the next day.

It stood on its own beside the main road North. I was not going that way now though. Instead I headed out on the top of one of the walls along what was now a flat cobblestoned street. This gently dipped down to the Southern part of the city where I took a left turn and headed towards the aquaduct and the many tourists that were there. It had two stories of arches, with many smaller ones on top of fewer but much longer and higher ones. They supported a gently dipping channel of water, over a hundred feet up that had once flowed into the town over 2000 years ago. It was still an incredible feat of engineering even in today's terms.

I followed the arches for a while as they headed back into the centre of the town. This was also where the cathedral was. One of the things I'd figured out when I'd left the hotel was that if I kept the Cathedral in sight over my left shoulder the whole time, I wouldn't get lost and that would be safer for me too. I had now run up the hill and into a large crowded square with the Cathedral at the far end. Although beautiful in design, it was not that old. It hadn't even been on put up on the site of the original cathedral. Just because of that I ruled it out from looking into it more deeply.

After about 20 minutes, with a few short stops to look at the sites, I was back at the hotel. It was not a long run, but enough for me to feel much better. I could feel my confidence returning. What I was looking forward to now was a shower and then going down to the hotel garden to read the last part of Otto Rahn's book with a chilled glass of white Rioja.

The book 'Crusade against the Grail' was an insightful account of the Cathars, their life and the difficulties they faced from the Roman church and the war that had been launched against them. It highlighted their secret paths, their idea of the Grail and its Middle-Eastern connection and it was easy to see how much Rahn had been inspired by them as well as by the Grail writer Wolfram Von Eschenbach.

What I found particularly interesting were the many references to the caves including two that were next to the Lombrives Cave. One was called the Hermits cave, the other the cave of Fontanet. I would have to ask Bernard if the one he'd taken me to was one of them or not.

There was also an interesting shepherd's story of the stone being hidden in a cave and being guarded by snakes. This included one that was biting its own tail. I'd done some checking on this symbol and found it was called the Ouroboros, the same symbol that the elderly gentleman had spoken about at the café opposite Chartres cathedral. It was said to signify eternity which is what the Cathars believed about life.

For some reason they seemed to think that when they died, their soul continued to live on in the next World. I still couldn't get my scientific mind around how that could happen though.

Of all the wonderful snippets of old folklore from recent and distant past literature, what my right brain found particularly intriguing were two other stories. The first was a fun tale about a dwarf called Gwion. According to the story he guarded a sacred Cup that contained water of regeneration. This water was apparently able to lift the veil from over our eyes so that we could see the mysteries of the World for what they really were.

Although this was just a story, the properties of this Cup now seemed to match the Grail properties that the other, later Grail stories had attached to the Grail. This was yet another example of something that our ancestors seem to consider quite possible. Ordinarily, this should be dismissed but for the fact that now several different people had been trying to associate these similar properties to the concept of the Grail. In addition to that, where these Grail properties were being said to be found, there now appeared to be a possible connection with the lines of sound and where they crossed.

The second story was about a Rose Garden. The Bertrand scroll I had found had also referred to sacred rose gardens as something the Templars had been looking for so I knew there was something significant about them. The story was obviously a metaphor for some secret knowledge but at the moment I was unable to say quite what. The rose connection with the rosy cross was also uppermost in my mind now too. Although these stories hadn't revealed anything to me at the moment, they did seem to spur me on a little into finding out more about these sounds. Who knows what they may be able to actually do and how they may actually help us.

It was Friday morning and I'd had breakfast and checked out of the hotel. I'd also changed my plans overnight. I was going to look at the Templar church this morning and then make a decision as to whether to stay longer here or move on to my last target. I drove down the road next to the Alcazar and then over the bridge above a small river and along and round to the Church. It was 10.30 am when I'd parked up, just the same time as it opened.

I was the first there and I started by walking around the outside of it. What had looked like a round section of the church from a distance was actually a perfect geometric shape made up of twelve straight equal length sides. Either side of the large entrance were two fading circular red Templar Cross symbols. The more I looked at them now, the more my eyes were drawn to the four 'flower of life' like gaps between the arms of the red cross. At the far side there was a tall square tower. I looked hard but could see no other signs or symbols nor any possible places where they might have been. Altogether though, it was a good start.

Going inside what was immediately visible was a central supporting octagonal structure in the middle. It had an arch in four of its eight sides and these arches were opposite each other. They led to a small central area. If any place here was a sacred place, it would be in there. The floor to the church had been made of bricks that had been laid down in a zig zag pattern. In one section of the floor there looked to be several horizontal gravestones. For a place of prayer, I'd never come across something quite like this before.

Why, I wondered, was this building built this way? If twelve sides on the outside was a significant part of the design, then why wouldn't there be twelve sides on the interior central supporting structure. Instead there were only eight. In Chartres, there had been six alcoves at the centre of the labyrinth. The numbers of sides then cannot have been important. But then again I was new to all this. The near circular shape may well be important though, I thought. It may even have been the empty space in the middle that was sacred to these Templars.

Could the round shape even have anything to do with the round castle shape symbols I'd seen on the Montsaunes ceiling? This idea seemed to have been supported by what I'd found out online some days ago. The

Templars had built quite a few round castle shaped places of prayer around Europe.

I looked around the inside some more. Modern wooden benches and chairs had been placed around the outside walls. Each had a more modern Templar cross sign on them. The difference was that these more modern Templar cross symbols all had straight edges. This shape nicely eliminated the petal designs between the arms of the cross Perhaps though this was intentional. In three other places I found the old style crosses with their curved lines. It was the curves that outlined the petal shapes. Each of these three older crosses seemed to have been specifically preserved.

Looking more closely though, I could see that one of the three was part of an old wall painting. A couple of pairs of legs were all that was now left to see. Most of the rest had been lost either due to being covered up by new plasterwork or they had perhaps just degraded over time. The other two old Templar crosses had been surrounded by new plasterwork which made them look as though they were set back into the wall. Who knew what originally lay behind the plaster. It was entirely possible that what was underneath it had been deliberately covered up.

I looked around more and saw that one of the chairs had a modern Chi Rho symbol on the back. It looked nothing like the Chi Rho at Montsaunes. From looking at it all, there was nothing here that really tied it to the Montsaunes chapel. If Thibault and his friends had thought this was the place of miracles, he would have left better signs than this that it was that place. They would also have done so in ways that would have stood the test of time. I now doubted that the Cathar stone had been anywhere near here.

I walked to the centre of the octagonal room and looked around me. No one else had yet entered the church and the attendant who had opened up was standing outside. I started to hum gently and began to lose my thoughts in meditation. My fingers waited expectantly. I raised the level of my humming and went up the frequencies. Still nothing.

After a few minutes I stopped. I hadn't expected to find so little here. I was completely nonplussed by it all. Maybe I was just not doing it all right. Either way, it didn't feel good. Perhaps the place used to be a sacred place and now it wasn't for some reason. Maybe the sound intersection used to be here, but now it wasn't. There was still so much I didn't know and didn't even know how to begin to find out. I took my mobile out to take a few shots of the place and then headed to my car. Inside it, I sat and thought about my next move.

Things really didn't seem to be working out for me in Spain. I was also still feeling quite vulnerable. It was still only just 11.15am in the morning. If I left now, I could be in Luchente by 5.00pm. Was it worth it though? It was a long drive down to the Mediterranean coast and then further on down South past Valencia. Would my car even make it, I wondered. It also meant I'd have a much longer trip back home.

Could I, Should I pack it all in now? Did I have enough to work on? Was there still something I should try and find out? What about following my path? Had I really given it my best shot here in Spain? Did I owe it to myself to keep trying in that regard, especially after everything I'd been through this week already?

If I gave it all up now, it would feel like defeat. No. I had to go on. Somehow I had to change my mindset on everything. I needed to become more positive – like I was in France. I pulled out of the car park and headed for Madrid.

For this longer journey I thought I might try a more eclectic combination of sounds. I hadn't listened to them for a while but I was now looking for a change. Out came Kesha, Carly Rae Jepson & Lana del Rey.

After some tricky navigating around the ring roads of Madrid, I'd found the R4 South East to Albacete. From there I could head East towards the coast. Luchente wasn't far from there.

Luchente, or Llutxent, was an old Roman site. The name meant pillar of light. What was of interest was that it had an old Muslim fort there called Xiu Castle. It also had a Monastery complex with a 13th century hermitage. This was significant to me because of something called the 'miracle of the corporeals' which was said to have occurred there back then.

There was also an old Gothic church that had been there and I wanted to see if there was any evidence of the Templars at that site. They could have either been connected to the Gothic church or the Hermitage or even to the Castle. I was also curious as to why the town got its name pillar of light.

It all sounded hopeful, but then again so had the other places. My mood hadn't improved much yet. The more I thought about this, the more I began to feel something wasn't right. It began to bug me as I couldn't put my finger on it. I turned up Carly Rae. I thought that if I could drown out my thinking an answer might come.

After about 5 mins it worked. I'd set out on this whole Spanish adventure in completely the wrong way. There'd been absolutely no synchronicity. I'd set out with four targets in mind. Admittedly they'd been all logically worked through, but it had not allowed for any natural deviation and discovery. They were all my predetermined goals. I never even allowed anything or anyone to influence that thinking.

Unconsciously I must have been thinking that deviating from my plan would have taken me off my path. If I was going to get anywhere and follow my own special path, I would have to create and look for synchronicity on the way. The more I set rigid goals for myself, the more I could be steering myself off my true path. I started to think back to what I'd found out so far through synchronicity.

I'd been given several signs in France. My path was leading me down into Spain. It should have been about showing gratitude for everything and everyone, staying positive and asking for help with the first question being to ask for signs of synchronicity. I hadn't really done that in Spain properly, but I could do it now.

I started to spend some time thinking about everyone individually in my recent past who had helped me. The policeman, the garage man, the café owner. I thanked them all in my mind and wished them each well. I then thanked each of my friends in the Ariége region and everyone I'd met there who had been so helpful. I even thanked Christian for his music. I then thanked everyone in turn that I'd met in Paris, on the train and in Chartres. It felt good to have remembered them all.

Slowly it began to dawn on me. As I was thanking these people, I realised just how much they'd all influenced me. My life had been permanently changed for the better by them all. Part of my knowledge now had originally been their knowledge. They'd given me their greatest gift. My teachers at school, at University, the writers of all the books I'd read, the researchers over the years who had found some of the big truths in life. We were all benefitting from their time and work.

I continued to thank everyone I could remember who had helped me in the UK. My Uncle, Katy, Aliya, my Dad. I thought about each of them in turn and wished them well. I was nothing without them and all their input.

I was still driving but I happened to look down at the clock. Goodness. I'd been thinking of and thanking people for nearly an hour. Time had flown by. I hadn't finished though. I had to thank everyone.

I continued on by thanking John. If it wasn't for him flirting in the pub I wouldn't have met all these lovely people and come to learn so much about life and the opportunities it could give. He'd also helped me a lot when my father had died. I really wished him well and hoped he'd find happiness and love. I had to admit it felt good to have done that. If I'd been told back then by someone that those kinds of incidents were defining moments that were really going to be positive, I probably wouldn't have believed them.

Having thanked John, I realised I could now thank my ex-supervisor at the dead-end job I'd had. If hadn't been for her too, I might have still tried to make it work back in the UK. I then stepped back further in time. I thanked my Mum. Life was not easy and some people find it harder than others. If it hadn't been for her though, I wouldn't be here. In my early life, she must have done so much for me. I wished her the best whatever she was doing.

The image of the teenagers appeared in my mind. Did I have to thank them too? Of course, but what could I thank them for? They were just kids really and probably highly frustrated in a World that was too ordered and controlling for their young free thinking minds. I was just someone to vent their anger on. They had though made me reflect on my current path in Spain. They'd in fact made me begin to consider if what I was doing, was the right thing. They'd led me to thinking about my fears and my ego and to finding out that I had to care more about others.

In fact, it had been partly down to them that I was now changing the way I was doing things. I took a deep breath and thanked them too and hoped that their lives would get better.

I then thanked Dr Benoite for kindly paying me so many Euro's for finding the scrolls. That would make a huge difference.

At the end I was getting the clear impression that my whole position right now in life was down to almost everyone else. Whether they had known it or not, or had wanted to help me or not, if it hadn't been for all of them, I would have next to nothing. I would know next to nothing and I'd have achieved next to nothing. Without everyone in my past, I was nothing.

It was then that I had the strangest of feelings. It felt that any ego I'd had, had now completely gone. It was a very new sensation and realisation for me. It felt like an 'emptiness' but there was a warmth to it. Maybe this was what it was like to not have an ego. If I wanted to be successful and to find the right path in life for myself, I had to not only lose my ego, but I had to connect with as many people as possible and focus my attention and my energy on them. In addition to that I just had to be positive and ask the Universe to guide me with synchronicity, just as it had in France.

I drove on in silence without thought. It was made easier with the road now not having any vehicles at all in front of me, or behind me, to distract me.

After many minutes driving like this, another thought then popped into my mind. There was absolutely no point in me going to Luchente. If I was supposed to go there, I would be guided there. It was Friday afternoon, the Sun was shining. I would just keep driving and see where I ended up.

It was not long before I saw the road sign for Luchente. If I was to go there, it would need something pretty major to happen and quickly………………….. Nothing.

I continued on along the CV-60. A few miles further on and the road began to turn to the left and head North East to a place called Gandia. The name had a nice Spanish sounding ring to it. The signs to the city centre didn't seem to appeal though so I just kept on driving going straight on ahead at the roundabouts.

Where I couldn't go straight on, I looked left and right and took the direction that felt best. It was crazy. I knew it. I had a rough idea where I was and the direction I was heading, but no idea of where I was going to end up.

It then dawned on me that I was driving in the same way that I'd been taught to follow my path. It was not about the end goal, it was about the journey. It must have been exactly what the Knights had felt when they crossed over the land and journeyed through the forests.

My sense of awareness heightened. I looked everywhere and yet in no one place. I could hear everything and yet no one thing.

Gandia

I was now entering a port area and crossing over a wide river. White apartment blocks with red tile roofs could be seen on both sides. I soon passed large supermarkets and shops and, before I knew it, I was facing the sea. On my right was an expensive looking marina filled with the masts of yachts. To my left were palm trees growing up out of a long straight sandy beach which lay in front of a long line of hotels and bars. I chose right. It just felt right for no particular reason at all. Things were looking up. Everything was now beginning to feel good.

A few moments later I saw the sign for the Hotel San Luis. That too felt right. It would do nicely. Not too big, not too small and with great views. I pulled over and went in to book a room. Being mid-summer, it was busy but I was in luck. There'd been a cancellation.

I could even see the sea from my room. It looked really inviting after having driven so far. A cold swim would also be just right for my bruised and battered body.

Less than ten minutes later I was in the water. It was another five through before I'd sunk my shoulders down into it and started swimming. The sea always looked warmer than it actually was.

Swimming again was truly liberating. There's a freedom of movement, a freedom of direction and a freedom of time to it all. I was constantly smiling. Maybe its freedom that really makes a person happy, I pondered. Right now, I'd never felt so free. Everyone deserved to feel like this. Without realising it, I found I'd started thanking everyone again.

Twenty minutes of swimming along the shoreline was just enough for me. A short jog on the wet sand back to my towel was enough to warm me up again. A few male looks on the way helped as well. I knew I wasn't looking my best though but I'd sort that out tomorrow.

301

The Hotel had booked me into a local hair and beauty Salon a few blocks away. It was a lovely sunny Saturday. I'd had a short morning run along the beach, showered and had had breakfast. I was now heading for my 9.00am appointment. After the long drive and my swim, I'd been too tired to go out the previous night and had gone to bed early. It had paid dividends as this morning I felt terrific. I now just had to try and look that way too. The cuts and bruises to my face had nearly gone, but with a good makeover, I knew I could look as good as new much sooner. My nails needed attention as well as my hair. The question on my mind though was what kind of cut and style did I want? The old me would have left it all as it was and just had it trimmed and smartened up a bit. What would the new me want though. I needed some help with this.

Nearly two and a half hours later I looked a new woman. My long straight brown hair look had gone. It was now a shorter lighter brown to blond colour. At the back it had been layered into a tousled, choppy and slightly spiky look. It was also much shorter and now exposed the base of my neck. At the front it fell above my eyes as it crossed my forehead. I'd still wanted my ears covered and they were.

It was a modern, strong and independent look that showed both fun and freedom. One look in the mirror and I'd wondered what had taken me so long. It was rocking and I was ready to roll. All that was missing was a new Spanish outfit. New shoes and a new dress perhaps and I'd seen just the place to look on my way to the salon. It was not far from the marina, so I guessed it might have catered for that market. The prices seemed reasonable though which surprised me.

What my eyes were drawn to was a white dress that was loosely fitted so that the skirt swirled in the air when you turned quickly. I liked the longer length at the back which would go down to my calves whilst the front would be up above the knee on the left hand side. It also had a short delicate lace trim to it which made it both feminine and daring. The top was more close-fitting. It had more of a gypsy look to it with thin straps. Low at the back but not at the front worked for me too. It also went well with my short silver necklace which was the only jewellery I'd brought with me. I checked the sizes on the rail. Great I was in luck.

Now for some shoes. It was now that I was really glad I came over on the car ferry. No annoying baggage limits at the airport. Somehow black didn't seem appropriate anymore. I had several pairs back home anyway. Another colour seemed far better and one without much of a heel to them. Light and comfortable enough to wear all day would be good too.

This was my lucky day. At the back of the same store there were several different types. I could see a pair of navy blue espadrilles with wrap around straps that could be tied just above the ankle. They also had a slight wedge. Great. They had my size too. Wearing the dress and the shoes, I paid for them both and headed outside. I now looked and felt fantastic again and full of confidence.

Time for a pasta salad. I'd had my eye on a restaurant that seemed to almost be sitting on the sea itself. The Ripoli had views of water on all sides as it was situated actually on the breakwater between the marina and the beach. It was Saturday lunchtime and likely to be full but I felt sure my luck would hold.

It was full. All the tables had been taken but I didn't give up. A young lady was sitting alone at a table for two. I looked at her and her eye caught mine. I glanced at the free chair and smiled back at her. She immediately got what I'd meant and stood up and beckoned me over. "Thank you so much." I said to her holding out my hand, "My name is Rowena. It's lovely to meet you." She shook my hand and I sat down.

"Sofie. No, thank you for joining me. I wasn't looking forward to lunch on my own. My husband is off on a fishing trip today and I really didn't fancy going on another one." Her English was good. She either had a Dutch or Belgium accent, I couldn't tell.

"You speak English well, but I can't make out where you are from with your accent."

"Hollande." She replied. "I do love your outfit." She remarked changing the subject. "It seems very appropriate for this region of Spain on a day like this."

"Thanks. I've literally just bought it. I've gone for a complete makeover this morning."

"Oh my!" she exclaimed nicely, "What brought that on?" I thought about giving her a full answer but then remembered that it was not about me anymore.

"I've just had some changes in the last couple of weeks that's all. You know work, partner, home, lifestyle. It's really been the first day though that I've had time to chill out and relax. What about you though, how long have you been here?"

"About three days already. We were staying in Valencia but my husband, Jaap, wanted to come down here to do some sea fishing. It was only supposed to be one night but he enjoyed it so much, he wanted to go again and again."

"What about you Sofie? What have you been able to do down here?"

"To be honest Rowena, I am really, really bored down here."

"I'm sorry to hear that," I replied. The waiter then arrived and we ordered some drinks and food. A seafood pasta salad and some sparking water was all I wanted.

"What line of work are you in Sofie?" I asked.

"I work in a PR company in Amsterdam. My husband's stockbroker business is based there." She replied without much passion in her voice. I guessed something was not right somewhere.

"How is it going?" I asked.

"Well, not that great actually. There are three partners and I have been hoping one day to become the fourth. Unfortunately we are losing clients and having to lay off one or two people."

"So why is the company not doing well?" I asked.

"I think it has lost a bit of direction. So much had gone into Social Media marketing recently and I think clients are becoming more wary of that. It doesn't seem to be giving the sorts of returns they are used to with their marketing spend."

"Maybe the clients just aren't making so much money these days and are just having to cut their marketing budgets." I suggested.

"Maybe, but I'm tired of it all though. I try and help the partners but they only seem interested in their own ideas and if I do come up with something they like, it always seems to be presented to the clients as their idea and not mine. I'm not sure I see a future with them anymore." She sighed.

"What would you do instead?" I asked.

"Well Jaap says, I don't have to work. I'm his second wife you see, he's 15 years older than me and he already had two kids. I think he would prefer it if I was just with him more." She looked about 28, I could see why he liked having her around too. She had a good shape, good looks and seemed intelligent.

"Well that's nice, that he wants you around." I stated, hoping that would help.

"Yes it is, but he's not always around which is the problem. Business meetings, entertaining clients etc. and I am left with time on my hands. I need something to get my teeth into. I have a HBO degree in Media marketing and I really want to use that in some way."

"When you did your degree what did you enjoy doing most?" I asked.

"Now that's an interesting question. Thank you Rowena. Let me think of that." The drinks arrived. I leant back and enjoyed the view.

"I think what I enjoyed most was making short funny adverts and making people laugh….. Hmm….. That was really fun."

"How did you do that?" I asked.

"Well as part of research into that project, I decided to find out what people found was funny to them. I asked them to tell me about things that had happened to them or things that they'd seen that had made them laugh - even parts in films. I then broke those scenes down into what the trigger points were and then tried to replicate those trigger points in my work."

"And it worked?"

"Yes, I got a distinction for that work." She smiled remembering it.

"So, does your company ask what the client's customers find funny?" I asked just as a matter of interest. There was no answer. I stopped and looked up at her.

She seemed frozen in time for about three seconds. She then slowly lowered her glass of wine to the table. She made a move to speak but then stopped. After a few more seconds of silence, while she thought, she finally spoke.

"Do you know something Rowena? You've set me to thinking. No is the answer to your question. They don't ask their clients customers. In fact we do too little of that sort of thing. We just buy in data. However we do know our clients customers marketing categories but I don't think anyone has done any research on what triggers people to laugh in each of these categories. If I knew that, I could tailor short funny video clips to appeal to a client's customers specific sense of humour. If it could be shown that certain types of humour could be more specifically linked to each of the different marketing categories, we could use that type of humour to much greater effect. I could then design more precise humour to appeal to those categories."

"Would that work?" I asked.

"If you can make someone laugh, and then present your product or service to them, it would very much work." She stated sounding much more excited. "But what is really interesting is that we already know that there are several different types of humour. We've been working on what makes board room executives laugh in order to win their business. Their humour though may not actually be the same as their target audience. All I would need to do is to prove that to them and I'm sure could win their business."

"Would you do this for your PR company? or is it something you would want to do yourself?" I asked again.

"They wouldn't want to do the initial research and probably couldn't anyway. Certainly not without me." She replied still thinking intensely while she was speaking.

We chatted some more on the subject until our food came. By the end of the meal, she'd decided to start to do her own research whilst she worked with the company for another couple of months. By that time, she would have done enough to see how she could best take it all forward.

"Let me get these Rowena." She said when the bill came. "You've given me more help and ideas than anyone else has in years. If it all works, I'll have to make you my personal consultant."

"That's very kind of you, are you sure?" I asked.

"Absolutely." She quickly replied, "Now what do you have planned for the rest of the day?"

"Well not much really. I was going to go out this evening to see what was on and then just see where things led me."

"Well this afternoon, I'm going to take you out. There are some shops near here you are going to love and after that we can have a nice cup of tea on our yacht."

"You have a yacht" I exclaimed.

"Not quite. Jaap, hired it for a couple of weeks. It's moored over there." She pointed to the Marina. "He won't be back until about 5.00pm so there is no rush. So would you like all that?" she asked.

"That would be lovely. Let me drop my bags back at my hotel first though. It's only over there."

Shopping with Sofie was indeed fun. I could see her creative side coming out as she tried all sorts of ensembles together to see if they went. By the end of it I had a wide-rimmed navy coloured straw hat to go with my shoes with a white rose on the side of it at the top. Sofie had around five bags for the clothes and the shoes that she'd bought.

Their yacht was about 40 foot in length. It was gleaming white with dark brown wooden decking. It looked very expensive.

"Do you like music Rowena?" she asked from the inside as I sat at the back.

"Absolutely. Please put on anything you like."

"I think you might like this one." Van Morrison just joined us for tea. Memories of my dad flooded back. He would have loved this.

His parents had come over from Ireland in the 1950's so he felt Irish through and through. Sofie came up through the hatch with a cup of tea and could see I was enjoying his singing. "You should stop by the Dublin bar tonight Rowena. They've a live band playing music like this. You'd really like it. We went last night. It's not much to look at from the outside, but everyone's having fun in there."

"Where's that?" I asked.

"Just along the beach and in a bit."

"I'd go again with you, but I think we're leaving tonight."

Her husband Jaap came back just after five. She wanted me to stay so I could meet him. He seemed a kind man and I could see why she liked him. She said she would keep in touch and let me know how things went with her new business and I left to go back to my Hotel.

It had felt good to focus on her for the afternoon and to have helped her. I wasn't sure where it would lead, if anywhere but that wasn't important. It was about going with the flow. If this whole synchronicity thing was right that meant an evening of Irish music at the Dublin bar.

I dressed down for the occasion, not sure what I would find there, but knowing a little bit about these sorts of places. It was about a 20min walk away. Most of that was along the beach front. A dead straight road lined with palm trees, apartments, hotels, bars and restaurants. It seemed that everyone was out doing the same thing – walking along the beach front in the cool evening breeze as the Sun went down. There were even still people lying on the sand.

It was 9.00pm by the time I got there and the live music had already begun. It was not a large place and was already quite crowded. Two musicians stood with guitars in the small area that was their stage. They sounded good enough for me to stay and get a drink. I found myself slightly surprised by that as I hadn't expected anything to be this good down here in a small bar on the Spanish coast. I bought myself a glass of chilled Cerveza and turned to listen to them. They were both Irish. I looked around at the audience. There didn't look to be any English or Irish people in here at all - a few Spanish, some Germans and even some Nordic looking tourists. Quite a mixed bunch really.

After about 15 mins a young man sidled up next to me. He looked at first as though he was going to order another drink but instead he turned to me. "Do you like them?" He asked in an Irish accent.

"They're good." I replied. He was dressed in jeans and T-shirt that seemed to have the name of a band on it. I couldn't read the writing though. It must have been an old favourite of his from some concert he'd been to many years ago. He had nice blue eyes but altogether far too much facial hair. Not my type at all.

"I'm their manager." He stated, "I like to find out what people think." So he's not just hitting on me I thought or was that his escape plan in case I wasn't interested. "Also their 'everything else' too - stage hand, electrician, driver." He half joked.

"They must keep you busy then." I replied.

310

"They do. Do you know I think you're probably the only person from the UK in here?" He pointed out, again seemingly trying to find out if I was interested in chatting some more.

"I was thinking the same thing a few minutes ago" I replied, happy enough to talk for the moment.

"This is our last night here," he spoke more loudly as the music was now louder. "We're off to do a really big gig down in Murcia next week..." He continued. "...should be several thousand people there too." He said. Was he deliberately trying to impress me now?

"That's a big difference." I replied, "Have they ever played in front of so many people before?" the question seemed to surprise him as though he hadn't thought of that. "I'm sure they will be fine." I added.

"Yes. Yes, they will, they will." He nodded in agreement, his Irish accent now sounding a bit heavier. At that point something went wrong with the sound. One of the microphones stopped working. The guitarist waved at him to come over and fix it. His partner kept playing and singing on his own.

Minutes later he was back next to me having switched microphones and given the guitarist a replacement one. He started to unscrew the head off the one that had gone wrong and looked inside. He shook it and played with the on/off switch a few times. The light went on and off. Something worked but there was no sound. Something intrigued me about this.

"What's wrong with it?" I asked.

"Not sure. I think the transducer may have worked loose and lost its connection."

"What's a transducer do?" I asked.

311

"It's what turns Sound energy into Electrical energy and Electrical energy back into Sound energy." He replied. "The voice is picked up and switched to electrical information which then goes through to the amplifier and then to the speakers which then change it back into Sound energy."

My knowledge of science seemed to be missing a whole sector of information. I knew nothing about transducers but because they were connected to sound in some way, I was now very interested. "How do they do that?" I asked.

"Well they have something called a magnetostrictive property. Metal combinations of Iron, Nickel, Cobalt all react slightly differently under stress. When sound waves put pressure them, they produce electrical energy. It's a bit like a quartz crystal in people's watches and something called Piezoelectricity. When pressure is put onto the quartz, it produces a constant electrical signal." I heard everything he said but my mind had been focusing on the words Iron and Nickel. I asked him to repeat that bit again. He did so sounding happy I was interested in that sort of thing. I then paraphrased it back to him to make sure I'd heard correctly.

"So if you put pressure onto a piece of Iron and Nickel, it would convert that energy into another form of energy like sound energy or electromagnetic energy."

"You've got it." He replied happy with his success. My mind was now racing around in all directions. The inner core of the Earth was thought to be Iron and Nickel – that was under intense pressure from the mass of the Earth above it. It was also surrounded by the Earth's magnetic field. What if the inner core was working like a transducer and turning those energies into sound energy as well.

Sounds would then to travel outwards in all directions, a bit like an Earthquakes vibrations, but in this case it would be like bubbles of sound growing and expanding out from the centre of the Earth. The sound waves would also be bouncing back off the different layers inside the Earth. That could make them behave like two way spherical standing waves. The solid inner core also sat inside the molten outer core. This meant there was a chance it could expand and contract just like the membrane in a loudspeaker moves in and out.

The vibrations must be really slow though. Could these match up with the low frequencies that were making the mysterious hum? I didn't know. What I did possibly now have though was the beginnings of a hypothesis that I could test. Spherical sound waves expanding in all directions out to the surface of the Earth would also produce very distinctive patterns of high and low pressure zones on the surface. I needed to research this on my laptop. Much now depended on what sort of patterns these might be. Maybe someone had already been working on this in some way. If these patterns then linked up with the song lines and their intersections that would indeed be encouraging.

All this time, my bearded new friend was watching me. I looked up at him. "Wow," he started, "you were really away there with it for a few moments. Really deep in thought. What were you thinking about?"

"Thanks." Was all I could say for the moment. The Universe had certainly delivered an answer for me, or at least a possible one for me to check out. "Sorry." I continued. "I think I need to learn more about these Iron Nickel transducers for a project I am working on – that's all."

"What's that?" he asked sounding genuinely interested in that now rather than in me. I owed it to him to tell him.

"I've been looking into the way sound plays a part at ancient sacred sites. I think that certain sound formations may occur that can, in some way, lift the mind of a person into being more positive. The trouble up till now is that I haven't been able to find any possible origin for this very low frequency sound. With what you've told me, it may be now coming from the Earth's inner core."

"Cool." He said. "Loudspeaker Earth. Hotblack would have loved that."

"Hotblack?" I asked.

"Nevermind," he replied, "I'm just a hitchhiker." He shook his head so I left it and continued on.

"I think that some areas are subjected to different frequencies or types of sound. Some of which are good for life and some places which are unhealthy for life. I study Geobiology you see."

"Well from my point of view, I can tell you this. I'm forever having to retune the guitars for the guys. They never sound the same from one location to another. I know there are well known reasons for this like temperature, humidity but there seem to be many other things that affect tuning on top of that. Essentially you end up having to tune them exactly where they are going to play and just before they play. It's as though every location has its own settings at every moment in time."

"Well. I don't know about tuning guitars but you could possibly add another variable that could be affecting them. The strings could be vibrating differently because of the different low frequency vibrations found in different areas." I suggested. "There are natural laws of harmony that occur. When any frequency of sound is played, both higher and lower octave sounds resonate in sympathy with it. Maybe it's these higher harmonics that interfere the tuning of your guitar strings in some way."

"Could be." He agreed. The band was finishing up their first session and he went over to help them. Moments later they all joined me back at the bar. "Hi. I'm Mikey, this is Connor my brother and it seems you've met our manager Sean. What's your name then?"

"Rowena." I replied

"Now isn't that a lovely Irish name now. Sean you eejit, you didn't even find out her name." Sean came up behind them looking sheepish.

"Come now let's all have a bit of the dark and retire upstairs to the lounge for a while till we have to go on again." said Mikey.

"So Rowena, what brings an Irish girl all this way to listen to some Irish lads play some crap music." said Mikey as we all went upstairs with our drinks. At the top we were really now on the roof of the building which had been decked out with tables and chairs. There was even a wooden trellis structure overhead that some vines were clinging to. It was getting dark too and some of the brighter stars could now be seen in the dark blue night sky. On other occasions, it could be quite a romantic place. Now though it was just a nicely chilled place to hang out.

"Long story," I started to reply, "but the short answer is that I'm looking for the Cathar Grail – a Holy stone. But what do you mean crap music. I thought you sounded great." I replied hoping perhaps to stimulate some further conversation with them.

"Would you hear that now Connor, we've got a regular little Grail hunter here. Now what on Earth do you mean by that and yes that was crap music. Our little Sean here contracted us to play other peoples popular Irish music in our first session. We get to play our own stuff next. Now that....I promise.... you'll love."

"I'll look forward to it." I said. I'd half hoped for an early night but now realised that that was going to be out of the question with this lot.

"But now what I'd like really to know is more about this Cathar Grail?" Mikey asked.

"I can answer that, but the full story would take a while. I can give you a short version if you'd prefer though."

"Good God Rowena, the short version of course" said Mikey. "I don't want to fall asleep before I've to go on again." He smiled in a friendly, half mocking manner.

"Well one of the Grail writers wrote that the Holy Grail was a sacred stone and that was thought to have been kept by a group of very spiritual people called the Cathars in Southern France. The Pope though saw them as a threat and wanted to wipe them out…"

"…I like these Cathars already." said Connor holding his pint mug higher into the air as though he was toasting them.

"Shut up Connor," called out Mikey with a smile on his face, "Let the poor woman speak."

"Well it seems that, to stop it falling into the hands of the Pope, this stone was split into four pieces and hidden in four sacred caves across the area around the South East of France. The French Ministry of culture has one piece, my Dad, who would have loved your music by the way, found one piece and about two weeks ago I found the third piece in a cave near a tiny village called Ussat le Bains…"

"Would you believe that? She is a bloody Grail hunter. What about the fourth piece. If you say it's hidden in France, what the hell are you doing down here in Spain?"

"Well I also found a couple of scrolls in another cave and when these were translated it appears the fourth piece was taken down into Spain to a place I am trying to find."

"Well you'll not find any caves down around Iass. Your best bet is further South. If you are looking for sacred places Murcia is apparently buzzing with them. Ain't that right Connor" half shouted Mikey.

"For sure, the girls are down there now 'taking the energies' at the sacred sites." Connor added smiling away at the thought of them doing that. He then took another long swig at his beer.

"Taking the energies?" I asked.

"Meditating" he replied, "They're off to some retreat down there next week too. For those in the know, it seems that there's an area down there that's 'off the scale' when it comes to these energies." Mikey playfully said with his hands making air comma's when he said 'off the scale.'

"Where's that?" I asked hopefully.

"I've no bloody idea at all. I think they're raving mad sometimes, that's what I think." said Mikey, "God love them though they are beautiful people – you'd really like them. In fact you should come down there Rowena and meet them if you are into that sort of thing."

"I'd love to." I heard myself saying without thinking about it. What on Earth had I just agreed to, was my next thought?

"Enough of that now little miss Grail hunter," Mikey changed the subject. "Sean tell us how the sound was from back where you were."

The guys talked shop for a while. They all seemed to be in their mid-thirties and had been doing this for at least ten years together. Summer in Europe and Winter in the UK and Ireland seemed to be their thing. They played and sung well but I couldn't really tell much more until I heard their own music.

Sean brought up my thoughts on an extra variable that might affect tuning guitars and they had listened keenly on that. Connor had mentioned that certain venues could be better to play music in than others. Although I hadn't produced any results to my research yet, it did look as though it could affect where and how sound and music was played. I promised to let them know if I found anything out.

It was 11.30pm when they'd finished. It had been a treat to hear them and I'd bought their album. It was hard to describe their music. It was not definitively Irish by any means. They had obviously been influenced by many different artists and had then added their own touch as well. They'd also given me a ticket for Monday night in Murcia in the Plaza de Toros – the bull ring. I wasn't sure I was going yet but they said that, if I was, I should ring them so I could meet up with their girlfriends beforehand.

I walked back barefoot along the beach. Not quite a full moon but still very tranquil. It gave me time to collect my thoughts on the day. If I'd not decided to have a makeover and to buy a new look, I wouldn't have had the confidence perhaps to head for the crowded Rivoli restaurant for lunch on my own. If I'd not had enough self-esteem to be able to nod towards Sofie to ask if I join her at her table, I wouldn't have been able to help her and I perhaps may not have found out about the Irish bar. If I'd ignored Sean and not engaged him in conversation, I'd have not found out about the transducer and a possible link to the inner core. If I'd gone home early, I may not have been given an invite to meet their girlfriends and possibly another clue to follow up with sacred places. I was nowhere nearer finding the 4th piece of the stone, but I did feel I'd got nearer to where I was supposed to be heading, wherever that was.

All I'd done was to focus more on others. That in turn seemed to reduce any fears I might have had. I'd forgotten about myself and instead had tried to care more for others. In just one day at Gandia with that approach, I'd achieved more than the all the rest of my time in Spain. I really felt as though I was now back to how things were working for me in France.

The next morning, I awoke late. It was a day to be beside the pool reading a good book - which, fortunately, was exactly what I had with Otto Rahn's book 'Lucifer's court'. I was aiming to read, sunbathe, swim, eat and drink and to also try and work out how to regain my hairstyle from yesterday. I hadn't quite got it right this morning. It was either the mousse or the small amount of gel that was not quite in the right place. My nails still looked gleaming red though, and they were still all my own. My bruises and cuts were now almost completely gone. Having said that, anything could still happen today. If the Universe wanted to change things, I'd ride that wave.

As it was she gave me a day off. Nearly everyone around seemed to be wanting a lazy day too – maybe that was just Sundays here in Gandia. For me it meant I could also get on with some much needed research. The first was to check up on the latest thinking on the composition of the inner core. The common consensus was that it was still a mixture of Iron and Nickel and maybe a small amount of other metals.

I then found out about some research on spherical standing waves and the patterns they make on the surface of a sphere. It seemed that they make straight lines of high pressure concentrations that ran around the sphere in great circles in several directions. The overall look was that in several places, six of these lines would cross over in one place.

That meant that if spherical sounds were coming from the inner core, straight line concentrations could also be found on the surface of the Earth. All that I needed to do now was to find some way to find them and then measure them and then find out where they crossed over. If these places then matched ancient and modern sacred sites, I'd be on to something.

What was interesting was that the spherical sound waves that made these patterns were standing waves. These were like echoes of sound coming off a wall. The sound waves would rebound off different interfaces like the different densities of rocks. This was much the same as Earthquake waves that bounced around the World and down through the ground and back as shadow quakes.

I'd also found out that an Iron and Nickel mixture works really well as a mechanical filter. This meant that the sound it converts and emits outwards is not found on all frequencies. It seems that it only makes sounds within specific ranges of frequencies.

In between these ranges there are large gaps where no sounds are made at all. These sound groupings were called eigenmodes. This was interesting to me because geophysicists using supercooled gravimeters in Antartica had also found eigenmodes of frequencies when they had measured this mysterious hum.

All I now had to do was to see if I could find and measure any eigenmode frequencies from the inner core and see if there was a match up with the eigenmodes measured in Antartica. If a match could be found, it would not only explain where the hum was coming from, but it could also go a long way to showing how low frequency sound reached the Earth where it could then affect life both in a good and bad way.

My guess was that most frequencies would be fine for life. A few would be really good but a few could quite probably be harmful. I remembered hearing some sounds that were utterly horrible which made my spine go rigid. It was such an awful feeling I'd had to cover my ears with my hands. On the other hand though some sounds were beautifully relaxing.

By the end of the day I'd also finished Rahn's book. There was so much in it that was interesting. Unfortunately I couldn't really see what might be helpful to me at the moment. I made notes of the things that resonated with me that I would have to look into more carefully in the future.

1. Rahn had highlighted a connection between the Grail and Rose gardens. He too thought the rose was a symbol for the location of a Grail. *(Gabrielle had talked about the Rose and the Cross. Rahn may have got this from Gadal.)*
2. Rahn had identified a connection between the Grail and the Flower of Life pattern. *(This matched with my thoughts about the symbols at Montsaunes chapel.)*
3. Rahn had said that to enter the Rose is to cross the threshold into natures secret Worlds of Enchantment. *(Flower of life rose petal design could be where something really special happens. Possible link with the grail properties spoken about in the later grail legends. No idea what 'Worlds of Enchantment' mean.)*

4. Rahn also reported that he had a vision of a Bee in the rose. He had later said that the bee was a symbol and known as the keeper of the keys of the inner self. *(An experience found at these grail sites, if Rahn was right, this was a spiritual one. Possibly to do with one's own inner relationship with the World around us.)* He also later said that the Bee was known in ancient Egypt to be the door to other Worlds. *(Not quite sure yet what this means either – weird)*
5. Rahn wrote about a skeleton key and a form of Rose magic that was the way to go through the gates and enter the rose garden. This he had later said was the feeling of love and a specific sound. *(A good link to sound at these grail sites.)*

I was beginning to think that the Templars at Montsaunes must have found this 'key' and had experienced some of these things. If only I could find this 'Place of Miracles', maybe there would be more that could be learnt from them there.

Unfortunately I had no more tangible clues to follow up. The best option I had now was to go further South and to meet up with Mikey and Connor's girlfriends and find out about the areas with 'high energies'. Maybe I could meet some locals down in that region and look to try and help them in some way. Some place further South must have once existed that was known at the time as the 'Place of Miracles'.

It was clearly off the radar at the moment though. I could find nothing about it at all on the internet. I'd searched for ages trying all sorts of words and phrases. I'd even searched under images, videos and maps. Places that might have been candidates all failed the date tests with the Moors and the Templars. The only thing left to do was some actual physical exploration. For that to work, I was left with only one thing to help me – synchronicity.

Murcia

I'd set off at 11.00am on Monday morning after a late checkout. I'd crammed in a 5km beach run with a 15 minute swim in the sea at the end of it and a full English breakfast. I'd also won with my hair. It now looked just as it had done when I left the salon. Today I felt like sitting next to Justin Timberlake again and watching him tapping a beat on my dashboard. He was easy to enjoy but two hours with him was more than enough for any woman. By then though, I would be in Murcia, the capital of the region of Murcia.

I'd booked ahead and found a nice hotel not far from the bull ring called the Arco de San Juan. It had been described as an antique neoclassical palace located in the historical centre of the city. Basically, for me, it was just really good value. It was near the shops as well and it had its own parking.

I was parked up and in the hotel by 1.30 in the afternoon. It gave me a couple of hours to look around the city and be back early enough to meet up with the Irish before the concert. I gave Mikey a call. "Rowena, lovely to hear from you. Listen. I'm a bit busy right now. But let me pass you over to Kayleigh." He said with the typical Irish staccato in the way he spoke.

"Rowena. Hi, it's Kayleigh. Mikey told me that Sean had met up with an Irish girl in Gandia at the Dublin bar."

"Hi Kayleigh." I started, now wondering what had been said, "Yes I met Sean there and later Mikey and Connor...."

"...Great," she interrupted me, "Listen, Mikey says you are into things like sacred sites and sounds and meditation and all that. Siobhan and I are really into all that as well, so why don't we all meet up before the concert tonight and have a chat. The boys are going to be busy from now on anyway so we won't be seeing them again until after the show."

"That sounds great," I replied, "What did you have in mind?"

"Where are you staying?" she asked.

"At the Arco de San Juan just down the road from the Bull ring." I replied.

"Ah would you know. We're just round the corner from you in the Occidental. We'll come over to you as it's on the way to the centre. We can meet you in the foyer over there in about half an hour. Would that be enough time for you?" She asked.

Everything seemed to be happening very fast. I had to stay with the flow. "That would be fine." I replied.

I'd unpacked and was now sitting in the foyer with a cup of tea watching the entrance for a couple of Irish women I'd never met before. It was strange - even for me. I picked up a magazine that was on the table in front of me - The Costa Colida Chronicle magazine. I was in luck, it was an English version. It had obviously been placed there for tourists. Soon I was thumbing through the pages. There were colourful festivals taking place all over the region. This place seemed alive with different celebrations.

One mad one caught my eye. The running of the wine horses at a place called Caravaca. Apparently each year on the 2nd May the young people in the town form teams and tie themselves to the sides of a horse. They then race their horses, with themselves running alongside them, up the hill in the middle of the town to a castle at the top. Every year people seemed to get hurt. Whether you were in the crowd and just standing too close or if you were a team member and you tripped and fell whilst tied to the horse, it was all taken in good spirit. One word caught my attention. Templars.

The events seemed to be commemorating a time when the Templars were under siege from the Moors. They'd escaped down the hill to find water for their colleagues and the townsfolk who were surrounded back in the fort at the top of the hill. All they'd found was sacks of wine. As this was better than nothing they tied the wine sacks to their horses and ran them back up the hill, through the enemy lines and back into the Castle at the top.

I was only half way through the article when I saw two girls outside the hotel entrance. I made a note to remember the name of the place in case it came up again. I wasn't about to shoot off on another wild goose chase. This going with the flow was working well enough for me at the moment.

The two young girls had now come through into the hotel. They both looked about my age and had been blessed with good looks and long hair. Instinctively I reached behind my own neck only to be reminded that mine now only came half way down it. I got up and went over to them. They saw me immediately and we embraced like old friends. "Hi I'm Kayleigh and this is Siobhan."

"Rowena." I said smiling.

"We're going to have so much fun, I just know it." said Siobhan. The three of us left the hotel and headed down to the River Segura and then along to Le Puente de los Peligros – the bridge of Dangers. The main shopping street in Murcia started from there.

"I'm going to need some food to begin with." I said to them as we walked.

"Yes. Great idea." replied Kayleigh enthusiastically and she looked at Siobhan.

"Tapas." they both shouted out at the same time as well as clapping their right hands together above their heads. They didn't seem to need much of a reason to be happy. It made me wonder. Were they always this? I didn't know but it kept me smiling.

We found a small tapas bar down one of the many side streets. This whole area was a gourmet shopper's paradise. Kayleigh ordered a selection of snacks and three glasses of white wine whilst we stood at the bar. "So how long have you been here in Murcia?" I began.

"A week and a half." replied Kayliegh. "It's been a sort of base for us whilst the guys have travelled around doing gigs up and down the coast."

"They've been to Cartagena, Valencia, Alicante, Gandia, which you know of course, and now they are finishing up here at Murcia." added Siobhan.

"So what do you both do?" I asked.

"We keep the guys happy." said Siobhan

"Grounded. Inspired." Kayleigh followed.

"Creative." added Siobhan.

"It sounds lazy and useless but we believe in what they're doing and the message they're putting out." reasoned Kayleigh.

"Having fun, being free, spreading the love." Siobhan said spreading her own arms out wide.

"Seriously though," I asked. "I can see you both do that easily, but what about work? Do you do anything to earn money back in Ireland for example." I asked out of genuine interest as I couldn't see how their lifestyle was going to be self-supporting in any way in the future.

"I know where you are coming from Rowena." replied Kayleigh. "We nearly fell into the trap of thinking that way, but we found we were becoming unhappy and making people around us miserable."

"We know we've no future with what we are doing. It is in many ways irresponsible. We get that. We also understand that if everyone did what we did, the World would come to a standstill." added Siobhan.

"I know but I wonder how lovely a World like that would be like?" mused Kayleigh.

"Some people are just needed though to spread some joy into people's lives. Look not everyone is the same, we understand that, but many people at the moment are really depressed" continued Siobhan.

"Many of them don't even know why they feel so down." added Kayleigh.

"All we know is that when people are happy, they do positive things and good comes out of it." Siobhan leant back with her hands now face up in front of her as though she was holding up an invisible ball. "So in a way, if we make people happy, we are making the World a better place." she continued now gently moving the invisible World she was holding up in front of her.

"We need to do this for our own sanity too." added Kayleigh.

"But what about earning money?" I asked sounding like a kill joy.

"The guys pay us." They replied almost together. I hadn't expected that and I think they saw the surprised look on my face. "They say they need us to be around them when they are writing new songs. We help them." said Kayleigh.

"They say they make better music when we're around and we believe that too." added Siobhan. "The World is changing Rowena. The old ways are on their way out." she added.

"We are helping people to re-programme themselves. It's hard for many of them though after years of indoctrination. They are told to work hard at school to get a job, and to then work hard to buy a house, and to then work even harder to raise some children." said Kayleigh.

"But people are finding that doesn't work anymore. They work hard but cannot afford to have kids and they cannot afford to even rent a house let alone buy a house." Siobhan added.

"Things are changing now though. The Universe is changing things." Kayleigh now spread her arms out wide. "New waves of energy are coming." She said now moving her arms from side to side.

"I'm not sure what that means?" I said, feeling slightly confused by the turn of direction.

"You will find out Rowena one day, it may even be your destiny to explain it to everyone, but we feel it." said Siobhan, "Keeping sane in an insane World is not easy."

"People are going to need to have a strong mind for what's coming." added Kayleigh. Several bowls of tapas were now placed on our table. They gave us each plates and the girls told me to pick away at whatever I wanted. They said they would eat whatever I left.

I was glad the conversation had been interrupted. I felt that they both had lovely intentions and they clearly radiated joy and loved to make people happy but they were also practically unique. There were not many people who could do what they did. My right brain loved them, my left brain though was screaming at me. "What music do you like Rowena?" I was glad of the change of subject. I told them about the CD's I had in my car and who I had been listening to recently. They approved excitedly. After I'd eaten enough, they snacked on what was left.

The rest of the afternoon was really fun. We tried on different make up and accessories trying to find a new look that might work for each of us. Just as I thought we were getting to the end of the main shopping street, the three of us stood in front of a large department store - El Corte Inglés.

They'd been saving the best till last. It had everything and on several floors – even a food hall with its own unique speciality section. I had no idea how long we were in there. Normally when shopping with anyone else I found it quite hard but with Siobhan and Kayleigh, they just blended in with everything I wanted to look at. They just seemed to enjoy everything. Their energy seemed to continually lift me.

It was time to head back and get ready for the concert in the evening so we started walking back to the hotels. I was also eager to find out more about the energies that the guys had mentioned they were on about. They must have read my mind. "Rowena. Have you any plans for the next couple of days?" asked Kayleigh.

"No, not really." I replied and at the same time thinking that that was strange for me.

"We like that about you. You seem to be following your heart." replied Siobhan. "Would you like to come to a retreat with us in the mountains?" she added.

"Just a couple of nights in a cabin. The guys are going to be busy for the next few days so it's cool with them that we take off." said Kayleigh.

"We have to be back on Thursday and we will then be busy helping them for the next few days. We also fly back next Monday to Dublin so it's the best chance we have to share some time with you and get to know you some more." She added.

"There's yoga and meditation there – that sort of thing." added Siobhan. The Universe was speaking to me again.

"Yes I would love that, thank you. I can drive us all up there if that will help." I replied now really looking forward to finding out where this would all lead.

El Berro

The concert was sensational. The circular arena with all its history added a dimension to their music that was just not possible to hear in a small venue. Relaxing and having a good crack with them afterwards in their hotel was hilarious. The girls were on top form and certainly knew how to bring the guys gently back down to Earth.

Now though the three of us were heading towards the Sierra Espuna mountains which were about 45 mins away from Murcia. Somehow we'd all crammed into my little mini. Instead of music though, they'd been asking about my research and what I had been up to recently. I let them know all I could and answered all of their questions. With the two of them it had been almost impossible for me to focus on them. They kept switching their attentions back on to me. I sometimes wondered if they either knew what they were doing or were just unconsciously caring about everyone else all the time.

What they seemed to like most though was the recent change of plan I'd had with regards to going with the flow. They'd said that that was what had resonated with them most with me.

As we headed through the small town of Alhama de Murcia with its streets lined with orange trees we were soon on a narrow windy, but still tarmac, road up to El Berro. The zig zags with their hairpin bends took us up to 2000feet and about 1500 feet above the flat plain below. The views with their different shades of browns, stretched for many miles to the North and to the South.

The trees up at this height were mainly pines. They were curiously all spaced quite wide apart from each other. It was probably because there were only certain places where they'd managed to burrow their roots down through the hard white limestone bedrock.

As we looked up to the top of the hills, we could see the taller ones silhouetted against the deep blue cloudless sky. We all fell silent as we looked at the scenery all about us. With the windows down, we could now feel a cooler wind compared to the warmer air that had been down on the plain below.

We drove over the crest of the main hill and were soon turning off to the right and following the road down to El Berro. I could see it now nestling down in the valley below us. "So how did you hear about this place?" I asked.

"Some friends of ours came here a few months ago." Kayleigh replied.

"They said the energies here were off the scale." said Siobhan.

"More than any place they'd ever been to in the whole of Europe." added Kayleigh. "They'd heard about it from a friend who lived in Aguilas – a town on the coast about an hour from here. She'd been told about it by an Englishman. He'd apparently spent weeks walking around the Sierra Espuna mountains before he discovered the power of this location."

"From what they say, this place has much higher energies than those found at Mount Shasta or Mount Sedona in the US." continued Siobhan. "Apparently they are almost as powerful as those at the holy mountain of Mount Kailash in China which some say is the most sacred place in the World." She finished in a voice like she was telling a fairy tale. All tops of mountains again, I thought.

"Nothing's ever been written about it. It's all just word of mouth. Apparently it's about being there and just feeling it for yourself." started Kayleigh again after we'd all thought about it for a few moments.

"That's why we just had to come." added Siobhan.

I wasn't at all sure what they meant by the 'energy' of a place. If they were referring to sound energy though, without realising it, then that would be of interest. I could only wait and see if I could feel it for myself. If I could though, I still had the problem of trying to find a way how to measure it scientifically.

We were heading for a camp site called Camping Sierra Espuna. They had several large cabins that could be hired out and the girls had managed to hire one of them midweek for a couple of days. This place was always fully booked on the weekends all through the summer with hikers, cyclists and climbers. The reason for that was because there were so many adventure trails running all though the forest. This place was a playground for the fit, the healthy and the adventurous.

We pulled up to the side of a horizontally slatted, golden brown stained, wooden cabin complete with shutters over the windows and a veranda that looked out at the mountains opposite.

As soon as we opened the car door we could feel a crisp freshness to the air. It made me want to get out quickly, stand up straight and inhale slowly and deeply several times. I did so. This place felt exhilarating. It had somehow already made me feel healthier.

Inside the cabin there was an open plan central kitchen dining room that led immediately into two small bedrooms and a bathroom. A moveable step ladder led to a couple of beds above these rooms. Those beds were part of the open plan space. Nearly everything was made from pine which had all probably been sourced from local trees. All in all it was very simple, basic and self-contained, just what you needed in order to spend most of your time outdoors.

It was only 11.00am. The plan was to visit the retreat in the afternoon. This was in an old house just outside El Berro. The girls had booked to do a special yoga instruction class in the afternoon. Tomorrow afternoon they'd also booked to do a session on 'meditating with the higher energies'. I looked forward to them both immensely and was hoping this would lead me further along with my own path down here in Spain.

We spent the rest of the morning walking around the camp site exploring. Even though it was nearly fully booked there was little sign of anyone. The manager told us most people were already up and out of here, running, walking and cycling through the trails. I picked up a photocopy of a map he'd made of nearby running trails. There was one that started next to the site and went up an old dry river bed. 3km up and 3km back – perfect for early tomorrow morning. The girls didn't seem keen to join me.

After a cup of tea at the café next to the pool, we got back into the car and headed off down the road to the retreat. We were greeted at the door by Mariana. She was a slim tall Spanish lady with long dark hair that fell a long way down behind her back. She was wearing tight fitting black yoga pants that just flared slightly at the ankles and a white bra top. It showed off a lean mid drift and her light brown skin. She looked mid-thirties but I discovered later she was actually mid-forties. "Hi, you must be Kayleigh and Siobhan. My name is Mariana. You must be Rowena. It's really lovely you are joining us this afternoon." She greeted us each with a warm hug and invited us through into her yoga room. Her English was good and I suspected she must have lived over in the UK for some time. "It's just the four of us today. I really like working with small groups though." Mariana continued to say as we walked through into the room.

The long full length sliding windows on the far side were wide open and we were greeted with views right down the valley back to El Berro. Even though we were still standing in the room it felt as if we were already part of the surrounding nature.

Mariana first took us through to her side office where we filled in registration forms whilst she told us a bit about the place and how long she'd been running it. She seemed to know the area around here was special too in some way, having been guided to come here herself over 5 years ago.

When we'd finished and had taken off our shoes and put our bags down, she took us back into the main room and asked us to sit down on the mats that were on the floor. "Have any of you done any type of yoga before?" she asked. We all answered yes. "Good. That helps a lot. It means we can begin at the beginning" I looked over at Kayleigh and Siobhan and we all had a slightly confused look on our faces.

Mariana continued. "Ladies, I have to start by telling you that I do not teach yoga with any typical style and indeed in any normal way." She walked slowly around the room and behind us as she spoke. "The way I do it, was just how I was guided to learn to teach others. Please do not judge me on what and how I teach you compared to other teachers. This is different." She had now stopped in front of us. "Also, please don't ask me any questions about what you have done, or have been taught, in the past. I'm just not able to answer them."

"I am not looking to teach you a new style of yoga either." She added. "I am though hopefully going to teach you parts of yoga that will help you with your own usual style of yoga." She now held her hands together palm to palm in front of her in a praying position. "If you wish to judge at all, please do so much later on after you have had time to see if you sense any improvement after your normal yoga sessions." She now relaxed her hands and arms back down to her sides and began walking around us again. Her movement was slow, precise and almost balletic.

"Living and practicing yoga here has taught me one or two things that I would now like to share with you." she continued. "Parts of what I will cover, you will know already, some will be new and easy to learn but some will also be new and hard to learn. It will take time but if you practice these things, you will find some amazing benefits."

She stopped now to look out and down the valley herself. After pausing for a few moments to take in the view she continued. It was as though she had been seeking inspiration on how best to start what we should be doing. "We cannot learn many poses in a short session like this and this is not, I think, the objective we should be aiming for today anyway." The inspiration seemed to now be slowly coming to her. "Good let's start. We are going to begin in pairs. Kayleigh you work with Rowena, I will work with Siobhan." This was different. I thought.

"I want you Siobhan and you Kayleigh to start in the Mountain pose with your eyes closed." We each started to stand up and get into the pose. "Stand with your feet together, bend your knees a touch and bring your stomach in slightly. Now move your shoulders back and down a bit. The palms of your hands should be against the side of your body. For the moment breathe casually but breathe from your stomach."

"Right Rowena, I want you to place your hand on Kayliegh's head and press down lightly." She did the same on Siobhan's head. "I want the two of you to now feel the pressure on your head going down the length of your body. Feel that extra weight on your feet as they seem to mould down into the floor. Can you feel it?" They both nodded and said yes. "Rowena please now change the pressure on Kayleigh's head, increase it then decrease it several times but do it slowly." Mariana did the same. "Can you now feel the slow pulsing pressure going down your spine? Good"

"Next I want you to start to slowly breathe in and only breathe out when you feel the pressure on your head from your partner's hand...... As you breathe out and in I want you to feel the pressure going down your spine to your feet and then back up again when the pressure is released when you breathe in again." It took a moment to get the pressure and the breathing synchronised.

"Put the pressure on slowly Rowena and then release it slowly..... Good. Kayleigh, Siobhan, I want you to give this feeling a colour..... Imagine this coloured feeling going up and down your spine and down your legs to your feet. Are you doing that?" Yes they both answered.

"Now Rowena I want you to take away your hand. Kayleigh, Siobhan, keep breathing and keep the two-way colour movement and feeling going.

"Rowena, can you now please stand behind Kayleigh and place both your hands on her shoulders and press slowly down as she breathes out. Feel the muscles in your body react to this pressure. Notice your back muscles, your stomach muscles, your glutes, now your thighs and your calves. Can you feel your muscles tense and relax as the pressure on your shoulders increases and then decreases?" Yes came the answer from them both. "Good, now give this feeling the same colour but a lighter shade of the one you used before." This was something new and not easy to begin with.

"Now imagine both the stronger colour going down and up your spine and the lighter colour going down and up all the muscles in your body. Good." This seemed harder to do. One moment it was feeling, the next it was visualising – not at all easy to do both together.

"This takes practice." Mariana said, "It will come though and with it, you will greatly benefit."

"Now I want you to open your eyes and continue to feel and visualise this colour and this movement that is now aligned with your breathing." She continued. This was harder again.

"Rowena, now take your hands away and ladies continue to breathe in and out and continue to feel and see the colour go up and down your body." She waited for about 30 seconds.

"Fine, now relax….. Excellent….. Now how easy did you find that?"

"Quite easy to begin with. Harder though when there was no pressure. I could still just feel it and see it though." Kayleigh replied.

"Same with me. Easy to begin with, but much harder when my eyes were open." answered Siobhan.

"It gets easier with practice." replied Mariana.

"Excellent. That's a good start both of you. Let's give Rowena a chance to try."

Mariana repeated it all with me and at the end I too was experiencing the pulsing tension and relaxation through my body matched with my breathing all with a yellow colour. Visualising and feeling together was not easy though. I was like inducing one's own form of synaesthesia.

"I like to start this with the Mountain pose as your muscles are not under too much tension compared to other poses. It serves to give us a baseline experience that we can draw upon for use in other poses. This is also just a physical feeling at the moment. Later on we will introduce another feeling." She had again started walking slowly around us whilst she talked.

"Right let's now change the pairings. Rowena you work with Siobhan now and I'll work with Kayleigh. This time we will do the same thing with the downward dog pose." We both got down and into the position with just our hands and feet on the floor.

"I am sure you will all know the position. Siobhan, I want you to now stand in front of Rowena's head and place your hands on her lower back by her glutes."

"Keep your legs straight and feel the pressure now coming down your legs into your feet and also up your back through your arms and into your hands. Rotate your arms so your elbows point slightly more towards each other to make sure your arms are really straight. Good."

We repeated the same feeling and breathing exercise in this position with pressure being felt in greater and lesser amounts on the lower part of the back. We again added a colour to the physical feeling.

"Can you feel areas in your body where there is greater tension and pressure?" Mariana asked.

"Yes" we replied.

"Good. What I want you to do now is to see if you can release that tension and pressure into other parts of your body by making small subtle movements in your position" Mariana instructed, "Either move your hands and feet nearer together or further apart. Remember only make small adjustments."

"Now also use your breathing and your movement of feeling up and down your legs and arms to help balance out any tension you still feel."

My hamstrings were indeed tight as were my shoulders, especially when Siobhan added some pressure. I rebalanced by moving my hands a bit further away from my feet. I then tried to breathe the pressure equally through my body. In the end I was so focussed on doing this I hardly noticed it when Siobhan took her hands away. It felt like I was breathing and visualising the feeling of stress and strain away through my body. I was now in a state of balance where I couldn't really feel any particular part of my body more than any other part.

"Ok that's enough." said Mariana, "Please slowly stand up again and let's switch and give Siobhan a chance." We did so and Kayleigh and I spent time in turns putting pressure on and off her back to help her feel the movement through her body. After about 10mins of this, we'd finished.

"That seemed a long time to be in that position," I said to Mariana, thinking it was about as twice as long as I'd had.

"Actually it was only slightly less than the time you spent." Mariana replied. "If you get this exercise right, time seems to rush by. It's because of all the extra mental work you are doing and the fact that you eventually find a position of balance and that then allows you to stay in that position more effortlessly." she replied.

"Wow." It was all I could say. I'd never spent that long in a downward dog position before. 2 mins and I'd normally had enough. I wondered about

Aliya's advanced classes. She'd told me before not to worry about the breathing and visualisation yet, maybe this is what would be yet to come. I looked forward to chatting with her about all this.

We did the same set of exercises in pairs for two more poses. One was the Triangle – which we did leaning to both sides in turn, the other was the first Warrior pose – the one with both arms above the head, front leg forward and bent at the knee and with the back leg straight and the foot at right angles to the front foot. Each of us now held the poses for far longer than we would normally have.

We'd spent nearly 45 mins on just four poses we all thought we already knew how to do.

"Ok," said Mariana, "What we are going to try now is to put all these exercises together ourselves in a sequence. Try and remember all that we learned with each pose. Follow me and change when I change and listen to my breathing. Try and breathe in and out with me."

We started with the 'Mountain' pose, then the 'Warrior', then the 'Triangle', for both sides, and then the 'Downward dog'. We must have spent at least 2 mins in each pose but I wasn't sure, there were no clocks anywhere in the room. At the end we were all standing up smiling.

It had gone so smoothly. It also felt as though I'd had a really good workout but without having lost any energy.

"Right," Mariana began, "This time we will do it again but now we will face the valley and I am going to play some sound. The poses will not be for so long. This time though when you think about each stage of breathing and visualising, I want you to feel the sound wash through you with the flow of movement too. One last thing I want to see is your smile. It's your chance to put it all together."

'What the heck just happened.' I said to myself at the end. I still had a stupid grin on my face and so did Kayleigh and Siobhan. Towards the end of each pose, Mariana had started to lightly sound a large gong. She beat it faster and faster and harder and had then left it to resonate. The vibrations had moved rapidly up and down my body speeding up my own movement of feeling. It wasn't quite like the feeling I'd had in Chartres but it was close. Sound was definitely at play in some way both here and back there.

At the end of the session I now realised that I knew very little about yoga itself. So much more to it had been opened to me and we'd only just scratched the surface of it all. I had so many questions for Mariana about how this would link up to my previous experiences of yoga, but as she'd said at the beginning, she couldn't help with what we'd done in the past. I guessed it was just something I would have to discover for myself. Maybe that was also exactly what she'd intended to happen. It was the most expensive yoga lesson I'd ever had by a long, long way but I'd learnt so much, it had been well worth it.

After a short discussion on what we'd all learnt and experienced, Mariana told us that this was just the first stage she had taught us. There were other processes she'd learnt that could be built on top of this one. What we would be learning in tomorrow's meditation session would touch on some of these. If it was anything like what we'd just had, I thought, it would have to be incredible.

The three of us talked of nothing else all the way back to our cabin. It was time for a shower and a swim followed by a meal in the local restaurant.

It was only 10.00pm, the three of us had been chatting on the veranda on nearly every subject there was as the Sun went down. Kayleigh and Siobhan were now enjoying turning nearly all of the conversations back to me and men. They had all sorts of ideas of who I should be with including suggestions of friends of theirs. I think they found matchmaking fun and felt it was something they were good at. Aside from still having some hope that something might come about with Bernard, I wasn't ready yet for any serious relationship but had eventually agreed with them that my frame of mind could turn in an instant if I met the right person.

What had been strange was that none of us had anything else but water to drink since we'd got to El Berro. Wine or anything else just didn't seem to appeal. The girls had said it was as though we were being fuelled by the energies of the place. I was at the point of beginning to agree with them.

Even though the energy during the day had been high, we were still physically very tired at the end of it. The cabin though had one last surprise for us. With the shutters closed and the lights out, it was pitch black and now heavily sound proofed on the inside. I had never slept anywhere so dark. There was literally no light anywhere for my eyes to adjust to. Lying in bed and noticing this was almost like realising I was going to sleep in a sensory deprivation chamber. As I wondered what that might be like I just dropped off into a deep sleep.

Around seven hours later I woke up feeling really well slept and raring to go. My mind was on a run up the old dry river bed before breakfast. Just enough light from outside was coming through the shutters for me to now see what I was doing inside the cabin. I carefully descended the steep wooden ladder into the front room and put on my running gear. The others were still asleep.

It was still only 6.30am. The Sun was up but the shadows from the mountains still kept the campsite fairly dark. It was just the mountain tops that were lit up. I started off running nice and slowly, enjoying the cold air in my lungs and allowing my body to gently warm up. The dry river bed trail was easy to spot and a path riddled with roots and stones ran alongside it - just how I like it. It was running mixed up with a little bit of dancing from side to side.

I passed to the side of dried up waterfalls and over old tree trunks that had fallen across the stream bed. I had to run with the occasional leap and bound to avoid some of the larger obstacles. I then danced some more in order to miss the minor ones. In one or two places there were clusters of wild ferns and tufts of damp moss with tiny wild flowers poking up through them. There must have been water still here in small pockets underneath the soil.

A cloudless sky was just visible through the tops of the pine trees that lined the steep sides of the stream valley. It was all just so invigorating that I wished everyone could experience this. After reaching a crossing point with another forest trail, it was time to head back. If I was staying for longer here, I would have definitely come back. The choices of where to run next were plentiful and each direction seemed to offer their own different attraction.

Coming back downhill was faster but a bit trickier. Stable rocks for my feet to land on were less easy to see and my legs were moving between them all like I was now doing a quickstep. I nearly tripped twice and had to roll with the flow when a stone had given way. Not good to turn an ankle this far away from the cabin but fear wasn't going to stop me loving this.

The others were still asleep when I got back. I grabbed my purse and a light jacket and headed straight out and round to the local bakery. I'd heard it was special from the online reviews. Apparently it was the only one around for hundreds of kilometres that only used organic flour. It was also a 24hour communal bakery which meant its ovens were always on. Locals without ovens in their houses regularly brought their meals over there to be cooked.

The entrance was just a wide door into a room with a few shelves. They were not there to sell you anything else but what they baked. Most of the racks were empty but there were a few with some freshly baked bread and pastries. I could feel the warmth from the oven coming from the next door room as a lady came through to serve me. She was in the middle of baking with flour all over her overalls but she seemed to have all the time in the World for a chat. The friendliness of the few people who worked here was overwhelming. They seemed so happy I'd come in. I was there for half an hour chatting to them as well as to the other locals who had come in during that time.

With my phone app translator and their few words of English we were all soon laughing away with each other. A Spanish hiker and his wife then came in for some rolls for their lunch. He spoke good English and was able to tell me that the bakery here was well known throughout the Murcia region. Because of the ingredients and the way they baked the bread, the loaves stayed fresh for weeks. I doubted mine would last that long, they'd probably all be eaten in less than a day. I said goodbye wishing one day that I could come back and stay in this lovely community for longer.

Back in the cabin I cooked up some free range boiled eggs, sour dough toast, fresh croissants and black coffee. The smell of it all was enough to wake the other two. "This is heaven. What is that lovely smell Rowena?" Kayleigh said in her soft, mellow Irish accent as she walked out of her bedroom wearing only a long T-shirt. It was one with their bands logo on it.

"Breakfast El Berro style." I replied. "Probably the only thing that's not from around here is the coffee."

"What time is it?" asked Siobhan emerging from her room.

"Nearly 9.00am."

"It feels much later than that." she added. "I feel so rested."

We all agreed with that and we were all soon sitting outside on the veranda in silence eating and drinking and listening and watching. I'd opened my car doors and had Clannad playing softly in the background. We all just sank up the magic around us.

We spent the rest of the morning relaxing, chatting and listening to music. By the time it came to go off to the meditation, we were all in a high state of expectation.

Mariana welcomed us at the door again and this time brought us though into a different room in the house. She explained it was her meditation room and that the energies were highest in here. I made a mental note to ask her about this later. There were cushions on the floor to sit on. We hung our bags up behind the door and took our shoes off and knelt down.

"This type of meditation today is something I learnt from a friend of mine." Mariana began, "She calls it meditating with the higher energies. She is one of the World's top healers and she very kindly has allowed me to teach her method. I feel truly fortunate to now be able to share it with you." Mariana now lowered herself into a full lotus position on the cushion in front of us and continued. "There is no way I can do the whole course for you in one afternoon unfortunately. If you like it though, there is more information available online about it."

Mariana then stated that the aim for today's session was to reach a state of mind where we could consciously ask a question and then go into an unthinking state of mind to see if our unconscious mind could offer anything that might help us with that question. Sometimes it might be that an image or a sound or a feeling of something comes to a person. This then would be something that could be possibly interpreted.

This was not at all what I'd expected and very different from what I'd thought meditation was all about. I'd thought it was about calming the mind and relaxing in order to distress and become healthier. It was about getting a better mind body connection. What Mariana had said though was something I could actually understand. It was similar to my own thoughts when it came to dreaming and being in an unconscious state and getting information from the Universe that way. What was interesting here though was that she was saying that through this type of meditation, we could access our subconscious without having to go to sleep.

Mariana then took us through four key learning stages breaking down this type of mediation initially into four parts. As the session progressed she began to build the four parts back up into one complete process. A mixture of 'key' feelings and visualisations were again combined into making a 'universal energy' move within the body in a way that allowed it to expand and contract within the heart. This was matched and driven by our breathing which was now also connecting us to the universal energies that were all around us.

For the first time, I felt I actually understood the instructions and what I had to do, even though I wasn't sure how it worked. I was also still none the wiser with regards to the term 'Universal Energy'.

We'd now reached the point where were going to put it all together including sounding and chanting the vowels. As we sang the different vowels, sound energy seemed to resonate up and down our bodies. Mariana had chosen to beat a drum this time so we could all breathe in and out together.

In the last part of the session she used a Cello and a bow and played a long low note that sent a tingling sensation up and down my spine and down my arms to my fingers. This apparently was just the beginning. We now had to ask for a sign or a symbol or a thought to come into our minds that would show us our path in life. We were to then go into a 'mushin', no mind state of silence.

I sat there patiently waiting for something to happen. I felt it would but all I could see were horses running together with men next to them. I dismissed it because of the picture I'd seen in the magazine two days before. Still nothing came. I waited patiently trying to rid my mind of any thoughts. It wasn't at all easy. Perhaps I was just not good at this.

"Right" said Mariana. "How did that go? Kayleigh, let's start with you."

"Ok, well. In the silence I had this image of me dancing dressed all in white as part of a large circle of people also all dressed in white. Inside us was another circle of people and also outside of us another circle. We were all dancing together with the circles moving one way and then the other. I'm not sure where we were exactly but it seemed to me that we were on a high up plain in between some mountains. I think there was a lake nearby too."

"Good. Was this something you remember doing before?"

"No it all felt very new and also very exciting for some reason. What does it mean?" Kayleigh asked.

"Well," said Mariana, "I felt the two of you….." she looked at Siobhan briefly before looking back at Kayleigh, "…were together somewhere in Europe. Maybe Hungary or Romania or Bulgaria. As to what it means, I suspect it may be some future event you will attend." She suggested.

"A bit more meditation perhaps another time and you will find out more. For some reason though I think it's probably important that you go there." She paused as though waiting to see if anything else came through or if there was anything else she had come across that she should mention or leave.

"Good, right Siobhan, did you get anything?"

"I got an image of being at a stone circle in some distant past. But as soon as I saw that, I had this feeling of fear. I think I was involved in some sort of ceremony but it was stopped. I remember feeling sad about that. Again I am not sure what it means."

"From what I picked up," started Mariana speaking slowly, "I felt you were in Ireland a long time ago. There seems to be a connection to your past or even a past life." I sat up a bit. Did she say a past life? What was this about? I was slightly disconcerted as to where this was all heading.

Mariana continued, "There may be something you need to do at this place you saw. Somehow you will have to find it and then find out if there is anything you need to do."

"Yes, I got the feeling there was something left undone but I was not sure what." said Siobhan.

"Well don't worry about it," said Mariana, "For now just take it as information to be aware of. I think you'll get given more in time. This is not a small subject that has been uncovered here." Mariana finished and paused again in thought for a few moments as if deciding if there was anything else she should say.

"Rowena, how about you?" she asked.

"Well," I started, "I have to say that during the silence I didn't really get anything."

"It might have not seemed like anything important Rowena. Anything you thought of at all might be relevant in some way?" she stated.

"Well I did think of something," I replied, "but that can't have been important. It wasn't something that just popped into my head because it was something I saw in a magazine a couple of days ago. I don't think it was relevant."

"It may well be though, what was it?" She asked again.

"Well I saw a picture yesterday of horses and men running alongside them at some place in Murcia. I just got this image in my mind now again."

"Very interesting Rowena. You see I got nothing specific for you apart from the fact that I already had some knowledge of something that you needed to know about. It may be to do with these horses and the men running alongside them. Can you tell me anymore about the picture?"

"It was some festival in a town where everyone came out and watched. The Knights Templar were involved in the past too, I think." I replied.

"Ah." Mariana sighed as though a light bulb had switched on and she could now see, "You mean Caravaca de la Cruz. The running of the wine horses in May."

"Yes that was it. Why do you think that place is important?"

"Maybe you need to go there. It's only about 30mins drive away. It's a very special place." She stopped to think for a moment, as though she was thinking about what next to tell me.

"Not many people know that the Roman Catholics say that it is the 5th holiest site in the whole of the Christian World. Miracles are said to have occurred at this place." The hairs on the back of my head began to stand on end.

"Miracles?" I asked. She smiled as though she'd known she'd been right in telling me that.

"Yes, indeed. The running of the wine horses was one of them. You should look it up online. It's a really quite a sacred place Rowena. In fact, come to think of it, you are supposed to be going there. I think this may be the reason you have come here Rowena." She paused.

"Have you been specifically looking for a place like this?" She added looking slightly confused herself and by what she has just asked. By now I was sitting bolt upright. The meditation, the message, Mariana's instruction, the energies, it was becoming overwhelming. I sat in silence trying to calm my mind again. I'd come all this way following some kind of 'going with the flow' and now it seemed like it was really working. It was great that it was, but how could that happen? I'd just been half holidaying and half hoping, and somehow, here I was now right back on the path again. The others were all looking at me in silence, waiting for me to say something.

"Yes," I replied, finally realising I'd been silent for a while, "I think you may be right. There is a place I have been looking for. It may well be this place. I will go there. Thank you, Mariana. Thank you very much." She smiled back at me with a kind of 'knowing without knowing' look.

It was already past the length of time we'd booked with Mariana. I had wanted to ask her what she meant about the energies in the room but we'd run out of time and it didn't feel right taking up any more of it. We again thanked her for the lesson and the next minute we were back in the car heading for the cabin.

Once there, I got online and started searching. Caravaca was indeed a very special place. It ticked all the boxes, the dates, the Moors and Templars all fitted with the information on the scrolls. This really could be the 'Place of Miracles' that the monk Thibault had written about. I just couldn't believe how I'd missed it in my earlier searches but it just hadn't come up at all.

Next I searched for meditation in the mountains in Eastern Europe. After a while I found something that might fit. I called Kayleigh and Siobhan over. A group called the Universal White brotherhood met in their thousands each year in between August 15th and 20th. White was their symbol for purity. It had nothing to do with race or colour. It was to do with the fact that they all dressed completely in white clothes. They did this up in the mountains behind the town of Rila in Bulgaria. There were seven lakes up there and, in between them, they all danced in large circles. The pictures and the videos were just as Kayleigh had seen.

"We have to go Siobhan" she whispered, "It's calling to me."

"Me too. What about you Rowena?" said Siobhan.

"It looks wonderful, I'd love to go." I replied, wondering when though. "I'll have a look at stone circles in Ireland next Siobhan." I added.

After much hunting I found that there were just too many possible sites in Ireland that could fit. Mariana had been right, Siobhan would need more information to help with this one.

After a late night swim and a home-made pasta meal along with the fresh bread from the morning, we retired for another night of complete darkness. We woke revitalised and ready for anything the World wanted to share with us.

As we drove away from El Berro, we each resolved to come back for longer next time. The idea of taking some more courses with Mariana was very appealing. Thinking of coming back helped as we left a place that we'd quickly come to love.

Caravaca de la Cruz

I dropped them both off at their hotel in Murcia. We hugged like old friends and agreed to keep in regular contact on social media. We knew we would all meet up again, we were just not sure where or when. The two of them were very different from anyone I'd previously known. They loved to be helpful, they were kind, sensitive and caring and fun to be around. Mikey was right they were beautiful people. The World would surely be a better place if there were more of them around. There would be far less wars but I am not quite sure just how much work would get done though. We were all different, and necessarily so, but we could perhaps all also learn much from each other.

It was now about 10.30am on Thursday morning. I was heading for Caravaca. El Berro had been the friendliest place in Spain so far. If Caravaca was only half like that, it would be another highlight for me. The main thing on my mind though was now seeing if I could find prove that Caravaca really was 'The Place of Miracles.'

I arrived at the outskirts of the town at about 11.30am. The Sanctuario church could clearly be seen at the top of the only hill. That was situated right in the middle of the centre of the town. It towered over all the other buildings around it. I drove slowly along a straight road into the middle of the town centre. There was a line of trees either side of it and in places it reminded me of France.

The Sanctuario was closed from 12.00 till 4.00pm so my plan was to book in to my hotel early and look around the outside of it. When searching for a place to stay, I'd been drawn to the Hospederia of our lady of Mount Carmel. It was an old monastery that had been restored and converted into a low key hotel. It dated right back to 1587AD and was only a 10min walk from the Sanctuario. It had its own parking which helped considerably. Everything had been adapted to make it look like it used to many years ago. There were cloisters a garden, simple rooms and even a small chapel. It was perfect.

The journey to Caravaca had been like crossing a desert. There really didn't look as though there was much around outside the town and I'd wondered how isolated this place must have felt many hundreds of years ago. The heat now in the middle of the day was also fairly extreme – nearly 40 degrees. I decided to stay inside for a while before venturing out. It would give me time to think too.

Since I'd been 'going with the flow', I'd learnt about Iron & Nickel transducers. I'd now come up with a hypothesis I could try and test. This was about the inner core behaving like a transducer and projecting spherical standing waves of low frequency sounds to the surface of the Earth. I'd also learnt that the pattern that this would make would be many intersecting straight lines. In addition to that I had also managed to improve my yoga and my meditation.

What I wanted to now try at Caravaca was to see whether I could sense these sounds and learn a bit more about them. I'd felt them at Chartres and a few other places, but if they were here, I wanted to see if I could find the high pressure zones and see if these followed straight lines. As for the 4th piece of the stone, if I was ever going to find that, the Universe would have to show me. There was really no other way it could happen.

At about 3.00pm I left the hotel and headed towards the Sanctuario church. The last part up there was up a slope that ran alongside the walls to the castle's main gate. Going through that led me to a large paved courtyard area with the church at the far end on the left. To the left of that was another building that seemed to be attached to the church.

On reading about the site, I realised that originally there was just a small chapel here back in the days of the Templars. It must have stood on its own right at the top of the hill. This small chapel had subsequently been built upon and around and eventually it had become this much larger complex. There were several long steps now leading up to an impressively high façade either side of wooden arched entrance doors to the church. The façade had matching columns and sculptures on both sides with lots of scallop shell designs. I had no idea why.

What I did notice at the base of both the main pillars were the carvings of the heads and bodies of what looked like two giant sea serpents. The other thing that was noticeable was the Caravaca cross set in a large alcove above the top of the arched entrance doorway. It had two horizontal strips across the upright. I'd seen crosses like this before, but normally in pictures of South American churches.

For the moment the Sanctuario was closed. There was another entrance to the left in the building alongside of it. This now seemed to be a museum. That too was closed.

I'd expected that though and had come up here early to get into a meditative state of mind to see if I could sense any low frequency sound energy with a tingling in my fingers. My thinking was that, if I did this in several places up here, I might find these high pressure zones of energy. I knew it was a long shot, but I had to try.

The first place I tried was in front of the main entrance. After a few minutes I felt my fingers tingling. It was enough for me to move on. I pulled out my free tourist map that I'd picked up in the hotel and ticked the spot where I'd been standing. If I found any areas where there was no sensation, I would put a cross.

After about 30 mins of this I was beginning to see a pattern. I'd divided the area up into squares and had meditated briefly in each section. I'd done nearly twenty sections and had found two lines of 'ticks' amidst a sea of 'crosses'. I had now run out of space and sections to test up at this height and in this courtyard area. If I wanted to test it further, I needed to go down to the town and try it there when I was not sure where I was in relation to the 'ticks' up here at Sanctuario.

If I got a line of ticks in the town that matched the line at the top, I might be on to something. As it was, the two lines of ticks seemed to be crossing in the middle of the church. That could be self-suggestion on my part though.

That testing could be done later as the church had now opened and I and about fifty others were now allowed inside. Once in, I started looking around for signs, just as I had with the other churches in Spain. I found nothing. The energies were still high inside though and my fingers were still tingling as I meditated.

I decided to try the museum next door. Inside was a long counter with all sorts of trinkets on sale. I was sure that tourists would love the mementos but I was not here for that. One sign on the counter did catch my eye and that was the time of the next tour. I was in luck, it was in a few minutes and the lady taking it spoke a bit of English. I chatted with her as she waited for others to arrive. She then very kindly gave me the following information. The double cross was down to an old miracle.

A King of the Moors in 1232 AD had been persuaded to convert from Islam over to Christianity. At a ceremony here, it was discovered that, for some reason, no crosses could be found. Without a cross, there could be no conversion. At that moment a host of Angels were said to have appeared though a small window bringing with them a fragment of the true cross. With this they were then able to make a Christian cross and carry out the conversion ceremony.

The Caravaca cross, with its extra horizontal strip, was made to commemorate the miracle of the Angels appearing that occurred here. All the other churches in the World that copied this, are essentially copying this same cross that was first created here. The extra strip of course was signifying the piece of the true cross.

I asked her about what was going on in this region back then. She told me that it was a time when both the Christians and the Moors were fighting for the land across Southern Spain. By 1243AD though, the Christians had taken back most of the Murcia region.

I remembered that it was 1244AD that brother Thibault had left Montsaunes to go down into Spain with the 4th piece of the stone. That meant that they could have heard about the miracle of the cross and they may have also heard that the 'Place of Miracles' was now a safe place to go to. Everything fitted so far. This really could be it.

Our group was ready to go. There were six of us. We were shown the cloistered area first next to the room with all the souvenirs for sale. In one corner of the central cloistered area there was a deep well. Our guide began to tell us more about it.

In 1250AD the Moors had again laid siege to the town and the townsfolk had all gathered up in the Castle to avoid being killed. Unfortunately the well was running dry and the remaining water in it had gone off and it was now causing illness and disease. The Templars rode out on their horses one night to look for new supplies of water. All they found was a number of large wine sacks filled with wine. They took these and ran them back up to the Castle with the wine sacks thrown over the backs of the horses. They then emptied some of these wine sacks into the well and this seems to have turned the water good and healthy again. This was hailed as a miracle by the townsfolk and they went on to survive the siege.

They were so happy with the Templars that the townsfolk eventually placed the town in their hands in the year 1266AD. It remained cared for by the Templars until their order was disbanded in 1313AD. This place has since had several miracles associated with it over the years. It was perhaps because of all these miracles, that there were now so many people coming here each year on a pilgrimage.

The Pope, in 1998, recognised this fact and awarded this place the title of the 5th Holiest city in the Christian World. This is behind Jerusalem, Rome, Santiago de Compostela and Santo Toribio de Liébana. The last two were also places in Spain.

Our guide then moved through the group towards some stairs. We all followed along behind her and were soon going up and through into the upper chambers of the church. It hadn't been possible to get to these areas from the ground level when I'd been in the church earlier. It now provided some good views down into the church and again another chance for me to look around.

A few moments later we were taken up some more steps right at the back of the church. This led to part of the original Templar chapel.

It was a small room but with a fairly high ceiling that was about 3 meters square. In the middle was a large wooden structure. No one was looking at that though. Instead everyone's eyes were drawn to a small circular feature high up by the ceiling of the open facing wall to the rest of the church. Around it were many strange symbols. Somehow I knew that this was what I was meant to find.

I could feel my heart beating faster. I slowly turned and looked around at the rest of the chamber. It was filled with all sorts of encrypted messages, drawings in the corners and on the walls.

Our guide started by pointing first towards the small circular feature. It was actually a piece of ornate plasterwork with several clear glass panels that had flowers set behind them. The quality of the leaves and petals behind the glass made it look as though they were still fresh but they couldn't have possibly been.

She described this as the 'Apparition window'. Before the window had been filled in, this was where the Angels had been seen flying in with a piece of the true cross. As this was the original chapel with the church having been built next to it, the window now didn't lead to the outside. Because of that, it had been bricked up and then covered with an enigmatic plasterwork design.

What made it really special though were these symbols around the edge of it. They could well be coded letters or even a mixture of parts of several different ancient languages. It was impossible to tell with just a quick look at it. It had to mean something really special.

Our guide started to speak in English again. "The symbols around the apparition window here have never been deciphered. There is a local legend in the town that says if ever they were, it would change the World for good. As you can see some of them have very strange designs and many of them have, so far, not been seen anywhere else in the World."

I looked at the symbols again. Could this be a hidden Templar message? Was this a message from the monks at Montsaunes? It was then that I saw one symbol in particular. I'd seen it before. It was just like the A sign or the Alpha sign above the front entrance of the Montsaunes chapel on the Chi Rho symbol there. The symbol here was drawn in just the same way. There was a horizontal line across the top of the A and the central line below it was a V shape. This must be the connection I'd been looking for.

355

My heart started to race faster. This could well mean that Thibault and his followers had made it all the way South to Caravaca and had left signs of that here. This had to be the place of miracles.

This enigmatic message around the 'filled in' Apparition window was quite possibly another message from Rossal's followers that now needed to be translated. The town legend about it leading to something really good for the World was baffling though. My mind just couldn't comprehend what that could possibly be. Somehow this message really had to be deciphered. I just had no idea how for the moment. More synchronicity perhaps?

Our guide was now leading us out. I wished I could stay longer and study it all further but I couldn't. I took my phone out and started taking as many photos as I could. Amongst the ceiling designs, there were four wall paintings in each corner of the room. Each one had a short Latin inscription on them. It seemed like these contained even more hidden symbolism. I quickly took pictures of each of them to look at more closely later on. These too all looked as though they were all part of an overall hidden message that this small chapel had been trying to hide for centuries.

I followed the guide out of the small room and back down the stairs. I felt elated at being very sure that I'd found what I'd been looking for but also slightly frustrated with even more questions as to what it all meant. So many critical secrets seemed to have been around back in those days and we just didn't know at all what they meant today.

Not long afterwards we were all back at the main entrance again and I found myself walking out into the large courtyard area again. It was nearly 5.00pm. I really needed to sit down, relax and go through the photos I'd just taken.

I walked slowly back down the slope that ran alongside the walls of the Castle and then down and round into a small café area. I was now in the beautiful Plaza del Arco. There were more people around now as the shops had reopened after the siesta. I stopped to buy some bottled water and some fresh fruit. Doing that then made me realise how hungry I really was. I'd not eaten since breakfast at El Berro. There was a table free in front of me at one of the restaurants in the Plaza. It was also right next to a full size Iron statue of a Moor and a Templar.

I sat down at the table. There were several trees in the paved area, each growing out of their own small round circular patches of earth that had been set amidst the paving stones. It seemed unnatural but their green was a pleasant contrast to the whites and creams of the buildings. On one side of the plaza was a two story building with flags flying from the first story balcony. Underneath it there was a large arch which was just wide enough for small cars to pass through. It made the Plaza feel nicely contained and isolated from the rest of the town.

The waiter came and took my order. Feeling prepared and ready, I took my phone out to look at the pictures I'd just taken. I scrolled through them all quickly first and decided to start on the wall paintings. One of them was just a pitcher of wine which probably represented the miracle that occurred here when the Templars had poured the wine into the well and the town had been saved. That didn't seem to tell me much more than the fact that these paintings all related to the Sanctuario. It had a Latin inscription under it that I decided to translate later as I wanted to flick through them all quickly first.

The next one drew my attention in much more. It was titled with the Latin words Lavacrum Sacrum. The picture was a chalice shaped object with a bird flying up and out of it.

To me this was further proof that someone who'd had Cathar beliefs must have been here and arranged for this wall painting to be done. The bird was clearly representing a dove. It was yet more proof that this was the place of miracles.

This looked easier to translate so I looked up a Latin to English page on my search engine. Sacrum was an old Latin name for sacred. It was also a

Greek word for sacred. Lavacrum meant washroom. "Sacred Bathroom" I whispered to myself. I could not believe it. Here in, writing, was actual evidence that these people believed that not all places on the Earth were the same. Some were much more sacred than others. This was exactly what I was going to investigate scientifically.

This place was obviously one of their really sacred places – a place perhaps even where the Grail could appear to those people who were holy enough to see it – however that could happen. The picture was now probably not a chalice, or a Grail, at all though. It was far more likely to represent a baptismal font. It would have been amusing to them, I guessed, that they'd drawn it to look like the Holy Grail cup. Seeing this picture on the wall here made me now fairly certain that this place was where there was a large sound energy intersection. Any bathing done here would be in the sound energy formations on that intersection. I remembered the Vortex and the Torus shapes on the Montsaunes ceiling. Their meditations and other ceremonies would therefore take place within these sound formation shapes.

I then remembered reading in one of Otto Rahn's books that the Cathars had preferred to be baptised by the Spirit rather than by water. It was another of those things that had really annoyed the Pope. If this was what the Cathars were referring to when they talked about being baptised by the Spirit, I could perhaps understand why. This was a baptism in a sound so low you couldn't even hear it. Who knew what benefits that could bring? Healing, Rejuvenation, Enlightenment perhaps? At this point the waiter came with my food. I put my phone down and started to eat.

It was only a small selection of tapas, but it was enough to keep me going until an evening meal. Having finished it all, and feeling much better, I decided to not do any more investigations into the locations of these sound energies on the streets. I could start afresh on that tomorrow.

Instead I headed back to the old monastery Hospideria. I fancied a shower and some quiet time to do some further research on what I'd come across today. I also needed to catch up with all my social media messages.

Sophie had texted me and so had Kayleigh and Siobhan and I'd had emails from the guys at Tarascon and a missed phone call from my Uncle.

Having showered, I was now getting back to everyone with a glass of red wine sitting at a table outside in the cloistered garden. Being as this was not a normal hotel, the outside area was also a bit different. There were large flat rectangular areas that had been filled with small flat shale stones that had a pinky, grey colour. These areas were crossed by white gravel paths. Growing up through the shale stones in these rectangular areas were several types of bushes, plants and small trees. It was all very minimal and slightly Spartan but completely in fitting with the monastic lifestyle that used to exist here.

Fortunately for me, that was now not the case. I had a soft comfy bed and there was a fine looking seafood paella on the menu at the hotel tonight. The restaurant wasn't open yet though so, having replied to all my messages and having called my Uncle, I took the time to search the internet for more information on the pictures in the corners of the chapel with the Apparition window.

After about ten minutes searching, I'd found very little. There were no images anywhere on the wall paintings in the corners and there were only two or three pictures of the window with the symbols. It all seemed to be really unknown, except perhaps regionally in Murcia and locally here in Caravaca. Outside the Murcia region though, I couldn't find any website that seemed to be mentioning anything about the Caravaca symbols and wall paintings.

It was almost as though it was all meant to be kept a secret and something that some people didn't ever want deciphered. I changed my searching to see if I could find out what the Latin phrases meant on the other remaining wall paintings.

The first was a painting of a snake on the cross. To me this was very strange to see in a church. Snakes have always been associated with evil in the bible.

The words above it read 'Deus Exaltivit Illum'. With some online searching I'd found out that the Latin message had come from a letter that St Paul had written to a group of people from a town called Phillipi in Greece. It could be found in the new Testament in the Bible under Phillipians chapter 2 verse 9. The meaning was 'God exalted him' and this probably referred to Jesus. However, I discovered that 'Illum' in Latin could also mean 'It.' This message with the snake in the picture could now mean 'God exalted it.'

This was really strange. Why would a Roman Catholic Church have allowed a painting to be seemingly praising, or 'holding up on high' the Snake? With a bit more searching online I found out about the Gnostic Gospels. In these Gospels the Snake in the garden of Eden had been viewed in a very different way. It didn't represent Satan or Evil at all. To the Gnostics the Snake represented the Instructor or the Teacher. This was such a different view point, I had to investigate further.

The Gnostic gospels were apparently a collection of 52 texts that seemed to have been written around 200AD. It seems that some of Jesus's disciples, other than Matthew, Mark, Luke and John had also written about the life of Jesus and what he'd been teaching. These other disciples and their gospels seemed to have been saying that the message Jesus was teaching was slightly different from that being put forward by the Roman Catholic Church. Their message now appeared to be much more similar to the message that the Gnostic Christians were following hundreds of years later.

I could now see where and when the two different schools of Christian thinking had emerged. In addition to that it seems that at some time in the 4th century the Roman Catholic Church had ordered that all the writings containing these Gnostic gospels should be found and destroyed. Unfortunately for them it seems that a few of them had survived.

In the 13th Century these two schools of thinking had obviously reached a point where one school felt very threatened by the other. I thought back to the Grail stories and their hidden Gnostic messages and the Cathar massacre at Montsegur. The schism between the two sides of Christianity had begun a very long time before that. On my mind now was that the people here at Caravaca seemed to have been much more in favour of the Cathari Gnostic interpretation of Christianity. This again tied in with some of them having come originally from Montsaunes.

Only they would have wanted to have a wall painting with the snake on the cross with those words under it. I was also now wondering if there was any connection with the Snake image here and the sound lines. I turned to look at the next wall painting.

This one was a drawing of a pair of straight horns that you would expect to see and hear at some mediaeval jousting tournament. Underneath it were the words 'Vox Clamantis In Deserto'. This Latin message appeared in two places in the bible. The first and original place came from the book of Isiah in the old Testament of the Vulgate bible Chapter 40 verse 3. The words under the picture were just the first few words of a longer verse.

The Vulgate bible seems to have been a work commissioned by Pope Damasus 1 in 382AD. Several people were said to have contributed to it and only selected Greek and Latin texts were used. It seemed that the Gnostic point of view had not been represented in it at all. The full verse read 'Vox clamantis in deserto parate viam Domini rectas facite in solitudine semitas Dei nostri.'

Translating it proved quite difficult and there seemed to be several ways it could be done. The Vulgate bible was probably the one the Templars would have been most familiar with so, even though it probably was not very gnostic, I had to start with it. Having managed to translate this verse into English it seemed to provide a different translation from the one found in the later 17th Century King James the 6th bible.

I wondered briefly why that might be until I realised that the Roman Church may well have wanted to further disguise some things in their newer version. I needed to get my translation checked out but, using the best online translators the following was obtained:-

'Call out the voice in the desert. Prepare the way of the Lord. Make straight in solitude the paths of our God'

It was a really strange message.

Two things stood out for me though. The first was the clear distinction between the Latin words Domini and Dei. The former translated to Lord or Master, whilst the second translated to God. Clearly the early writer was deliberately using two different words and each with a separate meaning. This was strange to me as the church had always seemingly gone to great lengths to say that they were the one and the same.

Looking at where the verse appeared for a second time in the bible showed that in the later New Testament, in the Gospel according to Mark, chapter 1 verse 3, the same Isiah verse is intentionally repeated by the later writer of that gospel. This time though this clear differentiation between the Lord/Master and God had been deliberately omitted. Someone had even changed the original Latin to cover it up.

The priests here at this chapel had perhaps chosen the short first part of the verse, which was identical in both testaments, in order to be able to interpret it one way for the Roman Church with Mark's verse, and another way, with Isiah's verse, for their own followers. This would allow their more gnostic way of thinking to be hidden in plain sight. The Roman church's deliberately composed viewpoint that the Lord/Master and God were one and the same was now much clearer to see.

The second thing that stood out for me was the fact that the word for 'paths', semitas, and the word 'straight', rectas, were in the same sentence. It looked to me as though the message was something about meditating on the straight paths in the desert. If it was anything like that at all, it provided a link with the straight paths and their intersections that I'd come across earlier. It also made me think of the crossing song lines in the Australian desert and the sacred Aboriginal 'dream time' sites.

The picture of two horns crossing was perhaps a clue here as well with regards to intersections. Questions kept started firing off in my mind. Could the Templars have been following these straight paths themselves? Maybe this was how they were searching for their Grail? It was then that I remembered Ethan Parker on the train to Paris telling me how the Aborigine's used them to travel great distances across the desert. This seemed just the same thing. Their 'dream time' sites must then be the same type of places as the ancient sacred sites that the Templars had been trying to find.

It really now did appear that this place really was an extremely sacred site to the Templars who lived here. At that moment a bell rang and distracted me from my thoughts.

The restaurant had now opened and the constant focus and attention of my research had made me tired. I decided to eat next and then have a think about the symbols around the window afterwards.

The seafood paella had been excellent. Having finished every grain of rice on the plate, I turned to researching the strange symbols with renewed energy. Throughout my meal I had had the picture of it open in front of me and it had fully absorbed my attention.

Deciphering its message around the window was, unfortunately, proving harder than I'd expected. I recognised one or two symbols but the rest I'd drawn a blank on. I'd spent ages online looking through pages and pages of symbols but could find nothing that matched or made any sense at all. To decipher it would take a whole new strategy. I decided to leave it up to synchronicity and went to bed.

My last thoughts before I drifted off to sleep were about the 4th piece of the Cathar stone. The monks would have certainly brought it to Caravaca. The question on my mind though was where they might have put it. There'd been no sign of it up at the church or the museum. There were some caves around Caravaca that I could search later on but for now I wanted to discover more about these sound lines.

The next morning, I awoke raring to get going. Over breakfast I'd being thinking about what I could now do to test these sound lines in a more scientific manner. Now that I'd found out how to find them using a form of meditation, I could place instruments on them and either side of them. I'd need to first find a wide area of fairly flat countryside with them running across it. I could then sink large flat, rectangular metal sheets made of Iron and Nickel into the ground so that they could act as transducers. I could then wire them up to recording devices.

Any sound energy coming from the centre of the Earth would then be converted back into Electromagnetic energy and easily measured. If the Inner core of the Earth was working like a transducer any electromagnetic energy going into it would be converted into very low frequency sound energy. I was going to convert it back again.

If I sank enough plates into the ground over a wide enough area, I could leave them recording the vibrations for a few weeks. Over time, and having eliminated as much background noise as possible, any inner core high pressure sound vibrations would then show up electronically.

Variations between the sensors should show up these areas I was sensing physically. I could then try using some more sophisticated equipment to see if I could find any Eigenmodes that might match harmonically with those already found associated with the mysterious hum. It was the start of a plan and it excited me. However, as I'd already found out, if I went with the flow, plans could even change for the better.

Right now though I was still in Spain and I wanted to see if I could find these lines down in the town and then check if they matched the directions of the lines I'd found the day before up at the Sanctuario. I'd selected several streets to start with and had obtained a new map of the town. I sectioned the streets up so that I had about thirty places to do quick meditation sessions on. If the lines crossed them, I wanted to find out where that was. Having packed up and settled my bill, I headed out on foot.

After an hour, I'd again found two lines of ticks running across several streets. I repeated the process to check it and definitely found that whilst I was in one section I could feel a tingling sensation and when I stood in the two sections either side of that, I could not. I then checked my 'tick' directions with the ones I'd found yesterday up in the Castle. I got out my first map. There was a clear match.

One line seemed to be heading to the South West, the other to the South East. A further look at the map and I could see that the one leading to the South East seemed to be heading towards the Sierra Espuna and El Berro. Could that be why the camp site and the village felt so energised? Who knew? I then had another thought. Could I track this line across in that direction to see where it went?

It might take a while but I could drive across to where I thought the line would be heading and then see if I could find it there. It felt like the right thing to do and I wasn't prepared yet anyway to check the local caves for pieces of haematite.

Following the lines felt more like going with the flow anyway. It would quite possibly even lead me to where I was supposed to be going next. I might then even find out more about the symbols around the window.

I went back to my car and drove to the outskirts of the town where I'd expected to find the line. I parked up and started walking, testing the sensation every 10 meters. After a few minutes I'd found it again. I plotted the position on my map. It was still running in a straight line. I projected the line further on the map and saw where it crossed another small road in the mountains.

It took about 20 minutes of driving to get to the site but this time I had Paulo Nutini with me so the time flew by. Once there I started the same process again and after about ten minutes of quick meditation in various places along the side of the road, I'd found the line again. I checked the map. The line was now not quite straight. It was bending South slightly. It still projected towards the mountains though.

I was now on M504 heading South West towards a small place called Burete. Caravaca was now out of sight but I knew it was to the North West of me. I stopped again and started walking along the road looking for the feeling in my fingers again. This time it felt stronger. Was that the line getting stronger or me getting better at picking it up? I didn't know.

I was now looking at the top of a hill to the North West. I checked the map. It looked as though the line had taken a definite turn Southwards to go through the top of the hill. If this was a high pressure concentration of sound, maybe that is what these things did. They would naturally gravitate towards certain places. It seemed likely now that this kind of high sound pressure concentration was why we get some high up places being thought of as more sacred than others. I thought of some of the many sacred mountains around the World.

Having recorded the line where I was, I checked the map again and projected the lines new direction. It was now not heading for El Berro. I felt disappointed for some reason but my left brain actually now spoke up. No this was a good thing. It means I am not self-suggesting where this line is heading. On the flip side though, I had no idea at all as to where it was going. I continued on beginning to realise how exciting this was now becoming. I was all a bit of a mystery.

After another hour of this I was now on the MU 503. The line looked as though it had run through the peak of a mountain called Pico de la Selva. It now seemed to be heading for the small town of Aledo. The road I was on swung round to the East again. To get to Aledo, it meant that the line would cross over the road again. About half an hour later it did, but now it looked as though the line was swinging slightly Northwards of a South East heading again.

This behaviour didn't seem to me to be a straight line at all. On the other hand, it could be that the overall direction was straight and, on a more local basis, it would snake along one side and then the other either side of this straight alignment.

Could that be why they were even symbolised as Snakes? An image of the Caduceus with its straight central staff and with two snakes coiled around it came into my mind. Was this a symbol for these as well? I couldn't tell.

Everything was going well but I was getting incredibly tired. I'd been doing this for around three hours and I needed a break.

St Eulalia Monastery

I stopped in the small town of Aledo and got out to stretch my legs. The streets were narrow and the houses were packed close together. After a few hundred meters of walking, I could see why. The whole town had been built on a rocky promontory that had steep cliffs on three sides. At the end there was a tall square tower – the Tower of Homenaje. It held a hugely strategic position across the vast plain below. There must have been a lot of history to this place at one time.

Having rested my eyes with the amazing views I headed back to my car. Just a short break made me feel much fresher. I checked my map again. The line seemed to be still running towards the South West but it had passed slightly to the North of Aledo. It now looked as though it would cross the RM-502 road in a couple of miles at exactly the same spot as an old Monastery and then again beyond that at a large statue of Jesus Christ on top of a hill to the South West of it.

My heart nearly missed a beat. Was this further evidence of a connection between these lines and places where people prayed and meditated? If these were high pressure concentrations of sound why would they even do that? More questions!

The Santa Eulalia Monastery came into view as I came round the corner. It was time to get out again and test to see if the line ran past here or through here. It was not a Monastery anymore though. It had been turned into a hotel. I pulled into the car park feeling as though I had been drawn to find this place for some reason.

After a few minutes of testing, a process which now seemed to be getting easier and faster, I'd worked out that the line ran right through the Monastery/Hotel. It also looked as though it was heading straight for the statue as well.

There was nothing else for it. I had to stay the night here. I got out my suitcase and went to see if there were any rooms free. Again I was lucky, the hotel was fairly new and bookings had been low. For no particular reason I checked in for a couple of nights.

I took my bag up to my room and sat down. I immediately felt a tingling sensation without even trying to find it. I checked by meditating. The line ran right through the room I was in. I must have been on some kind of auto pilot which was how I'd sensed it. I went outside and tried to work out just exactly how wide this line was. After about 5 mins of shuffling up and down the corridor I'd discovered it was about 35 meters wide.

I went back to my room wishing I had someone to talk to about this. I tried calling Pierre – no answer. He must be busy. It was early Friday afternoon, most people would be at work. I tried my Uncle. Again no answer.

Perhaps I was not meant to speak with them about this just yet. I decided to do some exploration and went for a walk. The hotel gardens were lovely but there was no one there either. I was now wondering why I had this urge to talk with someone. Was it because I wanted to tell someone what I had been finding out or was it because I still had so many questions and I wanted someone else's thoughts or guidance on it all.

Guidance. Yes that was it. At University there were always tutors we could talk to. Here I had no one. I stood in silence and realised I'd stopped in the garden at exactly the centre point of the sound line I'd been following. Somehow I'd been drawn back to the line again. The image of the Snake on the cross came into my mind - the Snake as the teacher. Of course, that was it. If I meditated on the lines, perhaps just as Mariana had taught us, we could ask for the information we needed. Maybe this was the 'way of old' and how knowledge used to be obtained over 2000 years ago. Meditating on the Energies and getting answers to your questions was like having your own teacher. The Snake must represent these linear concentrations of sound energy. Praying or meditating on these lines was a way to receive guidance in the past.

That must be why the Snake was regarded by the Gnostic Christians as the teacher or instructor.

My urge to talk to someone was really an urge to get some answers to my questions. I must have felt the urge because of the extra strong energies here. Why this should be the case though I really couldn't tell. I took a drink of water from the bottle I'd been carrying and looked around for a quiet place to sit and meditate. Before I began though, I needed to have a question on my mind to ask. There were so many to choose from though. What did the message around the window mean? Where was the 4th piece of the Cathar stone? What can really happen at these intersections? What is this Rose magic that Otto Rahn wrote about? Am I following the flow and am I on the path I should be on?

It was then that I realised that all my questions were selfish. All the answers would have been about making my position stronger and better as though I was fear full. This lack of knowing and understanding was a driving force for many scientists. It seemed that my own curiosity and quest for answers was making me fall into the same trap. It may well be that I am supposed to find out some of the answers to these questions, maybe even all of them, but was it the right time. Asking direct questions and receiving answers to these would surely help me but that may then take me off the path I was working to stay on.

If I was supposed to find out the answers, I would. If it was not for me to know, either not at all or not until later on, then that would be as it should be. 'If God wills it', the phrase from Perlesvaus, came to mind.

All I could really ask for is for help and guidance to follow my path. I could ask for help to notice these moments of synchronicity when they came along and to know how best explore them. If I received anything, either now or later, that would be fine, if not, so be it too. I relaxed, breathed deeply and followed the processes that I'd been recently shown. It felt good to be doing it again. This time though the energy seemed so much more powerful. The more I tried to send it out into the World, the more it seemed to be coming back into me.

Was this down to the energy of the place? Again I couldn't tell and instead I looked to ignore any more of my own questions. I remained in silence trying to get into an Alpha brain wave state - hearing no one thing and yet hearing everything, seeing no one thing and yet seeing everything and feeling no one feeling but feeling everything. Quite soon an amazingly warm feeling began to build in my stomach. It felt as though I was in the right place at the right time and that I should be patient.

I waited again in silence for at least another ten minutes trying to keep hold of a new feeling of growing confidence that was building up inside of me. Yes I had questions, yes I felt the urge to ask because of the energies, but now I had received the best response I could have hoped for.

It was time to relax and enjoy my time here and to watch out for any further synchronicity. That meant mixing with as many people as I could and focusing on them. I was here for a reason and I was in the right place at the right time so for the rest of today, I would stay at the monastery.

By 11.00pm I had played my music and had updated my notes on what I'd found out during my time here in Spain. I'd met a few lovely guests in the dining room in the evening and conversations had been varied but so far no coincidences seemed to have emerged even after exploring them.

What had been fun though was focusing on them for most of that time. Some people can be amazingly interesting. More importantly I realised that not every interaction I was going to have was to be for me, my journey and my benefit. Right now though, I was now wondering how I could possibly sleep right on top of all these energies. I shouldn't have worried. I dropped off into a deep sleep in no time.

I woke up at about 6.00am in the morning in a hot sweat. My dreaming had been incredibly vivid. I'd been living back in what seemed to be the Bronze Age in a small community down here in Spain - one which didn't seem too far away either. There were about five hundred of us living on a hill surrounded by giant fortifications at the base of it. At the top was our most holy sacred place.

Somehow I had been part of an exceptionally dangerous ritual that was being carried out right at the very top. Something was not quite right though and the ceremony had not worked and that was when I'd woken up. My sweating added to the realism of it all.

I took a shower and tried to figure out what it all meant. By the end of it, I decided I needed to find out if there actually were any old Bronze Age settlements nearby. There was a tourist office in Totana which was a town just a few kilometres down the road. I would ask there after breakfast.

La Bas Tida

I parked up and walked down towards the square in front of the town hall in the middle of Totana. The town sat astride a huge dry river bed that had strong concrete walls either side of it. I peered over one of its bridges and could see that there must be occasions when an enormous torrent of water must run down off the mountains at rapid speeds here. The phrase Flash floods came to mind from past Geography lessons.

The tourist office was open. I went in and asked about Bronze Age settlements. "Ah you must be looking for La Bas Tida" the young lady said in very good English. She picked up a brochure for me. I reached out to take it and noticed my hand was shaking. On the front of it was a picture of the place. It was on a large conical hill. It looked very familiar. "You are in luck if you want to see it," she continued.

"Why is that?" I asked.

"Well it is only open on Saturdays and you can only see it if you book in on a tour. There is only one today and that is at 6.00pm in the evening." That struck me as strange to start at tour that late in the evening but hey, this was Spain.

"Can I book a place?" I asked.

"Sure." She took my name and a contact number and then gave me directions on how to get there. I said thanks and left. There'd only been a very small price to pay for it as well – ridiculous value.

I couldn't wait until 6.00pm though. I had to go and see it now. I went back to my car and followed the directions.

After about 20 mins I was pulling up to a large gate that was closed. Behind it was a car park and a one story salmon coloured row of offices and rooms. It was the Archaeological centre. Behind this building was the hill.

It was not the highest hill in the area by any means but I couldn't stop looking at the top of it. For some reason I was not only connected to the top through last night's dream, but now I had the distinct feeling that the Monk Thibault had also been up there.

The more I thought about it, the more I now also thought that he'd buried the 4th piece of the Cathar stone up at the top. It sounded ridiculous, I know. I had no proof of that at all but the feeling inside me was utterly compelling. My left brain seemed to have given up from even beginning to pass comment on this.

It was still only late morning. There was no one here, no cars around. I could climb over the gate and be up at the top in under 15 mins. The devil in me said to go for it. I only wanted to see if the stone was at the top. If it wasn't I'd come straight back down. There was a problem though. If the stone was there and I took it, how could I then prove where I'd found it? What would that be worth? No I needed to do this by the book if there was anything there at all. The urge to go to the top though was growing stronger. In the end, I couldn't cope with it any more. I had to get back into my car and drive off.

It was unlike me to have thought all those things. With my rational mind having given up on me, my right brain activity had been left to its own devices. I put it down to the vivid dream I'd had last night. Having now actually been there though, I knew that my dream had been very real in some way. It felt that I'd already been there somehow.

I was at an impasse and again I had a head filled with questions. With five hours to kill before the tour started. I seriously needed to do something different. I decided to go for a run. I'd seen a canal waterway that I'd driven over on my way to La Bas Tida. Next to it was a narrow support road. It would make an excellent out and back run.

I was only about ten minutes from the hotel so I nipped back and got changed into my running gear. Not much later I was now running along the canal and enjoying the lovely views of the mountains of the Sierra Espuna on my left and the plains that stretched down past Totana on my right. The run was flat all the way but I had the bit between my teeth for some speed. I ran for 30mins on the way out and found that it had only taken me 28mins to get back. I'd shaken my demons away and had returned to some sense of reality. I drove back to the hotel for a shower and a change of clothes.

I spent the rest of the afternoon in my room reading about La Bas Tida online and watching a couple of short videos about the place. Apparently it was thought that the original Agaric people here had come from the other side of the Mediterranean Sea. The building architecture and the tools discovered here, matched those found thousands of miles away in the Middle East. I wondered why they might have done that.

It was a long way and it would have been a journey filled with dangers and hardship all that time ago. If it had been to escape some other warring nation, they wouldn't have travelled that far. If they were just looking for another good place to grow their crops and live in peace, well there were many places that would have been perfect much nearer. In those days there were really nothing like as many people around either so there would have been land available. The only seemingly rational answer to me was that they were on some kind of pilgrimage. They might even have been following some of the major sound lines like the Aborigine's did.

La Bas Tida had to also be where they wanted to end up as well. The reason for that was that they had arrived here around 4200 years ago and had lived there for over 700 years. The Archaeologists working on the site now thought that the tribal elders, and perhaps the wealthier people, lived in houses near the top of the hill and that this was where they now also thought was their most sacred site.

I had to agree with that one. What had surprised them though was that this was a strange place to build what has now been recognised of as one of the largest Bronze Age cities in the whole of mainland Europe. It was not next to a river, or an Estuary which would be good for trade. It was not even the highest place around which would have made defending it easier.

It was now 5.30pm. I'd arrived early. I was also in luck as the gates were already open so I parked up. The offices were also open. Their shade offered some protection against the searing heat that was still around this late in the afternoon. I wondered just how the Bronze Age people had managed to cope.

With all this in mind, I walked in through the entrance and then into a connecting side room. There were a few display cabinets showing some of the 'finds' from the site. There was also a Spanish gentleman in a small office at the far end. I went over and introduced myself as one of the people who had booked the tour. "Hi. My name is Rowena. I'm from the UK and looking forward to the tour around La Bas Tida."

"Good evening Senora" he replied, "My name is Alejandro. Yes I am your guide today." He paused for a while. "My English is not good. The tour is only in Spanish, I am sorry."

"I understand." I replied. I brought out my phone and switched on the Spanish to English translator 'app'. "Try this." He spoke a few words in Spanish. The 'app' translated it into English for me.

"The tour starts at 6.00pm and lasts for two hours" my translator said. Alejandro smiled. I switched languages around.

"Do you know how many people will be coming?" I spoke into the 'app'. A Spanish voice relayed my question to him. He nodded.

375

"Today only eight people." He said directly to me in English. There were other questions I wanted to ask him but a couple of other people for the tour had turned up. It could wait until later.

In the end there were only six of us. The others were all Spanish. The tour started by following a purpose built vehicle track around to the other side of the hill. Here we were shown the massive foundations to the walls which had once protected the place. The main excavations came next. There were helpful information boards next to each section that also gave an English description.

My 'app' unfortunately had given up trying to translate his descriptions. The speed of his talking, the background noise and probably the technical archaeological jargon was just too much for it.

After an hour, it was plain to see that only around 10% of the site had been excavated and that was around the base of the hill. The site of real interest at the top had been left untouched for the moment. I decided to ask why. "Alejandro," I began by speaking into my 'app', "Why is it that there have been no excavations yet at the top of the hill?"

"I am not sure why," he replied, "We have been told by the director to start at this level. In time, we will get to the top." He shrugged his shoulders as though he had no more to say on the matter. I left it for the moment. I needed to find the right time to ask him if I could go up there.

With some more descriptions, the group started to head back along the track to the offices and the car park. On the way we passed the only track that wound its way up to the top of the hill. The others had gone on ahead and I sensed my chance. I knew he wouldn't let me go up on my own so I tried another angle. "Alejandro. I want to ask you a very big favour. If I left my camera and my bag down here in the offices, after the others have left too, would you take me up to the top for just 5 mins. I had a dream last night that there was something there that I had to see. I know it sounds ridiculous but just a few minutes looking and not touching anything and staying on the track, is all that I would need. Please." I looked earnestly into his eyes.

"There is nothing up there to see Rowena, I can assure you." He replied.

"I appreciate you saying that but there may be something I can see that will remind me of my dream. You see, last night I dreamt that I was living here all those years ago. I was at the top and involved in some kind of ritual but I was woken up before I could find out what was happening. That's one reason why I came here today." He looked at me. I think he was wondering if I could have made all of that up.

"Ok. But only 5 minutes and only after the others have gone so I can lock up. Yes too because you were woken up from your dream. I know how annoying that can be." He replied with a smile on his face.

"Thank you so much." I instinctively gave him a quick hug. "I will be quick I promise."

"You don't need to leave your bag and camera behind either, that will be ok." He added.

With the others now having departed, we headed up the spiralling track to the top of the hill. "To be honest, we don't often come up here these days," he began, "so it's nice for me to come up again and take a look."

"What do you think went on at the top?" I asked

"Well. It's definitely their most special place here. The building at the top is very different – no one lived in it. It's not there now of course, but the foundations are." I then focused more on him and asked him questions on how he ended up here and what he was studying. It seemed to open him up and it made him want to talk more.

"Do you know that I was one of the first archaeologists up here in about 1986? A student who had been researching this place took me here. We looked around the top back then but couldn't see anything. A few fragments of pottery that was it. There may be more beneath the surface but that's unlikely at the very top. The winds and the rains will have washed them away."

In next to no time we were at the top. My eyes scanned the ground in all directions. Intuitively I somehow knew that the 4th piece of the Cathar stone had been placed here by the monk Thibault. He must have gone on to find this place after he'd reached Caravaca. Maybe the 'Place of Miracles' was not the most sacred place that the monk Rossal had heard about in Jerusalem, I wondered.

Maybe possibly instead an old Bronze Age city could well have become legendary over time for some reason. The people who lived here must have thought it was very special to have travelled so far to get here.

Maybe Thibault had somehow found this place and realised what it once was - an incredibly powerful sacred place. One that was much more powerful than either Caravaca or Montsaunes.

I went to the very centre of the top and started to meditate – nothing. I tried again. Still no sensation anywhere, not even in my fingers. I felt confused. I hadn't expected that at all. I looked around again. This time I was looking for a lump of reddish Haematite. It would have stood out like a sore thumb at the top though. There was nothing like it around here.

If it had been buried nearly 700 years ago, it would have almost certainly been exposed by the weathering by now. Being an incredibly dense stone too, it would have been very unlikely to have been moved by the wind or the rain either. My heart sank and my face must have shown that. To have come all this way and to feel it was where I should be and then to find nothing was a bitter pill. I squatted down and covered my face with my hands. If I'd been alone, I might have cried.

"Rowena. Can I help? What are you looking for?" Alejandro asked in a kind voice. I may as well tell him, I thought.

"This will seem very strange to you Alejandro, but I thought I might find a special piece of rock here which was completely out of place – a rock that shouldn't naturally be here at all."

"Would that be a very hard, very heavy reddish rock by any chance?" he asked. I looked at him totally thunderstruck by what he had just said.

"Yes, yes." I replied quickly, "But how could you know that?"

"Lucky guess," he replied, "We found a piece like that up here nearly ten years ago. You are right it was out of place completely so we brought it back down."

"Do you still have it?" I asked, desperately hoping he did.

"Possibly," he answered, "It was lying around at one of the bottom of the cupboards in the office for ages – ever since they were built in fact. It might have been thrown out by now. I don't know. Why is it so important and how is it that you knew about this stone and that it might be here?" He asked.

"It's a long story," I replied.

"Perhaps you can tell me as we head back down." He suggested.

"Ok" I replied, now very apprehensive with regards to the rock still being here or not.

"I've been looking for this piece of rock, which is a lump of Haematite, for a while now." I started as we walked down the track.

"If it's the right piece, it's one of four pieces that originally came from the South of France. As I told you I had a dream last night about having been part of a ritual at the top of this hill 4000 years ago. Something was telling me that I had to come here. However when I got here today, I found myself thinking that this piece had been placed at the top a long time ago and I just had to go up and see for myself. That's why I begged you to take me up there. I knew it was a long shot, but it was the only possible sign I've had as to where it might be since I came to Spain nearly two weeks ago."

"Well you must be quite psychic Rowena, that's all I can say. Even if it's not exactly the right piece your thinking about there being a strange stone up on the hill was spot on." He shook his head in part disbelief of it all.

I then explained more about the stone I was looking for and the other pieces and that I had two of them in the back of my car. Alejandro opened up the offices again and went into a back room. "You are in luck. It is still here." He called out from the other room. Moments later he reappeared carrying a large dusty ruddy coloured stone. He carefully placed it on the bench next to the sink and then wiped the dust off with a damp towel. I gasped. The unmistakeable markings of Haematite were immediately apparent. "What do you think?" he asked.

"It's the right size and the right shape." I replied. "Let me get my two pieces from my car."

In a couple of minutes I was back with both pieces at the bottom of my canvas rucksack. I lifted it up on to the table next to the other piece and lifted the two pieces out. The two of us then carefully began to move all three of them together. It was a perfect fit.

"Where's the fourth piece?" He asked.

"The 'Ministry of Culture' has it in Paris." I answered, "I already know that piece fits mine. I say mine, but really they are not mine, the Ministry owns all three pieces."

"So are you working for them?" He asked.

"Not exactly." I replied as honestly as I could. "They said they couldn't support me travelling down through Spain to look for this 4th piece. I just wanted to give it a try. I also had one of two other things I also wanted to do down in Spain anyway." I said. "Who technically does this stone belong to?" I asked.

"That is now hard to say." replied Alejandro. "It doesn't belong here, we don't have rocks like this around here. Clearly, from what you say, it was once from France as well. We had discarded it here and I think I remember being told to get rid of it sometime in the past. So technically, I suppose it belongs to the French ministry too."

"Would you be able to let me have it and take it back, if you gave me something to sign and I could take a receipt from you saying this is where it was found?"

"I think that can be arranged Rowena. The authorities higher up can then sort anything out if they want to after that. I would be happy to let you have it on that basis."

"Wonderful." I replied. Alejandro then went into his office to sort out some paperwork. Five minutes later he was back with two copies for us both to sign and date. I gave him my contact details and showed him my passport. He then took out a camera and took a photo of the one piece and one with all three pieces fitted together and one of my passport. When he had finished I put all three pieces into the rucksack.

"Rowena, I wish you all the very best with what you are doing. I have one other request if I may. If there is going to be any publicity about this Cathar stone, we would very much appreciate any promotion for what we are doing down here at La Bas Tida when it comes to explaining where the fourth piece came from."

"I think I can promise you that Alejandro." I smiled. "The story surrounding it is a fair bit of an adventure in itself. I'm sure lots of people will want to know how and why it ended up here." We shook hands and said goodbye and it was not long before I was driving back along the dusty roads back to the hotel.

It was only fifteen minutes away and the time had flown by. I'd done it, but ....I.... hadn't.

I'd been led all along the way. The dreams and the meditations were all important but most important of all were all my communications along the way with everyone else. I'd also not fallen into any traps.

If I'd illegally tried to find the stone by going up to the top of the hill earlier in the day, I would have missed finding it. If I'd lied about why I wanted to go to the top, I may not have found out about the fact that the stone was sitting at the bottom of a dusty cupboard. If I'd not even been open about everything I'd been doing, Alejandro may not have been happy for me to go off with the stone.

The whole success of my time in Spain had been down to everyone I'd met. If I'd not met, spent time and got along with Kayleigh and Siobhan, I would never have found El Berro and the retreat and learnt how to meditate more effectively. I may never have then come across Caravaca and the Sanctuario and its miracles and its strange esoteric symbols and wall paintings. If I'd not learnt how to find the lines and followed them to the monastery, I may never have been able to meditate and sleep on them and potentially get the information I needed to find out about La Bas Tida.

Everything was interconnected. It seemed to me now that the answers to everything in life were all within our grasp, if we went about it the right way. Each of us just had to play our own part and to follow our own path.

I realised that now but that didn't make it any easier to do. Giving up the ego, eliminating my fears and all the other things I'd endured in Spain were really tough challenges and I knew there'd be more in the future and they would be harder.

We are all tested. I'd learnt that over such a short period of time.

There was one other thing that I also knew though. I now knew how I was going to live my life.

I'd found my path and I was now determined to stay on it.

Epilogue

It was the first weekend in September. I'd only been back in the UK for about six weeks when I'd got the call. The scrolls had been carbon dated back to the 13th century and were real. Provenance had been accepted on the four pieces of the Cathar stone and this too had now been accepted as the Holy stone of the Cathars at Montesegur. Things seemed to have moved very fast.

It was here that I now stood in the 'Prat dels Cremats' at the foot of the Pog. I was wearing a jade green dress with pleats lower down and with a round neck collar. In one of my suitcases I'd found a wide navy blue suede belt with a gold buckle that went well with it. For shoes I'd chosen my navy blue pumps with a tiny heel. The ceremony was on grass so high heels were out. To go with the shoes and belt I'd bought a navy blue bolero jacket and I'd found a navy, cream and jade green silk scarf that matched. For once I felt appropriately dressed for the occasion.

It was midday and the Sun was only competing with one or two large white clouds. The sky on the whole was dazzlingly blue.

The Ministry had promised to fly me over to any celebrations and put me up and they had. Uncle David had joined me and he was now standing by my side in front of a line of French dignitaries. Having heard so much about the area from me, he was really looking forward to me taking him to see the Montsaunes chapel, The Cave of Lombrives and Rennes Le Chateau in the week we had down here.

The Minister of Culture himself had come down from Paris, bringing with him an army of photographers and TV crews. To his left was Dr Hugo Benoite and Gaston LeMaitre and to his right were several local mayors and members of Parliament from around the Ariege region. Apparently there was an important local election coming up very soon and they needed good publicity. This whole Cathar stone thing had fallen into their laps at just the right time.

The Minister was speaking now to the crowd below him on the gently sloping field. In front of him, on a tall square table covered by a long red cloth that went down to the ground, was the Cathar stone. The four pieces were now being held together by a wooden base with four support arms that had been specially made to keep each individual piece pressed towards the others.

I stood in front of it a few yards away and slightly downhill. Next to me were Pierre and Brian, Gaston's daughter Gabrielle and her mother and Albert, who had helped us with the initial translation and who'd put us in touch with Gaston. Gabrielle and I had had some time earlier before the ceremony to catch up and she'd had loads of ideas for me to consider, these included giving talks to lodges and their members about what I'd come across and how I'd found the last two pieces of the stone. I'd told her I would love to do that but that I'd have to put it off for a while until I sorted out my PhD. The extra funds from those activities would help me through it though. It was just a matter of timing and what the Universe had in mind for me.

Pierre and Brian were both on top form and had been keeping my Uncle and I amused all morning.

Behind me were Antoine and Amelie from the L'Escalère hotel in St. Martory. They were just so excited to be there. The news had already somehow spread fast and bookings at their hotel had just begun to go up both from people wanting to see the caves as well as the Montsaunes Chapel.

I still hadn't deciphered any more of the symbols on the ceilings and walls in there, nor had I managed to get very far with the symbols around the Apparition window at Caravaca de la Cruz.

There were so many questions and puzzles and I only had so much time. There would be others who would come along and probably do a better job deciphering them than me. Some of the symbols though seemed to be definitely connected to my research.

I could only follow my path and that, for the moment, seemed to mean trying find out more about why some places were sacred and why others were not. That was what intrigued me.

Most of my time though had been taken up persuading my PhD tutors to accept my project to study the effects of the Earth's low frequency sounds on life.

They'd seen it however as two subjects rather than one. The first was to prove that the inner core was generating these sounds. The second was to then measure the effects on life. I'd been suggesting doing both together. In the end we'd agreed a compromise.

Back in the UK, I'd done some more yoga sessions with Aliya and had mentioned what I had learnt in El Berro to her. She'd been eager to hear about my whole trip too. Katy had come along to do some classes with Aliya as well so we too had had a chance to catch up and have a laugh.

Shortly after I'd got back to the UK I sent a message and photo of the cave that I'd found in St Martory to my fellow train passenger Ethan Parker.

It was one with the cave art in. He's sent one back of a cave with some Aboriginal art on the walls and said that I was welcome to stay anytime I was over. He'd also said that if he'd had the time, he'd take me out into the bush if I wanted.

Sophie had texted that she would have loved to have come but she'd just left the PR company she'd been working for and had been setting up her own business. Her life was now incredibly busy. Everything was falling into place for her and if ever I was in Holland, I had to come and stay with her. She again said she was serious about consulting with me in the future. I'd texted her back that I'd be happy to do that once her company was up and running. It felt like I needed to 'go with the flow' in that direction but I wasn't sure why just yet.

Kayleigh and Siobhan were now on tour in Scotland and had messaged me that morning. We'd been in touch from time to time on social media. They'd gone to Rila in August and spent time up in the mountains with the Universal white brotherhood. They'd sent me loads of pictures of people they'd met up with. Everyone was so likeminded it had been like meeting old friends. They'd said that I absolutely had to drop everything to make it for next year and I'd know why when I got there.

Tania, the dancer I'd met at Chartres, and I had also kept in touch as well. She too seemed interested in going to Rila next year and had hooked up online with Kayleigh and Siobhan.

The Minister looked as though he had plenty of words left in him.

When he finished there would be presentations. I'd been warned. I'd only agreed to accept one though on the basis I didn't have to make a speech.

I looked over my shoulder and back to the car park.

Arnaud and Bernard had been cramming everything into this morning. As they'd both had to take the day off to be here, they'd got up early to go caving. Bernard had promised me they'd be here on time.

As the Minister continued to speak, my mind went back to another massive piece of synchronicity that I'd had on my way back through France. I'd stopped for the night at Le Mans having driven up through France. That evening I'd met an elderly lady called Francine who had been staying in the same Hotel. She had been visiting relatives there but had lived for most of her life in St Malo on the coast.

We were both in the restaurant and she'd been seated at a separate table from me but they were right next to each other. The place was nearly empty and it seemed ridiculous so we started to chat. I then moved over to join her at her table.

She'd led a really interesting life and had lots of stories to tell. One of the stories it seemed she wanted to tell me was that in the 1970's she'd met a young man in St Malo called Daniel. She and Daniel had become good friends. She was now telling me about the time she helped him gather up all his father's old research equipment and notes. His father was a man called Louis Rota. In the 1930's he'd had a research laboratory near Rouen at a place called Mont-Saint-Aignan.

The reason she'd told me this was that it seemed that his father had discovered a great secret during his research and she knew what it was. Daniel's father apparently had filed several patents in his life and had even worked for the British Admiralty. Unfortunately Louis Rota died in 1951 when his son Daniel was still very young. Rota though was only 65 when he died. Francine had almost whispered to me that she thought that he'd been killed because of this secret that he'd discovered.

At this point I'd felt that I was just being kind and listening to an elderly lady talk about her life. What she'd said next though shocked me to my very core. Synchronicity had just gone into overdrive.

Apparently his father had been investigating something called a Universal Energy. He had been doing this by burying metal blocks in the ground and measuring their electrical responses. This was exactly what I was planning to do. What this Universal energy was though I had no idea and nor had Francine. She had gone on to say that Louis Rota had found out that a certain combination of sheets of different metals, placed on top of one another and into a block, would produce a constant stream of free electricity. Rota had then used this to power his lights and heaters.

I'd dismissed that as something that was probably not possible but I could see why she thought it was relevant and why she'd thought he'd been killed because of it. I was just not into conspiracy theories though but what really interested me was what he'd actually discovered and why he'd been sinking metal blocks into the ground in the first place. Just knowing that alone could seriously help me with my research.

What had possibly started out as dinner on my own in a hotel had ended up as another enjoyable evening listening to a lovely old lady. From out of just caring, and showing interest in others, had come this huge synchronicity which had provided me with another avenue of investigation.

I looked around again at the sound of a car pulling up and braking quickly. It was Arnaud and Bernard. It wasn't long before they were both running up the path and into the field trying to button up their shirts on the way. Bernard and I, my Uncle, Pierre and Brian had spent last night together in Tarascon. I'd only had a few moments alone with Bernard though.

We'd spent a day together on my way back from Spain and had kept in touch since with regular messaging. He'd said that he'd loved my new hair style. That comment made me feel that there was still hope for us. Bernard was becoming a good friend. Unfortunately, it seemed like things would have to stay that way for a while longer. When I'd made a suggestion to meet up, he'd said he couldn't commit to anything too far ahead just yet. He did though ask me to be patient with him. I felt slightly 'in limbo' with that, but at least it allowed me to focus on my work.

I would have moved on from trying to make things happen between us but knowing the circumstances of his rather unique situation at home, I felt it was worth trying to help in any way I could. I'd therefore asked him if he would do something for me and that was to go and see a counsellor. He promised he would. That gave me slightly more hope too. Perhaps after a few months of that, he'd want to see me again on a proper date.

All I could now do was to 'go with the flow' with it all. If was to be, it would be.

My ears caught the sound of my name being announced. It made me think of my Dad. He would have loved to have been here. Who knows, perhaps he was in some way. I walked up and shook the hand of the minister who gave me a rather nice looking medal. I could see Bernard and Arnaud now cheering at the back of a crowd of about 200 people.

What followed was a mass scramble by the waiting photographers trying to get their pay check shots for their papers. Everyone was clapping. It was all quite surreal as I couldn't understand anything that was being said around me as everyone was talking in high speed French.

It was then that I remembered the last time I'd been here. It was when I'd met Paul Cloutier and he'd told me that I was special and that one day I'd be running my own business. If he was here now I am sure he'd have a wry smile on his face. I decided to send him a picture. I took my own phone out and called to Pierre to come and get it and to take a photo of me and my medal with the minister next to me, the Pog behind me and the table with the Cathar stone in front of me. Pierre joined the group of photographers, took a shot and then handed me back my phone.

Moments later Gaston and Hugo's names were mentioned. They were also being presented with awards for what they had done. This really seemed to be a big thing for them all. I guessed that it would considerably help the tourist industry and that would be good financially for the whole region. I watched and clapped along with the others as they too were rewarded by the Minister.

I then looked down at my photo. It looked good so I emailed it to Paul with the words 'Back here again at Montsegur. This time with the sacred stone of the Cathars and the French Minister of Culture who has just given me a medal for helping to find it. Thanks again for calling me special. All the best Rowena'. Some time later on he'd sent one back. 'Well done. Glad to see I was right about you. Keep in touch and let me know how it all goes. Paul C.'

Dr Hugo Benoite then began to talk to the crowd about how we'd each found the four pieces of the stone. I just smiled and got back thinking about my recent synchronicity.

I'd had time on the Ferry crossing to investigate Louis Rota further. He had indeed filed patents. They were on detecting the proximity of mines and submarines. It turned out that he really was a well-respected scientist in his time. Even Lord Kelvin had accepted these Universal currents existed and had agreed that their origin was within the Earth itself. Rota himself had said that they were definitely not electromagnetic in origin but that they did couple with this energy in some way.

For me this opened up the possibility that they were somehow connected to low frequency sounds. This was given added credence when I discovered that Rota used to use earphones to listen to these blocks in the ground. What clinched it for me though was that two of the metals he'd used, amongst combinations of six or seven metals, were Iron and Nickel. He'd even used the word Transducteur to describe it. This apparently was one of Rota's greatest secrets. My research into Rota's work had now given me lots of ideas to test. I'd even found diagrams of how he had set these blocks in the ground.

When I was in Spain and I'd found the 4th piece of the stone, I still had many questions left unanswered. I had no idea if I was the person who was supposed to be finding answers to them. All I knew for the moment was that I was meant to be studying low frequency sounds coming from the solid inner core of our planet and their effect on life on this Earth. After all I was a Geobiologist.

The presentations and speeches had come to an end. It was now time to celebrate and the time for the TV cameras and the interviews.

I was now standing amidst a whole throng of people all wanting to talk to me. I was handed a glass of Champagne and asked to stand behind the table with the stone. Out of the corner of my eye I could see Bernard moving through the crowd towards me. He was smiling. That seemed positive.

I was now being asked a question in French by a man who had a female interpreter between me and him. How did I feel when I'd found the fourth piece of the Cathar stone? I did my best to answer but was still looking at Bernard coming towards me. Maybe he'd changed his mind I hoped.

"What made me start looking for the stone?" was the next question. I started to talk about my dad and his piece and finding mine matched. Bernard was now just behind the cameraman. If only things could work out between us, I thought. I could then do my research down here in France.

I was asked another question "What did I think when I found my first piece of the stone and how was that?" I told them about meeting Bernard and how he took me into a cave. This seemed to interest them. "Who is Bernard?" they asked.

"He is behind you." I replied. They now all turned round towards him. He really was good looking. With a half unbuttoned shirt and a rather wild and unkempt hair style from his early morning caving with Arnaud, he could have easily passed as a male model.

He held his arms out towards me. I felt as though I could have leapt over the table in front of me in that moment. Bernard was now speaking in French answering a question but his eyes were on me and his arms were still waiting for me to move round to him.

As I reached him, he pulled me into him and kissed me. My legs almost gave way but he held me strong against his chest. Amongst the sound of all the camera clicks, I heard Bernard whisper. "Cherie. The thought of you leaving again was too much for me. I really want to be with you more."

That was more than enough for me to begin with. "I think we can work something out." I replied smiling at him.

Fact or Fiction

All the characters in this novel that are engaged in the ongoing dialogue have been made up. Any resemblance to anyone, either through similar names or character or even both, is completely and wholly unintentional.

With regards to the factual content of the novel it has to be said that the two scrolls that Rowena Colleen finds are fictional. The holy stone of the Cathars is definitely thought to have existed but its whereabouts is currently unknown. That it was split into four pieces is just part of the fictional storyline.

All other places, symbols, events and organisations that are mentioned in this book actually exist and can be seen today.

Some characters, past and present who have been mentioned in the story, but are not part of the actual narrative, are real people. They have been included based on their expertise in the area being discussed. Their actual names have been used as they deserve full recognition for the excellent work that they have done.

Two examples of this are Louis Rota's work on Universal energies and Christian Koenig's wonderful panpipe music. (A recital of his in the cave of Lombrives can be heard here (www.youtube.com/watch?v=SKGwsv8uoPI)

The coming sequel to this book is:-

Rowena Colleen & The Invisible Grail

www.roryduff.com

Printed in Great Britain
by Amazon